WORTHY OF FLOWERS AND FOREVER

Fox Grove

Book 1

PAMELA GAUTHIER

Pamela Gauthier Publishing, LLC

ISBN: 979-8-9932673-0-2

This is a work of fiction, created without the use of any type of AI technology.

Any characters, names, places, locations, or events are products of the author's imagination and thus used in a fictitious manner. The resemblance to any actual people, places, or events are a coincidence or fiction.

Cover design: Pamela Gauthier

Kaitlin Slowik: copyeditor

References used: The Chicago Manual of Style, 18th edition; Merriam-Webster Collegiate Dictionary, 11th edition

A note from the author

Dear reader,

Worthy of Flowers and Forever is a work of fiction, however there are many topics covered that dip into difficult subject matter.

If you would like to go into the book without knowing any hints or spoilers, please know that the next page has all of the trigger warnings—read them at your will, but always take care of your mental health first and foremost.

This book is intended for mature audiences, 18+

Trigger Warnings

Dear reader,

This book is intended for audiences 18+

The triggers for this book include . . .

- cheating (not between the main characters)
- open door sexual scenes
- childhood trauma
- childhood sexual assault
(talked about, not explicit on page)
- stalking (not between the main characters)
- death of a military spouse
(not main characters/not on page)
- scenes inside of a hospital
- birth
- water PTSD
- fire trauma
- animal in danger
- conversations about drug abuse
- discussion of drug overdose
(OD not on page)
- attempted murder (on page)

- arson
- vomit (on page)

*At the time of writing this book, there were no Safe Haven Baby Boxes (which are briefly mentioned) located in the state of Virginia.

Playlist

- "Deserve You" Justin Bieber
- "Till There's Nothing Left" Cam
- "Building Chemistry" Cody Francis
- "There You Are" ZAYN
- "Any Man of Mine" Shania Twain
- "cut my hair" Tate McRae
- "Have You Ever Been in Love" The Ivy
- "Everyday" (E) Ariana Grande ft. Future
- "Missing Piece" Vance Joy
- "NIGHTS LIKE THIS" The Kid LAROI
- "Rare Love" Cody Francis
- "Burning Down" Alex Warren
- "Another" Adam Doleac
- "Dead In The Water" James Gillespie
- "Fire" Augustana
- "Dusk Till Dawn (feat. Sia) - Radio Edit" ZAYN ft. Sia
- "I'm a Fire" David Nail
- "Your Bones" Chelsea Cutler
- "I Believe" Jonas Brothers

- "Living My Best Life" Jessie J
- "invisible string" Taylor Swift
- "Bones - Wedding Version" Russell Dickerson
- "Alive" PRKR.
- "The Few Things (with Charlotte Lawrence)" JP Saxe, Charlotte Lawrence
- "Showing You Off" (E) Jake Miller
- "Baby I Am" Dalton Dover
- "BUTTERFLIES" MAX, Ali Gatie
- "Easy Does It" Emily Ann Roberts
- "Nobody (from Kaiju No. 8)" OneRepublic
- "Shivers" Ed Sheeran
- "Slowly - Acoustic" Jordan Hart
- "Home to Me" Alexis Arnold
- "Banks" NEEDTOBREATHE
- "For You" Liam Payne, Rita Ora

The way I choose songs for my playlist is all about vibes. Some lyrics hit true to the story and who Remington and Lainey are, so I needed them on the list. Other songs might be mentioned in the book. Some I heard and thought "this is just so ____ scene" and popped it on there. All this to say, there is no particular order they <u>need</u> to be listened to, but my hope is that when you miss the book and can't read it, you can turn on this playlist and get the vibe of the book until you can pick it back up again.

For the little girls that grew up feeling like their best was never enough, which made them afraid to chase a dream.

You are enough.

1

Lainey

Daddy issues. That is what got me here. In this worn, old chair at the wobbly wooden table that never gets fixed at the Sugar Cube, our small-town cafe that has stood the test of time. I always pep-talked myself that I would *never* be "that girl" with the classic daddy issues written about in pages, portrayed on screens, and gossiped about in grocery checkout lines. And yet, they were all right there from the very start. There was absolutely nothing the little girl I used to be could do to stop the parental flood damage from carving my future.

He used his words instead of his fists to leave bruises on my soul. Marks that are permanent. Places that partners push on, making me ache, making me feel like I deserve the scraps of attention they gave me. So yes, daddy issues were the reason I was right here, right now, having this insane conversation with my boyfriend.

"Like I was saying, we just don't get to spend enough time together. So, I am going to head back to the city tomorrow," Brett says with total exasperation.

"Let me get this straight," I say, trying to stay calm and keep my voice contained to our wobbly table. "We have been dating for over a year, been long distance for eight months. I haven't seen you in person in three months. You came here to celebrate my birthday, which was a week ago, by the way, *and* you were supposed to stay here for three more days."

"Riiiiiight . . ." Brett drawls, listening to me bullet point our plans that we had made weeks in advance.

"Now, you are telling me the big issue in our relationship is not spending enough time together because of the distance? And instead of actually spending time together that we *planned,* y-you are really going to leave? It makes absolutely zero sense," I say to him, baffled.

"Babe, I just think we need some space," Brett says, looking anywhere but me and taking a big, sloppy bite of his double club breakfast sandwich, egg yolk and tomato juice running over his fingertips.

"Are you freaking serious?" I exclaim, not caring that eyes are being drawn to us, and people are starting to listen to what should be a very private conversation.

"Hey, hey, hey! *Keep* your voice down, Lainey. I knew that you were going to have an overreaction when I told you I think we need a break." He sighs like I am the problem.

"I see," I hiss, "you took me here to keep me quiet and calm. To not cause a scene because we are in public? Well fine, let's go finish this conversation at my apartment where it should have been happening in the first place." I abandon my favorite wild blueberry muffin and fruit platter combo, untouched on the table, my stomach having turned to lead. Brett is finishing his own food, acting like he didn't just drop a bomb on our life, when his phone screen lights up on the table with a text message.

And then another . . .

And another . . .

JuneBug: Are you finally free yet, Big Daddy?

JuneBug: I miss you . . .

JuneBug: I need your big cock.

Brett tries to snatch his phone, but I get to it first.

What. In. The. Actual. Fuck.

"Babe, I can explain, please. Let's go to your place and talk," he whispers, eyes darting nervously around the cafe.

"Explain what exactly? That you are a total lying, cheating, piece of shit?" My voice carries across the now silent cafe. All eyes are on us, and I don't care. We are in our own wobbly bubble and it's about to burst for everyone to witness. "We were committed to each other, made promises and plans. Did that mean nothing to you?"

Brett looks at me like I am someone to pity, like I am childish. "I have needs, *Lainey*. I am a man, and being so far away has been hard. June is there and you are here. This is exactly why I think we need some space. To see if this is what we really want." He glances around, looking for some manly support from the crowd, gaining nothing but gasps and looks of disgust.

"No. *YOU* want 'space' so you can feel good about cheating on me and getting your dick wet with your little Junebug while I am here, waiting and fully committed to you. Because you know that I would not want space, and if we had it, even with the distance . . . I would not cheat on you. You know that I wanted a life here and a partner."

I grab all of my things, slamming his phone back down onto the table. I look at his unremarkable blue eyes; lightly freckled, pinched face; and cinnamon-colored hair that has a bit of a curl around his ears. How did I ever find him so attractive? How could I not see the snake under his plain, unassuming, business-frat-bro charm. I was so desperate to have attention and affection I settled.

This is not love.

This is not the life that I deserved.

What am I doing with my life? He is such an idiot . . . but I am too, for wasting so much of my time and letting assholes like this take pieces of me, hoping to get anything in return. I spent all my time convincing myself that the scraps they tossed my way were as satisfying and nourishing as a full meal that I got to see served all around me but never actually tasted myself.

Enough. I deserve so much better.

With as much steel in my spine as I can muster, I spin fast on my heel, march toward the door, and yell, "Fuck you, Brett! Junebug can have your tiny dick and faking her orgasms all to herself. Enjoy the freedom."

I hear clapping from the Sugar Cube patrons, some laughing, and Brett yelling back, "It's not true!" I walk over toward my small SUV, not giving a shit how Brett will get back to my place. He will find his bag on top of his car, if nobody steals it before he comes to pick it up. But let's be real, this is Fox Grove, nobody is going to mess with something that isn't theirs.

2

Remington

The feisty, beautiful woman with long chestnut-brown hair, a pink sweater, and denim shorts marched her perfectly toned, long legs out the door. Leaving that asshole, Brett, scrambling and the Sugar Cube buzzing.

"It's not true!" he yells. "My dick is huge and I get tons of pussy. She is just being a petty bitch."

Storming out the door after her is the only thing that saves him from me leaving my place at the counter and rearranging his too-straight teeth. I am not a violent person. I have the reputation of being "the nice guy," albeit a little grumpy from time to time, but never out to start shit. However, something about that woman has me as fired up as the flames I saw in her eyes when she was laying into that moron. Hearing him say anything negative toward her is making every cell in my body sing.

Thank fuck I am going to work. I can hit the gym, work out my frustration there instead of on his face.

When I get to the fire station my best friend is waiting at the three open bay doors. The old brick building fits the charm of our small town, but the inside, equipment, and trucks are all modernized and top of the line. We are lucky to have a community that supports our efforts and department.

We do two fundraisers each year, a pancake breakfast in the fall and a car wash in the spring. Each one brings the people out in droves to support whatever extra things we need to fundraise for. Last year we were able to get funds and resources to help make some updates so we could install a Safe Haven Baby Box. We are one of the first fire departments in the state of Virginia to have one, and it has already been used once. A baby girl was placed safely in the box just three months after we put it in. People talk a lot of shit about small towns, but there is nowhere else I would want to live, to build a life. The people I care about most are all here in Fox Grove. We take care of our own, and now we can help even ones that are some of the most vulnerable in a new way.

Eli takes one look at the box in my hands and grins, knowing that I have a full order of sugar cookies from the cafe. It's their signature dessert, and they sell out fast. That's why I try to put in a weekly standing order before my final shift. I like to do something to give all the crew a little morale boost, plus I won't get stuck having the temptation of eating too many cookies alone, gaining five pounds, and getting a stomachache.

"Were you there for the show?" Eli asks with an excited grin. Popping open the box and snagging two cookies, he takes a big bite of one, crumbs dusting down the front of his navy-blue FGFD T-shirt.

"What show?" I ask, knowing exactly what he's talking about. The blowup I witnessed is sure to be spreading through town faster than a fire, sparking the interest from anyone willing to listen. Gossip like that will be catching a back draft with every retelling from now until dinnertime, making it the hottest town chatter for at least the next week.

"Some hottie tore her dipshit boyfriend a new one in front of the whole place? I was hoping you got a VIP ticket, could give me a play-by-play." The smirk tells me *exactly* what he's hoping for. He's as bad as the old ladies at the Dip and Dye salon at the corner of Main and Booth.

Eli Hargrove is the biggest extrovert out of all my friends, and I swear he can make anyone melt in about three minutes of meeting him. He's got zero issues with his game and runs around proudly waving his "bachelor forever" flag. Women know the deal, and they are happy to be in his company for whatever time he will give them. His dark hair, olive skin, deep-blue eyes, and signature dimple are weapons he is an expert at wielding to his advantage.

"Yeah, I was a VIP alright. At the counter. The asshole had the audacity to tell that beautiful woman that he cheated on her because they were apparently in a long-distance relationship, and 'he had needs.'" I blow out a breath, feeling my blood starting to boil again thinking about the look on her face. "Oh! *And* then when she left, she said the new chick could enjoy his tiny dick and faking her orgasms." I smile thinking about her sass.

Eli chokes on the last bite of his second cookie. "Hooollllly shit, Rem, I wish I was there. That's small-town gossip gold!"

"I know. He's lucky I wasn't closer to him after she walked out. When he claimed to have a huge dick, gets tons of pussy, and said she was being a petty bitch." Eli flinches at those harsh words, and his eyes turn dark. He might be a huge player and highly allergic to commitment in romantic relationships, but he loves and respects women. He has a single mom and three younger sisters that think he hung the moon.

"Maybe we should go teach him some manners, then go find that beautiful mystery girl so I can show her how a *real man* treats a woman. I can promise she won't have to fake anything with me." He gives me a devilish wink, and I level him with a cold stare. "Ohhhmmyggoood," he mumbles around a third cookie. "You like this girl?"

"I don't even know her. Saw her all of three minutes. I was in the Cube to get my order," I grumble.

"Yeah, but that look you just gave me tells a totally different story, brother. Don't worry, 'beautiful girl' is all yours. I won't steal your woman." He laughs, carrying the box of cookies off into the fire station for the rest of the crew.

Rolling my eyes, I follow my best friend. What *are* the chances of seeing the beautiful girl again? Yeah, this is a small town, but I don't even know if she is from here. As far as size goes, I'd say we are more of an envelope than a postage stamp. Small, but not out of the question to meet a new face once in a while. I didn't recognize her, and her name hasn't been connected to the story floating around yet. All I can hope for is that she really did dump that tiny-dicked asshole and finds someone that shows her how worthy she is of a committed relationship.

The kind of relationship that always feels just out of reach for me. Once upon a time I thought I was so ready for forever, but I keep hope on that future door locked tight. I won't let my heart be open to that kind of ambush ever again.

After my shift I was exhausted and ready to go home, turn off my brain, and decompress. We had a hard accident on the outskirts of town. It kept me there several hours after I was scheduled to leave. Fatals are always devastating, and compartmentalizing only works for so long. Sometimes we all need to be in the same room, together as a crew, a family, and process things. Shifts and schedules don't matter when the mental health of the people you walk into the flames with are more important. The ties in the station are thicker than blood, we are a family.

As I drive through town toward my house, I see a stream of thick smoke coming from the back of the Fox Hollow apartment complex. Hitting the gas and turning the emergency lights on in my truck, I drive over in that direction as fast as I can. I call into the fire station on my truck radio.

LeBlanc: Dispatch this is Sergeant LeBlanc. Do you copy?

Dispatch: Copy.

LeBlanc: We have an unidentified, active fire situation at the Fox Hollow apartment complex. Heavy smoke present, situation unknown.

Dispatch: Copy that. Sending out trucks to the location.

LeBlanc: Tell them I am two minutes away.

Dispatch: Copy that, Sergeant LeBlanc.

Whipping around the back of the building, I slam on the brakes of my truck. When I see the cause of the smoke I have to blink and rub my eyes, thinking I must be having a hallucination. Sleep deprivation? What the hell is going on?

There is no way my beautiful girl is *here*, behind this apartment building playing pyro. Her smoke signal calling me right to her.

3

Lainey

Red flags. So many freaking red flags. But do I do anything about them? Of course I don't. I ignore them. I pretend they are pink and hope they will bloom into something pretty that can be planted into a garden one day. Stupid. But I should know better, I only propagate weeds in my life, and I am never fast enough to pluck them before they start to rot everything around them.

Me. *I* am the thing that suffers and rots.

"When people show you who they are you should believe them." That saying is popular for a damn good reason. I'm an optimist to the point of pain. Pain that has obviously done some serious damage. I want to be loved and accepted so badly I've allowed bad behavior in *every* one of my relationships. Brett's red flags have been there all along, but the ones waving right in front of my face from just this trip alone should have been much more obvious if I wasn't so busy trying to grow a garden in a pile of toxicity.

I should know better, flowers have no place in my life.

The lukewarm hug and dispassionate kiss he gave me after not seeing each other for *three months*? Red flag.

Telling me he had to ask *my mother* for a birthday gift idea for me, even though we have been dating for over a year? Red flag. Especially since he should know my mother wouldn't know what to get me. She doesn't really know me well enough to be able to hand out sound gifting advice like a good mother should. One of her many red flags, but we are not talking about her right now.

Last year Brett gave me a thoughtful, nostalgic gift that was absolutely terrible. But I could tell he actually put in some effort, and for me it really is the thought that counts. This time he brought me an ugly yellow tumbler—I freaking *hate* yellow—and a drip coffee maker for my kitchen. I don't even drink regular coffee, and at home I always have tea. It is like he shopped for a total stranger, not his girlfriend. Red-freaking-flag!

The red flag that makes me want to puke and has me out behind my apartment building burning things in the community barbecue pit? Brett had sex with me—terrible, unsatisfying, uncomfortable sex—an hour before our miserable Sugar Cube breakfast. He knew full well he wanted to break up, had been cheating on me, and *still* slept with me. I have an appointment with my doctor tomorrow to be tested for alllll the things. Even though he always wore a condom with me, I feel completely disgusted. Five hot showers later, practically rubbing my body raw, and my skin is still crawling thinking about that slimy asshole.

Did Junebug know he was going to fuck me? What kind of bullshit lies and story was he telling her? Ugh, I was literally going to be sick.

The few pictures I had printed of the two of us that I had pinned to my fridge and an old newspaper article about the gala burned first. Our happy smiles from our first picture together, the night we met at a charity gala event my PR firm put together, singed, melting the plastic and the pretense of what could have been. That is what our whole relationship was for him apparently: an elaborate flash of smoke and mirrors. Tricking me and trying to mold me into something convenient to fill his time or a fuck when he felt like it.

Brett's favorite hat, any lingerie I had worn for him, and his college fraternity sweatshirt all went up in flames quickly. Next went my bedsheets we unfortunately shared and his cologne. A giant ball of smokey heat engulfed them as they caught fire. I yelped and jumped back, landing into what felt like a brick wall . . . but a brick wall that apparently had arms?

I screamed again, fighting against this stranger until I heard his smooth, deep voice in my ear. "Hey, hey, sorry. I didn't mean to scare you. That fire is getting a little out of control, and I'm gonna need you to back up now."

Whipping around, ready to fight for my fire-cleanse rights, but the words get lost when my eyes land on his honey-dipped amber ones. His sandy blond hair, cut jawline, and slightly crooked nose are lit up by my little bonfire. I simply nod and do as he says.

I suddenly hear sirens in the distance and my eyes go wide. "Oh no! What's that?"

"That would be my guys, coming to help with your little pyro party for one apparently. What the hell are you burning? This is a family barbecue area. Is that some kind of . . . clothing?" he almost murmurs to himself, looking into the flames and ashes that are much more smoke than fire now that the sheets are fully engulfed.

"Ummm, it's my bedding," I whisper as the fire trucks pull up, and I hope the noise blocks out my reply. Suddenly, a small explosion comes from the fire, and before I know what's happening I am pressed flat on the ground, covered up by the impressive height, weight, and strength of a stranger. My brain is slow to catch up to what is happening, but as he flips me over to my back the heat that rolls through my body has absolutely nothing to do with my bedding bonfire.

"Are you okay?" he gruffly asks, pulling away from me and helping me back to my feet. He backs up a few steps, brushing off grass and dirt from his long-sleeve, navy-blue Fox Grove Fire Department shirt.

Am I okay? "Yeah, yeah . . . I am so sorry about that. I guess I wasn't, umm . . ." My voice trails off as I look back to the fire and then to the flashing lights of the fire trucks. Men are coming toward us in a rush, and I gulp in embarrassment. "I guess that means you're a firefighter?" I ask my stranger-turned-hero for saving me from blowing myself up with the world's most basic cologne.

"I am, and I need to ask again, ma'am . . . what exactly were you burning?"

"Ugh, I was trying to cleanse myself of my stupid ex-boyfriend's existence in my life and wasn't exactly thinking totally straight. After burning some pictures, fortunately his favorite hat and hoodie, unfortunately my favorite lingerie, and my bedding, I also tossed his bottle of cologne onto the sheets. Probably not the best idea, but I just needed it *out* of my apartment and . . ." *And I am rambling.* I look up to see him smirking at me.

"I definitely have some follow-up questions to all of that, but first how about a name?" he says keeping his tone of voice serious but trying to hold back a full grin that would most likely make me combust exactly like that cologne bottle.

Before I can answer, three other firefighters reach me and my hero. *Yeah, I have already claimed him as mine in my brain after just swearing off* all *men at the start of this disaster of a do-over. What the hell is wrong with me?* He shakes hands with the older man that must be in charge and gets him up to speed on what is happening.

Thankfully, all that's left in the barbecue pit are some small flames, smoldering ashes, and my dignity. They are talking, and all I can think about is how fast *my* firefighter sprang into action. The way he felt pressed against me, protecting me from the fire and from *myself,* if I'm going to be honest.

"Ma'am," the older man in charge addresses me. "We are glad that you're safe and this was not a more serious situation, but we have to ask that you do *not* use the community cookout area for your, ahh, fire cleanse." His dark, wrinkled brow creases even further as he says those final words.

"Yes, and I am *SO* sorry. I promise that this will never happen again. It was the result of a shitty breakup and me not thinking it through all the way, clearly. Science 101 and all that. I really know better than to put that in there." I sigh, adding, "And please, call me Lainey. I'm Lainey Quinn."

"Quinn? You must be Ann's little girl. Well, not so little anymore, I guess. I'm Chief Roberts. I have known your momma for a long time. She talks 'bout you when I see her up at the bank. She must be happy to have you back around all the time?"

Chief Roberts smiles at me kindly now that he knows that I am the daughter of the most passive lady on the planet—unless you are her daughter. Hopefully my mom has earned me some points here today. She works at the local bank and has a good pulse for what's happening in town. When I told her I was moving here two years ago after my internships and other obligations were complete, she was as surprised as I was. We don't have the best relationship, but I wanted Fox Grove to be a place where we could start fresh. So far, it's been a *really slow* start, making me wonder why I'm still trying so hard and if moving here was the smartest choice.

"Yes, sir. She's had me home for a while now, and it has been good for both of us. I will be sure to let her know you said hello when I tell her my embarrassing story of how I wasted your time and the town's precious resources today." It's a lie, all of it. *I will not be telling her this story, now or ever. All she will do is lecture me and make me feel like garbage.*

Chief Roberts huffed. "Lainey, no need to worry, we are happy to help, and happy that you're safe. I was glad when your momma moved back to town. My wife missed her when she left all those years ago and they lost touch. It has been nice to have her back in Fox Grove where she belongs. As for you, young lady, let's just take out the trash the traditional way next time, shall we?" My mom was always good at letting people see the sides of her she wanted them to in DC, and it seems like that's not any different here in Fox Grove.

"Yes, sir." I smile as I shake his warm, rough hand, and then he leads all his men away to the waiting trucks.

I only had one thing left to burn, and I have it clutched in my hands. The nostalgic gift from my birthday last year. It is a Lisa Frank knockoff notebook. Covered in kittens and butterflies. Absolutely hideous. Not my style and not up to par with the epic art that made Lisa a legend of my childhood. I kept this stupid thing and even used it for something that *actually* mattered to me because I was trying to give Brett the benefit of the doubt that he tried to get me something that was meaningful, thinking that he paid attention and cared about a story from my past.

I used it because I was too nice, a people pleaser through and through.

I used it because I wanted to make *him* happy, placate his ego, and make him think that the bare minimum on his part was worthy of a gold star, a blow job, and seeing me write special things in the most un-special journal.

Now, I stand here waiting for the fire trucks to leave so I can toss in another thing I shouldn't have to give up because a man can't keep his promises—or keep his dick in his pants.

As soon as I reach out my hand to toss in the cat-covered nightmare, I hear, "You can't be serious!" I shriek, jump back, drop the journal, and trip over my shoe. Once again, I'm being saved by a pair of strong arms.

"You scared the shit out of me! What are you still doing here?" I ask my firefighter, who is not looking thrilled to be saving me *again.*

"I told Chief I would stick around and make sure the fire was totally out, and I wanted to make sure that you were okay. Why the fuck are you still burning shit after what just happened, Lainey?" he asks gruffly.

My name coming from his lips sends a shiver up my spine. I have never loved my name more than I do right this very minute.

"Well, you see, I umm Ionlyhavethisonethinglefttoburn," I quickly mumble at him.

Rolling his eyes, he picks up my journal that landed at our feet when I jumped out of my skin. He gives it a disgusted look, like he can't believe he is even touching something so hideous. "What the hell is this thing?"

"It was a gift."

"It's a nightmare. That dickwad actually thought a woman like you would want something like this?"

"Wellll, to be fair I had told him about my Lisa Frank notebook that I loved when I was a little girl . . . But mine had puppies on it," I say with a frown, not knowing why I'm being defensive about it. Looking at the knockoff kittens, one has a lazy eye, and I swear it kind of follows you like those creepy haunted house paintings. I shiver, and not the good kind.

"Why would you keep it? He is such an idiot," he grumbles. "This is obviously *not* Lisa Frank, and not what you told him about. A gift is supposed to mean something to the person you are giving it to, not be some check mark and nightmare fuel." His eyes meet mine with a sincerity that takes my breath away.

Who is this man?

"The reason it wasn't the first thing in the fire is because of what I wrote in it." I shift on my feet uncomfortably.

"What did you write in it?" His voice softens with the question, like he knew he was peeling back a delicate piece of me that might tear off and blow away like the ash from my bonfire if he wasn't careful.

It made me want to give him honesty.

"I, um, like to write down things. Like quotes, song lyrics, or stuff that people have said that are memorable or mean something to me. Memories. So, I have one journal for each year and write down things throughout the year. On my birthday I pick out a new one and start over, saving the last one. Like my only little memory collection of moments that touched me or random things that I didn't want to forget about that happened. *This* was last year's." I reach out to take the journal back, but he pulls it away.

"So, you were going to burn a whole year of your life, your memories and traditions, because your ex is an asshole?" His eyes search my face, a soft kind of desperation asking me to give him more.

"I cannot have *that* journal in my house, my life. I can't look at those stupid, creepy-eyed cats and not think about him, no matter how important the things I wrote inside are to me. I won't ever be able to open it up again. I don't want to touch it, so it doesn't matter. I might as well burn it. Cleanse it and the whole year of bad decisions and being with him. There were so many red flags. How could anything I wrote last year be worth keeping anyways?" A wave of shame rolls through me as I turn my face away from him.

"I think you're being way too hard on yourself. I think you are letting the bad choices of a guy that took advantage of the best thing that will ever happen to him ruin something that has made you happy for a lot longer than he was ever around. Don't let that piece of shit have any more power. Isn't that the whole point of your little pyro show out here today? Don't let him win, Lainey."

"I can't keep it, I absolutely can't." I can feel the tears starting to swell in my eyes, and the flood of emotions coming up is from trauma that has nothing to do with my breakup and everything to do with my upbringing. The constant reminder that I am not good enough for a man to choose me, love me, stick around, and pay attention to all the pieces of me that make up my soul.

"What if I help you out with it?" His calm voice once again pulls me from my spiraling thoughts.

"Help me how? You don't even know me? I don't even know you . . . I don't even know *your name*. All I know is that you are a firefighter and probably think I'm insane."

He chuckles. "Well, that is easy to sort out. First of all, you are Lainey Quinn, queen of a post-breakup barbecue cleanse. Your mom apparently knows my fire chief. I do *not* think you are insane, just insanely beautiful . . . And my name is Remington LeBlanc."

Freaking. Swoon.

"Okay, Remington LeBlanc. How exactly do you plan on helping me?"

"I am going to take your nightmare cat journal notebook, transfer what you wrote into a new journal, and give it back to you. Easy." He looks at me like he's calm about this whole thing. Meanwhile, my insides are a riot of butterflies . . . and rocks.

"What is your ulterior motive?" I can't hide my sarcasm or my skepticism.

"There is none. I'm just trying to be nice, help you out. I was there. I saw you at the Sugar Cube—with Brett." He growls out my ex's name with deep contempt.

My eyes nearly pop out of my face. Shock and embarrassment ripple over me like a choking wave. *Ohmygodohmygodohmygod. This man, this heroic dreamboat, has been witness to* two *of my most humiliating days.*

I bury my face in my hands.

Warm, callused ones wrap around my wrists and gently pull my arms away.

I feel like I have been zapped back to life from a simple touch.

Looking up into his face I see a strong, slightly stubbled jawline, the rumpled blond hair that is buzzed shorter at the back and sides but is a bit longer on top. Those deep, warm, honey eyes . . . I inexplicably feel a wave of safety that I have been missing my entire life.

"I can't believe you were there, saw that whole thing." A tear slips down my cheek without my permission.

He wipes it away with a callused thumb, letting his hand linger over my jawline for a single moment. "You were such a badass. I was completely in awe of you that day. He was such a dick to you. I could not believe the things that came out of his mouth. My biggest regret was not punching him in the face for how he treated you."

"I would have paid to see that, but honestly Brett is not worth it."

"Exactly, Lainey. He's not worth it. *But you are.* Please, let me help you."

"Why are you being so nice to me?" I whisper.

"Because I can. Now will you please let me have that

stupid journal . . . and your phone number?" Remington asks with a sexy smirk.

I gasp and laugh, smacking my hand into his muscled chest. "See! I knew there was an ulterior motive!"

"How else will I get the finished journal back to you, Lainey?"

"A smoke signal?"

We both laugh.

4

Remington

Remington: What's your favorite color?

Lainey: Who is this??

Remington: . . . You know exactly who this is, little pyro.

Lainey: I thought we were not going to talk about that night ever again . . .

Remington: Impossible. It was the night I met you and is my new favorite day of the year. I am going to petition for it to be a national holiday.

Lainey: OMG you are ridiculous

Remington: So color?

Lainey: Why?

Remington: I need to know so I can pick out a journal that you won't want to burn.

Lainey: Pale lavender.

Remington: Favorite food?

Lainey: How will that help you pick a journal?

Remington: Absolutely vital! What if they have food-themed journals? All this info is a must—Journal Picking 101 😉

Lainey: French toast.

I smile at my phone as I walk down the block toward my sister's shop. I knew that I would be able to find just the right thing there. I also knew I would not be picking an ugly-as-fuck journal that Lainey would hate, so I at least wanted to know her favorite color. Which gave me the perfect excuse to text her—and keep texting her under the guise of Journal Picking 101. I also learned that her favorite coffee order is a flat white, but at home she likes to drink tea. Her favorite season is summer. Her favorite hobby is reading. She has one best friend that lives in town, and they like to share a bottle of wine together once a week.

I like to keep my group of friends small, but it made me sad to think that Lainey only has one good friend here, and I wonder why that is. My sister would probably embrace her into her fold of loud, wild friends in two seconds with or without her permission. Not that either of them needed it. *Shit.* I was already feeling protective over this woman, and she wasn't even mine. Getting close to the storefront, I fired off one more softball question.

Remington: Favorite flower?

Text bubbles appeared and disappeared three times before

a response finally came back to me, one that left me feeling confused.

Lainey: I don't have a favorite flower.

Remington : How is that possible?

Lainey: . . .

Lainey: It isn't something I really talk about, but I guess I have no reason to not tell you. I have already embarrassed myself more than once, and you have my journal, and who knows what you will uncover in there that I forgot about writing.

My heart twists. There was no way I thought a simple question, one that most girls could easily answer, was going to cause her such trepidation. She is nervous and rambling, but in text, like she was last night. I feel like a dick.

Remington: You can tell me anything, Lainey. Always.

Lainey: I was not really allowed to have a favorite.

Remington: I don't understand?

Lainey: My umm dad . . . He always said that they were useless and a big waste of money.

A waste of time. Talking about useless things upset him.

So I didn't allow myself to pick a favorite, to like them, want them.

It doesn't matter.

They just die. You don't get to keep them.

The fuck? I could feel my blood heating with the rage I felt toward a person I never knew. How could a man, a father of a little girl, treat her that way? Make her feel like she couldn't even have a favorite flower for fuck's sake? That they are a waste of time and money? I am sure there is so much more she isn't saying, a deeper meaning behind everything, and I am determined to make Lainey not only see the beauty in her own life, but in flowers and favorite things.

I also know exactly what I am going to do with her new journal.

The bell in Sutton's shop rattles gently to announce my arrival. She pops her blonde head up from behind the antique wood counter and says, "Welcome to . . . Oh, hey, Rem." When she notices that it's only me, her barely one-year-younger brother, she cuts off her normal "Welcome to Brooks and Books" song and dance for customers. Usually I am here to visit or check up on her, but today I will actually *be* a customer.

"Nice to see you too, big sister," I say with a drip of sarcasm while I scoop her tiny frame into a gentle hug, being mindful of her belly.

"Calling any pregnant lady 'big' is a dangerous choice of words, Rem. Deck would kick your ass if he was here," she says with a sniffle. Her husband Derek Brooks, or Deck as we all call him, is a Navy SEAL and currently deployed. Sutton is sixteen weeks pregnant, and Deck left eight weeks ago. She had just found out that they were expecting, in the first trimester sickness that made her feel awful, and it was a really hard time.

Still is a hard time. But we are all here for her. My mom stops at her house daily and calls her lord only knows how many times a day. My dad does all her mowing and yard work, and he even brings her a grocery delivery every few days. I work a lot, but Sutton knows I am always a quick call away, when I am on or off duty. Even Deck is still sending her care packages when he can. Amazon boxes and random things show up at the shop or their house constantly for her or the baby. That man cannot wait to get home and spoil her and that baby in person.

"Sorry, Sut. You're right. Hello, older sister, lovely one that is making me an uncle and going to help me pick out exactly what I am shopping for today," I tell her with a smugness, hoping the last bit of information will perk her up.

"Shopping?" Sutton's shimmering brown eyes lock on me, and she smiles widely. "You aren't just here checking in on me? You *hate* shopping. What are you shopping for?" Her words spill out in a flurry, like if she doesn't get me to admit to talking about the dreaded *s* word that I may change my mind.

Laughing I say, "I make exceptions when I need something important. And I knew that your store would be the perfect place to get what I am looking for." I can feel a flush creeping up my cheeks, realizing I am going to have to tell her more.

"Holy crap, Rem! This is about a girl, isn't it?" Sutton, of course, wouldn't think I would be shopping for myself. "Who is she? What happened?"

"It's not a big deal, I just need a new notebook. Well, not a notebook. I need a nice journal," I explain.

My sister's place is like the quintessential small-town gift shop, bookstore combo. It is the perfect fit for Fox Grove locals, the influx of out-of-towners we get from being not too far from base, and summer vacationers. She and my brother-in-law have worked hard to make Sutton's vision come true, and it has been worth all the hard work. She runs the store full time with the help of a couple dedicated and trusted employees that Deck of course put through hoops and background checks before letting them on to the team.

Brooks and Books is full of earth tones, plants, and organized in a perfect, "chaotically Sutton" way that makes it feel warm and welcoming. The shelves of reclaimed barn wood and thrifted tables are the exact right mismatch blend, displaying everything that has been brought in with a lot of intention. The store offers a unique selection of items curated by Sutton and Deck along with locally made things that also help other small businesses and makers. Each local artist has their own little area showcasing their work.

Sutton spins on her heel, marches toward the back wall of the store, leaving me to follow. The large wall is lined with a selection of cards, notepads, stationery, and most importantly, journals.

"We finally got in some new things that I was waiting on. Put them out and organized it all yesterday. What did you have in mind . . . Or should I ask what did *she* have in mind?" Sutton side-eyes me, the line of questions as subtle as an elephant.

Sighing I say, "Sutton. I met someone and she, ugh, she is really great, but she just went through a shitty breakup, and I am trying to help her out with something. That's why I need that journal. Her ex was a total asshole. She has this thing where she gets a nice journal on her birthday every year. I guess she told him about how she liked Lisa Frank when she was little."

Sutton squeals with delight. I know all about Lisa because my sister was obsessed. She had a big poster of the little tiger above the desk in her bedroom, and she always wanted all the folders and shit for school. "Lisa Frank was THE best! I wonder if Deck would let me do the baby's room in that theme." She starts laughing, tapping a thoughtful finger on her chin. I know that as much as she used to love Lisa, her style has changed drastically, and she would only suggest that to Deck to drive him crazy. And he will love every second of her playful torture.

"Yeah well, you would not love the stupid-ass notebook her ex-boyfriend got her. It's a nightmare knockoff and would make your baby cry. Creepy kittens and butterflies, and she *told* him that she had a puppy notebook when she was little," I say with deep irritation. I fill her in on the coffee shop scene, the fire cleanse, and officially meeting Lainey.

My sister looks at me with soft eyes and says, "Wow, first of all that guy sounds like an idiot. Good for Lainey for breaking up with him in a Sugar Cube–gossip-mill-worthy fashion. I love that *that rumor* I heard about is *her*! So badass. But most importantly, Rem, you are down *bad* for this girl." Sutton looks delighted.

"No, I'm not. I know it's only been a few days . . . But I feel like I was meant to know her. We have a connection, and I am honestly just trying to help her out. Write the stuff from her old notebook into a new journal so she doesn't have to ruin a year of work and memories or her tradition because of him. Hopefully, it will help me get to know her, and maybe she will give me a chance to prove to her that not all guys are assholes."

"Just be careful, Rem. I don't want you to get hurt." Sutton softly delivers her sisterly warning.

Sutton knows I long for a real relationship, and that I have a hard time letting anyone get too close. She also knows all the shit in my past that makes it hard for me to let people in, even when it's the thing I crave the most. I think back to the way Lainey bravely handed over her journal to me, a stranger, and then opened up to me again when we were texting about the flowers. She has every reason to be closed off, and I have a feeling that she is with other people, but with me she opened the door. She let me in, and it makes me want to let her in, too.

Eli is always telling me that I need to relax and play the field like him. He swipes his apps, hits it and forgets it, but that is not what I want. I have always been ready for more, but my past burned me so badly that I swore off any kind of real and meaningful relationships and had only been casually dating.

The minute Lainey Quinn's eyes locked on mine, I think I knew I was ready to jump back into the fire, especially if she was the one starting it.

5

Lainey

How could I have been so stupid? Why did I tell Remington all that stuff about the flowers? I should *not* have given him that much honesty. I should have made up an answer. Told him a white lie. Why can't I just have a normal answer like a normal girl? Every other girl I know loves flowers and knows exactly what kind they liked the best.

I should have said roses. But then would he think that is too flirty, forward? Are roses too sexy of a flower to be your favorite? Maybe that only applies to red ones? Should I have said a daisy? Or is that too simple or plain? I don't even know. I *can't* even know. I haven't allowed myself to like flowers, as I explained to Remington. The idea of thinking about them, figuring out what I truly enjoy without judgment is so overwhelming.

God, he must think I am insane.

It has been a few hours since our text exchange, and I have not heard from him. It says he read my message. I am trying really hard not to overthink everything, but that is not how my mind or my anxiety works. Thankfully, I had some work to do at my desk, and also had a quick meeting that just wrapped up.

I love my PR job, and the fact that I get to work remotely now is a blessing. I was in the city, Washington DC area that is, for eight months for a special training program that my company wanted me to do. I kept my apartment here because they paid for my small temp place there. Brett was also in the city, and I was so excited about it. I thought that I would spend a lot of time with him, but looking back on it now, I really didn't. We only saw each other a couple times a week. I would meet him for a lunch or dinner, maybe hook up a couple times a week. We would rarely spend the night together, and if we did it was always at my crappy little apartment. He said he was busy with work, that his place was on the opposite side of town so my place was more convenient, that he needed to get rest for early morning meetings. Looking back now, it should have been so obvious.

When I came home to Fox Grove once my training was over, and Brett and I were doing long distance, I was the one making all the effort. I was the one that cared. He said he missed me and that I was important to him. He knew all the things to say to keep me hooked enough to keep me happy, or so I thought. Now, knowing what I do, I think he was just full of shit. I was a placeholder for I don't even know what. We were definitely not on the same page as far as what a committed relationship was, and I can't believe that once again, I picked wrong.

Shutting down my work programs for the day and thinking about what I should do for dinner, there's a buzz for my apartment door. I walk over to the wall unit, leaden anxiety swooping in and nearly stealing my voice with the press of the button. "Hello?" I say down to the front buzzer of the building.

"Yes, I have a delivery for a Ms. Quinn," a young man's voice says back.

"Okay, thank you," I say and press the button to allow the person access to the building. I hate answering the door, having to sign for packages, unexpected deliveries, knocks on the door. I normally know exactly what I order and when they are coming. I know that I have some new sheets ordered from Amazon, due to come tomorrow, but maybe they are a day early? I guess I can shove down the uncomfortable swell of anxiety from having an unplanned interaction with a delivery person knowing I will have the reward of getting to wash my pretty sheets and slip into crisp, clean, soft bedding that only *I* have ever slept in.

The light tap on my door shakes me from my drifting thoughts and I check my doorbell camera on my phone that I set up. What I see is not the Amazon guy leaving my box, but a high-school-aged boy with shaggy brown hair, a baseball hat, glasses, light bomber jacket, and beautiful bouquet of flowers. I unlock and open the door, and the boy smiles. "Ms. Quinn?" he asks cheerfully.

"Yes, that's me," I confirm.

"Great! I have these here for you," he says, handing over the pretty mix of reds, pinks, oranges, yellows, and whites of the same type of flower mixed with some kinds of greenery. "I hope you have a fantastic day!" The high school boy spins down the hallway before he can hear my whispered thank you.

Shutting and locking my door, I carry the flowers to my coffee table and sink down into my soft cream couch.

Shock. I am in shock.

There is only one person that could have sent me these flowers, and only one person that I *want* to have sent me these flowers. I stare at them for several long minutes admiring the bright, cheerful colors before realizing that there is a little white envelope tucked into the bouquet. I lift the card with trembling fingers and slide out the note.

LIFE IS THE BEAUTY, LAINEY. EVEN THE THINGS THAT MIGHT NOT LAST FOREVER, THEY ARE STILL WORTH TAKING THE TIME TO ENJOY THEM. A DESSERT, A SUNSET, AND DEFINITELY FLOWERS.

WE ARE GOING TO TAKE THE TIME. WE ARE GOING TO FIND YOUR FAVORITE.

-R

PS: THESE ARE RANUNCULUS.

THEY SYMBOLIZE CHARM AND ATTTRACTIVENESS.

I read his words over and over, and I let tears fall. Nobody has ever done something like this for me. Not only the flowers, but the words that went along with them. Remington had shaken me to my very core. I assumed that after texting with me, after hearing more depressing honesty from me, that he would be sprinting in the other direction . . . not going to the local florist, picking out flowers, and hand writing me a note. This handsome, strong, alpha, heroic firefighter has a caring, sweet side and I wonder if he does this for everyone.

My stomach drops at the thought. He offered to take my journal only because he was being nice, he even admitted it. I'm positive that this is just part of it. It has to be. We were texting and I shocked him with my truth. He felt sorry for me. He might *truly* be a nice guy, so he went out of his way to do this, to make me feel better.

The ever present, mean, unworthy voice hisses in my head that this is all that it is.

He doesn't have feelings for me, he doesn't like me-like me. I am just the basket case, weird, pyro girl that he feels sorry for. That man, the sexy hero with the deep voice, caring soul, and matching eyes doesn't want a mess like me.

A different kind of tear slides down my cheek as I pull out my phone.

6

Remington

After reading those texts from Lainey I knew that a simple reply back was not going to be enough. I wanted to show her that she is worthy of more, and I want to be the man that gives it to her.

I can't stop thinking about her stunning, stormy blue eyes and the way they welled with tears the night of her little fire. I can also imagine them filling back up texting me about flowers, something that should, in most instances, make you fucking happy. I am determined to give that woman some sunshine and happiness in as many forms as possible. Starting with figuring out her favorite flower. I have a sinking feeling that she has been let down by a lot of men in her life—beginning with her dad, and most recently with Brett. Who knows what she has experienced in any of her other relationships?

Just the thought of her with any other man makes my blood heat in an insane, caveman, possessive manner. Lainey is not mine. She isn't even my friend, technically. We have known each other for a matter of days, but it feels like I was meant to know her, like I explained to my extremely nosey sister. Shit, Sutton will not let me off the hook. The way that she lit up when I was at her store, and then when I told her why? It makes me happy I came to her to pick out the journal for Lainey.

I love my sister, but I don't open up to her about my personal life that often, especially after my one and only long-term girlfriend, Cora Tyler, completely fucked me up. What made it worse was that she was one of Sutton's best friends. I know that my sister carries guilt that is not her own burden to hold when it comes to the cataclysmic failure that was mine and Cora's relationship. Sutton had dreams of Cora being her sister one day and all the family things that go along with it. I thought I wanted that too, until Cora showed me who she really was. After that, my desire for love, marriage, and family never went away, but I never trusted anyone with that part of myself ever again.

The scary thing about Lainey is I don't even know much about her, but she has cracked open that hope chest I had locked up tight. It was firmly placed in the back of my mind, a shitty attic space that collects dust, forgotten dreams, and ghosts. I saw something in her that mirrors my own desires, and I want to shine the light into all my dark and forgotten spaces in the hopes that maybe she will let me in, help her get rid of some of her own shadows and whatever haunts her pretty eyes.

But I guess she *has* let me in . . . I go to grab her journal. *A whole year of her*. Things that she was drawn to and loved so much that she needed to write them down so that she could remember them forever. I can't believe she was planning to torch the whole thing because of that dick. I mean, I get it, I wouldn't want anything from Cora sitting around on a shelf seeping toxicity into a cherished tradition. I am happy I can help Lainey with this, save what was written inside, and get rid of the evidence that fuckface, Brett, ever had anything to do with her favorite thing.

I hadn't looked at her writing yet, wanting to give myself time for more than a quick passing glance at it. As I walk through my living room I wonder what Lainey would think of my house—*shit. I really am down bad like Sutton teased me.* But I can't help not picturing Lainey curled up on the worn leather couch with me, writing in a new journal. Or watching me cook her dinner. Does she like to cook? I know one thing for sure, I want to make her French toast in my kitchen and bring her breakfast in bed after a long night of staying up way too late, memorizing every inch of her perfect body. I am sure her brown hair is as soft as it looks and is the perfect length for me to wrap my fist around. I let out a groan as my cock twitches behind my zipper at the idea of my dream girl in my bed all night. Before I can get too lost in my thoughts, I sit down and flip open the first page of her journal.

Happy birthday to me . . . I was really looking forward to going to pick out my new journal this afternoon, but then Brett surprised me with–this, um, special one. So, I am going to make the most of it and use it. It seemed to be what he was expecting me to use it for, so it made him grin at me when I told him I would.

Next year I can pick something else, go crazy in my own way. Maybe even something with some actual cute animals or something different on it?

"Blessed is he who expects nothing, for he shall never be disappointed." –Alexander Pope

Shit, Lainey couldn't even allow her full feeling of frustration and displeasure to be put down in the journal. She was still trying to people please even on paper. That was really sad and obviously so conditioned she couldn't see any other way. There was a mix of the kindness, her pure heart, and of what she felt was expected of her . . . but there was also the flicker of defiance with the quote. A little pushback. It was not positive or happy, but it was there.

My phone dings signaling a new text. I grab it expecting it to be Eli with plans to hit up the gym, but the name I see makes me grin.

Lainey: Thank you for the flowers. They are beautiful, and that was very kind of you.

Image: Lainey wearing a soft, almost sad, smile and holding the bouquet of flowers.

Jesus, she takes my breath away. Examining the photo on my phone, I wonder why she looks kind of sad. I thought she would be happier. I hope that I didn't already mess this up, push too much, freak her out . . .

Remington: You're very welcome. They are the second most beautiful thing in that picture.

Lainey: Doubtful.

Remington: I don't lie, Lainey. That is something that's important for you to know.

I will always be honest with you.

Lainey: You are a good man, Remington. These are officially my favorite flowers, no need to try and figure out if I like anything better.

I laugh at that. I might not know Lainey well yet, but I knew *that* was bullshit. You can't pick your favorite flower after only seeing one option.

Remington: Beautiful . . . I just told you I would be honest with you, that means you have to be honest with me.

Remington: You can't pick a favorite yet when you haven't seen all your options.

Lainey: 😳 ALL my options! Remington LeBlanc, you are not allowed to send me "all" the options.

Remington: Why not?

Lainey: 1- That's impossible.

2- That's crazy.

3- You will be bankrupt.

4- You don't even know me.

5- I am not worth any of this effort.

I knew that cracking Lainey's walls would be hard, but the first thing I needed to do was prove to her that she was worthy of my time, attention, and effort. How many people did she have in her corner to help take care of her, or was she always taking care of other people? This woman was drop-dead gorgeous but brushed aside any compliment I gave her. She tried to stop me from simple acts of kindness, fully thinking that I must have some devious, twisted ulterior motive. It pained me to know that the interactions and people that had paved the path before had woven this mistrust and lack of self-worth into Lainey. *Fuck that.*

Remington: 1- I can give you as many flowers as possible, one way or another.

2- I am very creative.

3- I minored in finance and am pretty good with money, so I am not worried.

4- Let's fix that.

5- You are worth everything.

7

Lainey

I stare at my phone. He could not be a real person, right? There is no way possible that I, Lainey Quinn, found this gem of a man and he's being this kind to me . . . telling me that I am worth *everything*. And it doesn't feel insincere, slimy, or like some overused line to try and get something from me. Every interaction with Remington is different. I know that he's genuine.

I have been my own worst enemy when it comes to men and relationships, always giving them too much credit when they have not earned it yet. I am a glass half full, believe in a better world, fairy tale love can happen kind of girl. I have seen friends fall in love and find their perfect match. It just doesn't happen for me. I find the rotten apples disguised in candy coating. Poison that slowly drips into my system, making it too hard to feel because I'm in deep, numb and wanting to give the person the benefit of the doubt, while they are simultaneously whispering *doubts about myself* to me.

It takes me too long to pull myself out of bad situations. I have the unfortunate life-experience receipts to look back on to confirm my self-loathing right now. This is not just a "one bad boyfriend" whoopsie. I am historically awful at picking the right men to have in my life.

When I met Remington I felt this draw to him, and I told myself it meant nothing. This had to be rose-colored glasses for the first person being a little bit nice to me after what happened with Brett. But deep down, I know I am wrong. There is not one speck of my body or soul that gets a vibe from Remington that says he is full of the deception or toxicity that I am used to. Every other man, even if I never wanted to admit it at the time or upon reflection, had red flags right off the bat. I swear to all the saints I am like honey to a bee when it comes to those toxic men. It is like they can feel the daddy issues, vulnerability, and need for more pouring off of me even when I try to lock that all in. And then they pounce.

I want to give, and they love to take.

And it's always painful.

Leaving me with scars deeper than the skin, imprinted on my soul. Whispers of *unworthy and unlovable* scratch through my brain on the most unhealthy record player of all time. So, when a man like Remington LeBlanc walks into your life, wipes tears from your face with strong, callused hands, and offers to help you out of pure kindness, then sends you flowers? He tells you he wants to help you even more, to *know you*?

God, *that is everything.*

It also scares the shit out of me.

I should not allow myself to have any kind of feelings for anyone right now. I don't have a problem being alone. Relationships, as awful as they have been, are not a chronic problem for me. I have only seriously dated three people in my twenty-six years. Then, the handful of casual dates scattered in between were unsuccessful setups, or thankfully never turned into more than one or two dates.

Remington wants my honesty, so I guess that is what I will

give to him. Not only because I want to, but I think he might be the first man that actually deserves it.

Lainey: I don't even know what to say to that . . .

Remington: Say that you will let me take you to dinner tomorrow night?

I blush reading his immediate response, like he was waiting for his chance to ask me out. *Is he asking me out? Is it a date or just going as friends?* I want to go back and overanalyze all the things he said to me and try and figure it out, but I know he's waiting for me to answer, and I can't sit here debating in my own head, leaving him on read for too long.

Lainey: Dinner sounds great. I should be done with work around 5.

Remington: Perfect.

Lainey: Where should I meet you?

Remington: I will pick you up at 7.

Lainey: You don't have to do that, I don't want you to go out of your way.

Remington: I'm picking you up at 7, Lainey. Nothing for you is out of my way.

Lainey: Okay see you tomorrow, Remington ☺️

Remington: It's a date 😉

A kaleidoscope of butterflies take off in my stomach as I read the exact words that confirm what I desperately wanted to know. And they make me race toward my closet, already worried about what I am going to wear.

8

Lainey

As I smooth a shimmery, copper eye shadow lightly on my eyelid, classic ’90s country playing on my phone, I glance at the time.

Shit, shit, shit! It’s 6:55 and I am *not* ready.

I had a total anxiety spiral about what I was going to wear even after I tried to do early prep yesterday. I didn’t want to wear anything I wore on any previous dates, which ended up making me clean out a huge bag of things to donate. *Donate, not burn.* It seems so stupid to get rid of tops and dresses that I genuinely like and flatter my figure, but I can’t let go of the memories attached to them. This is my time to start over, and “Lainey 2.0” is not taking bad energy into what will hopefully be good. The fire was apparently just the start—I needed a closet cleanse, too.

I had put on one of my very best dresses of all time. A sapphire-blue sundress with cap sleeves, a scooped neckline, and little pink polka dots in a delicate, almost transparent pattern all over. It was feminine, fun, soft, but also sexy. Perfect for a first date, any date in my opinion, which is why I remembered that I wore it on a date with Brett. We had gone to dinner in the city when I was doing my training program for work. He didn't even compliment me, instead gave me a scoff as we left, asking if that was really what I was going to wear to the French place he was taking me. Evidently it was not up to his standards, too casual. He had no problem taking the dress off later that night and using my body to get himself off in less than five minutes, leaving me laying in my bed alone, disappointed, and having to "compliment" myself once he left. So, yup, that dress was in the *absolutely not* pile along with several other things that another woman would hopefully stumble upon in the thrift shop and create her own favorite memories in. That dress deserved happy thoughts, not morose ones.

The closet overhaul left my room in disarray, kept me up until midnight, and still hadn't been rectified since I had a full day of work, and a final team meeting that ran later than expected. That had me rushing my hair and it turned out terrible. My curls never look good when I need them to. I am not one of those fancy YouTube girls or influencers that know all the tips and tricks to make your looks flawless in fifteen minutes—or ever. I should have called my best friend over for help, but it was too late for that now. The frustrating hair was tossed into a messy bun with a few loose curls framing my face. It was as good as it was going to get. My make-up at least was cooperating, and I didn't ruin my eyeliner with my shaky hands. Anxiety was eating me up from the inside out as I applied my mascara, and I prayed that Remington was a few minutes late so I could finish panicking and getting dressed in Shania Twain peace.

I cranked up "Any Man of Mine" trying to hype myself up and told her that just this once "my man" *could be late for this date* . . . not that he was my man, but wouldn't that be something?

Lainey! Snap out of it, girl . . . Shimmy your butt into an outfit, so you don't scare the man. Good lord, even a few wandering thoughts about Remington were so distracting.

My door button buzzed just as I was going back to my closet.

"No, no, no!" I grabbed my lavender robe and tossed it on as I rushed to the door. "Hello?"

"Hey, Lainey." Remington's deep voice came through the speaker. "Sorry, I am a few minutes late." I look at the clock on the wall and it literally says 7:04.

I laugh and say, "No worries, I'm still getting dressed. I will unlock the door, so just come on in when you get up here." Then I hit the buzzer, unlocking the security door downstairs, and run to my bedroom.

I quickly find my favorite pair of skinny jeans. I don't care if they are trendy or not, nobody can make me stop wearing them. Next I put on a cute lavender front-knotted V-neck top with lace detailing along the neckline. The floral pattern on it is muted and complements the slides that I grab from my closet. As I slip my feet into my shoes I hear the front door open and shut. Looking into the mirror above my dresser, I give myself a nod, take a deep breath, and decide on a pair of simple silver hoops.

"I can do this," I tell my reflection.

"I want to do this."

"I deserve to enjoy this."

As I step out of my bedroom, I suck in a breath when I see Remington standing so casually in my living room. He takes up so much space, but in the best way. He fills the room with his safe, comforting presence effortlessly. Remington's eyes lock with mine as I take him in slowly, head to toe. His blond hair is perfectly mussed, like he'd ran his fingers though it recently. The deep olive-green, long-sleeved Henley hugs all of his hard-earned muscles, and makes his amber eyes stand out even more. The jeans he's wearing are a dark wash that travel down his perfect, thick legs to his booted feet. *Jesus, I am a sucker for a man in boots.* And these are not the ones that are just for show, they are well worn, but cared for, and I am sure will do amazing things for his ass if he turned around and I got a peek.

From behind his back Remington pulls out a bouquet and steps toward me, handing the flowers to me. "You look so incredibly stunning," he rasps as his eyes trail over my face, lingering on my lips.

Goose bumps race across my skin, and I bite down on my lip. "Thank you. You look very handsome yourself. And thank you for these, they're so pretty. What are they?" I ask, finally giving the flowers the attention they deserve. There are a mix of two different flowers this time in pinks and whites, each uniquely shaped but interesting and textured.

"The pink ones are snapdragons and the white ones are dahlias. I know people typically do roses for first dates, but I think you require something unique," Remington says with a smile that tugs at something low in my belly.

"Unique, huh? Because I am the crazy girl you meet burning stuff, and roses are too normal?" I ask with sarcasm directed at him and that constant skepticism directed at my own heart.

Chuckling with a low, sexy hum he says, "Absolutely not. Unique because you are special and deserve something with thought and care behind it, not just grabbing the easy thing that everyone else might pick."

"Oh," I say, feeling unexpected wetness gathering in the corners of my eyes as he continues.

"Mm-hmm. Flowers represent a lot of things to a lot of people. Mean a lot of different things, too. Including these ones. Do you want to know why I picked these for you, Lainey?"

"Yes," I whisper so softly I'm not sure Remington can even hear me.

Stepping even closer to me he says, "Dahlias have a whole list, but for you I picked them because they can represent beauty, inner strength, and growth." I suck in a breath. "Snapdragons can not only represent strength, but also mystery. And they are just really fucking fun." Remington gives me a full-on, world-spinning, heart-racing smile. I watch as he takes one of the delicate pink flowers from the snapdragons in between his thick fingers. I assume he is going to crush the petals, or pluck them off, but instead he gently pinches the flower, and it pops open revealing the hidden inside of the plant.

I grin back at Remington. "I want to try it!" Pinching the flowers myself carefully, the little heads of the petals pop in my fingers—open and shut, open and shut. It's magical, simple, and whimsical. I look up to see Remington already watching me with so much emotion written all over his handsome face. "I had no idea a little flower could be so much fun," I admit to him, and my shoulders slump.

"Hey, hey," he says, wrapping me in a hug, his clean soap and cedar scent and strong arms comforting me. "I figured you wouldn't know the fun of this if you didn't *really* know about different flowers. My mom had snapdragons planted all along the front porch of our house growing up, and my sister and I used to spend a lot of time playing with them. Watching all the different bugs come to them, my favorite was always the praying mantis. Anyways, I want to give you all the flowers, Lainey. The simple ones, the romantic ones, the unique ones, *and* the fun ones."

"I love them," I say earnestly. "Thank you, Remington."

He smiles at me and asks, "Ready for dinner?"

"Yes! I am starved. Probably not best first-date etiquette to say that, huh? But I was so busy with work, a meeting that ran late, and then getting ready that I didn't get a chance to eat much today."

Frowning at me he says, "There are no fancy rules or etiquette for dating me. The only thing I want is your honesty. I don't like that you didn't eat all day today, that isn't good. Let's go remedy that, shall we?"

"Okay, let's go." After putting the flowers in water, I grab my purse, phone, and keys to lock up. We step out into the hallway, and I shut and lock the door. Lacing his fingers through mine, Remington makes my heart rate take off as we head toward the elevators.

"By the way," Remington says as we step into the open elevator car, "I don't like that you buzzed me up and left your door unlocked. I wish you would have waited for me. I tried to text you that, but you didn't respond."

"Oh, I didn't even see that, sorry," I say, tension souring my gut. "I really wasn't ready when you buzzed, and was in my robe, and needed to get dressed. I was in a hurry, and I didn't want to waste your time, and was trying to just be as fast . . ."

Remington cuts my flurry of words off as he leans his body into mine against the wall, strong hands framing my face. His eyes looking deep into mine, thumb running along my jawline halting my rambling. "Breathe, Lainey."

I instantly obey.

"I don't mind that you needed some more time to get ready. I would have sat and waited twenty minutes, two hours, as long as you needed. All I cared about was you being safe. Leaving your door unlocked and just letting me come in isn't safe. What if someone other than me walked in? I know that this is Fox Grove, but you never know. Next time please wait for me to come to the door, okay?"

I grin at him. This man. He is flipping my world upside down with every sentence that comes out of his mouth, and he has no clue. It's just him being *him*. "Next time, huh? We haven't even completed our first date. That's some confidence you have there, Remington."

"Oh trust me, beautiful, there is definitely going to be a next time." He winks at me, steps back, and pulls me off of the elevator, out of my building, and into the fresh spring air.

9

Remington

Jesus, Lainey is absolutely stunning. When she walked out of her room it left me speechless and just staring at her for way too long. Thank fuck she was staring right back at me, tracing her alluring blue eyes over my body, going wide when she realized what she was doing. Having her hand in mine as I walked her to my truck felt like slipping my hand into a tiny, warm pocket that was meant only for me. I didn't want to let her go as I opened the passenger door and helped her inside the cab. She quietly thanked me, and I rounded the black hood, taking a deep, steadying breath before I allowed myself to join her, knowing that the second I did my truck would be engulfed with her sweet, honeyed scent. I prayed the deep-grey fabric would soak it up and let me hold on to a small part of her even after tonight was over.

I swear to God this girl is already sinking in so deep. I know that once I really get to know her more there will be no going back. Lainey Quinn is fucking me up, and I am here for it.

"Where are we going?" Lainey asks, snapping me out of my Lainey-fueled spiral.

Coughing to clear my throat, I reply, "There are only a handful of places here in Fox Grove, but I thought we could order from Gino's and then take it to one of my favorite places. If that sounds okay with you?" I was hoping that a casual, relaxed date would be the best thing for tonight. I wanted to get to know Lainey, and also have time alone without the pressure of the gossiping grandmas and anyone else that might be out tonight.

"Oh, I love Gino's!" she exclaims with a genuine smile. "They have such a great menu for a small-town family place, but my guilty pleasure is the cheese bread. Sometimes I just order a box of that and have it for my dinner." She covers her face as she finishes her sentence, seemingly embarrassed, like she admitted something she shouldn't have.

"Damn that bread could be the only thing that Gino's sold, and I think that they could still stay in business. There is nothing to be ashamed about admitting that you have excellent taste." I look over at her, and she looks at me with eyes that almost shimmer with tears. I have no idea why my simple comment makes her have this reaction, but I want to know why, and then kick the ass of the person that hurt her. Or likely more than one person . . . but hell, she could order ten boxes of cheese bread, anything she wanted.

"What is your favorite thing to get there?" Lainey asks.

"You mean besides the kick-ass cheese bread?"

Laughing she says, "Yeah, Remington, of course! Besides the bread, what's second place for you at Gino's?"

"I'd have to say the chicken parm. I think they put something in the breading, some kind of secret spice that is so good. I tried to replicate it at home, and it's disappointingly not the same. I can never get it right." Sighing, I think about the failed attempts. My parm turned out fine, but I didn't want *fine*, I wanted Gino's.

"You know how to cook?" Lainey asks with a healthy dose

of surprise as I swing my truck into the restaurant's busy parking lot.

"Of course I do, I am a grown-ass man. I cannot live on boxed mac and cheese, takeout, and cereal. Also, we take turns cooking at the fire station. So, even the guys that don't necessarily *like* to cook know how to cook a couple dishes for their turn. But I *actually* enjoy it. It's relaxing, and I like cooking for people I care about." I say the last thing, giving her a pointed look, hoping she can tell that means I would like to cook for her someday. The French toast fantasy comes to mind, and I shut that shit down immediately. I don't need to get out of this truck and freak Lainey out with a hard-on after just talking about cooking food for fuck's sake.

"I think it's really nice that you know how to cook and enjoy it. I like to cook, too. My mom and I spent some time cooking together, but we didn't get to do much experimenting," Lainey explains with a frown, fidgety in her seat and looking out the window.

Huh, definitely more there to unpack. This woman is an onion, and I want to peel back all the layers. She opened up to me in so many ways, told me a lot of things that I think even surprised her so far, but there is obviously so much more. Underneath the cheerful, sweet, caring demeanor there is also a layer of hurt, mistrust, and pain. I am not a therapist, but I have a feeling it had very little to do with limp-dick Brett and their split. Whatever pain Lainey was harboring was much heavier, carved from places in her past that went back way further than a couple of years.

With a double order of chicken parm, three boxes of cheese bread, and Lainey's shock, protests, and laughter, we headed out to one of my favorite places—Eagle Point. People around here had a real affinity for naming shit after animals, but this spot actually fit its name better than most. The lookout point gave a panoramic view of the town, and we made it just in time for sunset. I pulled the stack of pillows and blankets from the back seat of my truck that I had packed and made a cozy spot in the bed of my truck. After helping Lainey up and making sure she was comfortable and warm enough, I grabbed our food and joined her.

The few locks of hair that were not in her bun blew gently in the wind, and she closed her eyes, taking a deep breath. I couldn't look away from her if someone paid me. The soft glow of the sunset kisses the apples of her cheeks, warming her skin even as the temperature around us started to drop. A shiver goes over her skin and she pops her eyes open, finding mine already locked on hers. And then she smiles at me, fully, without any kind of hesitation or shyness, which I was expecting.

"Hi," she says.

"Hello, beautiful." I smile back at her. "Are you still warm enough?"

"Yes, I am, thank you. I can't believe how much thought and effort you put into all of this. I have never been up here. Heard about it but have never made the drive up to see what all the fuss was about. I definitely get it now," Lainey says looking out at the pink and orange clouds blanketing our small town.

"It's been a while since I have been up here," I admit, "and I forgot how much I used to love the peace and stillness. And as far as the effort, there wasn't much. It's just grabbing a few things to make sure that you're comfortable, anyone would do that, Lainey."

"Remington, you aren't anyone. And nobody, and I really mean it . . . nobody, has taken the time to do thoughtful things like this for me, take my comfort, wants, or opinions into consideration. So these things that seem really small and easy to you are actually huge for me." Lainey peels back another layer of herself and slices me to my very core as she does it. How is it possible that nobody, *nobody,* has treated this woman with the most basic effort, let alone anything extra?

Reaching out, I take her hand in mine, still a perfect fit, and say, "If there ever comes a day that I don't do these things for you like it's second nature, not because it's just a habit, but because it's what you fucking deserve, then we will have a serious problem. I will never give you anything less than what you should get. And to be honest, I hope to exceed that as much as I possibly can. I understand we are still just getting to know each other, Lainey, but I feel that every ounce of time and effort I put toward whatever *this* might be is exactly how I should be spending it."

I let my words sit with her, a soft and peaceful silence hanging between us. I will prove myself over time with my actions toward her. That's the only way a woman that has been treated like Lainey has in the past will ever believe me. Words mean a lot, but actions often speak so much louder.

Determined to shift the mood, I ask, "What was your favorite memory growing up here?"

"Actually, I didn't grow up here," Lainey says. "My mom is from here, both my parents were from here."

"Oh, I assumed you grew up here and I just didn't know you or your siblings? Somehow I missed you, which seems unlikely. Chief said he knew your mom, and she was happy you were back?"

Lainey sighs. "Yes. Well my dad *hated* this town. Hates this town. He said that anyone that stayed here was a loser and would never make anything of their life. So when he and my mom left for college, and then eventually got married, they never came back." Lainey picks at her food, taking a small bite of chicken, not looking at me.

"Geez, that is a bit of a harsh view of small-town life," I say, trying not to take my offense from her dad's words out on her.

"I agree," she says soothingly. Surprising me, she reaches out and rubs her hand over mine. "My mom likes this town, didn't want to leave, and always dreamed of raising me and my brother here. That is what I am working with in the sibling department, by the way. One brother, Calvin. He's five years older than I am."

"Are the two of you close?" I ask her, keeping her hand in mine.

"Ha! Definitely not, and thank God for it. We were not friends growing up, or now. I have very, very limited contact with him. He is cut from the same cloth as our father. They both don't like that I am very much like my mother as far as wanting to live here. She came back to Fox Grove my senior year of college when they finally got a divorce. When I moved here, my dad and brother both threw a fit. Threatened me, told me I was making the biggest mistake of *my* life."

My protective instincts were beyond a simmer, and now my lid is about to blow. "They fucking *threatened you*? What did they do, Lainey?" I needed to know as much as I needed my next breath of air.

"He told me that he would blacklist me from every PR firm in DC, cut me off financially. All the usual manipulation and BS. Don't worry, Remington. I'm safe, it was not a physical threat from my dad or anything like that. Although my brother got in my face on behalf of my dad, he backed off when I threatened his precious balls. And I'm doing fine. I have a great job that I love, and it has zero connections to them or their businesses. Also, I have not relied on my dad financially for anything since my sophomore year of college when all he paid for was my books. He thinks he has all kinds of control over me, but he doesn't. Which he hates, which makes him lash out. Trust and believe that I have spent many hours, and much of my hard-earned money in therapy working on my 'daddy issues,'" she says, using her cute little hands to make air quotes and rolling her eyes.

"Why the hell are you smirking at me like that?" she asks in a much higher voice than just previously.

Smiling fully I say, "You are so goddamn cute when you get all worked up and feisty. And it's really, *really* hot when you stick up for yourself like that."

"You don't even know if I stuck up for myself," she says indignantly. "You weren't there."

Oh now she is getting so worked up, and extra sassy. It makes me want to grab her face and kiss the shit out of those pouty lips, but I resist. "I can tell you stuck up for yourself just by your take-no-shit attitude right now, Lainey. Had you *not* gone through with it and set some boundaries, probably something that was really hard to do, we wouldn't be having this conversation. You would probably still be in DC."

Lainey blinks at me like a little owl. Taking another big bite out of a stick of cheese bread, she chews slowly, obviously needing time to think of how she wanted to respond—how deep she was willing to let me in.

Fuck, baby, please let me all the way in.

Finally she relents. "You're right."

"I know," I reply smugly, giving her a raised brow.

"Ugh." Lightly smacking my forearm, she continues, "Boundaries *are* very, very difficult for me, especially when it comes to him because all I ever wanted was to make him happy and gain his approval. However, nothing was ever good enough. No test score high enough, no effort was the best I could have given. I was a B student, but in my parents' eyes it might as well have been straight failing. Anything I did was bottom of the barrel according to him, even if I had killed myself for the results. I never once heard him say he was proud of me." She is looking at me this time, as more of her trust spills out around us, pouring into the quiet air. The deep russet-gold-colored clouds fill up the sky as the sun dips low, about to tuck in for the night. One last spectacular burst of warm light for the day.

When Sutton and I decided what to do with our lives, the most important thing to my parents was for us to always work hard, do something we are passionate about, and make *ourselves* proud. My parents have a great life and are happy. They love us and our family endlessly, however they are absolutely not living vicariously through us because they have always lived the life they have wanted. My mom said she doesn't need to try and relive any kind of glory days. Every day she wakes up next to my dad and gets to have her family is her best day. Glory days are for people that don't have anything good and purposeful in their current lives. High school and college, or whatever time people get stuck in, do nothing but hold them back from fully embracing the happiness of the life they are living in the here and now.

Lainey looks out at the sunset, and the pain from her words hits me in a sharp place that I can't even really name. My parents were always so supportive, loving, and kind. Still are. Charles and Renee LeBlanc are the type of people that are easy to look up to, and most definitely told their children they were proud of them. Good grades were praised, sure, but overall effort was more valued. Also, when we made hard choices, went down a path that was unexpected but the right thing for us, when we wanted to take a chance they supported us and loved us through the ups and downs, still do. We have their pride and their support. It's the kind that is expressed with their words often but carried with us in our bones. I remember my dad telling us to be fierce, be kind, be true to ourselves. Most of all, he wanted us to, no matter what, know that we were enough. He would always say, "You are the *best* part of me. I am so proud to be along for the ride." To not have that kind of support from a parent is unimaginable to me.

"Lainey, I am really sorry that you had to deal with that," I say, hoping she can feel my honesty and concern. "What about your mom? Are you close with her?"

Lainey pinches the bridge of her nose, stress running over her creased brow. "That is a whole other conversation. A complicated one. She is good at hiding who she really is and letting the world think we had a picture-perfect DC family." Her sigh carries a weight that must feel like a mountain. "It's fine." She tries to brush off my comments, but I won't let her.

She is still looking out at the sky that is quickly turning inky, and a cool breeze is picking up. She shivers and pulls a blanket up farther on her lap. I tuck one of the stray hairs behind her ear, and she looks over at me, a sad smile on her lips. I can see that she is trying to bury her past, her pain, her thoughts. Hide in her usual place that she thinks she needs to when she is with other people to make them more comfortable. Well she needs to know, right here and now, I am not other people. *I want to be her person.*

"It's far from fine, Lainey. No child should ever have to grow up like that. Wondering if they are enough? Begging for affection, and having to live off scraps?" She sucks in a sharp breath at my words, but I don't stop. "Nothing about that is okay. A parent is supposed to have unconditional love for their children, and it sounds like your father, and even your mother, had nothing *but* conditions. That is not love." I rub my thumb along her cheek and down to her jaw, a habit I apparently can't quit when she is close to me. Her striking blue eyes study my face as she absorbs my words.

"Thank you." A soft whisper carries her words to me.

"For what?" I ask.

"Seeing me. Telling me things that nobody else has. Talking to a therapist is not the same thing. They are trained, and paid, and have helped to a certain extent. It was instrumental for me in learning how to handle conversations and dealing with my father and mother, but there was still a lot that has not healed. A lot that I still have to work through. But you don't even really know me, and yet I feel like you might be the first person in my life that has *truly seen me*. I try to hide my feelings and be fine for everyone else, and they usually allow me to get away with it. But . . ." Lainey sighs deeply.

"But?"

"You are different. This feels different." Her eyes look up at me, and I swear she is burning herself into my very soul.

"Yeah, Lainey, this is different." I tug her close to me and lean back against my truck. We watch as the stars start to pop into the dark sky, and she relaxes in my hold.

Yeah, this is definitely different, and I really hope I don't fuck it up, because I will never get enough of Lainey Quinn, or proving to her that *she is enough* exactly as she is.

10

Lainey

He didn't kiss me good night. We had a perfect date. I could not believe how thoughtful and planned out everything was. I had zero intention of telling him most of the things I did, especially about my parents, but there is something about Remington that makes me want to tell him everything. That terrifies me. If I give him so much of myself, my fears, my past, my dreams, all of it, any of it—that gives him so much power to break me. More than any other man, any other person has had the ability to in the past.

After the heavier conversation, we laid in the bed of his truck for a long while talking about everything and nothing. Lighter topics that helped us get to know each other better. I learned that he hates blueberries but loves apples. His favorite color is blue. He wants to have a dog someday, but his schedule at the fire station doesn't really allow for that right now. His parents have been married for almost forty years, and he has a deep respect for their relationship. I had a pang in my chest listening to him talk about them, and I desperately want to meet them. They must be special to have that kind of enduring relationship and admiration from their son.

Once I started to shiver, even under the blankets with Remington's body heat and his warm hands caressing my back and shoulders, we packed up and headed out. He held my hand all the way back to my apartment, walked me up, and I had that riot of wild, uncontrollable butterflies in my stomach the whole time as I unlocked my door. He cupped my cheek sweetly and looked into my eyes, his darkening as he licked his lower lip. I thought *this is it, this is happening!* He told me he had a great time and asked if he could see me again, and all I could do was grin like a fool up at his handsome face, nodding. Remington smiled back and said, "Great." He ran his finger across my lower lips, making my panties instantly damp . . . and then he kissed my cheek. "I will talk to you tomorrow, beautiful. Go in there and lock the door."

I looked up at him, speechless. Stumbling back into my apartment, I shut and locked the door. I was too stunned to do anything other than follow his simple directions.

What the hell! What in the actual fuck had happened? I thought we were on the same page. He for sure looked like he *wanted* to kiss me. Our bodies were screaming to each other with every single touch all night long. Or was it just my body? Maybe this was one-sided. Maybe all the things I told him on our date finally sank in, and he was starting to see that I was a lot. A lot of baggage. A lot of emotional damage. A lot of family drama to deal with. That must be it. Remington is too good of a man, from too solid of a family for someone so broken and trampled on like me.

I have worked really hard in therapy on my self-confidence and self-worth, but it is not a switch that flips on and you are just suddenly perfectly healed. The wounds are deep and the doubts are plaguing. That voice *especially* loves to try and take away the good things in life when they are trying to take root.

Taking some deep breaths, I steady myself. I am spiraling, and I need to get it together. I pull out my journal for this year and decide to write about tonight. I don't want to forget the good, the happy, the wild butterflies. From the flowers to the extra cheese bread, which Remington insisted I keep the left-overs to snack on while I work from home, to the stunning sunset and raw conversation.

After writing it all down, I know that I didn't imagine or fabricate our connection. There must be a reason he didn't kiss me. Remington is thoughtful, the most thoughtful man I have ever met. Maybe he wants to take this slow, not rush things and scare me off? I am sure that he thinks I'm like a baby fawn, ready for fight, flight, or freeze after all the things he's learned about me.

The last thing I feel around Remington is afraid. He makes me want to do things for myself, including opening up to a man that has the power to break me or bring me to life. The only way to find out is by taking the chance. And after tonight, I know he is worth it . . . as long as he still thinks that I am as well.

Brett always wanted me to keep my hair long. It falls just under my shoulder blades right now. It's thick, heavy, and I have not really changed it much my whole life. I wanted to do things to it so many times over the years, but I knew it would be overly critiqued and fussed over by my mother and deeply criticized by my father. Once I told Brett I was considering getting a shoulder-length bob-style cut, and he was mortified. I wanted something fresh and different. He told me that it would not look good with my face shape, and it would limit my options for styles when we had formal events in and around DC. We had only ever been at the one charity event together that we met at, but he acted like we needed to be ready at all times to rub elbows with big executives and politicians at the drop of a hat. I felt so much shame and disappointment. That was the last time I brought it up, and I ignored the massive red flag waving right in front of me with his controlling nature and the expectation to be an ornament on Brett's arm like my mother had always been for my father.

I was so stupid for so long, letting these awful people control, manipulate, and dictate so many of my decisions, worried about their opinions and optics. I was D-O-N-E with that. Lainey 2.0 doesn't let anyone decide these things, and I need to shake up my life a little bit. Apparently, according to other girlies, haircuts can make you ready to take on the world. I didn't necessarily need that much power, but I did want a boost to take on my own life. They also say hair holds memories, and like the clothes I was donating, I was ready to let go of more things holding me back.

That new attitude had me marching into Dip and Dye the morning after my date with Remington, ready to meet up with my bestie Kendra. She works here at the salon, and also runs her side business for her pottery through Etsy. She is hoping that she can sell some things locally soon and cut back on her shipping costs. I love her work so much, and being her best friend comes with the perks of being gifted beautiful mugs whenever she is trying out new designs. My cupboard is filled with one-of-a-kind Kendra Powell creations. And today I am finally ready to let her get creative with my hair, something she's been begging me to do for years. She might totally pass out when I tell her I am not here for just my usual split-ends trim!

I also need to catch her up on all things Remington. The last time I gave her a text update I had downloaded her on my embarrassment of a bonfire, and I purposely left out some key details . . . like texting with Remington, our insane connection, the flowers, and everything else since then. Kendra is the only person in my life that I am myself with, but even with her I keep things closed-up sometimes. We met when I moved to town, and it was like our souls recognized each other instantly. She grabbed on to me with both of her little, strong hands, literally and figuratively, and never let me go.

Her big, boisterous, artsy personality is perfectly her, and sometimes it can overwhelm me when I need time to think about things. I needed to have time to process my feelings about Remington and decide what I really wanted. I know that after my spiral last night I made the right call in waiting to tell her about all the details. Relying on myself and my own mind to sort things out feels scary but necessary right now. Journaling helped, and now I am ready for Kendra to add her perspective.

The whimsical chime of the salon signals my arrival as I push through the door. There are only a pair of older ladies toward the front getting their hair done and chatting quietly. Kendra turns from her station with a huge bright smile. Her unruly blonde curls, streaked with bright pink, are barely contained in a claw clip, make-up done to perfection. A trendy jumpsuit in navy hugs her petite curves perfectly, and a pair of cute pink Converse complete the look. Her five-two frame is three inches shorter than mine, but her personality often makes her feel much taller when she gets excited and starts bouncing around.

"Heyyyyy!" she sing-songs. "I am so glad your morning meetings were canceled! We are so dead in here this morning, and I need some girl time, girl!"

Striding over to her I give her a hug and say, "Me, too. I have some things to catch you up on."

"Oh, reallllly? You have been holding out on me, your very best friend on this perfect planet?! What gives?" She fakes her annoyance.

I smirk and roll my eyes. "Well for one thing, you know I love you, and you will always be my number one. I just needed to process some things . . . and I also made some important decisions."

The cheerful teasing drops off Kendra quickly, like I just splashed her with a bucket of water. "What? Are you okay? Are you moving? What happened?" Concern is laced in every question she shoots at me in rapid-fire succession.

"Deep breath, bestie! I am doing good," I reassure her with a smile. "The first thing I want to tell you is that I have made a major hair decision, and I am ready for you to make it happen."

Kendra drops her worried hands from her cheeks and lets out a squeal that I swear dogs in the next town could probably hear. The two other old ladies in the salon are probably going to have to reset their hearing aids if they have any. "Are you pulling an April Fool's joke on me right now?"

Laughing I say, "Noooooo, it's still March. Also you know I can't stand that 'holiday,' so I would never do that to you."

"True! Okay, tell me ev-er-y-thing! What made you finally decide to change things up? What are you wanting to do?" Excitement buzzes over Kendra like a wave of bees ready for her twitching hands to attack my head the second I say go. I would be slightly terrified if I didn't know that she was so talented at everything she does, including wielding her shiny shears.

"Remember when I wanted a long bob, and Brett told me it was a bad idea?" I ask, frowning.

Glowering, Kendra scrunches up her nose, slams a hand on her hip, and rolls her eyes at me. "And remember that I told *you* he was an asshole and had no idea what he was talking about. Fuck him."

"Exactly. Let's do it. I want you to do the bob, with long layers on the ends." I can't help but smile and feel proud of myself as I lock in my choice. It feels good to do this for myself and only myself.

"Shoulder length?" Kendra asks, remembering what I wanted from previous conversations.

"Yeah, I want it to barely brush them." I show her with my hands.

"Let's freaking do this!" Kendra claps and pushes me to the washing station. It is like I told her she just won the lottery. I know that as happy as she is to cut my hair, she also knows this is a big step for me. She tips me back and wets my hair with the perfectly warm water in the deep sink. I love this part, when she massages my head and I can close my eyes and just be for a few minutes. The honey scent of my favorite shampoo, which Kendra knows I prefer, floats through the air as she says, "I need to know what else has been going on with you. You told me you have *things* to catch me up on. We didn't have our wine night this week, and as HUGE as this hair sitch is, I know there's more, right?"

"There *is* more," I sigh, and peek open my eyes to see her bright silvery-blue eyes looking at me expectantly while she works the lather through my long locks one last time. "So, do you remember the firefighter?"

"Uhhhhh you mean the hot-as-fuck hottie that saved your cute pyro butt and took your journal? How could I forget? I have been dying to know what happened. Did he give you back the journal?"

"No, no, he hasn't had nearly enough time to transfer over what was written. But a looooot more has happened." Kendra rinses my conditioner, wrings out my hair, and wraps a towel around my head. She tips up my chair with a practiced ease and we make our way back to her station. Sitting down, I settle in for what comes next—my hair transformation and catching my best friend up on all things *Remington LeBlanc.*

An hour and a half later I feel lighter. I feel settled in

myself. Cutting off my hair really did give me a huge boost and pep to my confidence. When Kendra spun me around dramatically in her chair, because of course she wouldn't let me see a damn thing until she was done, which included a full blowout and soft beach waves, my jaw dropped. I looked like me, but a me that was . . . *more*.

It was like I cut off the dead weight and expectations of others that I was carrying. I let go of a piece of myself that I was holding on to so tightly, trying to please everyone other than myself. My head felt lighter, my neck felt less stiff, and my smile hasn't left my face.

"Thank you, thank you so much," I whisper to my best friend as she pulls me into a tight hug.

"You look just as beautiful as you always do, but I am so happy that it's finally on your own terms, bestie," Kendra says. "And you are going to make Remington fucking *drool* whenever he sees you next. There is no way he won't be all over you." She grins as she finishes organizing her station.

I narrow my eyes. "Well, it doesn't matter because this hair and decision has nothing to do with him or any other man."

"Damn straight!" Kendra cheers. She ate up every crumb I gave her when I spilled details about Remington. I told her all about the texting, the flowers, the date . . . and the not kissing me. I was embarrassed about that part, but of course she helped me get out of my own head, calming my anxiety before I could spiral about it again. It was helpful to get her perspective because I hadn't realized that she actually kind of knows Remington. Her nana was from Fox Grove, so Kendra spent a lot of time here in the summers off and on. Small-town life had her crossing paths with lots of people in this town long before she officially became a resident a few years ago when she moved into her nana's place. Kendra is convinced that Remington is totally into me and trying to be a gentleman. I am sure she's right, but damn it, I still really wanted him to not be *so gentlemanly* last night.

"Alright, thank you for this wonderful metamorphosis. I've got to get going so I can grab a few groceries before I hop on my last afternoon meeting. I am really glad you could squeeze me in this morning and we could catch up."

"Same! I need you to come to the studio next. New mugs are happening for my summer line, and I need to show you the samples. I know there is one you are going to want for your collection for sure. Think *strawberries*." Kendra beams with a flourish of her hands.

"Don't I want all of them for my collection? I'm your number one fan!" I say back with a smile as I bounce back out into the warm spring day with a wave at my best friend.

A soft breeze blows through my freshly cut hair, and I know this really is a new beginning for me. But it didn't start with a haircut . . . It started the night Remington helped finish one fire and set a brand new one.

11

Remington

I really wanted to kiss Lainey last night. I almost kissed her. I felt like an idiot as I walked away after I heard the lock on her front door engage, knowing she was tucked safely inside. I wanted to be in there *with* her. As much as I craved those things, and so much more with her, I also do not want to rush or push Lainey. I will not fuck this up.

When we were laying in the bed of my truck I made a promise to myself that I would take my time with her and not scare her off. I have feelings for her—big feelings. Feelings that if I expressed them to anyone else at this point in our fledgling relationship, people would probably think I was insane.

I am not insane. I am just in, all in.

But now I'm second-guessing walking away last night.

So that is why I am here at work, beating the shit out of our heavy bag in the gym, and taking out my pent-up frustration through punishing my body with Eli. He's over in the corner working on some new jump rope move he is trying to master. It takes a hell of a lot of concentration, effort, and practice to make the skills and tricks he can do look effortless—and it pays off big time for him, too. He has gained a massive social media following posting exercise thirst trap videos and clips of him jumping rope. The last time I looked he had a quarter of a million followers. Absolutely nuts.

"Son-of-a-fuckin-nutcracker!" Eli yells as the neon-green rope he's working with whips him across the chest. Yeah, that is going to leave a nasty mark. Sometimes he gets going so fast and intense there are a few injuries, but he will be okay. And it truly makes him that much more motivated to master the skill.

"You alright, man?" I call out.

"Yeah, that one just got me good. Damn. I need a break. I got sloppy." Taking a gulp of water, he strides over to where I am pulling off my boxing gloves and hands me an extra bottle.

"Thanks," I grumble, taking it and downing half of the bottle in one long guzzle.

"What's got your panties in a twist today, dipshit? I thought you would have rainbows coming out your butt after your date last night." Eli pokes at me. I have told him a lot more about Lainey. Eli Hargrove is the greatest friend I could ever ask for. He has been my best friend since kindergarten when Tommy Gentry pushed me down, and Eli came to my defense. He's always had my back, has had the biggest personality on that and any other playground, in any other room for that matter, and is the most genuine human I know. He is also the best firefighter in this building. I know that once Chief is done someday, Eli would be a good man for the job. When it comes to this work, he knows how to flip the switch. That fun-loving side of himself is the balance he needs for all the hard shit we see and deal with, but there is nobody that I want next to me more when we are walking toward a fire. Eli is a natural leader, and all of the people in this station rely on him in more ways than one. We are all a family, but we often tease him and call him "daddy" when he gets on our asses about stuff. That discipline versus fun balance? Definite dad energy.

"I think I might have fucked up by trying really hard to not fuck up." I wince.

"Dude, you are making my brain hurt. What did you do? It has only been *one* date, Rem." He rubs his temples in a mocking fashion.

"The date was amazing, that's not the issue. She is amazing, also not the issue. I don't want to scare her off or rush things. So, at the end of the date, I didn't kiss her, and I think that she wanted me to." I look over to see Eli studying me, no longer joking.

"So that's the problem?" he asks. "You are worried that you made her mad, offended her, or something?"

"Yeah, I have no idea what she thinks about the end of our date. I walked her up to her apartment, then . . . I kissed her cheek." I groan.

"For fuck's sake, that is weak sauce, man. I know you don't want to rush things with Lainey, and you want to be respectful and everything, but a kiss would not have been a bad thing. It is not like you banged her in the back of your truck and then sent her on her way." He laughs.

I whip him with my sweat towel. "Fuck off! Of course I wouldn't do that to her!"

"Well, have you talked to her today?" he asks pointedly.

"No, not yet. I came here to work out, get my thoughts together, and talk to you."

"Awww you needed my sage advice, some best friend time. I knew you loved me more than you could ever love some chick." Eli lives to push my buttons, and right now he's pressing a little too hard.

"She is not some chick, so shut that shit down right now, man." I sigh, exhausted and not ready to get into more rounds with him.

"Damn, Lainey really is different, isn't she?" Eli asks me.

His question sends me back to last night in the bed of my truck and my conversation with Lainey.

"You are different. This feels different." Her eyes look up at me, and I swear she is burning herself into my very soul.

"Yeah, Lainey, this is different."

I look at Eli, and simply say, "Yeah, man, she is."

"Well, then, Rem. You better man up and do something about it." Eli's "sage advice" rings through the gym like a final bell. And I know I'm ready to do what it takes to fight for my girl.

I have never been so nervous to text a girl . . . a woman . . . after a date, ever. Until now.

God, please don't let her hate me for not kissing her last night.

The last thing I want is for her to think that I am not into her. But that would be impossible after our date and the insane chemistry we had, right? Lainey had to have felt it, too.

Please, God, let her have felt it, too.

Remington: Hey, beautiful. How is your day going?

Lainey: . . .

Oh my God, those dots are going to kill me.

Lainey: It's great! I had my morning meetings get canceled, so I got to go see my best friend, Kendra.

Remington: That's nice.

What did y'all do?

Lainey: She was at work so I went to see her there.

Remington: Cool. Does she work around here?

Lainey: Yup! She does pottery and she also works at the salon.

Remington: So did you ladies have fun talking about me?

Lainey: Ha! What makes you think we talked about you?

Remington: Post-date best friend debrief?

Lainey: Is that what you did?

Remington: Yes.

Lainey: . . .

Oh shit. She's going to think that's a bad thing.

Remington: I told Eli that I had the most incredible date of my life last night.

Lainey: You did?

Remington: Yup . . . But there is only one thing that I regret about it.

One thing that would have made it even better.

Lainey: What's that, Remington?

Jesus, I loved that she full-names me all the time. Nobody does that. Everyone's called me Rem, even my family, from the time I was young. But hearing Lainey use my full name, in text or in person, makes my body spark. I think her doing that just unlocked a new kink I never knew I had, because she is the only one that has held that particular key.

Remington: I should have kissed you good night.

Nothing. Silence.

No dots bouncing along my screen. Nothing.

Fuck.

Minutes drag out.

And then . . .

Lainey: You're right, you should have.

Holy.

Shit.

12

Lainey

I can't believe I just said that, but it was the truth. Remington *should* have kissed me. I wanted him to kiss me. At least we are on the same page. Now I know for sure that I am not alone in my feelings, and I am not crazy thinking I am being burned alive by our chemistry with no way to control it. We are both being consumed just as quickly by whatever is happening between us.

I love the flexibility of working from home. Thankfully, this afternoon is a conference call that I have to phone in for, no video. I can listen to it while I bake. It is only a monthly meeting that I don't contribute much to. Lots of listening, and "uh-huhs," "I understands," and "yes, sir, I will get that going," followed by more listening. Very boring, very time consuming, and my least favorite meeting of the month. So having this distraction to keep me busy will help pass the time. I usually try a new cookie recipe or make myself my perfected apple pie.

When I first moved in here and tried to make a pie, I burned it to an inedible crisp and I cried. Me a few years ago would have just given up and never baked anything ever again, but my therapist encouraged me to keep going until I mastered at least one recipe. One thing that was hard for me that I was not allowed to try making with my mom growing up, that I would have loved to have done, was pie. So I tried again, and again, and again. I feel bad for all the apples, sugar, and crust that I sacrificed in the process of my healing. However, in the end it was worth it, because now I can confidently say I make an amazing apple pie that I am proud of. And I happen to know a man who loves apples.

Remington is working today, a twenty-four-hour shift, but I would really like to see him again. The fire station has long, demanding hours, and I know that Remington doesn't just cover fires. He is fully qualified as an EMT as well. They get called out to all types of accidents and emergencies. He works really hard, gives so much of himself to everyone. That makes me think of a plan to surprise him after I am done with my work. I had exactly enough time to run to the grocery store to get my weekly shopping done and the pie ingredients I needed before I got back to my apartment for the afternoon meeting. Plus, I really hope that it will make Remington smile. He went out of his way to make our date special and thoughtful. He also puts so much effort into his flowers for me, and don't even get me started on the journal.

My phone dings as I am pulling into the Fox Hollow apartment complex. I look down and smile to see the man that consumes my thoughts has finally responded to my last text about kissing me. I was really starting to worry I had been too forward.

Remington: I promise, Lainey, I won't be making that same mistake twice.

Remington: I have been beating myself up for not kissing you from the minute I walked away.

I feel my cheeks heat, and those wild butterflies come back in full force. I am not sure if I want to laugh with giddy excitement or sob with relief.

Lainey: Please don't hurt that handsome face. I don't want our first kiss to be me kissing it better.

Remington: I will try and stay injury-free until I see you again.

Only punching the heavy bag today.

Lainey: Promise?

Remington: Pinky ♥

Lainey: Are you allowed to have visitors at the fire station?

Remington: Yeah, we have family and friends pop in all the time when we are on shift.

Lainey: Would it be okay if I came up to see you after I get done with work?

Lainey: I have something I want to drop off for you.

Lainey: I promise I won't stay long.

Remington: Nothing would make me happier than seeing you today. All you need to bring me is your smile, and you definitely don't need to rush off.

Lainey: Okay.

Remington: Shoot me a text when you leave so I know when you're on your way.

Lainey:

Thumbs-up?! I was too frazzled and nervous to think of what else to say.

The meeting seems extra boring and extra long, but I know that it is simply because I am clock-watching. I can't wait for the workday to be done. Good thing I am not so distracted that I ruin my perfect pie by swapping salt and sugar like I did for pie number eleven. It was so awful I took one bite and spit it out, ran to the sink, and had to rinse my mouth out. Unfortunately, I also had to do that for pies three, seventeen, and twenty-six, but for reasons other than salt. That was one problem with buying bulk and not being as organized as I should have been. I shudder thinking of the dark days of my pie mishaps. I've come a long way.

My boss finally wraps up the meeting just as I slide the pie into the oven and set the timer. This gives me enough time to complete my notes and work for the day, organize what I need to have set up for tomorrow, and shut down my laptop for the night. I pull the pie out to cool, make my way into my bedroom, and freeze. Oh my lord. *Lainey, you are a one-woman tornado sometimes.* My room is still experiencing my pre-date outfit disaster. I was so blissed out from a wonderful date, but also spiraling about the non-kiss, that I went to bed with tunnel vision and didn't even register this mess. I start to clean up as quickly as I can, not wanting to come back later to yesterday's problems.

My hair still looks amazing from Kendra, so I go to my bathroom and carefully fluff it a bit and add some hair spray. I brush my teeth, touch up my make-up, and smile at my reflection. It falters for a minute, thinking about previous men in my life and how much they would hate my new look. I briefly worry about Remington and what he will think. I know he liked my long hair. My stomach does an uneasy twist. Taking three full, deep breaths I think back to this morning and what I told my best friend—that I did this for *myself.* If Remington doesn't like it, well that will be red flag number one. This is the first time I have felt this confident in a long time, maybe ever. I don't want this feeling to go away by letting that negative voice crawl back in and ruin my day. Clicking off all the lights, I carefully grab the pie, my bag, keys, phone and head out the door. Once I am in my car, I send a quick text to let Remington know I am on my way to the fire station.

When I pull up to the visitor lot, Remington is standing outside waiting for me. I nearly swallow my tongue at the sight of him. He has on navy-blue tactical pants, black boots, and a tight navy T-shirt with the Fox Grove fire department emblem in red on his chest. As hot as his uniform is, it's the full sleeve of dark tattoos on his left arm, disappearing under the cuff of his T-shirt, that makes me feel like I am going to pass out. I had no clue Remington had any ink, and honestly this whole picture right now is too much for me to handle. I am not sure if I should take a picture so I can remember this moment forever or jump out of my car and embarrass myself by trying to Velcro myself to him like a human koala. My lady parts are definitely screaming their vote for the latter.

I get out of the car, smoothing my blue, paisley-covered maxi dress so I have something to do with my nervous hands. Was I a bit overdressed for a pie delivery? Sure, but I wanted to look as good on the outside as my new hair was making me feel on the inside.

Remington starts to walk toward me, but then his eyes slightly widen, and he falters for just a moment. My heart starts to sink.

"Holy fuck," I hear him murmur.

"Hi," I say, giving a small wave as he stops right in front of me, his eyes devouring my face and his tongue licking his full bottom lip.

"You are the most gorgeous woman I have ever seen," Remington says, nearly breathless.

"W-what?" I stammer in disbelief.

"You look incredible. Did you do this today? With your friend?" he wonders, looking at my hair.

"Yeah, it's something I always wanted to try and never had the guts to do it," I admit, casting my eyes to the ground.

A warm, rough hand tips my chin back up, and his golden eyes are locked in on me. Remington's attention does not make me feel uneasy like every other man I have been with. It makes me feel a comfortable warmth that starts wherever he's touching me, whether it's his stare or his hands, and pools out, running along some kind of invisible plane of existence that he's charging. That warmth burns deep in a place that hasn't existed before him. It's safe and sacred, and I'm trying to not be afraid of its power.

"I really want to touch it, run my hands through it. But I know from my mom and sister women have hair rules, especially when they just got it done all fancy." Remington smirks at me.

Laughing, not able to hold back my own smile, I tell him, "I don't have any hair rules, you can do whatever you want to it, Remington."

His eyes go to a molten smolder as he laces one hand around my hip. Nearly growling, he pulls me close, and says, "Good, because I wanna fucking ruin it." He slips his other hand into my hair, and he bends his massive frame over me. His mouth finally doing what I wanted it to last night, he devours me in a kiss. His lips are soft but commanding, and I melt into his embrace. I moan as his hot tongue sweeps across the seam of my lips, and I let him in, allowing him to deepen the kiss.

Never in my life has a man kissed me like this.

I never want another man to kiss me like this.

I go up on my toes so I can hold on tighter, and he tugs the hair at the nape of my neck. I let out a tiny yelp of surprise, and Remington immediately pulls back. A cold rush of air running where his heated body was just pressed against mine makes me shiver.

Worry creases his brow. "Sorry, too much?" he asks, sounding a little embarrassed.

"More" is all I can manage to say and pull him back to me, his smiling mouth consuming me all over again.

Slowly we pull out of our smoldering kiss and stand with our foreheads connected, breaths heavy, lust thrumming thick in the air. If we were not standing in the FGFD parking lot, who knows if we would have been able to stop.

"Hi," I whisper again.

Remington looks down at me seriously, and says, "Hi. Can you forgive me for not kissing you last night?"

Beaming up at him, probably looking like a total fool, I say, "As long as you keep kissing me like *that*, yeah, all is forgiven."

Remington pulls me into a tight hug and kisses the top of my head. "Deal, beautiful. Can I give you the grand tour of the fire station now?"

"I'd love one! But I have something for you, remember?" I unfortunately have to leave his warm embrace to go back to my car and get his pie. Handing it to him he looks so surprised, like it's the first pie he's ever seen.

"Did you make this?" His voice is warm and reverent.

"Yes, it's my special apple pie. I spent well over a year experimenting and perfecting it," I tell him, suddenly feeling worried again. "I thought you might enjoy it because you told me apples are your favorite."

"Hell, yes! Thank you. This is amazing, and so kind. Nobody has ever made a pie just for me before." His smile is so bright and happy, it could power our small town.

"You are actually the first person I've ever made it for." My hands feel the need to fidget again with my admission, so I fiddle with the strap of my bag that I grabbed off the passenger seat.

Remington surprises me again with a sweet, quick kiss on my lips. "Nothing will taste as amazing as your kisses, but I am willing to try anything you make."

Blushing, I start to laugh uncontrollably, tears stream, and a side stitch forms. Remington patiently stands there, grinning and waiting to be let in on my inside joke. "What is so funny about that?"

"*Trust me*, you didn't want to try all my practice pies before I perfected this recipe, Remington."

"Sure I would have!" he defends himself.

"No, really. They were *so* awful most ended up in the trash. Working on this pie was part of my therapy. Allowing myself to experiment and learn and grow in the kitchen . . . in a way that I wasn't able to when I was growing up." I sigh, swallowing a lump of emotions, hating to bring down the moment.

Remington, still happy and smiling, says, "I think that's great! And I pinky promise that if you want to experiment with any new recipe in the future, I will try them all, even the trash batches." Grinning still, he takes my hand, kisses the back of it, and leads me toward the station doors.

"Who even are you?" I ask in disbelief.

"Your man." He states it so effortlessly, like it was meant to be, and I think maybe he's right . . . because there is nothing that would make me happier than having him claim me.

13

Remington

Everyone at FGFD loved Lainey. How could they not? She is kind, sweet, and has the perfect amount of sass to keep me on my toes. She's also incredibly thoughtful. I had no idea what would happen when she pulled up to the station, but when she stepped out of the car looking like a damn snack, I knew I needed to get my hands on her. Needed to remedy the epic fumble from the ending of our first date and show her just how much I wanted her. And then when she gave me the green light, told me I could mess up her sexy new haircut? I could have died right there before our lips ever touched, but thank fuck that didn't happen, because that was the hottest kiss of my life.

It didn't feel like a first kiss. It felt like the kiss I have been waiting my entire life for. It's not just because Lainey is a great kisser, and I'm getting hard just remembering the feel of her lips on mine and the little moans she made. No, kissing her cracked open that closed-off place inside of myself. She fully shattered the illusion I built up years ago when I told myself that I didn't really need *this*—a connection that is so real there is no point denying it or trying to run from it.

Wanting something and having it are two totally different realities. I thought that I had "it" with Cora. We had so many plans for our future, and she ruined everything. I thought I knew who she was, after all we grew up together, and she was Sutton's best friend. They loved the idea of being "sisters" and would talk about how the day Cora and I got married would make it official. Cora and I never even really talked about marriage explicitly, it was just kind of assumed that it was going to eventually happen. I felt a numb contentedness in our relationship, happy with where my life was headed . . . until I wasn't.

My unsettled feelings didn't even have anything to do with Cora at first, they came with my chosen career path. I started college as a finance major. Being good with numbers and thinking about comfortable jobs, it felt like a solid, safe plan. The coursework was not overly challenging for me, but still interesting. Cora was going to school for a hospitality degree, minoring in business. She wanted to pursue being some kind of wedding or event planner. She *informed me* that I was going to help her with the business and money side of things because my degree would snap right in place with her plan. She had it all mapped out, spreadsheets to match. I told her I was happy to help her figure things out, but I didn't want to be full-time in wedding and event planning when I graduated. My parents wanted Sutton and myself to follow our passions, and mine did not march down aisles next to bridezillas or manage finances for overpriced parties. Cora just laughed.

The more I thought about it, the less appealing *any* kind of finance position felt. I went to a job fair put on through the different college departments trying to see what was out there and hated all the options. I felt sick, like I was wasting time and money not knowing what I really wanted to do. There was only one table that day that stirred any kind of excitement in me that I saw when I was about to give up. It was one that had a display about earning a degree in fire science. I talked to the guys at the table for over an hour. I had some previous knowledge of the degree because of Eli, but I didn't know the full ins and outs. A lot of entry level firefighting jobs don't require something like that, but it would open up different opportunities for the future. I could be a fire investigator, fire safety inspector, teach different aspects of fire safety and preparedness. There were a lot of things that were interesting, and I had always felt a pull toward doing some kind of service, but I didn't know what I was called to pursue until that moment.

Walking away from that job fair, I knew exactly what I wanted. I switched my major for a degree in fire science with a minor in finance so I wouldn't lose all the credits and time I had already put in. I worked my ass off to take extra classes for the fire science degree so I could still graduate on time, which meant going to school year-round. I was so excited and motivated. I didn't care that I had little time for anything else. This was going to secure the future that I could be proud of. One that wasn't dull, dreary, and constantly about punching a clock. I would be helping my community in a meaningful way, and the best part was Eli was also going to be a firefighter.

Eli knew from the time he was little that was his passion, and it never changed. He dressed up as a firefighter for Halloween every single year from the time he was in third grade. Eli was happy to share his dream with me, encouraging me every step of the way, just like I should have expected him to. He was already in the program when I changed my plans, and he helped me catch up. I was worried he would be upset or feel like I was stepping on his toes. When I told him that, *he told me* I was an idiot, and then dragged me to the gym for a hard workout so he could kick my ass in the boxing ring. He's my brother in every variation of the word, that will never change.

Cora was not thrilled with my choice. She was tepidly supportive, and it was wearing on our relationship, but we stayed together through graduation. As soon as caps were tossed, and gowns were taken off—Cora looked at me expectantly. She had on a short white dress, and her dark hair barely had a dent from the cardboard hats we were just sweating in. Our families were all there, ready to celebrate and then move us back home. As the day went on, Cora became colder and angry. Turns out, she told everyone that I was going to propose after the ceremony. I absolutely was *not.* That wasn't on my mind at all. There was no ring. Even if our relationship was in a good place, which it wasn't, I would never want to do something like that publicly. I think that moment should be special, thoughtful, and personal . . . not rushed and showy. Surrounded by our family, maybe—but not thousands of other strangers. That night at my apartment, as I was packing up my last few belongings, she dropped bombs that broke apart the pieces that were left of our struggling relationship, leaving nothing but shrapnel behind.

"Now that graduation is over we can finally really get the business going," Cora had stated as she sifted through my things in the half-packed box on the dresser.

I looked over at her, confused. "Yeah, you can set everything up how you planned and make the event business what you want. You have been dreaming about this for a long time, it will be great."

"It is *our* dream, silly goose! Don't you remember all of our plans? You promised me you would run the business and finances. I need all my focus to be on the creative side and the clients. Now that school is done we can really get cracking. I already have two potential brides lined up in Fox Grove, and one big party in Norfolk." She spun to me, flipping her long hair over one shoulder, and smiling in a weird way that didn't sit well, like she was convincing me that this was my idea all along.

What the fuck? Cora knew this was not happening. I told her when I changed majors years ago that my dream was being a firefighter, and she supported me. Albeit, reluctantly, but we had been together the entire time I had gone to school for this.

"Cora, I'm a firefighter. I already interviewed and I have a full-time job lined up at Fox Grove Fire Department. My dream is *that.* Not to run a finance department for your business." She glared at me. *Jesus, if looks could kill.* "Or *any* business," I emphasized.

"Firefighting? Really, Rem? That is seriously what you want to do with your life?!" Cora shrieked, her face reddening with anger that was unfair and misplaced. "I thought this was a stupid, childish phase, and I was letting you live out your little GI Joe, macho fantasy while we were in college."

"What did you just say to me? This *IS* my life, Cora. I am a dedicated, highly trained, highly qualified firefighter. I am going to serve my community, save lives. There's nothing fucking *childish* about it. There is no fantasy or romanticizing the danger or the sacrifice of this commitment. *How fucking dare you.*" I looked at her, and it was like I was seeing her for the first time. And I hated it.

Being with Cora was easy until it wasn't. I should have ended things with her a long time ago, but our lives were so tangled and twisted together. Breaking up with her was not like ending things with a typical college girlfriend. Cora had been my girlfriend since high school. She was ingrained in every part of my life. Our little town looked at us like we were the prize couple and put pressure on our relationship—I despised that, but Cora loved it.

Standing there with her arms crossed, Cora said indignantly, "So you're not going to do this with me? What's going to happen?" Her phone beeped with an incoming call on the bed before she could fire off more stupid questions. I picked up the phone and looked at the screen, blinking at a familiar, unwelcome name.

"Why is Jared calling you?" I asked in a hushed voice, knowing I was not going to like her answer. There was no reason this dick should be contacting *my girlfriend*. He was a TA for one of her previous classes, and they had an inappropriate relationship. She promised it didn't go past the extremely flirty banter and him asking her out a few times. She chalked it up to her being inexperienced and unable to see it for what it was since we started dating so young. That was a year earlier. I told her I would forgive her and forget about the whole thing as long as she never spoke to him again. So his name flashing on her phone signaled nothing but doom for our relationship.

Cora's entire haughty, angry demeanor shifted on a dime. Tears welling in her brown eyes, she said, "Please, Rem, I-I-I can, let me explain. It, you, I mean, you were always so busy, and so many classes, and working . . ." She was stammering, scrambling to put a coherent sentence together, but I cut her off.

"So all this time I have been killing myself to finish my degree on time, so we can graduate, move home. *Home*. Where I thought we could finally have some more time, hopefully get our relationship back on track, and have time to work things out. Because you and I both know it hasn't been great. I was willing to at least try . . . But you have been fucking around behind my back? How long, Cora?" Not one of her pretend tears had fallen onto her cheeks yet. I just stared at her, waiting for an answer.

"The whole time," she whispered.

I ripped my hands across my hair. Rage ran through my veins. I was furious, more with myself for not seeing what a selfish, manipulative, opportunist Cora was—had apparently always been. The red flags had been waving right in my face, and I decided they didn't matter because I prided myself on being a man that could be relied on and stuck to his commitments. And look what that got me? A cheating girlfriend that shit on my dreams.

"Get the fuck out." I shoved the ringing phone into her hands and pointed to the door.

"What about the things I have here?" Cora had the nerve to pout at me.

"I'll fucking burn them," I roared at her and she scrambled out the door, seeing that I was not going to listen to her bullshit for one more second.

Snapping out of that long-buried memory, I am actually smirking thinking of that last thing I told Cora. That I would burn all her shit.

I didn't, but I really wanted to.

Never in a million years did I think I could ever remember that night and not be stabbed with the deep shame I experienced, pain twisting my heart where I thought love for a girl I knew my whole life was housed. But today, I feel grateful that my life with Cora ended the way it did—forcing me to let go of something I had been holding on to for too long, assuming it was love because everyone around us expected it to be.

We have a lot more in common than Lainey realizes. I guess she was the only one that got to live out the "burning your ex's shit fantasy" between the two of us, and honestly thank fuck for it because that night brought me to my dream girl. Spending time with Lainey is proving just how much of my life I wasted with Cora, because that wasn't living, and it certainly wasn't love.

14

Remington

Lainey's journal is like diving into her brain, seeing little glimpses of who she was, and how she felt throughout the year. She mostly put down song lyrics, book quotes from things she was reading, or random stories. But every once in a while she would write about her day or thoughts she needed to get out. Those are the pieces that really get to me. Sometimes the things she said made me laugh at her surprisingly sarcastic humor. Other times my heart ached when I could feel her anxieties seeping into each word. I wanted to reach into the pages and pull those worries away. It was hard for me to sit here and rewrite all her doubts and insecurities, but it would be wrong to not give her what I promised. I told Lainey I would copy what she wrote and give it back to her.

Feeling the rain soak my clothes when I ran today was just what I needed. These past few weeks have been a mix of emotions and overwhelming anxiety attacks that I don't feel like looking at too closely. I'd rather let the water today sweep them away.

Raindrops on my skin . . . the only kind of water I love, or brings me some sort of comfort, well, bedsides a soak in a deep claw-foot tub of course.

I am also going to add my own improvements to her pages and hope she doesn't kill me for it. With every transfer from the old journal, I add to the page, filling the blank space with my own drawings . . . of flowers.

Every single kind I can think of from memory, and when I run out of those I Google more images and work from there. I told Lainey I would find a way to give her *all* of the flowers, and this is a great way to help accomplish just that. Each one I draw, I add the name and a little description at the bottom of the page. I want her to be able to name them and understand why I chose each one for that particular page or matched it with what memory she wrote. I knew as soon as Lainey told me about her flower situation through our texting that I was going to not only fill her apartment with flowers but also figure out a way to give her something more permanent.

Not many people know that I love to draw. It's not something I intended to keep a close secret necessarily, but it definitely isn't a talent that I openly like to broadcast. Cora had lots of nasty little quips about me "doodling" and after that, I kept to myself when I pulled out my artistic side. When someone takes something that is so personal, so woven into who you are, which all forms of art seem to be, it's impossible to disconnect yourself from a partner's dismissive and demeaning attitude toward it, even years later. Protecting myself from prying eyes and any kind of further persecution has just been easier than opening myself up again.

Normally I draw at home on my back deck or in my art space in my office to decompress. So me sitting here at the fire station drawing flowers of all things has caught the attention of my friends. Eli, of course, knows that I draw. More than half of my tattoos are based on the concepts I sketched, and my friend Keller Shore, in Norfolk who is part owner of a shop there and an amazing artist, inked them all for me.

"Hey, Rem, what are you doing?" Adrian Garcia asks me, as he sets down a huge pan of his mom's famous enchiladas. We all love it when it's his night to cook because his mom passed on her chef genes to him, and he spoils us. My mouth starts to water, and I close up the journal as the rest of the crew come to the table, drawn in by the aroma and the rumbles of impatient bellies.

"Oh, uh, I am just working on a project. Lainey needed help with an old journal, and I am transferring what she wrote into this new one," I say quickly, rubbing my neck, hoping he doesn't press, but of course he does.

"Why do you need to redo what she already wrote down?" Adrian asks.

All eight of us that are on shift, including Eli, have settled into the table and are grabbing plates, eyes on me, obviously ready for a story. Most of them met Lainey, and they all are invested. I look to Eli, and he gives me a nod, confirming that it's a safe space to share this hidden part of myself with the guys.

Blowing out a deep lungful of air, I relent. "Lainey has this tradition where she gets a journal on her birthday every year and writes things down that are important to her. Her asshole ex gave her this hideous one." I hold up the old journal, watch the table full of grown men visibly flinch away from it, and laugh. "Yeah, it's awful. So, anyway, the night of the fire at her apartment? She was burning a bunch of shit from him and their relationship, like a cleanse of her life from him, which would include this journal. The problem is that it was more important to her than just a picture or some dumb shirt. I could tell she didn't really want to burn what was in the journal, just the actual journal."

Nods go around the table along with bites of food. Darius Jacobs says, "So you took it for her, so she didn't have to burn it but doesn't have to look at the nightmare?"

"Exactly." I add, "I didn't want that idiot to take away something that important to her."

"But what were you drawing?" Adrian asks. "Did she draw things in there, too?"

I glance at him, clearing my throat. "No, I uh, I am adding to it."

Eli grins and claps his hands. "Our boy is finally using his hidden talent to lock down his dream girl, making Daddy proud." He winks at me, leaning into his nickname and making me groan.

A chorus of questions rumble across the table, and I hold up my hands. "Yes, I can draw. I don't talk about it because it has always been just something I do for myself. But I am trying to get this done for Lainey and don't want it to take a year, so I'm working on it here in our down time."

"So what are you drawing?" Chief asks from the doorway. We collectively turn to look at him, not realizing that he was late to dinner.

There was no way around any of this now that the cat was out of the bag. Nobody was making fun of me for being able to draw and all had genuine curiosity, but how were they going to react once I told them I was drawing flowers?

Running my hands nervously though my already tousled hair I say, "Flowers."

"Why flowers?" Eli asks, already knowing the answer.

Rolling my eyes at him, I say, "Because Lainey deserves as many as I can give her."

Adrian, Jacobs, Eli and the rest of the table all have shit-eating grins, and Chief says smoothly, "Yes, she sure does. That girl is special, Rem."

"I know she is, sir." The guys all nod, and look at me, knowing that me taking a chance on someone is not something I would do lightly. If I am making a grand, time-consuming gesture, one that also exposed a hidden part of myself to all of them, she must be really important to me.

"So, can we see them?" Adrian asks.

"No," I snarl at him. "Nobody. Nobody sees Lainey's journal but me. She trusted me with it, I'm not about to sit here and pass it around like it's show-and-tell." Adrian's face pales as he realizes what he asked for, and I feel bad for snapping at him. That is definitely out of character for me, but Lainey makes me feel fiercely protective. I look at Adrian and say, "Sorry, man."

"No, no I should have clarified, I don't want to see *her* journal, Rem! That is a major invasion of privacy. I was asking if we could see some of *your* drawings?" He glances around the table, and the guys chirp in with agreement and excitement.

I rub my jaw and say, "Well you actually see some of them all the time." Sticking out my arm, I show them my sleeve of tattoos on my left arm, pointing to the ones I sketched out for Keller. The details of the American flag wrapping my forearm with a Celtic cross on the inner side, the mountain scene with the eagle flying across the top of my shoulder, and few other details of the ink on my skin that have become as much a part of me as my eye color, height, or hair.

"Damn, Rem!" Ryan Banks, one of our rookies says, "I knew you said you could draw, but this is next-level talent.

Can you draw up something for me?" His eyes shine with excitement.

"I don't know, Banks, I have only ever drawn for myself." The idea that someone else thinks my drawings are good enough to want me customizing something for them is kind of baffling. I mean, Keller told me before that he could take me on as an apprentice and have me tattooing like a pro in no time, but I always thought he was messing around. The ideas I gave him he had improved on, and I made sure that everyone knew that when I explained them.

"Please think about it." Banks smiles at me and goes back to his dinner as conversation turns to other things. I look over to Eli, and that fucker just gives me another confident wink.

Later that night, I'm working on the journal in the common area of the fire station. There are lounge chairs, couches, and a big TV. The guys are all occupying themselves doing different things—napping, reading, and a few are playing cards at the dining table in the kitchen. I grin when I flip to a page from mid-spring of last year, her perfect pie day . . .

I did it! I did it!! I did IT! Finally after 109 tries I did it, I made the perfect apple pie. I didn't give up. I wanted to. I wanted to so many times. I cried, ruined so many, burned so many—burned MYSELF (see the scar on the back of my wrist for proof) but I didn't give up. I never would have been allowed to make so many messes or mistakes in my parent's kitchen—in my father's home. This pie is for me, my heart, my healing.

Nothing has tasted better.

I am not going to make this pie for anyone else until I know they will really appreciate it as much as I do, it is too important. This is my perfect pie.

I read that entry over and over, swelling with pride and something else I'm not ready to name. She tried so hard, for so long to make that pie. Her excitement was palpable through the page, and then the last lines hit me right in my heart.

She made me her perfect pie. She felt that I was worthy?

I did appreciate it, but more importantly—I appreciate her. Lainey is so special, exactly like Chief said. I want to work every day to be included in all of her important moments.

I write down her journal entry.

Then I fill the entire page with an explosion of apple blossoms.

15

Lainey

Kendra and I are going to a cute store in town to meet the owner. It's for Kendra, but I am just tagging along as moral support. Brooks and Books is an adorable local shop that has the perfect mix and vibe. I have browsed inside on occasion but am excited to spend more time there and meet the owner. Kendra said she is great and I will love her. She told me this with a suspicious twinkle in her eye when she invited me along, so I'm not sure what her ulterior motive could be. Because let's be honest, out of the two of us, Kendra is not the one that usually needs bestie backup for situations of any kind. She has a spine of steel that I admire and my anxiety definitely cannot relate to.

"I hope that she wants to carry my mugs in her shop," Kendra states as we walk toward that storefront, pulling me from my own thoughts.

"She would be crazy not to! Your work is exquisite, and I am not trying to blow smoke up your butt to make you feel ready for this meeting. Everyone on Etsy loves your work, you have never gotten a bad review, and you take a lot of pride in each piece you make." I smile at her, hoping each of my words wrap her in the sincerity I feel in my heart.

"Damn! That makes me feel ready to take on the world, girl! If I wasn't carrying this big old box of my samples, I would hug the shit out of you right now. Okay, let's do this." Kendra pauses at the antique wood door of the store so I can swing it open for her.

We step inside, and happy door chimes are followed by an equally sweet voice that must be the owner welcoming us into the shop. "Hello! Welcome to Brooks and Books." A beautiful petite blonde woman steps out from between some tables toward the back of the store. I have been in here a handful of times but have never met her and would have remembered her jubilant personality. "Oh, hey! It's so good to see you again, Kendra. Here, come bring your stuff over this way. I was working on clearing off a space so we can look at what you have." She points to a pretty reclaimed-wood table to her left.

"Thank you, so much!" Kendra strides over with confidence and smiles. "I hope it is okay that I brought my best friend along today. She is my pottery hype woman, and she always looks at all my samples before I make my final designs official." Kendra grabs my hand after setting down the box and pulls me to her side.

The shop owner smooths a hand over her small but obvious baby bump. "I am always happy to meet new friends. I also can't wait to see all this pottery. We are lacking a good selection of handmade mugs from local artisans, so this could be a perfect fit. I'm Sutton Brooks, by the way." She holds out her hand to me, and I take it, my jaw slightly ajar. Now knowing why Kendra was acting funny.

"H-hi," I say, stumbling over my greeting, "I'm Lainey Quinn."

Sutton's beautiful, soft brown eyes widen in realization,

and she lets out an excited squeal. She is a good couple inches shorter than my five foot five, like Kendra, but her energy outsizes me by a mile, also like Kendra. "Oh, holy crap." She covers her grin and looks at Kendra who's also smiling. "You're *Rem's Lainey*?" she questions.

I am not exactly sure how to answer Sutton—Sutton, as in *Remington's sister.* I knew she had a store in town, but we really didn't get a chance to talk too much about it, or what else his family does. After the heaviness of talking about my own family, we steered our conversation toward other topics. The only other things I know about Sutton are that she is pregnant and her husband is in the military. I just nod and say, "Yes, I know Remington."

"Oh, she *knows* him alright," Kendra so helpfully chimes in, and I give her an elbow. "Oww." She snorts. "What, it's true!"

Sutton's smile is a full-on tractor beam at this point, and she is practically bouncing on her toes. "I am SO happy to finally meet you! Rem told me all about you when he came in here to buy your journal, and I about *fell on the floor*. I could not believe he was shopping, for one thing, or telling me about his love life."

"Umm, oh." I go pale, and my hands feel clammy as anxiety crawls up my spine. "He told you about my journal?" I ask feeling so embarrassed.

"Yes! I was a huge Lisa Frank fan too growing up, by the way, but sounds like your old journal was terrifying. Rem came in here all nervous trying to pick out the replacement one and told me what he was doing. Don't worry, Lainey, he didn't show me what was written in the old one or anything like that. He just wanted to pick out something nice for you and asked for my help . . . which he barely ever does anymore." Her happy, cheerfulness slips for a moment, but I see it before she can put her smile back in place.

"Well, that was really nice of him. I am still shocked that he offered to help me with this at all. It's pretty crazy. I probably should have told him to forget the whole thing." I'm nervous now, and rambling. An unfortunate default mode. I feel guilty for taking up his time, knowing that I wrote a lot down last year, and it will take him time to transfer it all over. Time he could spend doing other hobbies that I have yet to find out about.

"One thing you need to know is that Rem loves to help people when and where he can. And if he offers to do something, it's because he genuinely wants to do it. So, let him help, and don't feel bad about it, Lainey. Plus, he was *so* freaking cute in here looking at my wall back there." Sutton points to the back of the store. "He spent forty minutes looking at them before he finally decided on the one he wanted."

My brain halts.

My heart melts.

He really cares that much about doing something for me?

I suspected that when Remington LeBlanc does something, he does it with a lot of heart and intention. And Sutton just confirmed that for me with her story.

"So . . . Remington doesn't like shopping?" I ask with a smile.

Laughing and helping Kendra pull her mugs out, Sutton says, "Ha! Absolutely not. The only time he shops is for groceries or when he really needs something. You won't find him tagging along for the fun of it, grumbles the whole time. My goodness," she gasps, pulling out a mug. "Kendra, this is stunning!"

Kendra is smiling ear to ear from our whole exchange, but an extra warmth lights her eyes and pinks her cheeks at the compliment. Sutton is holding one of my favorite mugs. It is cream colored, oversized, which I love for my tea, and is speckled with different shades of blues and green, heavier colors at the bottom, and light at the top. She did two colors in that collection. There is also a pink-and-orange speckled one that reminds me of a sunset.

"Thank you so much. I know that mug is Lainey's favorite." Kendra smiles at me.

"Well she has excellent taste. Everything that I am pulling out of this and unwrapping I want for my own house, which is exactly how I know that I need it in my store!" Sutton exclaims. "I think that this table is officially yours, Kendra. If you want it?" she asks, hopefully.

"That would be a dream come true! I am really wanting to have more of my work sold locally, and I have always loved your store. I appreciate you taking a chance on me," Kendra says sincerely.

"Kendra, trust me, friend! These mugs are going to *fly* off this table. We won't be able to keep them in stock. I hope you're ready to be one of our best sellers," Sutton says with a clap. I see so much of Sutton and Kendra in each other's personalities. It's like they are twin flames.

We spend the next hour chatting and setting up the mugs that Kendra brought in. She and Sutton decided on inventory, pricing, and signed a contract. It was so easy and natural to talk with Sutton. She fit right into the dynamic with me and Kendra. It was never easy for me to make friends, especially when my anxiety and past experiences poisoned the well. But having Kendra as a buffer, and the fact that Sutton was so warm and friendly, made my worries vanish, and I was able to relax and enjoy my time spent there with them. In fact, we were having such a good time we all exchanged numbers and even decided to have dinner together once Sutton closed up the shop for the day.

We landed on pizza after talking over our local options, apparently a major craving for Sutton right now. Her grin and excitement is matching both of ours as she looks toward the large front windows when suddenly, she gasps. Sutton's face goes a sickly white, and she grips the counter where she was getting things closed down for the day. Kendra and I rush to her sides, and I hold on to her arm.

"Sutton, are you okay?" I worry.

Breathing deeply, she shudders, and replies in a low, sad voice, "Yeah, I-I just saw something and I . . ." Sutton trails off.

"It looks like you saw a ghost," Kendra quips.

"I think that I did, and not freaking Casper," laments Sutton.

16

Remington

I have not seen Lainey since she dropped off the apple pie. I worked a forty-eight-hour shift, and I am ready for my time off. Normally we work twenty-four-hours shifts every other day for five days then get four days off. I did forty-eight to cover a shift for one of the other guys, Matt Ryder, who had to go home sick. It was not a problem; we are a family and jump in when and where we can. I know that he also had three little kids and a wife at home getting laid out with the twenty-four-hour flu. I hope and pray they are all feeling better, especially the little ones. Their baby is only one, and the flu is scary at that age. Being a trained EMT makes me run all the scenarios in my mind all the time, even when I am not the one living them.

I did the full EMT coursework and training three years after I graduated college. I wanted to be as knowledgeable and versatile as possible as a firefighter. We all have skills for that side of the job, but I wanted *more*. I don't live for the EMT role as much as the firefighting stuff, but knowing I can help on a deeper level in every situation, knowing the rig like the back of my hand, and having top training and knowledge makes me feel more confident and in control. I *need* open eyes and control, especially after Cora made me feel totally out of control and taken advantage of. It's about knowing that I have a clear path, no lies, and secure ways forward in my future if someone pulls the rug from underneath me again.

Right as I am leaving the grocery store with everything I needed for my weekly haul, plus a couple bags of essentials and Popsicles I got to drop off at Ryder's house, my phone starts to ring. I answer my sister's call. "Good mornin', Sutton," I say, happy to hear from her.

"Rem, hey." She sounds tired and worried.

"What's wrong? Is it the baby? Deck?" I gruff out my questions, not ready for her answers.

"No, no, no everything with the baby is fine. I have not heard anything from Deck, you know how that goes. He sent me a little care package before they had to go off the grid. I have no idea where he is, or when he will be back. No news from him or his superiors is always good news." She's right—we all know the drill when Derek is gone. He is highly trained, and in a highly classified group of SEALS that get called away to do things that we don't have clearance to know any information about—before or after they go, or even when they get home most of the time.

I let out a deep sigh of relief. "Okay, good. It's just that the way you sounded when I answered made me worry, you seem upset. What's going on, Sut?"

"I met Lainey yesterdaaaay," Sutton announces in a smug but cheerful way.

"What the hell? How did that happen?" I know that I told Lainey very briefly about my sister and was planning on making introductions soon myself. I was very sure they would get along, so I am still wondering why Sutton was upset before.

"Rem, she is seriously *so sweet*. I adore her! I can see why you are totally smitten by her," Sutton says.

"I'm not *smitten*," I deny indignantly.

"Remington LeBlanc, do NOT lie to your older sister! I happen to know that Lainey is also smitten with you too, so you should admit it." I can hear the smugness still dripping in her voice.

"And how exactly would you know that having only *just* met her?" I ask.

"Lainey came into the store yesterday afternoon with her best friend Kendra. You remember her, right? She was around in the summers when we were growing up and was friends with Eli's sister, Hannah. Anyway, Kendra does pottery and is going to sell mugs in the shop, they are amazing, by the way. We all got to chatting, which led to exchanging numbers, and we ended up going out for pizza when I closed up the shop. It was the *best* night!" Sutton is talking a mile a minute, and I can hear the excitement pouring through the phone.

"I'm really glad you ladies had fun, and that you got to know Lainey. I was going to introduce you two soon, but I guess y'all took care of that for me. I wonder why she hasn't said anything. We've been texting . . ." I leave the thought hanging. Lainey and I had been texting off and on the whole time I was at the fire station and she was working from home. I can't wait to see her again. I can't wait to *kiss* her again.

"That's because I asked Lainey to let me tell you, actually," Sutton says, pulling me back to our conversation.

"Why?"

"Something happened at the store that I need to tell you about. Lainey and Kendra were there, but they don't really know what happened." Sutton sounds nervous and worried now.

"Are you okay? Do you need me to come over right now?" I am instantly on high alert.

"No, I needed you to hear this from me, and I want you to try and stay calm." She takes a deep breath, like she is trying to give herself a few more seconds before she has to deliver whatever this news could be to me.

"What the fuck happened, Sutton? You're worrying me." I feel my hands getting sweaty as my grip on the leather steering wheel tightens.

Just as I pull into my driveway and park she says, "I was looking out the window of the store . . . and, and I saw someone lingering, walking past, looking in. Well not just someone, Rem. It was Cora." She says the name in almost a whisper. The name of her former best friend, and the woman that I have not seen since the night I kicked her out of my apartment six years ago.

"Why the hell would she be back in Fox Grove?" I growl at my sister. "She has no family here anymore. Her parents don't live here, her granddaddy passed a long time ago. She has no reason to be in town."

"I have no idea why she's here, Rem. But I wanted to tell you what I saw. I wanted you to hear it from me. I didn't like the idea of having you just run into her walking down the street or at the store or something." I can tell that she is trying not to cry, and I wish we were having this talk in person.

"Thank you for telling me. Shit, Sutton, you said Lainey was there? Did she see her? Does she know, or did you tell her about Cora?" I ask in a rush.

"No, Rem! I told you, I tried my best to kind of brush it off. I told the girls that I thought I saw a weird ex of mine. Then we went and had dinner. It is not my place to tell Lainey about your past. I wouldn't do that." She sighs.

"Alright." I slam my truck door and carry in my bags of groceries. "Thank you for telling me. Warning me. Hopefully I don't see her. Hopefully she stays the hell away from me."

Sutton lets out a weak chuckle. "She will if she knows what's good for her."

"Love you, Sut. Call me if you need me, okay?"

"Love you too, little brother." She loves to call me that, even though she has the age difference and I tower over her in stature.

I hang up my phone and stare at the bags of food, lost in thought. Finally I notice the extras that I purchased and the Popsicles. *Shit.* I hurry and put all my stuff away, toss Ryder's stuff back in my truck, and head off to his place a few blocks over to do a surprise drop-off of supplies. One small mention of Cora and my plans and my head are all screwed up.

Except her being back in town doesn't feel small. It feels like an ominous cloud coming right for me, and the only thing that will make me feel better is my own personal ray of sunshine . . . Lainey.

17

Lainey

I swing open my apartment door to the most handsome man I have ever laid eyes on. Remington is wearing a fitted black T-shirt, dark-wash jeans, the same boots he wore on our first date, and a sexy grin. In his hands he's holding "Tulips," I say with a smile, welcoming him in.

"Hi, beautiful." Remington wastes no time once I shut the door. He drops the flowers on my little blue entry table and scoops me into his arms. His lips are on mine instantly. Soft, warm, hungry. I lean deeper into him and a low rumble vibrates through his chest. Before things get more heated, he pulls back and I can feel the pout on my face. Remington's deep laugh snaps my eyes open to see him smiling down at me. "Jesus, I missed you," he says tucking a piece of my hair behind my ear, then running his thumb slowly across my jaw.

"I missed you too, more than I should probably admit," I whisper.

"Why should you not tell me that? I just told you the same thing." Remington runs his hands down my arms slowly and back up again making me shiver.

"I don't want you to think that I am needy or clingy or

whatever," I say, looking away from him in embarrassment, and with the whispers of past partners' voices plucking my memory.

"Lainey, look at me, please," he says gently. "I like that you think about me as much as I am thinking about you. That we miss each other. That we are excited to see each other. That we want to spend time together. Okay?"

"Okay." I nod, looking directly into his handsome face. "Thank you."

He gives me a soft, sweet kiss, and hands me the tulips he brought. "So you know these ones, huh?" Remington smiles at me with mischievous playfulness.

"I don't live under a rock, I do know *some* flower names, Remington," I say with a heavy dose of sass, which makes his smile grow impossibly wider over his straight white teeth.

"I know you don't live under a rock," he laughs, "but I also have to cover all my flower bases here. So today is tulips. They can symbolize lots of things, but I picked them as a representation of happiness."

I run my fingers along the silky purple petals and ask, "Oh yeah? Why is that?"

"Because nothing makes me happier than being able to spend time with you. I have not been able to stop thinking about when I'd see you next after you left me with that pie. Which, by the way, was the best pie I have ever had. I had to fight off the guys to keep them from eating it. Normally we share food, but there was no way I was going to let them have that one. Although freaking Eli did get one forkful, and his eyes rolled back in his head, so I think you have a fan for life out of him." Remington is laughing, picturing his best friend. I can't even imagine all the trouble those two have gotten into together.

"I'm really happy you liked it." I can feel blush on my skin growing from the heat of his eyes on me.

"It was the perfect pie," he says taking my hand, kissing the scar on my wrist, and leading me over to the couch. "I heard that you got to meet my sister?"

"I did," I tell him excitedly. "I hope that's okay? We hit it off when I went to her store with Kendra, and then we all had pizza. She asked to be the one to tell you for some reason, and I said that was fine." It was hard for me not to tell Remington about being with his sister. I want to just tell him everything. He makes it easy to be open and honest. Not telling him about Sutton felt weird, but she insisted on talking to him.

"Yeah, she called me, and it's great that you are getting to know each other. I knew that you would hit it off and be friends. My sister is awesome and one of my favorite people. She also wanted to talk to me first about something that happened in the store," Remington says, sounding a little nervous.

"I didn't do anything to upset Sutton, did I?" I try to think back to our afternoon together and start picking over each moment in my memories.

"Of course not!" Remington puts his hand on my thigh, and I feel the heat of his palm travel up my entire body. My mind wonders what it would feel like to have his hands roam all over my bare skin, and another shiver sends goose bumps rippling all over me. Slowly rubbing his thumb in circles, and being very distracting, Remington keeps talking. "Sutton wanted to tell me about something that she saw at the store when you were there."

"Oh, yeah. She looked really worried. I thought she might pass out. She said she thought she saw an old ex-boyfriend through the window or something, and it kind of freaked her out. Is she okay? They aren't bothering her, are they?" I ask.

"No, Sutton's fine, and she didn't see one of her exes through the window. She actually saw *my ex*, and she didn't tell you because she wanted me to be the one to be able to talk to you about my past when I was ready. But if she really is around town, and I hope she isn't, I wanted you to know." Remington is tense all over. Not the charming, relaxed man that strolled in a few minutes ago. I can tell this is not a conversation he wants to have.

"It's alright if you're not ready to tell me about her. I don't need to know," I reassure him. As much as I have opened up to Remington, there are still things from my past that I'm not sure I am ready to share with him. Things that I have not shared with anyone, not even my therapist knows all the little details. So I won't push him to tell me anything, ever. He has to come to me openly, in his own time. Hopefully I can be a safe space for him the way he is becoming a safe space for me.

"No," he surprises me, "I want to tell you so you know more about me. More about why I am the way I am. A lot of it has to do with what happened with her, with Cora." He says her name on a hiss, a tone of disgust so deep, one I haven't heard from him.

"I'm here," I tell him. "You can tell me anything, Remington. I know who you are, and more importantly what kind of man you are."

Taking a deep breath, Remington lays out everything. And there is *a lot*. He grew up with Cora, she was Sutton's best friend, and they are all close in age. They started dating in high school, and he told me about all the pressure he felt from everyone about them being a couple even that young. The more he talked, the more my heart ached for the boy that grew into a man with a person by his side that did not see him for who he was. Cora sounds like a selfish, self-centered person. I can't see Sutton being best friends with someone like that. I can't see *Remington* dating someone like that, loving someone like that. Hot discomfort licks my gut, and I know I am feeling jealous of a relationship that is long gone, but obviously still has a hold on the man sitting in front of me.

His past wounds are not fresh, but they are deep, just like mine.

Remington ends his heartbreaking tale with the night he kicked Cora out of his apartment, the day they graduated college. He is vibrating with the anger of the memory, and I am raging on his behalf. Furious that anyone could hurt the man I am quickly developing deep feelings for, making him question his life and judgment.

"I can't believe she did that to you. How dare she disrespect your relationship that way. But the thing that makes me the most upset—and honestly I can say this because you know I have also been cheated on—is the way she spoke about you being a firefighter. She thought it was something you were just messing around with at college and were going to get over? Give it up for her own company?" I stand up and pace my small living room, unable to contain the buzz of contempt rushing through my muscles, needing the movement.

"Yeah, I know," Remington agrees. "I was upset about the cheating, obviously, but being a firefighter is what I am called to do. I didn't know it right away, it took time to figure it out, but once I did I was locked in. She acted like it was a joke. Even after she watched me spend years working hard to earn my degree and make up time for my first year and a half pursuing the finance degree."

"Remington, you *do not* have to justify your decision to me. Most college kids change majors at some point, sometimes more than once. I know that you are meant to be a firefighter. I can feel it, see it with how passionately you talk about it. I got to go to the station and meet your friends and coworkers. They all love you. You're a family there and it's special. *That woman* has no idea what she is missing out on. Thank God she ruined her life so that mine could be made better by knowing you." I pour my words out, standing in front of Remington while he's still seated on the couch.

"You really believe that?" he asks, voice rough with emotion. His hands grip my hips and pull me closer, pull me down toward him.

I straddle Remington's lap, and frame his face in my hands, a light stubble scraping across my fingertips. "You are the best man I have ever met. There's nobody else like you." I lean my face in and go to gently seal the sentiment with a kiss, but Remington meets me halfway with passion. One large hand grips my waist while the other slides into my hair.

This kiss feels raw, primal, and opposite of the sweet and gentle one I was aiming for, but I don't want it to end. I moan when his delicious tongue sweeps into my mouth. He's like a man starved and I am the only thing that can satisfy him in this moment. My hands run along his hard chest, and his muscles ripple as his arms explore more of my own body. I grind down on his lap and gasp into his mouth when I feel his hard length press against my wet center. I am so turned on, just from this kiss, I might explode from barely being touched.

"You feel what you do to me, Lainey?" Remington says, kissing me, biting my bottom lip, and sucking it seductively into his mouth.

"Y-yes." I whimper when he switches to slowly trailing kisses down my neck, then nipping my collarbone.

"You are the most beautiful woman. I haven't been able to get our first kiss out of my head. Thinking about what would have happened if we were alone." Claiming my mouth again, he kisses me deeply, pushing his hips up into me as I roll back into him. And oh, holy shit does that feel good, feel so right.

"What would have happened?" I ask breathlessly.

"This. A lot of this. I want to touch every inch of you, know every part of your perfect body, Lainey." Remington pauses his kisses, looking into my eyes for permission.

"Yes, don't stop," I plead.

He flips us onto the couch and grips my ass. Our kisses feel molten, and the fire in my soul is sparking all along where his body is making contact with mine. I want more. I want to feel more of him, of us. I reach up and pull my shirt off, leaving me in a lavender lace bra and my yoga pants.

Remington is grinning down at me like a wolf. He licks his lips and runs the tips of his fingers ever so softly over the top of my bra, where the scalloped lace is brushing my skin. "Lavender," he whispers. I just nod. He bends his head and kisses along the swell of one breast then the other, and when he looks up at me with questioning eyes, I nod again. That wolfish grin comes back and he yanks the cups down, exposing my breasts to him. His stare and the cool air make my nipples instantly pebble. "*Fuck*," he whispers, then sucks one nipple into his mouth, rolling his tongue around the aching bud, and I gasp.

"Oh my God," I say. "That feels so good." I let out a needy moan and run my fingers through his blond hair.

Remington pops my nipple out of his mouth, and says, "Nobody here but me, Lainey. You only get to call out *my name*." His hard length presses firmly into my hip, driving home his point, and his hand slips into my pants.

"Holy shit," I whisper, "Remington."

"That's right, beautiful. How wet are you going to be for me right now after everything we have been doing, hmm?" he says in a sexy, questioning tone.

"Soaked," I reply honestly. He is only seconds away from discovering for himself what he does to me.

Slipping his fingers lower, he finds my slit and hums, kissing me deeply as he pushes one finger inside, making me gasp again. "Yeah, you are absolutely dripping for me." Remington slides out the one finger and replaces it with two, circling my clit with his thumb and kissing me like I have never been kissed before.

I feel like I'm drunk. It's all too much. I have never in my life been touched like this, worshiped like this. My hips buck wildly as he pumps his fingers and finds places deep within my inner walls that I didn't even know existed before this moment. My clit is throbbing and my whole body is tingling. "Rem-Remington I'm so close. More," I plead.

"I know, baby, I know," he whispers in my ear, kissing up my neck, moaning and grinding into me harder, bringing unrelenting pleasure to my body. Heat rushes through me, and stars explode behind my eyes, body locking in a tight, perfect release. Remington groans before slowly pulling his hand from my pants. My eyes flutter open in time to see him licking my release off of his fingertips, his greedy eyes locked on my face.

"Oh, my . . ." I trail off, lost for words, having never seen something so hot in all twenty-six years of my life.

When he's done, he leans in and gently kisses me, smiling. I readjust my bra cups and look at him.

"That was, that was beyond words," I tell him. "But umm, what about you?" I ask glancing down. I know he must be painfully hard, and I want to satisfy him as much as he just satisfied me.

Laughing roughly, he kisses me again. Remington says, "I'm good."

"What? What does that mean? I felt . . . things, big things, *a big thing.* And I don't want to have you be uncomfortable." I am feeling embarrassed and inexperienced. Rambling. Again.

"Baby, that was so hot you made me come in my pants." Remington smirks and has a pink blush staining his perfectly chiseled cheeks. "I feel like a fucking teenager, and I am going to have to go grab my gym bag out of my truck so I can change." He laughs.

I grin at him. "Oops." Shrugging, I lean in and kiss him.

"Yeah, oops. You should be so proud. You are so sexy you just made your boyfriend come in his damn pants." He laughs, and I blink at him. He smiles at me, knowing *exactly* what his words did to my brain.

"What did you just say?" I ask in a hushed voice.

"Lainey," he whispers, "are you really going to make me repeat what just happened?"

I know he is messing with me now, because he can. This is his playful, cocky, button-pushing side and he's trying to get me all riled up. I think he likes it when I am sassy. "You just called yourself my boyfriend," I state, eyebrow raised.

"Yup," he states right back, tucking my hair behind my ear.

"We aren't even going to talk about it? You are just going to appoint yourself to that role?" I chuckle, sitting up straight and fixing my shirt more.

"Okay, let's talk about it. I know it might be fast, but fuck it. And for the record, I think I have been pretty obvious about the fact that I want to make you *mine*. Lainey Quinn, would you please be my girlfriend?" Smiling, he holds my hand and runs his thumb along the back waiting for my answer.

"Nothing would make me happier." I lean in for a kiss.

"Not even a whole room of tulips?" Remington asks.

"Not even acres of tulips." I kiss him with a smile on my face and butterflies fluttering under every inch of my skin.

18

Remington

It's been over a week since Lainey and I have become official. Every day that I have not been working I go over to her apartment, but today is the first time that she is coming to my house, and I can't wait. I have been dreaming of having her here, in my space, for weeks. The more time we spend together, I see Lainey's walls slowly coming down. I know there is more that she has to share, maybe things I won't ever get to know, and that's fine. What I *do* know is that I have never been so happy and hopeful. Today is a Friday and I don't have to work tomorrow. I am hoping I can talk my girl into a sleepover. We spend a lot of time together, but since the time on her couch we haven't taken it further. I don't want to push things. I just want the chance to wake up next to Lainey and make her breakfast.

My doorbell rings, and I open it to see her standing there with a bottle of wine, a plate of cookies, and the most stunning smile. "Hi," she says a little nervously.

"Get in here," I say, grinning and welcoming her into my home. I give her a kiss that doesn't last long enough and guide her into the open-plan kitchen and living room area. I set down the wine and cookies, watching as her eyes scan over the space. My house is not overly large; it's a ranch that I have slowly updated on my own since I bought it a few years ago. The kitchen is my favorite part, with warm butcher-block counters and mossy-green cabinets. It gives the house a cozy, lived-in feeling. The rest of the walls are a soft cream color that allow the kitchen to be the star of the open space. I don't have a lot of decorations or clutter. I like to be clean and organized, but my house definitely lacks the warmth of a woman's touch that I feel when I am at Lainey's apartment.

"Your house is lovely." Lainey turns to me with a smile. I stride over and wrap her in a hug, not able to stay away from her.

"Much more lovely now that you are here." I kiss the top of her head, take her hand, and give her the very quick grand tour of the rest of the place. The laundry room off the kitchen, two guest bedrooms (one that is my office), a guest bathroom that I am in the middle of remodeling, my bedroom with its finished en suite bathroom, and finally the basement complete with a small home gym and some storage. "It's not big or fancy," I say, rubbing the back of my neck, "but it works for me."

"I lived in big and fancy, Remington. It was cold and lifeless and felt like a prison. This is perfect. You have made this place a wonderful home, worked hard to get it how you want, and be able to welcome people here. You should feel nothing but pride when you show it to me, or anyone else." She is looking right at me, smiling softly, and seeing so much more of me than I think she even realizes.

I want to be able to provide, have a family, and have the woman I choose to build a life with be proud to be *with me*. Cora was never going to be that person. I have a feeling that I could have worked my fingers to the bone, done everything she asked, given up my own dreams, and it still would have never been enough for her . . . because I was not enough for her. Lainey sees the effort that I put into the everyday things that I do and appreciates me. She thanks me for the big things and the little things. *She sees me.*

"Thank you, that means a lot to me," I tell her, kissing my way up her jaw and finally placing one on her lips. "I have been thinking about having you here, at my house, since I met you."

"Oh yeah?" she asks with a playful grin.

"Oh yeah . . ." I quickly sweep her into a fireman's carry, and she yelps and holds on to my back, laughing.

"Remington!" Lainey yells.

I gently deliver her safely to my brown, buttery-soft, worn leather couch, and drop down next to her. Pointing at the coffee table, her blue eyes sparkle when she notices the small arrangement of flowers I had placed there earlier today. When I went to my parents' house this morning I asked my mom if I could take a couple cuttings from her hydrangeas, and she was happy to share. The pinks of the tiny flowers pop against the dark wood stain of my table.

"These are wow! What are they?" Lainey asks, sliding closer to examine them.

"Hydrangeas. They can mean different things for the different shades they come in, like most flowers. Pink though, is harmony, romance, and true feelings," I tell her.

"How on earth do you know so much about flowers, Remington? You are like an encyclopedia." She looks back at me over her shoulder, distracting me with her long lashes and pouty lips.

Clearing my throat and sinking deeper into the couch, I explain, "My parents own a landscaping company. So, plants and flowers were a big part of life growing up. My mom *loves* to rattle off names, meanings, and flower facts. What I don't remember from her I Google," I admit and Lainey laughs. "She runs the office side of the company, and my dad is the dreamer and designer. He runs the crews and all that."

Lainey sinks back and snuggles close to me. I wrap my arm around her, breathing in her honey scent. "You didn't want to be part of the family business?"

"No. I mean, I like flowers, but landscaping and everything my dad does is not what I'm passionate about. My parents named the company after our family, LeBlanc Landscape, just because it has a nice ring to it. They didn't put any pressure on me or on Sutton to join them in the business."

"They sound really great." Lainey sighs.

"Sutton and I are lucky, they are really great parents. If we had wanted to be a part of it, they would have welcomed us with open arms. But ultimately, they truly wanted us to figure out what would make us happiest and pursue that. They have always supported us." I know that talking about my parents could be a sore spot for Lainey, but I want her to know them. I want her to understand that they are good people, and once they get to know her, they will love and support her the same ways they have and continue to for me and my sister. Lainey deserves that kind of parental embrace more than anyone.

"What will happen to the company when they want to retire?" Lainey asks.

"My cousin, Felix, actually works with my dad. He has the green thumb of the family. My dad has one brother, and my mom has a sister and two brothers. Felix is her sister's son. My dad is going to hand over the whole thing to him but still be part owner. But that won't be for a long time. My mom will probably give up the books before my dad hands over the planning, dirt, and shovels. Although, my mom's gardens can rival anything my dad does. She's a master gardener," I tell Lainey as I gently play with her hair.

"What does that mean? Master gardener?"

"She went through this like intense gardening education program and got a certification for it. So she knows a shit ton about plants and how to take care of them. What should and should be planted together, where they can be planted depending on climate and zones. Lots of stuff. She is way into it." I try to explain the best I can.

Lainey smiles up at me. "It's her passion."

"Yeah, it is. I actually got those flowers from her garden this morning." I point to the hydrangeas.

"Really? I guess I shouldn't be surprised." Lainey looks at them with an expression I can't really place.

"I told her all about you when I was there." This makes Lainey sit up straight and look at me.

"Y-you did?" she asks, nervously. She starts to fidget her hands. I notice that she does this when her anxiety starts to kick up, so I place my hand over hers and squeeze gently.

"Of course I did, Lainey. I wanted to tell her all about my amazing girlfriend. She can't wait to meet you. I got scolded for keeping you all to myself for this long. And then scolded *again* when I told her that you know Sutton and have already hung out with her." I laugh.

"I would love to meet her, Remington. Your dad, too." She says it quietly and looks down.

"Hey, if you are not ready that's okay. She can be overly excited . . ." Lainey cuts me off.

"No, it's not that. I really do want to meet your parents, especially your mom. They sound lovely. It's just that, Remington, my family is *not* like your family, and when you eventually meet them I am scared to know what you will think of me." She looks at me as those tears that rip me apart and send rage racing along my nerves any time she talks about her family are welling back up in her deep-blue eyes.

I swipe a fallen tear off of the apple of her cheek, and tell her, "Your family dynamics do not change the woman that I am holding in my arms. The person you are today is resilient, kind, warm, and strong despite all the shit they did to you. You could have gone down a totally different road, but you chose to be *this version* of Lainey Quinn. You have a lot to be proud of. It doesn't matter that we come from different backgrounds because we fit together perfectly."

A little sob chokes Lainey's laugh as she buries her face in my neck, and she says, "You don't know that yet."

I growl. "Oh, she's got jokes now." I poke her side, and she squirms. "I do know. I think you know it, too."

Lainey looks at me and wipes away a final tear. "We do. And it scares me."

"I know." I kiss her softly, hoping she can feel what I can't put into words.

Pulling back she says, "I . . . we did a lot that one day at my place, well it was a lot for me, and it was amazing. But that's not like me. I want every part of you, Remington, but I also don't want to go too fast." She bites her lip, obviously worried about my reaction.

"I'm okay with that, baby. We can take this as slow as you need."

"Really?" Her disbelief is written across her face, and I want to punch every asshole that has made her feel uncomfortable or pushed her for more than she was ready to give in the past.

"There is no rush, I am not going anywhere." I kiss her again softly.

"Thank you," she says, a shimmer of tears starting to form again, the hurricane in her eyes swirling back to life.

"No more tears, I can't take it. Let's have dinner." I link her hand in mine and lead her to the kitchen.

I grab out all of the ingredients I need to make blackened chicken with fettuccine Alfredo. Lainey opens the delicious bottle of wine she brought. We spend the rest of the night dancing in the kitchen while we are cooking, talking, laughing, kissing, and making my house finally feel like a true home.

19

Lainey

This must be what heaven feels like. I am surrounded by the masculine smell of cedar, soap, and something that is uniquely Remington. His even more rugged arms have slipped around me, holding me close, and I have never felt this kind of peace before. I look down at his left forearm and try not to drool at the combination of muscle and tattoos.

Remington asked me to stay the night last night after we had the best dinner and spent a couple hours relaxing and watching *Parks and Rec* snuggled up together on his couch. It was late and he didn't want me to drive home. I didn't want to leave, either. After our talk earlier, when I asked if we could take things slow, I knew he was not just trying to get me to stay so he could have sex with me. That's not who Remington is.

We got ready for bed together, and it was not ever even a question as to where I was going to sleep: In his bed, in his arms, was the only option. He gave me an extra toothbrush and one of his T-shirts to sleep in. Being that he's six-three it fits me more like a nightgown. When I walked out of his bathroom, his eyes darkened as they roamed a hungry glance over my body, lingering on my bare legs. He gave me a quick, firm kiss, walked into the bathroom, shut the door hard, and turned on the shower.

When he came back out, I was scrolling on my phone. It slipped right out of my hands when I looked up at my boyfriend. *Holy freaking shit . . . This man!?* I get to call *this man* my boyfriend? We need a new word, there is *nothing* boy about this *man*.

He walked out of his bathroom with only black basketball shorts on, sandy blond hair slightly damp and messy from toweling it dry. His muscles have muscles. His abs have abs. And that sexy V thing that I thought was a myth? Nope, it's a real thing, and Remington has it—complete with a tattoo on the right side of his ribs running down to his hip with flames and script in black and grey ink. That tattoo reads "bringing calm to chaos."

I also got to see the full sleeve on his left arm for the first time. It goes from his wrist all the way up his arm, wrapping around his shoulder—and it is *stunning*. Again, there are no bright bursts of color. All black and grey tones, which fits Remington perfectly. His upper arm has a fireman's face with helmet and face shield in place surrounded by flames and Celtic designs. His inner bicep has the Fox Grove fire department logo, and there is an American bald eagle flying across his shoulder in a forest scene. There is a large, intricate cross on his inner forearm and the American flag wrapping around the front of his arm. There's so much detail to all of his tattoos. Trees, flames, rivers of intention and hours upon hours of complex artwork fill up his skin. He is a walking canvas, and my eyes are hungry to take in every little detail.

I am gently running my finger along the very realistic stitching of the flag when Remington's arms pull me even closer, a rumble from his chest and his hard length announcing that his body is very much awake. Hot kisses are peppered up my neck until he gets to my ear, and whispers, "Good morning, beautiful."

"Mmmm, good morning," I whisper, pushing myself back into him and he grips my hip, trying to still me.

"Lainey," Remington warns.

"I'm sorrrrry," I whine, annoyed with myself and my stupid requests.

What were they again?

As if he can read my mind, Remington says, "Baby, if you keep rubbing that perfect ass against my cock, the last thing that will happen is us taking things slowly like you asked last night. I promised you snuggling and a French toast breakfast. And you are literally making it very hard to stick to that promise." He kisses my neck again and I moan.

He throws the warm covers off of himself and launches out of the bed. I can't help but let out a giggle as I look down at the *massive* problem tenting his shorts right now. "Please for the love of . . . don't laugh at my pain right now. I am trying my best here." Remington adjusts himself as he walks into the bathroom. I hear him turn on the water and start to brush his teeth. Snuggling back into the pillows, I suck in a deep breath and float in my feelings of happiness for a few minutes before I force myself out of bed, too.

After Remington leaves the bedroom, I go through my very short morning routine of going to the bathroom, washing my hands, and brushing my teeth. Looking in the mirror, my hair is messy but manageable, and my eyes have a new brightness to them, one that has been sparked to life by the presence of one man.

I meet Remington in the kitchen. Still shirtless and in his shorts, he has coffee brewing, a teapot warming on the stove, and is whipping up the ingredients for French toast. It already smells amazing and has my mouth watering. I walk up behind

Remington and wrap him in a hug as he works, pressing my cheek against his strong, warm back.

"Can I help you with breakfast?" I offer.

"Nope," he says, shifting so he is facing me, holding me in his arms. Tucking the hair behind both of my ears, he frames my face in his hands. His rich, honey-colored eyes look extra pretty right now with the morning light picking up little flecks of bright gold that are normally well hidden. "I have been excited to make you your favorite food since you texted me about it. So all you need to do is take a seat at the counter and enjoy your cup of tea while I cook for us." Remington kisses me and I want more. I roll my tongue along his lip, and he lets me in, then he takes control and devours me just the way he knows I like him to. We stand there in his kitchen kissing, touching, and getting lost in each other until we pull apart breathing heavily.

I bite my lip and blush. Remington gives me a look that tells me the last thing he wants for breakfast is French-freaking-toast, gives me one more fast kiss, and puts me on one of the three barstools lined up at his island countertop. "No more distracting me. I need to feed my woman."

Swoon.

I think my nipples just cut his T-shirt open.

I think I might climb over this counter and keep distracting him.

Hearing him call me "his woman" . . . nobody has ever called me that before. I never knew that's something I would like or want. Now it feels like a *necessity*.

"Say that again . . . please." I look at him shyly. I am not used to asking for what I want, but Remington makes me feel brave.

"I need to feed my woman?" he asks, confirming my new kink.

"Yes," I say in a breathy whisper.

"Do you like it when I call you *mine*, Lainey?" Remington dries his hands on a dish towel and walks to me in a confident prowl, spinning me so he can stand between my legs.

"I really do," I admit.

"Good." He bends down and whispers in my ear, "Because I plan on claiming you in every possible way, baby." He kisses my neck, walks away, and keeps cooking like he just didn't totally turn my world upside down and leave me a dripping, needy mess all over his barstool.

It is a perfect spring day, and we decided after the incredible breakfast that Remington managed to finish cooking to take a walk around his neighborhood. Once I finished getting redressed in what I had on last night, jeans and a tight sweater, he hopped in the shower and said to make myself at home while he got ready.

Remington's house is exactly the kind of place that I would want in a home. It is not too big, there is room to grow, and he's put a lot of thought into the finishes and work he's done. The second bathroom he's remodeling now will look so nice when it's complete, but I can't even imagine how much work it's going to take. Right now it is all gutted down to the studs, and the only thing in there is a toilet.

I am doing one last wipe down of the kitchen when I hear the doorbell ring. Looking down the hall I don't see Remington coming, so he must still be getting ready for our walk. Anxiety creeps up and turns my breakfast over in my stomach. Answering a door should not be this hard. What if it is Sutton? Or what if it's an important package that needs to be signed for? *Be a grown up, Lainey* that nasty voice hisses, *get over it and just answer the stupid door.* It's never that simple, but I want to win this time, I want to be the one in control, not my anxiety.

Taking a deep breath to try and calm my nerves, I plaster a smile on my face and reach a shaky hand toward the door. Opening it I find a stunning woman standing there. She is dressed impeccably in a black, belted sheath dress that matches her long black hair. Her gold, chunky sandals complement her bangles and earrings. She slides off oversized sunglasses down her sharp nose, highlighting her look of annoyance as she takes me in. Her brown eyes don't hold an ounce of warmth or friendliness the way Sutton's do.

"Hello," I say. "Can I help you?"

"Who are you?" she snaps at me. Her voice is shrill and irritating.

"Who are you?" I fire right back, crossing my arms.

"Rem is expecting me. Put down your cleaning supplies and go find him." She glances at the dish towel I forgot I was holding, gripped tightly in my hand.

"Excuse me?" I say.

"You are the help, right? A cleaner, a maid? Whatever the hell you call yourselves these days." Letting out a dramatic sigh she continues, "It doesn't matter. Let me inside right now, and then go get Rem." She is so aggressive, and there is not a chance in hell I am letting her step one gold-covered foot in this house.

Just as I am about to tell her as much, I hear footsteps come up behind me. Remington bands a strong arm around my stomach and pulls me close to him, my back to his chest. I instantly feel relieved to not be alone with this awful woman anymore until he says . . .

"What the fuck are you doing here, Cora."

20

Remington

As I was pulling my T-shirt over my head, I heard a voice I never wanted to hear again. It was shrill, rude, and being directed at the one person I never wanted it to touch. I stomp down the hallway, reaching Lainey as quickly as I can, needing to have her in my touch to ground me in this moment. I wrap my arm around her stomach and pull her little body close to me. She lets out a sigh of relief and grips my forearm.

"What the fuck are you doing here, Cora," I say in a very unwelcoming tone of voice.

Cora's whole demeanor instantly shifts once she has my attention. I see her stand a little taller and stick out her chest a little more, as if it's going to help her case. "I was telling your maid here that you were expecting me and . . ."

The fuck? I cut her off immediately. "No, absolutely not. First of all, this is my girlfriend, not my maid, don't act so ignorant. Second, I was *not* expecting you, nor are you welcome here."

Cora steps back with a gasp, as if I smacked her with my

words. "Rem," Cora says with a fake quiver to her lip, "what about the deal we made?"

Lainey looks up at me with questions written all over her face, ones I have no answers to. I give her a squeeze, trying to reassure her without any of my words.

"I have no idea what the hell you are talking about. We have no deals. I haven't talked to you or seen you since the day we graduated." There is something off about Cora, and it's making me uneasy. I want her gone. I want her far away from me and more importantly, Lainey. "How did you even know where I lived?" This question slams into my mind and makes that uneasy feeling double down. As a public servant I keep myself unlisted and as private as possible. I don't take women or dates to my house and have been careful. The only people that know where I live are the ones I choose to let know about it.

Cora rolls her eyes at me and says, "I knew you bought this place *years ago*, Rem. I did your realtor's little sister's wedding up on Casterview Lake. Chitchatting is currency in my business. I pick up all kinds of interesting information that people don't even realize they're giving away." She smiles at me in a sickeningly familiar way.

"Doesn't change the fact that you're unwelcome and need to leave." I turn and guide Lainey back inside, then feel the claws of the past grip my shoulder. I hiss and spin back to Cora, batting her hand away. Pointing at her I say, "Do *not* touch me, Cora."

"Mmm, I missed the way you say my name when you get all riled up, Remmy." Lainey sucks in a breath behind me. This needs to end. Now.

"You know I hate when you call me that. Get off my property, and don't come back."

"What about our deal," Cora whimpers at me pathetically.

"I have no idea what you're talking about," I say, getting more annoyed by the second.

"We. Made. A. Deal. We said that if we were not married by the time we were both thirty, we would marry each other. We swore it to each other." Cora is looking at me like we sealed this promise in blood. In reality, we were children saying childish things.

"Cora, you cannot be serious. That is some bullshit, stupid kid thing we said when we were in *middle school*. That was not real." I step back inside and take Lainey's hand in mine.

Cora looks at our hands, and steam is practically coming from her ears. "We are almost thirty. A deal is a deal, Rem!" she shouts at me.

"I'd never make a deal with the devil, Cora." I shut the door in her face and throw the deadbolt in place. Looking out the front window I see Cora stomp away, get into an old white BMW and zoom off at a speed way too fast for a family neighborhood.

Turning to face Lainey and my own shame, I see nothing but compassion on her pretty face. "Are you okay?" she asks quietly.

"Not really. I had no idea why she was in town, hoped she would just leave and I wouldn't have to deal with her. But that was beyond anything I would have ever guessed. Cora was always a bit ridiculous and had wild plans, mostly they were silly and harmless. That version of Cora you just saw, that was someone different. She was unhealthy, unstable." I rub my hand along Lainey's jawline in a way that has become a habitual comfort to both of us.

"Yeah, that went from zero to unhinged pretty fast," she agrees. "I think you should call Sutton and warn her. What if Cora shows up to Brooks and Books and bothers her?" Lainey worries, her hand finding the hem of my T-shirt, fidgeting with the fabric.

"We are definitely going to tell her what happened. I will call her right away. I don't want Cora anywhere near you again or Sutton." I am mortified that my past literally showed up on my doorstep for Lainey to have to deal with.

"I wonder what *my* eighth-grade marriage pact buddy is up to . . ." Lainey teases me.

"What! Who was he?" I playfully growl and spin her in a circle.

Lainey cracks up and says, "*She* was Abbie West, and we made a pact to marry each other because boys were the worst."

"Oh, really? And what do you think of boys now?" I ask sliding my hand along the back pocket of her jeans and slipping my hand inside.

Grinning, Lainey says, "I still am not a big fan of boys and all the stupid games they play." She takes her hand and runs it through my short hair. "But I am pretty crazy about one *man* in particular."

"Is that right?" I smirk at her.

"Mmhmm." Lainey kisses me and makes the warmth and sunshine that Cora dimmed with her sudden appearance shine brightly again.

21

Lainey

The "incident" with Cora was three weeks ago, and we have not seen or heard from her since then. Remington thinks that she is gone and took her crazy elsewhere, but my anxiety won't let go of it. The whole interaction with her felt so desperate and off. Why would she just show up after all this time and basically throw herself at Remington like that? The man obviously has nothing but disdain for his ex-girlfriend—I have no worries on that front. What actually worries me is her behavior and how Cora was trying to force him into a stupid childhood deal, one that thousands of kids make on playgrounds all the time. Hell, even friends in college make those promises that are a little more serious, but *not really*. Desperation and loneliness can make you say and do silly things.

Remington and I have fallen into a sweet routine. Whenever he's at work I stay at my apartment, but when he's off we stay at his house. On days I have to work, I set up at his dining room table. It has become my own little home-away-from-home office. We've gone on several dates, hung out with Eli and Sutton, Kendra and I have enjoyed our wine night on

Remington's deck instead of her house or my apartment on more than one occasion, and now I am going to meet his parents.

Tonight they invited us over for dinner and I am a nervous mess. My clothing options exploded all over again, but Remington is here to witness my breakdown this time. I did not want him to see my anxiety spiral, but just like with everything else, he knows exactly how to ease my fears and help me walk into his family home with more confidence than I thought I was capable of.

"Lainey, they are going to think you are wonderful no matter what outfit you have on." Remington stands behind me, rubbing my arms as I look at my reflection in the full-length mirror.

"That's not true! This is very important. I have to have just the right thing. This is the first impression they will have of me, Remington. I don't want them to hate me." Tears are welling and my anxiety is building.

"Jeans versus a sundress is not the make-or-break situation that you think it is. I am partial to that pink sundress though, if you want my unsolicited opinion. I know my parents pretty well, and I think you can trust me." He kisses my temple, and I take a deep, needed breath.

"I do trust you. I'm really nervous." My eyes meet his in the reflection.

"I know, it's okay. But we have to leave in like five minutes, so can we agree on the outfit and head out soon? I promise that I'll be with you the whole time, and if you get overwhelmed we can leave." I turn to look at him.

"We cannot just *leave*!" He silences my protests by running his thumb along my jawline in the way that makes me want to melt like ice cream in his hands.

"Lainey, we can do whatever we want. We are grown adults with free will. If you're overwhelmed, not having a good time, are tired, or just plain and simple are ready to go home, then we come home." Remington explains this like it's easy for him to set those boundaries—and stick to them. I know I told him about some of the boundaries I had to put into place in my life, but those took years of therapy and a near mental breakdown.

"Okay, I will wear the pink sundress." He smiles at me as I finish getting dressed and we finally get going.

Remington was right, of course he was right. We walked into his parents' house hand in hand. Charles and Renee LeBlanc were everything I hoped they would be and more. They welcomed me with warm embraces, genuine excitement over meeting me, and a meal that was prepared with obvious love. We ate on their garden patio, surrounded by Renee's stunning flowers and the landscaping that Charles spent years perfecting.

"Lainey, thank you so much for bringing us this lovely bottle of wine," Renee says to me as she tops off her stemless glass. "I'm going to be picking up a few bottles to have on hand for us! It's officially my new favorite."

"Oh, it was the least I could do. I appreciate you having me over. Tonight has been really nice." I blush looking between her and her husband. They are sitting across from me and Remington at the patio dining table. Our dinner of perfectly seasoned and grilled chicken, fresh salad, homemade bread, and crispy potatoes was delicious. Now we are enjoying the conversation, fresh air, and being in each other's company.

"The first of many dinners to come! You are always welcome here, sweetheart," Charles says with a warm smile splitting his bearded face. The kindness and genuine words pouring from Remington's parents is overwhelming. There is no show or pretense here, they actually mean every word they say.

Being with all of them made my anxiety vanish. All night I

have been able to talk, laugh, and be myself. I can't even be myself around my own family. I have to be the polished, up-to-par version they want, and even then they will find some flaw to pick at. What the LeBlancs had was rare, and I wanted to do whatever I could to stick around and soak up more of it.

The whole time we were there, Remington did what he promised. He stayed close, always touching me in comforting ways—an arm around my shoulders, holding my hand, a kiss to the top of my head, his thumb rubbing the inside of my thigh. He also kept checking in to see if I wanted to stay or leave, but no part of me was ready to bolt like I thought I would.

The night was made even more fun when Sutton showed up for dessert, a fresh blueberry buckle that his mom swears I will be capable of making on my own, but she insisted on teaching me sometime soon. When she said that she would love to bake with me after Remington went on and on about my apple pie, I felt like my whole heart was going to pound right out of my chest. It was about to land right in his hands, and I have a feeling I won't ever ask for it back. The more time we spend together, the harder it is for me to keep taking things slow physically when my heart is in an absolute free fall.

Today is another family meal of sorts. Remington invited me back to the fire station for "family dinner." He explained that this is different from the meals that the crew eat together on a daily basis. Once a quarter they have a big meal for the whole fire station crew, their significant others, and kids. It's a good way to bond and enjoy seeing everyone at one time. I asked what I could bring, but Remington told me that they all pitch in to have it catered so that nobody has to cook. This time Gino's is making the meal, and Remington told me he had them order extra cheese bread—to make sure I would get as much as I wanted.

Since Remington is on shift today I had to meet him here. I am looking forward to being introduced to more people and hopefully getting to know some of the wives and girlfriends. We have spent a lot of time with Eli because he's Remington's best friend, but he is a self-proclaimed bachelor, so I doubt he will be inviting anyone to family dinner anytime soon.

Walking into the fire station I feel overwhelmed by the amazing smell of Gino's waiting to be eaten by everyone and the sight of so many firefighters. Muscles, mustaches, and men are everywhere along with kids and women. Everyone is smiling, chatting, and enjoying themselves. My eyes scan the room for the one person I want to see most, finally locking in on Remington all the way across the room talking to Chief Roberts. Feeling my gaze, he looks over to me, and a smile lights up his handsome face. He points my way and Chief waves to me, slapping Remington on the back.

Remington makes his way to me, meeting me in the middle of the chaos. He palms my cheeks gently and kisses me deeply, not giving a shit that we are in a room full of people. Whoops ring out, echoing around us, and he pulls back from my lips with reluctance. "Well, hello," I say, feeling like my cheeks must be as red as the fire trucks.

"Hi, beautiful. I missed you." He takes my hand and leads me over to a group of people. "Hey, Ryder, Jess. This is my girlfriend, Lainey. Lainey, you remember Matt Ryder from when you came before? And this is his wife, Jessica." Matt is a few inches shorter than Remington, but a solid wall of thick muscle. He has dark hair and even darker eyes, and olive skin. His wife, Jess, is his exact opposite. She has fair skin and a dusting of freckles on her cheeks, white-blonde curls fall around her shoulders, and she has piercing, icy-blue eyes. She's holding an adorable baby in her arms that looks about a year old.

"It's so nice to meet you," I say and shake both of their hands. "And who is this cutie?" I ask looking toward the baby, who's now drooling all down his chubby arm.

Jess looks down at him with a dreamy smile and says, "This is Cooper, he's one. We have two more playing over there." She points to a large area with lots of toys and kids of various ages. "Noah is seven and Liam is five."

"Wow, they are all so cute," I say easily spotting which of them she is pointing out to me in the crowd, their blond hair matching hers and Cooper's. "Remington told me all of you had the flu a while ago. That must have been terrible." I look back to Jess.

"Yes, that was the most miserable couple days. Matt had to leave his shift early because he was sick. We all got taken down hard. It's one thing when the kids are sick, but us both having the flu too, and having to take care of all three boys . . . It was so rough. Thank God for Rem." Jess bounces Cooper on her hip.

"Oh, what did he do?" I ask curiously. Cooper babbles and reaches his arms out toward Remington, who scoops him up with ease. He blows a raspberry on Cooper's belly, which sends him into a fit of giggles, and then he snuggles into Remington's chest like they have done this a hundred times.

And my ovaries freaking explode. Good lord, as if he wasn't hot enough already?

"He covered my extra shift for me right after working his own. And then dropped off several bags of essentials that we couldn't go get ourselves, including the kids' favorite Popsicles. We didn't even ask, he just did it, and didn't even tell us." Matt grins at Remington.

He shuffles on his feet, uneasy with the attention and

compliments. "It was no big deal, I just knew y'all were stuck in the house, and I figured you could use a few things."

Matt looks at me and says, "We wouldn't have even known it was Rem had we not caught him on our security camera. He was just planning on dropping everything and sneaking off like a flu delivery service elf." We all laugh, and I smile at Remington, loving getting to see this side of him. I know he does so much for me, but he is selfless with everyone in his life. It flows from him naturally and pulls people into his orbit, making others want to be better, do better, just by his example. He probably does not even realize the impact he makes just being himself.

As if I wasn't already in deep with him . . .

The rest of the night is so much fun. Gino's was delicious, of course, and I got plenty of my favorite cheese bread thanks to my boyfriend. Remington was right: This is more than a job for him. It's a calling, and these people are his extended family. They have all welcomed me in and made me part of the group without question. Jess took charge, making introductions to other wives and partners. They were so easy to get along with and opposite of most interactions with any new "girl groups" that I have tried to become friendly with in the past. I got to know the firefighters that were on the other shifts and the paramedic teams that included a couple of really awesome women as well. I was added to the "significant others" group chat. Jess told me that they all keep each other up to date with parties, announcements, things that are going on, and most importantly if something big happens during a fire or emergency.

With full bellies and sleepy kids, we were all sitting around, laughing, and talking when all of a sudden the alarms in the station went off and madness erupted. Everyone went from relaxed to responsive and moving instantly; even the women and older kids seemed to know exactly what to do.

Remington, who was sitting next to me with his hand on my thigh when the alarms started, grabbed my face in a kiss so quick I am not sure it even happened, telling me, "Jess will tell you what to do, baby." Then he was rushing away with more than half the people at the table. I just stood there in shock, twisting my hands, trying to stay out of the way.

Jess, with all three of her boys wrangled around her, came up to me and said, "It is really overwhelming, especially the first time you witness it. Don't worry, Lainey, you get used to it, come on." I obediently followed her like one of her kids.

Sirens were still blaring as we walked into the visitor parking lot in time to see the three department trucks and the two ambulances fly out of the station. I catch a quick glance of Remington in the driver seat of the second truck, which takes my breath and heart with him as he drives away.

"Are they all going?" I ask Jess as worry for Remington takes over my mind, knowing that he and all of the people that just left, the ones that welcomed me into their found family, are racing off into a dangerous situation without any hesitation. I obviously knew what his job was, that it was intense and difficult, but until today I had not let myself truly register the very real uncertainty that Remington faces. It makes me feel naive and unequipped to handle this. I don't know if I am strong enough to watch him walk out the door every day and not know what will happen to him.

Jess rubs my arm, bringing me back to the moment and says, "Dinner and everything was wrapped up. Only the guys on shift go, unless they need more backup called in once they assess the scene. So, we're all going home now. There's no telling how long they will be out. There is no point in waiting around. We will get some updates on the group text, and I am sure Rem will call you later if it's not too late."

"Okay, thanks, Jess," I say sincerely as she pulls me into a tight hug, Cooper sandwiched between us giggling.

"Don't mention it. And you have my number if you ever need anything. This life is an adjustment, so don't hesitate to reach out. We will get together soon, promise." She shifts Cooper on her hip and opens her van doors to let the other kids climb inside.

"I'm so grateful to have met you and the other girls today, Jess. It means a lot that you're taking me under your wing." I smile at her as she clips the youngest Ryder into his car seat. I am in awe of how she seems to have it so together, managing all three kids and seeing her husband drive off the same way I just watched my boyfriend leave. Jess doesn't seem rattled at all.

Reading my mind again, she pulls open her door and says, "It tears me up every time they get called out too, but I can't let the fear take over. For Matt, for me, and especially for the boys . . ." She shakes her head. "What they do is too important for my own fear to be a weakness that holds him back from his dreams." With a final nod, she hops in the van and drives off toward her house.

22

Lainey

I barely slept last night. When I got back to my apartment, I went through my nightly routine in a numb, robotic haze. Anxiety parked itself firmly in my chest, squeezing harder with every breath I took. The FGFD significant other text group was a blessing *and* a curse. I was happy to get updates from them, but at the same time they kept the reality of what the guys were facing at the forefront of my brain. It played like a movie in flashes that I was unable to turn off. Every imagined image of a flame-filled building and Remington amongst them made me feel dizzy.

Apparently there was a massive fire at a farm outside of town. One of the silos that holds their grain caught fire, which spread quickly to multiple structures on the property. The house was spared and no humans were injured, but the loss was still devastating. The Rockfells, third-generation farmers that owned that land, lost a lot of their livelihood, including some livestock that was in one of the barns. It was horrible and so sad. Fire is unforgiving.

Remington had called me when they finally got back to the station. They had been up all night, and he had gotten no sleep, either. He was off shift but asked if he could come see me. I was awake anyways, having given up on any real sleep hours ago. He told me he was going to take one more shower and then head my way. When I came home last night, I had slipped on a comfortable pair of silk sleep shorts and one of Remington's T-shirts that I smuggled from his house that I liked to sleep in when he was working. Too exhausted to bother changing, I just brushed my teeth again, sat on the couch, and waited for Remington to text that he was here.

I must have dozed off for a little while, because a knock on my front door startled me from where I had slipped down on the couch cushions. Looking at my phone, I noticed that I had a couple missed texts and a missed call from Remington. *Crap.* Going to the door, I open it in my exhausted state without even looking to see who's there, which is so unlike me.

"Oh my God," I gasp when Remington's exhausted, but still devastatingly handsome face greets me.

"Good morning, beautiful." He steps into me, holding me tightly with one arm, the other occupied with a to-go tray of coffee and pastry bag from the Sugar Cube.

I let out a shaky sigh of relief. His strong presence and body brought me a calm that was impossible to find on my own all night. I hold his cheeks and kiss him fully, needing to make sure he is really here, really fine. I pull back and search his face. "You're okay?"

"Of course I'm okay, baby. I already told you that on the phone." He pulls me to the couch and we sit down together.

"I know, I know. But seeing you in person is different, better. It makes me feel better." I feel cold and want to get closer to him, but I am not sure anything will be close enough to fix what I am experiencing right now.

"Last night must have been a lot for you, and it's all my fault. I feel like such an asshole," Remington says with frustration, handing me a coffee cup. I take a sip. It's a flat white, my one and only coffee order that I like. "I know you drink tea at home, but I figured you might like the extra-large caffeine boost today." Again he's taking care of me, knowing what I need without me even having to ask for it.

"Thank you, this is perfect." I take another sip. "Why exactly do you feel like an asshole though? We had a nice time last night."

"I meant about the fire alarms at the station, us rushing out on the call. We never talked about that being an option. I am so used to that life, and I have never brought anyone else into it. I didn't prepare you at all, Lainey, and I should have. I had to just *go*, and I hated leaving you." Regret is painted all over his face.

"I understand that you had to go. I'm not upset about that at all. I am so grateful that you're safe, that's all that matters." I kiss him reassuringly.

Leaning his forehead on mine, Remington threads his thick fingers gently through my hair confessing, "Last night was the first time *ever* that I didn't want to get on that truck, Lainey. I was so worried about leaving you like that."

My conversation before I left Jess pops into my mind. How she has to control her fear so that Matt can do his job, and in this moment I truly understand what she was telling me.

"Remington." I pull his attention back to my face, needing him to really listen to what I am saying. "The last thing I want you to do when you get on that truck and head out to an emergency or a fire is to be worried about *me*. I do not want to be a distraction for you."

His eyes go wide, worry and panic running wild, and I know I must have said something wrong. "Does, does this mean that you don't want to be with me anymore?" He almost chokes out the words, like he has to force them out of his own mouth.

"WHAT!" I squawk, actually shouting, which makes his

worried eyes go impossibly wider. "No, no, no. That is *not* what I am saying, why would you think that?" I can feel tears forming fast from emotion and exhaustion.

"I'm sorry, I just assumed it was doomsday," he says, his face pinching in a pained admission. "I thought you were about to break up with me. A whole it's not you it's me, this is better for you, kind of thing." He groans and puts his elbows on his knees, hands covering his face.

"Sorry, not sorry, but you are stuck with me, Remington LeBlanc. You can't get rid of me or scare me off that easily," I say, sassily. My tone works to pull a small smile from him as he looks over at me and rolls his eyes.

"God, I love it when you are feisty," he grumbles, pulling me into his perfectly hard chest.

"I know," I say, and he blows out a breath.

"But really, this is not too much for you?" His question has layers upon layers of questions underneath, and I know exactly what they are, where they are stemming from.

I straddle his lap and he groans, gripping my hips firmly. "This is not too much for me. *You*, Remington, are not too much for me." Emotion ripples in his eyes and his breathing becomes labored.

Time seems to stand still as he stares into my own eyes, like he's waiting for something. I wiggle a little and feel the length of his very hard cock against me. The only thing separating us are his jeans and my barely there sleep shorts. Something snaps in Remington's gaze and demeanor.

"Fuck it," he says, scooping me into his arms, my legs banding around his chiseled waist, as he carries me to my bedroom.

He spins me toward my bed, but we don't make it that far. Instead, we collide with a wall as his mouth finds mine in a hungry pursuit of passion and lust. I can't stop the moan that rumbles up my chest when he dips his greedy tongue in my mouth and I taste him fully for the first time since yesterday.

I needed this. For him to touch me, hold me, kiss me.

But I need more.

I am tired of waiting.

I am tired of slow.

I want everything Remington has to give me, however he wants to.

I want him to take control.

23

Remington

Hot flames of desire lick up my spine and threaten to consume me. This burning I have for Lainey is hotter and more out of control than any real flames I have faced. No woman has *ever* made me feel things like Lainey has. Over the weeks we have been together it had gotten harder and harder to not break the barrier that she put up. She requested that we take things slowly, and I was trying my best to respect her wishes . . . But today all that went right out the window.

However, before this goes even one moment further, I need to know if she is on the same page. Because as hard as my dick is right now having her pressed against this wall, and it might just fall off if I don't use something other than my fist soon, I refuse to move faster than what Lainey is ready for. I won't lose her because I am a fucking caveman.

"Baby, I need you to tell me *exactly* what you want," I say to Lainey, looking into her blue eyes that are drenched in longing and lust.

"Everything," she says, her breaths making her perfect chest heave under *my* goddamn T-shirt. "Please, Remington. Give me everything, take control."

Take control.

Lainey has no clue what she has unlocked with those two words. I want to give her everything she desires, take everything she has to offer. I grin at her wickedly and say, "My pleasure."

Finally laying her on the bed, I move over her body kissing her neck. "Where did you get this shirt, hmm?" I tease her.

"Oh, this old thing?" She hums, grinning at me. Yeah, she knows *just* what the hell she is doing to me right now. Sassy as fuck.

"Take it off," I demand.

"Yes, sir." She responds instantly, and my dick goes impossibly harder. I never knew I wanted someone to call me that in the bedroom, but it sure as fuck is doing things for me, and I don't want her to stop.

She whips off the shirt, and I am left absolutely speechless because she had on nothing underneath. The last time I saw her amazing tits was weeks ago, and she wasn't totally naked. This time it's an unobstructed view of creamy skin, rosy nipples that are peaked to perfection and just waiting to be sucked—and that is exactly what I do.

I suck a nipple into my mouth and tug just enough, swirling my tongue around, moaning at the taste of her warm skin. "Remington, ahhh!" Lainey exclaims as I give the same attention to the other nipple. I continue my trail of kisses down her stomach and reach the waist of her pink satin shorts, so tiny and smooth.

I want to fucking tear them off of her.

"Are you wet for me, baby?" I ask.

"Yes," she whispers.

"Let's see." I slowly slide the shorts down, forcing myself to have some modicum of self-control, even if it kills me.

No panties. Holy fuck.

"You have been bare for me this whole time, Lainey?" I suck in a breath.

"I don't like to sleep in underwear," she replies, as if it's an innocent answer. I nip her inner thigh, and she yelps.

"All the nights we have spent together in the same bed, and your wet pussy has only been a thin strip of fabric away from me? I have been dying, Lainey. To touch you again. To taste you. Feel every inch of your skin. Sink my cock deep inside your perfect body." Her eyes are locked on me as I lean back and pull my shirt off over my head one-handed. "What do you want, baby?"

"Yes, yes. Th-that. All of that." She gulps nervously.

"I am going to take such good care of you," I tell her, leaning in and kissing up her thigh. When I am almost to her shimmering sex she starts to wiggle more, seemingly apprehensive, and I say, "Is this okay?"

"You don't have to do that, it's fine," she says in a quiet voice, barely a little whisper.

I prop myself up on an elbow and look at her. "Explain."

"It's just that I don't have, um, a lot of experience, well, and I have only been with a couple of guys." I let out a low rumble that I have no control over, and her cheeks turn pink. "I've never done *that*." She glances down toward her pussy and back at me, eyes widening, hoping to get her point across.

"Are you telling me that nobody has ever gotten to taste you, Lainey?" I demand.

"Yeah," she says, biting her perfect bottom lip.

"Good," I growl.

"Good?" She is shocked.

"Yeah, baby, good. Now I get to be the first and the last man that *ever* tastes you—and I'm fucking starving." I grin at her wide, surprised eyes and slowly run my tongue along her wet center, getting my first hit, and I already know I am addicted to her.

"Oh, holy shhhhit." She squirms and I hold her hips in place. I work my finger into her tight center and feel her constrict around me. I can't get enough of the sounds she is making, her sweet, heady release dripping onto my tongue, the way her clit is pulsing as I suck on it.

I want to stay in this moment as long as possible, unrelenting and free. I don't hold back, feasting on Lainey until she cries out, shaking in pleasure as her orgasm rips through her body and she soaks my face.

I sit up and look at her. "I was wrong," I tell her.

"Wrong about what?" she asks with breathless worry.

"I just found something that tastes even better than your kisses *and* your apple pie." I smile at her as she buries her face in her hands and mumbles unintelligible things under her breath. "Hey, no hiding from me." I pull her hands away and kiss her, letting her taste the sexiness of her own release on my lips. She moans and tugs me closer.

"I think you are overdressed," she says. Pulling at my jeans, I quickly stand and unbutton them, shoving them and my black boxers to the floor. My leaking cock springs free from being confined and points directly at Lainey, who once again gasps.

"What's wrong?" I say looking down at myself.

"That can't happen." She is still staring.

"Remember what I told you before, baby?" Cupping her face, I kiss her softly, soothing her nerves. "It *is* going to fit. I know you are thinking it won't." She huffs at me sassily and I laugh. "It will, because we fit perfectly together in every other way, Lainey. Trust me?"

"I trust you." She looks deep into my eyes, my very soul, and I know that the moment we come together, nothing will ever be the same.

I turn around in search of my wallet, but Lainey grabs my hand.

"Wait," she says.

My stomach drops. *Maybe she changed her mind and isn't ready to take this all the way.*

"Can we . . . not use a condom?" She searches my face shyly, like she is asking for something her heart and mind might not have totally communicated properly.

"Are you sure about that?" I have never in my life not wrapped it up, but with Lainey, there is nothing I want more than to give her this, give us this kind of intimacy I have never had with anyone before.

"I'm positive. I don't want anything separating us, Remington. I need to feel all of you. I can't explain it." She has so much emoting from her trembling body right now. Maybe I was wrong, maybe her heart and body are totally in alignment, and I need to catch the hell up.

"Okay," I say climbing over her and settling between her legs.

"I'm clean, I swear. And I have an IUD," she rambles, nervous again.

"I trust you, baby. I am clean too, promise." She nods her head and smiles.

Grinding myself against her I can feel that she is still soaked. She sucks in a sharp breath, still so sensitive from the first orgasm I just gave her. I take her hands and slide them above her head, holding them in place. Lainey widens her legs for me, and I kiss her with a slower, passionate, possessive kiss, wanting and needing her to understand the way I feel connected to her at an atomic level.

She rolls her hips up toward me, begging me without words to fuck her, and I can't wait any longer to be inside of her. I slide my tip up and down her clit making her shiver before I slip lower and slide inside her hot center, pulled in by her greedy body. I try to go slowly, letting her stretch around me. Her breathing picks up and I look at her, eyes pinned shut.

"Look at me, beautiful." Her eyes snap to my face. "Eyes on me," I command, taking control, giving a few shallow thrusts of my hips before finally pumping forward and sliding every thick inch into her perfect body.

"Fuck," Lainey cries out.

"Shit, are you okay?" I instantly worry that I went too hard, too fast. That I should have given her more time to adjust.

"I'm okay, promise. More, I need more. Please," she begs.

Begs. And I will gladly give her any damn thing she wants.

I grab her leg and hitch her thigh forward, driving my hips deeper. She pulls me in, kissing me wildly, and tugs my hair. Her teeth scraping my bottom lips, her nails run down my back.

"You're so deep, Remington," she exclaims on a whisper. "I'm so close."

I adjust my balance and grasp the front of her neck, squeezing just the right amount. Her eyes lock on mine. The stormy blue blown out in pleasure, and then they roll back as I feel the tight walls of her body pull me deep as she comes again. This time I can't hold back. "That's it, baby," I say. "Take everything." We both explode, our universe coming undone and being recreated, rebound around each other in the very same moment.

Collapsing in a sexy glow, Lainey smiles up at me as radiant as the sun. Her chest rising and falling in a mesmerizing pant, I slowly slide my half-hard cock from her body. I watch as my cum drips out. She moans and looks down. The primal fucking caveman in me snaps, *again*, and I do something I have never done before. I swipe the cum dripping from her throbbing pussy and push it back inside of her, looking at it and then directly at her, not able to even say anything.

Then Lainey shocks the hell out of me, grabs my hand, and sucks my fingers clean. I swear to God, I almost faint.

Like I told her before, *perfect fucking fit.*

24

Lainey

Soft afternoon light is drifting through my bedroom windows when I open my eyes. Rolling over, my whole body is blissfully sore, especially the hollow ache between my legs, reminding me of what happened this morning, that everything is different. I look at the man responsible for the changes in my body and soul to see his eyes already on me, drinking in my sleepy, sex-hungover body. I can't help the grin that splits my face when I catch him looking at me so openly.

"Hi," I whisper.

"Beautiful," Remington rumbles, leaning over and kissing me as if he'd been waiting patiently for me to wake up so he could do just that.

"Did you sleep? What time is it?" I ask him.

"Yeah, I only woke up a little while ago. It's almost three." Leaning back he hauls me to his hard chest, engulfing me in the strong comfort of his arms.

I run my fingers through the light dusting of his chest hair and sigh contentedly. This is the first time Remington's been in my bed. All of our other sleepovers have been at his house. It had been so hard in the previous weeks to not take things further. To just be satisfied with kissing and cuddling, especially after how incredibly hot things were between us on his couch, lord it was nearly impossible. But I'm so glad we didn't rush and gave it more time, that *he gave me* more time.

What happened between us this morning was unlike anything I had ever experienced. I'd only been with a couple people previously, including Brett, and my pleasure was *never* a priority. I always felt like sex was take it or leave it, not very necessary, and that passion you read about was exactly that—fiction.

Remington proves that all wrong.

He has passion and definitely knows how to pleasure me. I try really, really hard not to think about why he is so good at it, how he got so good at it. Green vines of jealousy rapidly twist their way up my spine, and I quickly remind myself that he is here with *me* in *my* bed. I also don't think that the connection we feel, the flames that engulf my very soul when he touches me, are something that just happens to anyone and everyone. This is special, this is life-altering, and I am so worried I am going to say the wrong thing and ruin it.

Remington's deep, sexy voice pulls me from my spiraling thoughts. "We should probably get up and eat something, but I don't want to let you go."

"Then don't." I snuggle deeper into the bed and run kisses down his chest.

"Lainey." A pained rumble vibrates under my lips. "I need to take care of my woman, I need you to eat and have some water. You are also probably sore, and you doing that is making me want to flip you over and do very dirty things, which won't help with that."

I suck in a breath and instantly feel wetness pooling between my legs imagining it.

Yes, please.

But I also know that he is trying to switch into that caretaker role that he takes very seriously, so I let him. "Okay, I agree to eating some food, but only because you need to eat, too. And only if you pinky swear that we can come back here after and you do that whole *'flip me over and do dirty things'* thing to me . . ." I prop myself up on an elbow, letting the sheet slip down, trying to give him a look that is innocent. I hold up my hand and stick out my pinky finger to him.

Remington groans and bites his lip, running a hand over his lower body. "You are *killing* me, baby." He slips his pinky around mine, kissing it. I giggle and roll off the bed to find clothes, putting back on his stolen T-shirt and rummaging for a different pair of shorts. I can feel the hot, lingering gaze coming from the bed with every move I make.

Turning around I say, "Come on, let's order takeout so we don't have to cook or go anywhere."

"I like that plan a lot." Remington gets up, and I might be just as distracted and turned on watching him re-dress as I am watching him undress. We need to hurry the hell up and get some calories in the both of us so we can get back to this room as fast as possible.

"Remington, we are going to be late to meet the girls if you don't let me get in the shower to get ready." I try to loosen his arms and get out of bed. We spent the night wrapped in each other's arms and had mind-blowing, sweaty, toe-curling sex this morning. I can't believe that my body is already aching for more. I don't think I will ever get enough of Remington or the way he touches me, makes me feel seen and sexy for the first time in my life. I am discovering a whole new side of myself with him, and I know it's only the beginning.

"Let's shower then," he says, whipping the bedding back in a cold rush. Remington scoops me up in a bridal carry and walks us to the bathroom.

"I *am* capable of walking, you know?" I snicker as he sets me down and turns on the shower.

"I distinctly remember you telling me that I 'turned your legs to complete Jell-O' after the last two orgasms I gave you this morning. So I was just helping you out, baby," Remington says with the most proud, male smile.

"Oh my gosh, you are *sooo* cocky, aren't you?" I jest.

"Damn right," he says, glancing down at himself and his thickening length. "And Every. Single. Inch. belongs to you," he says, kissing me between words. The kind, caring, sweet side of Remington is one thing. But when he flips this switch to a little bit cocky, take control, with stupidly sexy confidence? I might as well just pour myself right down that drain with the shower water. All I can do in response is bite my lip and moan.

We step into the warm shower spray where our kisses become just as steamy as the air around us. Remington pushes me up against the tile wall, and I gasp at the coldness against my skin. His hot body presses to my front and I melt into him, relishing in the opposite temperature.

He lifts me easily and I grind my hips against him, feeling how hard, how ready to take me again he already is. I want him too, but I am extremely sore from everything we did yesterday and this morning. Remington grinds onto my sensitive clit, and I suck in a breath, not being able to handle it.

I push him back a bit so I can explore his body better, something I haven't been able to do enough of yet. Running my fingers down the ridges of his abs, I look deep into his honey-soaked eyes that are about to eat me alive with desire. I bite my lip, and I finally wrap my hand around his impossibly long, thick cock. "Lainey." He grunts and thrusts forward—

smooth, silky perfection sliding through my hand as water pours over our bodies.

"I want to taste you," I tell him. "But, but I'm not very good at this," I admit with reluctance. Pleasing Remington and sharing this kind of intimacy is something I desperately want but don't have very much positive experience in. I have given blow jobs to exactly two people. My college boyfriend once, which happened when we were sloppily drunk, and then a couple times with Brett. He *demanded* that I try, even saying I "owed it to him" on his birthday. I was not turned on in the slightest, but being the people pleaser I am, instead of telling him to suck it himself, I did it. When it was over, I felt nothing but shame, especially when he told me that I wasn't any good at it.

"Baby, I am about to come just from having your hands on me. Anything you do with that sexy mouth of yours will be fucking heaven." Remington reassuringly runs his thumb along my jawline. I kiss him one more time, then get on my knees.

Licking the tip, I taste the salt of his skin mixed with precum and can't stop the hum reverberating from my chest as I suck him into my mouth. I can hear Remington muttering curse words under his breath, trying to hold still and let me explore. I pull him in deeper and he groans, fisting my hair.

Yes, more of that. I want him to use me, to take control.

Gripping what I can't fit in my mouth, I work my hand and lips in tandem. My tongue glides along the throbbing veins of the thick cock filling my mouth. I never thought I would like doing this, or even *want* to do this again, but I am so turned on right now that I can feel my own wetness starting to drip down my thigh. I rub my legs together, trying to get some relief.

Remington notices and says, "Yes, baby. You are such a

good girl on your knees for me, sucking my dick. Is this turning you on, Lainey?"

I pop him out of my mouth, breathing in a deep lungful of air, eyes on his and say, "Yes, sir."

Remington growls and tugs me back toward his cock, which I hungrily take back into my mouth. I hollow out my cheeks and suck him back as far as I can. When he hits the back of my throat I gag, and he immediately pulls out. "Are you okay?" he asks, that caretaker side of himself peeking through.

"Yes, Remington. Please. Use me." I look up at him, begging him with my willing eyes.

His own eyes flicker with something unrecognizable and undeniably hot. "Fuck your fingers while I fuck your mouth then, Lainey. Be a good girl and come for me." I nod as he shoves himself back in deep, giving me what I asked for, pumping in and out of me, making drool slip from the corners of my mouth.

I reach for my dripping wet center and moan when my fingers dip inside. I am so close it only takes a few deep pumps of my fingers and circling of my tender clit. I am an explosion of lust and fire and newness. Remington is right there with me and says, "I'm coming, baby." And with a roar, he releases everything he has left in him down my waiting throat.

Remington yanks me to my feet and kisses me, and I feel like I might float away if he doesn't keep his arms around me. Grabbing my wrist, he takes the fingers I just came all over and he sucks them into his mouth, eyes closed with appreciation at the taste of what is on his tongue. "Holy shit. That was . . ." I trail off, not able to unscramble my brain enough to give him my thoughts.

"Whoever told you that you weren't good at that, Lainey, can get fucked. You are perfect in every possible way." Then he kisses me again with a tenderness that mends a part of me that I thought would be broken forever.

"Don't you two look all cute and couple-y," Kendra says as we walk into the Sugar Cube ten minutes late. We are meeting her and Sutton for brunch. It's the weekend, Remington had today off, Sutton has the store covered, and we made this plan to get together last week.

Neither of us actually wanted to get out of my bed this morning and get ready to leave, but we managed to compromise. That resulted in more experiences I can't wait to try again. I look over at the man that makes my heart pound, remembering why we almost canceled this brunch all together.

Sutton rushes in the door and comes to a halt at our table. Her growing baby bump is looking adorable in a pink wrap dress. Her flowing blonde hair looks perfectly imperfect and her brown eyes shine with happiness. "Sorry I'm late," she says slightly out of breath.

"We just got here, too," Remington tells her, pulling Sutton into a hug and kissing her cheek.

"What's got you all extra happy this morning?" Kendra asks her.

"I talked to Deck!" Sutton exclaims, her enthusiasm pouring over us, and we all shout out cheers of excitement.

"What did he have to say? Is he headed back?" Remington asks, taking my hand, lacing our fingers together.

Sutton gulps the water that was waiting for her on the table. "He told me that the mission they just finished was a success, which is all he can say. You know how that goes. All the top-secret stuff we don't get to know anything about. But I am so happy it's over and he could finally call me. He said they have to wrap up a few things, but they should get to come back stateside in the next few weeks." She rubs her belly and sighs.

"You don't get to know a date?" I ask. I can't even imagine never knowing where my husband was or what was going on the way Sutton and other military spouses and families do. There is so much sacrifice and stress. I know it will be good for Sutton and the baby to have Derek back home, for however long he gets to stay.

"No," Sutton explains. "We never get any concrete dates. That's too dangerous for many reasons. Usually it is just a vague window of time. A lot of the days, Deck just shows back up. Walks in the door and surprises the hell out of me. It's different with *his* SEAL team though—it isn't like normal, planned deployments. They get called out at any time for any amount of time, until the mission is complete, and they let them come back."

"Wow," Kendra and I both say.

"My sister is the strongest woman I know." Remington looks at Sutton proudly. "Military life is not easy, especially on the ones that are left behind."

Sutton gives him a knowing look. "A life of service is never easy, no matter what path you take. But this was what Derek was meant to do, and I know that he is making a difference in the world by doing it. Me and this baby, we are proud of him." She rubs her belly again.

Conversation turns lighter as we eat our meal, and it's a wonderful way to spend our day. Kendra is making us all laugh about a story of her misthrowing some pottery clay in her studio and the mess she made last week when we are interrupted by a voice I wish I never heard again.

"Remmmmmmy," Cora's nasty voice purrs.

His body stiffens at the sound, and we all turn to see the unwelcome guest approaching our table. I immediately glance over at Sutton, and she looks like she is about to simultaneously puke up her meal and use her butter knife to stab Cora.

"What the hell are you doing here?" Sutton stands, shoving her chair back with a squeak.

"Hello to you too, old bestie," Cora says, flipping her dark hair over her bloodred dress. It is one size too small and more worn than the outfit she had on at Remington's house. She has on the same accessories, but her shoes are black, spiked heels with scuff marks today. "I am here getting a coffee, saw my man, and came over to say hello."

I swear Sutton's eyes are going to pop out of her head. I want to crawl over Remington to get to Cora for calling him "her man" and scoop her eyes out with my spoon because *absolutely fucking not.* Kendra has gone quiet, which if you know her is scary and dangerous.

Remington stands, putting a protective arm out toward Sutton and motions for her to back down. Cora takes this opportunity to give Sutton a long, unimpressed once-over.

"I know it's been a few years, Sutton, but you really have let yourself go," she mock whispers behind her hand. "I can give you some really good low-carb recipes to get back on track if you want." Cora directs her eyes to the table of food we just had, nose scrunched.

"Oh no she fucking didn't," Kendra yelps, tossing her napkin down.

"Don't," Remington says, his tone deathly calm.

"Remmy, I think it's time we go someplace quiet." She glances over his shoulder at the rest of us, giving me a nasty look. "Alone. So we can discuss our situation. We have a lot of planning to do." She looks back to him with an unnatural smile, showing too many teeth, red lipstick smudged on her front tooth.

"Cora, I have nothing to discuss with you now or ever." Her face turns sour, smile evaporating into a scowl. "And most importantly, I am *not* your man." Remington steps back and loops his arm possessively around my waist.

My whole body hums, this move by him screaming *mine* more than me scooping Cora's eyeballs out with a spoon would.

"I will get my lawyer involved if I need to," Cora seethes.

Remington barks out a laugh. "You are off your goddamn rocker if you think some playground pact between children holds any kind of weight in the eyes of the law. Leave me the fuck alone, Cora. This is the last time I'm gonna warn you nicely."

He throws down more than enough money to cover our whole bill, plus a generous tip. Kendra loops her arm through Sutton's and they walk away. Remington leads me from the table and Cora yells after us, "It was always supposed to be you and me, Rem. This whole town knows it. You are the only one that needs reminding."

Ignoring her, we walk into the sunshine, and I have a sick feeling that my dream of never seeing her again won't come true. Someone like that doesn't let go of things, even things that clearly don't belong to them anymore.

25

Remington

The only time I have been able to work on Lainey's journal is when I am at the fire station. I don't want to let her see anything until I am totally done with it, so taking the journals home isn't an option. Every night I'm not working, we are at my house. She was staying at her place when I was at the station and then my house when I was home, but that changed, too.

I want her in my space all the time, even if I am not there—it just feels *right*. I gave her a key last week and asked her to stay whenever she wanted. Her stunning smile and hungry kiss were answer enough to show me how she felt about it.

My dining room table has officially become Lainey's office. I cleared out half of my dresser for her, and I already had plenty of closet space for her to add whatever she wanted. Her make-up bag on my bathroom counter looks like it has lived there all along. Her honey-scented shampoo sits in the shower, and her favorite tea is next to my coffee in the kitchen. We even have a mix of Kendra's mugs added to the cupboards.

Melding our lives together in these little ways felt easy and comfortable. Besides the drama with Cora, the most uncomfortable thing is dealing with the idea of Lainey's family. My parents, and sister obviously, have welcomed Lainey into the fold without question. She is very happy and relaxed anytime we go to my parents' house. She and Sutton are becoming super close, and I love that for both of them. Everyone at the fire station is very excited that I finally have the kind of relationship I always wanted but never had the balls to pursue after college.

Lainey's mother and father got a divorce a few years ago, and her mother moved back to Fox Grove where she grew up. According to Lainey, her mother probably would have stayed with Patrick Quinn forever had he not been the one to leave her for a younger woman. The whole thing was a shameful mess, and her mom didn't want to stay in DC. Of course Patrick didn't care about the repercussions of his actions for his family or the younger woman, a relationship that only lasted a year.

The relationship Lainey has with her mom has always been strained and uncomfortable. I had yet to meet her, and today was the first time that was going to happen. Lainey, understandably, was a ball of nerves, her anxiety on full display rippling through the house as we got ready and now wrapping around us.

"We've gone over like ten different talking points. I won't talk about your dad. I know not to bring up the Newell Christmas party of 2015, even though I have no clue who those people are or why it was so traumatic. I don't think we really need to prep this hard for a simple dinner with your mom, Lainey." I take her hand in mine. We are in my truck as we drive to her mom's house in a nice neighborhood on the north side of town.

"Remington," Lainey sighs with nervous exasperation. "I told you, going over everything helps prepare for what she might say or what might happen. Any compliment I get is backhanded, and she is critical of *all* my choices. You won't be any different."

"Okay, ouch," I say. Maybe I *am* unprepared. My neck starts to sweat.

"Exactly! *Ouch.* I told you, meeting my family is *not* like meeting your family. I warned you." Her voice starts to tremble.

"It's alright, baby. We are in this together, just like everything else. But I do have a question," I say cautiously.

"What?" She looks over at me, picking at the pink polish on her manicure.

"If you have such a hard relationship with your mom, why did you move to Fox Grove?" I glance at her and then back at the road, slowing at a four-way stop.

"I thought that after she divorced my dad, left his toxic orbit, that things with her would be easier. That maybe the reason she was critical of me was because of him." The sadness in her voice makes me wish we weren't in my truck having this conversation. I need to have her in my arms.

"It's not?" I ask.

"Not fully," she says. "He was a big factor, and some things have gotten better, but not to the point that I thought they would. I heard my mom talk very rarely about growing up here, but I always liked the idea of it. Living in DC was suffocating for me. I know a lot of people can't wait to leave the small-town bubble and go off to bigger places, but I was the opposite. I want a smaller, simple life. And people there can't understand that, *especially* my dad."

I grunt, holding my thoughts back about a man I have yet to meet but already can't stand.

"When my mom told me she was coming back to Fox Grove, I was *excited.* I felt like it was my chance to live a small-town life, and maybe it was a sign that I could build a different kind of relationship with her. I'm at least getting one of those two things." She smiles over at me and rubs her gentle fingers through the hair at my temple.

I grasp her hand and kiss her fingers. "You can build any kind of life you want," I tell her sincerely. I want Lainey to have anything she wants, support whatever dreams she has in her mind, but she has yet to lower that wall for me and tell me what those dreams truly are.

She sits back deeper into her seat, lets out a sad hum, and looks out the window.

We pull up to her mother's house, a big, newer-construction home. It's stark white with black-framed windows and two stories. There is a large concrete porch with little personality, no landscaping other than grass and a few sparse bushes. As a landscaper's son, I cringe. It has so much potential but has obviously not been a priority.

I get out of the truck and go around to Lainey's side, helping her out. She is holding a bottle of wine, the same kind she brought to my parents' house the night she first met them and my mom raved over it. "Hang on," I say. I open the back passenger door and pull out a small bouquet of yellow and white daisies. They are cheerful, soft, and friendly.

Lainey looks at me and back at the flowers, questions in her eyes that she is unable or unwilling to speak.

I clear my throat and tell her, "I did not want to show up empty-handed, and I figured your mom probably never got many flowers, either. So daisies for meeting your mom because they mean new beginnings." Lainey sucks in a breath, and a wave of emotion rolls thick through the air between us. I didn't know what she would think of me bringing her mom flowers, but I wanted her to know that they were not just for Ann, but for Lainey as well.

"You are not real," Lainey says, stepping up to me on her tiptoes and kissing me.

"Yes, I am, and I am not going anywhere." I wrap my arm

around her waist, tugging her closer, and she relaxes into the familiar sweep of my tongue against hers as I kiss her again.

A front door opens, and Lainey stiffens in my hold, pulling back and locking her eyes with mine, an apology already written all over her beautiful face.

"Lainey!" A sharp voice clips across the sad lawn. Sighing, Lainey grips my hand and turns toward the sound—her mother. Standing with arms crossed is a tall woman with a sharp nose and hard blue eyes. Her brown hair is twisted into a tight bun at the nape of her neck, and she is wearing an expensive linen pant suit in a lemony color that washes her out.

"Hello, Mom." Lainey greets her mother in a kind but artificially happy voice. She has on a tense mask, ready to perform for this woman, and I do not like it at all.

"Please come inside. I hardly think it is appropriate to be standing out here kissing your . . . friend," she says looking at me, her eyes locked in on my tattoos.

Great, she is one of those people.

Walking up to the porch, I put on a smile and try not to judge her mom before I give her a chance. But the stress rolling off of the woman I *care* about—*fuck, fine way more than care, but I am not going there right now*—has me on edge, too.

"Mom, this is Remington LeBlanc, my boyfriend. Remington, this is my mom, Ann Quinn." Lainey looks at me with a sweet, genuine smile—no mask for me in sight.

I reach out my hand. "Hello, ma'am, it's very nice to finally meet you."

Ann takes my hand gingerly, like I might snap hers or give her some kind of disease. *Jesus, take the wheel. This is going to be a long-ass dinner.*

"Reming-ton," Ann repeats. "That's an interesting name."

"My parents thought so. Everyone calls me Rem," I say, trying to keep my tone cordial.

Turning to the door, Ann welcomes us in and we make our way to the kitchen. For having lived here a few years, you really couldn't tell. The house feels like a cold showroom. No family pictures, no warmth, no personal touches that make it feel like a well-loved and lived-in home. When Lainey first saw my place, she told me that she lived in a big house with her family in DC and it was like a prison. If her mom was in charge of the decor and her dad was even more controlling of her mom's choices back then, I can only imagine how sterile and suffocating Lainey's life had felt growing up.

"We brought wine," Lainey says cheerfully to Ann, holding out a bottle of red.

"Yes, so kind." Ann looks it over. "We will try and save that for another time, it doesn't go with the chicken I prepared tonight." She takes the wine out of her daughter's hands without another look, shoves it on a side counter, and moves to the oven.

Lainey visibly wilts.

"Mom, look." Lainey tries again. "Remington brought something else for you, too." She gives me a half smile as Ann turns back to us.

I give her my best smile and hold out the small bouquet of daisies. Ann's eyes go wide, and she takes a visible step back, a hand going to her chest. "Wh-what's this?" she asks me, genuine surprise and a flicker of real emotion taking over her face.

Maybe we are getting somewhere after all.

"I can't show up to dinner empty-handed, my mother would never forgive me," I tell her. "And I know how much Lainey loves it when I bring her flowers, so I thought that you might enjoy these." I hold them out to her, kindly.

Ann looks at them for so long I am not sure she is going to take them.

"Mom?" Lainey prompts.

"Yes, well that was very nice of you. Very unnecessary, and a waste of your much *needed* money, but thank you. They will look fine in the kitchen." She rushes to the cupboard, looking for a suitable vase.

Lainey looks at me with pain in her gorgeous blue eyes. I know this is not going the way she wants it to. I know she is worried her mom's behavior is going to change my opinion of her, but it doesn't. It just makes me feel even more deeply for her, seeing what she has overcome. Seeing how she decided to be a different person than the examples she was given.

Sitting down to our meal doesn't improve the mood. Ann keeps giving me uneasy glances from her seat at the head of the table. The conversation is awkward, stilted. She glares at my tattoos as if they are going to jump from my skin to hers, permanently marring her. It feels especially irritating to me knowing she is judging not only my ink but my own artwork—not that she knows that, not that it would matter.

"I cannot understand why you would do that to your hair, Lainey. It was so long and pretty." Ann slices into her food and her daughter at the same time. Lainey is sad, uncomfortable, and the confidence she radiates daily is completely absent in the presence of this woman.

"I think that she looks stunning, no matter what she chooses to do to her hair," I insist, cutting Lainey's mother off before she can keep jabbing at her.

"So, Remerton," Ann says directing her attention where I want it, and I try to not roll my eyes. "What do you do for work?"

"Well, Ann, my name is actually *Rem-ing-ton*," I correct

her. I live in the South. I am not the first or last man with the name Remington. And I specifically told her to call me Rem, like everyone else. She is just being rude on purpose at this point.

"Of course." She smirks at me. "My mistake." She scoops a bite of overly salted veggie mix into her mouth.

"No problem, I usually have to meet people a few times before I get their names to stick, too." I look across the table to Lainey, her cheeks pink with second-hand embarrassment, and wink at her. "I am a firefighter for the Fox Grove fire department," I say answering her mom's original question.

"Hmmm." Ann looks to Lainey and then back to me. "Is that all?" she asks.

Lainey drops her fork with a clatter, gasps, and harshly whispers, "Mother!"

"What, Lainey? A lot of men kind of dabble in it, do that as a volunteer thing, not a career. I can't imagine it provides a suitable livelihood." She glances over at me and back at her daughter, as if she is going to exclude me from this conversation.

"Actually, I have been a full-time firefighter in Fox Grove since I graduated college with my degree in fire science." Ann sucks in a tiny breath and reaches for her wine, wine we did not bring. "Yeah, it probably shocks you that I actually went to college and got a degree, but I did. I also am a fully certified EMT as well. I love my job, and *my livelihood*, as you say, suits me just fine, Ann." I level her with a hard stare, all of my warmth and friendly effort is obviously wasted on her, and I am done playing nice.

Ignoring me completely, she turns to Lainey. "Darling, do you really think this is a good idea?"

"What is a good idea, Mom?" Lainey asks, a cold steel hardening her eyes.

"Being with, with a man that has a job like *that*?" she

hisses. "It is dangerous, first of all. And it makes him untrustworthy, unreliable!" Her voice grows with each point she's trying to make.

"Remington is *exactly* the kind of man I should be with. He makes me happy, Mother! There is nobody that is as thoughtful or compassionate. He is the best man I know." Lainey looks at me, eyes shining with tears.

Scoffing, her mother tosses her cloth napkin on the table next to her bland chicken. "That means nothing. This is new, he's manipulating you, showing you what he wants you to see and then the rug will be yanked out, Lainey. Plus, everyone knows that the men in emergency services or the military are all cheaters."

"The fuck!" I exclaim, not able to hold it in.

Lainey abruptly stands up, points a shaky finger at her mom and says, "How dare you? How dare you," repeating herself with more confidence. "You don't know the first thing about Remington. He is a *hero*. A man that sacrifices himself for others every single day, and I could not be more proud to be with him." Her words make my chest ache, and my heart pounds. "He is a man that I happen to be crazy about, and I was excited to introduce you to him. All you have done from *the second* we got here was judge him, and I am done, Mom. Done!"

She rounds the table to where I'm seated. I stand up and take her shaking hand.

"Lainey, we need to discuss this. I'm sorry, but a firefighter? That is not the life I want for my daughter. He is not good enough for you." Ann's glare is aimed at both of us now.

"I am a grown woman, and you don't get a vote. There's nobody better for me than this man right here, and if you can't accept that then you don't accept me. I will not let you treat me like shit an—" Lainey is cut off with Ann's anger.

"I have never mistreated you a day in your life, Lainey!

I'm your mother. How could you say that?" She looks at Lainey like she is talking crazy, then looks to me and rolls her eyes, as if I am going to suddenly switch sides. *Get fucked, lady.*

"You have made me second-guess myself my *whole life*. You have gaslit me into thinking that I am not enough as a person, as a daughter, as a partner in my other relationships. You are a terrible example of 'do as I say, not as I do.' If I was in a miserable relationship, like what you had with Dad, but the person had a fancy title or big bank account you'd rather me be with them? You're finally free from Dad, and you still let him control you. I thought it was all him, but clearly you've had a big impact in the hurt that was caused. I refuse to let you damage any more pieces of my life . . ." Lainey looks up at me, tears slowly rolling down her cheeks. I nod at her, squeezing her hand hoping to give her a little more strength to finish what she needs to say. "I especially won't sit here and let you insult and disparage the person in my life that means the most to me. If you cannot love and support me like a mother, *a loving and kind mother*, then I don't have room for you in my life right now."

We leave her mom gaping after us at the dining table, looking like Lainey's words kicked her right in the gut. I hope they made a deep impact because I know that finally saying them out loud like that sure as hell will have left Lainey with wounds that won't heal easily.

26

Lainey

I'm staring at the stunning bouquet of flowers on Remington's coffee table. After the absolute disaster that was meeting my mother, I thought he was going to drop me off at my apartment and need some space from me. However, he took me to his house, wrapped me in his arms, and held me all night long while I cried.

Bright pink flowers are arranged in a round glass vase, their scent filling the house, and there is a card laid out next to it. Remington had to work today, so he must have gotten up early to leave this before going into the station. I was so emotionally exhausted from our dinner and all the crying that my body completely shut down. I didn't even wake up or hear Remington leave. When I finally rolled over to an empty bed, my head throbbed painfully and my throat was dry. I felt hungover even though I barely had a few sips of the wine my mom paired with her terrible chicken.

I bring my cup of tea to the couch, wrap up in my favorite knitted throw blanket, pick up the card from the coffee table, and flip it open to see Remington's distinct, blocky handwriting.

Good morning, beautiful,

I am so sorry that I had to leave you and go to work today. There is no place I want to be more than right next to you this morning. I know I told you this last night, but I will say it over and over again—

I'm so proud of you for standing up for yourself.

Text me when you wake up.

XO, R

PS: These are hyacinth flowers. They are meant to represent comfort, and the scent is used a lot for aromatherapy and stuff. I guess it helps make you feel calm and relaxed when you smell them? I don't know if it will help or not, but I thought it was worth a try.

Hugging the card to my chest I let out a shaky breath, tears I thought ran out last night slip past my lids and trail across my raw cheeks. I don't bother wiping them away. Remington was unable to be here this morning when I woke up, but somehow managed to still find a way to take care of me. I shut my eyes and draw in a deep breath, really focusing on the scent of the flowers in front of me. I'm not sure the "aromatherapy" is the reason I feel calmness start to pool in the center of my chest. I think it has everything to do with Remington and the peace, comfort, and happiness he has brought to my life.

Last night was beyond horrible. Worse than any practice scenario I could have possibly role-played in my mind. I knew it was not going to be smooth sailing introducing Remington to my mother, that is why I was trying to prepare so much beforehand. He thought I was going way over the top with all the questions and information dump I gave him, but in the end none of it mattered.

Ann Quinn took one look at my tall, rugged, tattooed boyfriend and turned her nose up. I saw it instantly. Remington had worn nice jeans, a pressed blue button-down shirt with his sleeves rolled up, and of course his signature boots. He was so handsome I had to try not to drool when I looked at him. I had hearts in my eyes when I looked at him, but my mother had daggers.

Bringing a significant other home is always cause for anxiety, and this felt so different because Remington is more important to me than anyone I have ever dated in the past. I was deeply embarrassed by the way she was treating us, but when she started in on how Remington was not good enough for me, demeaning his job and his morals, I snapped. Never in my twenty-six years of life have I ever spoken to my mom like that. It ripped something open in me doing it, but at the same time it also set something free.

Living under the Quinn roof meant I was always expected to do as I was told, stay quiet, and mold my opinions to my parents' whims. Calvin was the golden child that could do no wrong, would carry on the family name, and is my father's pride and joy. When I was younger I dreamt of Cal being my best friend, but he made it clear he wanted nothing to do with me. I was his annoying little sister, and he had much more important things to do than play with me, pay attention to me, or even try to be nice to me.

I was an extra burden that never lived up to the unrealistic pressure my parents placed on me. They wanted to make me into a replica of a robotic doll they could prop up at parties, have on the Christmas card, or bring up as a point of conversation to try and make my parents more relatable to other people in their circle. I wanted genuine attention and love, as any child does from a parent. What I received was constant criticism. Tepid warmth from my mother and cold disinterest from my father. It was a very lonely existence in their world. I often wished I would stumble upon secret adoption papers that would explain why I was so *other* in the Quinn house.

One thing I have learned being around Remington and his family is how horribly dysfunctional my family truly is. I obviously have been working on myself and my issues in therapy for years, but sometimes it takes a major moment in life to unlock a part of your brain which allows you to see things from a different perspective. Once your eyes have been opened, you can't go back. The excuses you made in the past and used as tourniquets can't ever cover up the gaping wounds that are left behind from your trauma—the experience leaving you bleeding out and broken all over again.

That is how I felt last night. After we left my mom's house I was numb the whole ride home, not saying a word. Remington just held my hand, his strong silence riding shotgun with us, holding me just as tightly. When we got to his house my entire body began to shake. He came around to my side of the truck, scooped me into his arms, and carried me inside. We went right to the bedroom where he gently changed my clothes and slipped one of his softest, most well-worn FGFD T-shirts over my head. Remington stripped down to his boxers, guided us to the bed, and wrapped me in his arms where I completely shattered. He held me for what felt like hours and let me cry, rubbing my back, running his hands through my hair, and whispering comforting words that only he could deliver to my heart in that moment.

Reading his card again, I have an overwhelming need to see him. Knowing that I would be useless at my own job today, I had already put in for a sick day first thing. I needed a mental health day, and I was not going to talk myself out of using it. I know Remington's working today and I do not want to be a distraction, but I was told by Chief and everyone else that I was always welcome at the fire station. I decide a quick visit will be good for both of us after last night.

A long hot shower, quick breakfast, and some extra time getting ready to my favorite '90s country playlist has me feeling more like myself. I grab my things and head out the door, making sure to lock up properly with the fresh set of house keys that Remington gave me not long ago. My navy-blue SUV is parked in its usual spot in his driveway, the sun reflecting off the paint and . . .

What the hell!

I race toward my car and see the driver's side is sporting an extra layer of paint today. Bright red spray paint to be exact. It is offensive in its color and the nasty word written along the entire length of my car.

WHORE

Tears of anger fill my eyes, and fear has my hands feeling instantly sweaty. Why would someone do this? I can't drive my car around town like this! And how much is this going to cost me to have fixed? Obviously I have insurance, but I don't know what kind of vandalism is covered on my plan.

Jesus, this is Fox Grove. I moved away from the city to a quiet town with "low to no crime" to avoid things like this. Well, not THIS exactly but . . . what the fuck!

Pulling out my cell phone I dial the one person I need right now.

He picks up immediately. "Good morning, baby. How are you?" Concern is thick in his voice, and I know he will be even more worried when I tell him my news.

"Hey, yeah. Thank you so much for the flowers and the card. They're lovely," I try to say calmly, even though the longer I look at my car the more panicked I feel.

"I'm so sorry I couldn't wake up next to you today, but I just needed you to know I was thinking about you—I am always thinking about you," he rasps.

"I miss you," I choke out.

"I miss you, too, beautiful. Why don't you come down to the station and hang out for a little while? You can bring some work here if you need to," Remington suggests hopefully.

"Remington, I was going to come. I was actually just on my way but—" I pause.

Hearing my distress, Remington is on high alert. "What's wrong, Lainey? What happened?"

Holding back a sob I say, "My car, when I came outside, Remington, someone spray painted my car."

"What the hell!" he shouts, and I hear a chair screech, and other guys in the background can be heard voicing concern.

"It's red and says 'whore' all along the side of my car, in huge letters," I whisper to him.

"Baby, listen to me. Do *not* touch anything. Go back inside, lock the door, and I will be home soon," Remington tells me with a demanding calmness.

"You can't come home! You're working. I will try to call my insurance and figure it out. Have it towed or something." I do not want to be a burden to him, and this isn't his problem; the problem is me obviously.

"No, Lainey. This is a crime, and we are going to be reporting it. Sit tight, I'm on my way. Go inside, promise me," he demands again.

"I promise." I nod, even though he can't see me.

"Good girl." His reply has a shiver running up my spine as I shut and lock the front door.

Less than ten minutes later I am looking out the front window and Remington comes flying up to the house in his black truck. He quickly gets out, Eli tumbling from the passenger side as they rush over to examine my car. A look of pure anger ignites both of their handsome faces. Remington's rage makes him seem even larger and holds a fury that Eli can't match.

He looks up at the house and locks eyes with me through the window, which has his feet quickly moving my way. I open the front door and his arms are around me instantly. I am so sick of crying, but I can't stop the tears from coming. The past twenty-four hours have been too much.

"I'm here, I'm here," Remington rumbles into my hair, kissing my temple and stroking my back. "It'll be okay, baby."

"Why would someone do this?" I ask, pulling back to look up at Remington as Eli joins us in the house, closing the door behind him.

"Hey, Lainey," Eli says, giving me a quick kiss on the cheek. "I am so sorry."

"Thanks, Eli. I appreciate you coming, too." I never expected anyone else to come, or care.

"The whole station wanted to storm over here, but we told them we'd keep 'em updated," Eli says.

I bury my face in my hands and groan. "Oh my God, they all know? This is so embarrassing."

Remington winds his hands around my wrists, and I look up at his face. He looks angry and I start to worry. "Lainey, you listen to me right now. *You* have nothing to be embarrassed about. This is not your fault. This is my fault."

Now I know his anger is more toward himself than me, but I don't understand why.

"Why would this be your fault?" I ask Remington and glance at Eli, who's rubbing his jaw and looking at his best friend with concern.

"Baby, there is only *one* person that I can think of that would vandalize your car. And seeing what they wrote only confirmed their jealousy and hate." Remington looks at me, waiting for me to connect the dots that should have been so obvious to me in the first place.

"Cora," I breathe out angrily.

"Exactly. So it *is* my fault. I didn't protect you from her psycho bullshit. I should have been more firm with her the other day and I wasn't. I'm so sorry." Agony plays across his face and I can't stand it.

Gripping his forearms I say, "Her being batshit crazy and jealous is not your fault! Do not put this on yourself, please. You had no way of knowing she would do something like this. You handled things at the cafe like an adult, because you are one."

"She's right," Eli chimes in. "You told me everything that happened, and I know the full history. Cora has always been a bit strange, but this is unhinged, man. We need to report this. Call Danny. He's our buddy that we graduated with," Eli explains to me. "He's a Fox Grove cop."

Remington nods and steps into the kitchen to make the call. Eli puts a reassuring arm around my shoulders while we wait, and I have never been more grateful for the people I have in my life right now.

When Danny McEntire showed up with his partner, Megan Grove, they introduced themselves and got to work. Of course there were no prints, but they still needed to check. They took lots of photos, but the most damning thing for Cora was the video footage from Remington's security cameras around his house. She didn't even try and cover her face or hide the fact that it was her doing the damage to my car. She had come after Remington had left for the fire station. The entire time she was working she mumbled to herself incoherently. It was really creepy to watch and left us all feeling uneasy.

Danny told us that he strongly suggested we file charges and each file a restraining order against her. We have no idea what the hell is going on with her or what she has been up to since graduation. She had her business planning weddings and events, but she never came back to Fox Grove to run it. Remington has not had any contact with her; he cut all ties the night he kicked her out of his apartment and broke up with her. Cora being back here now and demanding that Remington fulfill some stupid marriage pact from when they were little kids made us all uncomfortable and not in a "haha" way anymore.

Cora just went from an annoyance to a real threat. And nobody knows where she is.

27

Remington

The only thing that made me able to walk away from Lainey and go back to my shift at the fire station was my parents showing up to the house. I texted my dad to let him know what happened and they dropped everything and knocked on my door twenty minutes later. My mom had Lainey all mothered up on the couch with blankets, snacks, water, and was camped out right next to her. She told me they were not leaving "their girl" alone for one second and promised to take good care of her for me. After the horrible dinner with her own mother less than a day ago, this was exactly what *my woman* needed. To be shown love, care, and affection not only by me but the other people that are in her life now, too. She needs to know she is not alone anymore.

Danny promised he would get all the paperwork going to file a restraining order against Cora on behalf of both myself and Lainey. Never in a million years would I think we'd have to take this step when Cora knocked on my door. I wanted her to stay the fuck away from both of us, to protect Lainey, but it was hard to believe a couple pieces of paper would be helpful at all. Not knowing where she was also made it kind of hard to enforce it or even press charges for the vandalism to Lainey's car. Just thinking about those disgusting red, dripping letters spelling out Cora's clear hatred and jealousy made the fury I felt when I first saw it rage through my blood all over again.

"Hey." Eli clapped me on the shoulder. "Do you wanna hit the gym?" He could probably feel my mounting wrath and knew I could use a few rounds with my gloves on and some punishing miles on the treadmill.

"Yeah, I do, but I think first I am going to give Rodger Tyler a call." I look at Eli, who rightfully looks shocked.

"Seriously? You have not talked to him in years," Eli replies.

"I know, but he might have some information, and I don't like feeling like we're in the dark on this. I need to know what the hell is going on. Trust me, I don't want to make this call, but I will do anything to keep Lainey safe," I say honestly to my best friend, and he nods in understanding.

"Do you want me to sit here with you while you call him?" he offers.

"I appreciate it, but no, man. I got this." His willingness to do anything for me, because he is my brother through and through, makes my throat feel thick. He had no hesitation to jump into action today for me, to be there to help comfort Lainey, and I know he wants to help protect her, too.

Eli gives a mock salute, his way of trying to lighten the mood, and heads off toward the kitchen. I pull out my phone and bring up Rodger's number, hoping he will actually answer the damn phone.

It rings and rings several times before connecting. "Rem?" A voice graveled by decades of cigarette use crackles over the line.

"Yeah, hey, Mr. Tyler. It's been a long time, thanks for picking up," I say.

"What's going on?" he says with a cough.

"It's about Cora." I cut right to the chase. I am not about to play years of catch-up. I need information, not chitchat.

A deep, exhausted sigh leaves Rodger before he says, "What did my daughter do now?"

"She showed up here demanding I marry her, based on a pact we made as children. I told her I wanted nothing to do with her a couple times. Made it clear that I'm a happily taken man and in a committed relationship." He grunts in response, and I continue. "Then this morning my girlfriend went to get in her car and found the word 'whore' spray painted in red along the whole side of the car."

There is a long beat of silence, and I look to be sure our call is still connected.

"You sure it was her?" Rodger asks.

"We have her on my goddamn security cameras, Rodger!" I exclaim, feeling my temper rising.

"I am so sorry, Rem. Cora is not the same girl that ya knew back in the day. She has been hurtin' a lot of people for a long time, including me and her mother. Now it seems she's swingin' back 'round hurtin' ya even more." The pain and exhaustion in Rodger's rough voice is palpable.

"What happened?" I push.

"Jared happened."

I growl at the name.

"Yeah, that asshole, one of many of Cora's horrible decisions over the years. But he helped her with some of the party plannin' stuff, setting up her business, and that was a big mistake. He got her some investors, but they were not the kind of people ya wanna be mixed up with."

"Shit," I say, my mind reeling.

"Then Jared just took off after about four years, leaving Cora with a pile of debt and a drug habit," Rodger admits.

"What the hell, Rodger. I can't believe that. Drugs?" I feel like this is my fault. Had I not kicked her out the night of graduation and worked things out with her, maybe her life would have turned out better, different. But Cora was Cora, and her manipulative self-centered ways would have destroyed us that day or one in the future. Plus, if I did not end that toxic relationship I wouldn't be where I am today, where I am meant to be. As sad as I am for Cora and the shitty path her life took, I cannot look back or take on any responsibility for her self-implosion.

"Did she move the business back to Fox Grove?" I ask Rodger.

"No, she lost everything almost two years ago. Everything she does now is to try and keep the guys she owes money to off her back and fuel her drug habit. We *tried* to help her. Tried to get her into rehab, but nothin' has worked. She's stolen money and medication from our house. Rem, she even took the three pieces of heirloom jewelry that Nancy had in our bedroom. They were the only thing she had left of her mother, ya know what those meant to her." Rodger is a broken man. The sadness laced in his voice is paired with exhaustion and a loss of any hope he might have been holding on to. Cora is his only daughter, and I know telling me this must be so difficult.

"Rodger, I had no idea. I'm so sorry," I tell him sincerely.

"Listen, Rem, you and your girl do what ya need to do. Cora needs a wake-up call and to be held responsible for her actions. I am sorry it's been so long since we spoke. Nancy and I have always loved ya like a son and hold no ill will toward ya. Cora treated ya so awful, and you were nothin' but good to her. You're a good man, Rem." Rodger's words are something I did not realize I needed to hear so badly.

"I really appreciate you saying that." I clear my throat, feeling surprised by such a closed-off man expressing so much to me after all this time.

"Seriously, Rem. If Cora is coming 'round causing problems or trying to rope ya into any crazy plan she hatched, it is all 'bout money. She needs it for those damn thugs that constantly shake her down and for the drugs. *Please* don't give her anything. Don't let her ruin what ya have goin' there that's good in Fox Grove." Rodger sounds worried that she might be able to pull the wool over my eyes, like I am certain she did with him more than once to get her way. She did it a lot when we were growing up, so I can't imagine what it is like now that she has an addictive motivator.

"I promise to be careful, Rodger. Do you have any idea where Cora might be?" I ask.

"Yeah, a little apartment complex on the south end of town. It's week-by-week rent and cheap. I think it's called Riverview? Not sure why, no river in sight, and it has the shittiest views in town." He huffs.

"I know the place, thanks, Rodger," I assure him.

"Anything you need, Rem, I mean it, ya call me." His rough voice is stern, but I believe him.

"I will, thank you."

I hang up the phone and feel exhausted from the whole conversation.

After a grueling workout with Eli, an emergency call on the highway, and coming back to the station I need to decompress. I take out Lainey's new journal, my drawing supplies, and her old, ugly journal. If I can't be with her tonight, I can at least work on this and draw her flowers. Hopefully I can give it to her soon, watch Lainey flip through the pages, and surprise her with her own personal garden at her fingertips.

28

Lainey

Kendra and I are at Brooks and Books dropping off her first full order of mugs to display and sell in the store. Sutton was right, of course, and Kendra's samples she left when we first came in sold out almost immediately. Today, she brought in enough to fill the table—a wide variety from several of her past collections.

My jaw dropped as we kept pulling beautifully crafted mugs from the wrapping. "Kendra, how on earth did you have time to make all of these and keep up with the online orders *and* the salon?"

She grins at me and tells us, "Well, I decided to pause the online store for the time being. I wanted to focus on getting a lot of mugs made for my table here. I was really inspired and excited to see my work in an *actual* store. So, I have been spending all of my extra time in my studio working my sexy butt off . . . and I must say it's some of my best work." Kendra holds up a teal mug with delicate wildflowers hand-painted on it, a design from her spring collection last year that was very popular.

Sutton, organizing the mugs just so, says, "Kendra, these

are stunning. I have a really hard time letting them go every time somebody buys one because I want them all. But I also know that they will bring so much joy to each customer. I think you should stick around sometimes to see people buying them."

"I would love that!" Kendra claps. "With an online order you don't get to see how the person reacts when they see the final product, the joy, as you say."

"What if you did a pop-up shop?" I suggest. "Like a day where people know you will be here at a certain time, and they will be able to come in and 'meet the artist.' We could advertise for it, make it like a little party or something?"

"I LOVE that idea!" Sutton nearly lets a daisy-printed mug slip from her hands in her excitement. "Oh, shit!" She carefully places the mug down and wipes her hands on her legs.

Kendra lets out a relieved, slightly nervous, sigh. "Why don't you take a break, mama, and let me and Lainey finish the unpacking? You need to get off of your feet anyways."

"You're right, they *are* killing me. I also wanted to ask you a favor, Kendra?"

"Of course," Kendra says, placing down the last few mugs. "Whatever you need!"

"You might say no." Sutton looks pointedly at her, crossing her arms and not looking at all intimidating.

"Doubtful," she says, laughing. "You know I would do anything for my girls. Need to bury a body? Pllllease tell me it's Cora's," Kendra begs playfully.

"Unfortunately and thankfully no." Sutton snorts. "I am hoping this will be something fun for you to help me with."

I can't wait to hear what this is going to be.

"Deck should be home anytime now, and I know the baby's gender, but *he doesn't* since I am going to all the appointments by myself. They asked me if I wanted to know last time, and I said yes," Sutton tells us, eyes shining with excitement and bursting to share her secret.

"Oh my gosh!" I exclaim. "We had no idea you knew already. Sutton! This is huge news."

Sutton is beaming, rubbing her prominent baby bump, her cheeks pink with emotion, and tells us, "It's a GIRL!"

We all collectively freak out. Laughter, hugs, squealing, and so much happiness fill the entire store. I could not be more happy for my friend. Babies are such a blessing, and I know that Sutton is going to be an amazing mom. I don't know Derek yet, but from everything Remington has shared, he is crazy about Sutton and can't wait to be a dad. Being a girl dad, I am sure, will make him even more overprotective. It will be fun to watch a big, strong, military man like Deck be wrapped around the finger of a tiny, precious, little girl.

"What favor do you need from me though?" asks Kendra.

"I want to do something special for a gender reveal when Deck gets home. He loves coffee, and we even have that little coffee bar area in our kitchen. I was thinking of setting it up all cute with decorations." Sutton describes her plan.

"Love that!" we tell her in unison.

"I was hoping Kendra could make me a special mug?"

"O-M-G, *yes*!" Kendra shouts, making me and Sutton giggle.

"What did you have in mind?" I ask Sutton.

"I was thinking of an oversized mug with teeny, tiny, pink hearts all over, and then script on the front that says 'Girl Dad.'" She looks to Kendra with a hopeful smile.

"This is going to be so freaking cute! I'm on it." Kendra nods and starts packing up her boxes and paper she had wrapped the mugs in.

Laughing Sutton says, "I don't mean right this minute! Aren't we getting lunch?"

"Ugh, I guess," Kendra says. "But you got my creative juices going, and I am ready to get my hands into my clay."

"Well, I am glad you're excited, and I really, really appreciate you making my vision come to life. He's going to love it."

The girls hug, and a warm fuzzy feeling spreads through my body. There has been so much bad happening with my mom, Cora, my car, and dealing with the restraining order. I needed this today. Good news and time with my best friend and someone who is also very quickly becoming another best friend.

It feels like I have known Sutton so much longer than I have, and friendship with her came easily. Same with Jess and the fire station girls. They have been blowing up our text chain, checking on me, and making sure I don't need anything. Jess even had me over for dinner a few days ago with her and the kids. Matt and Remington were both on shift, and Remington is still uneasy about me being home alone the whole time.

Our family and friends are rallying around us, me specifically, and I have never had this kind of love and support in all my life. I feel unworthy of it, honestly. The broken parts of myself feel like if I let these kind, wonderful, normal people too close I will cut them unintentionally.

The hot sun warms my skin as I sit out on Remington's back deck. I was trying to relax, read, and distract myself from my anxious thoughts after getting back from lunch with the girls, but I was exhausted and found myself nodding off. I barely go back to my apartment anymore besides picking up things I need and checking my mail. We've basically moved me into

Remington's house, especially after Cora ruined my car, but haven't labeled it yet.

If you would have told me when I was burning my ex-boyfriend's things on a late night in March that by now I'd be sitting here, I never would have believed it. To some it would seem fast that I spend all this time here, but to me Remington has always just felt *right*. I've never felt more safe or more seen. It makes me think about how I had the foreboding earlier in the day with the girls, worried about how my brokenness could hurt them.

Remington has seen a lot of that brokenness. I have not shared all of it with him, but he knows most of it. Witnessed and felt the vitriol of my mother firsthand, has heard the stories of my father and brother. He knows the unhealthy history I have with men and dating. And yet he still embraces me and has not made me feel like I need to hide any pieces of myself, smooth over my emotions or hide things to keep the peace. I let the comfort of his solid presence in my life wash over my body with the warm breeze, pushing back the nagging worries.

I am in so deep with this man.

29

Remington

"Pack a bag, Lainey," I announce as I walk in the door after my final shift of the week. I am about to have four days off, and I plan on spending every second with my woman. More importantly, we are getting the hell out of here and away from the stress and the constant looking over our shoulders wondering if Cora is going to pop up and wreak more havoc.

Lainey comes out of our bedroom, *yes, I am calling it our bedroom*, and that feels so fucking good to say. She is here all the time, and I don't plan on letting her go back to her apartment. It feels so right coming home to her, sharing space with her, knowing she is here even when I can't be. Jesus, she has me wound so tight, if I don't focus I am going to toss her right back on the bed and fuck her, and then we are never going to get on the road.

"What? Are you kicking me out?" she teases, coming to a halt in front of me and running her freshly painted, summery pink nails up my chest.

"Never, baby. You are totally stuck with me." I dip down and take her perfect, soft pout in a kiss. Being away from her, even when I'm just at work kills me, and this moment, kissing her when I walk in the door, lights me up in a way she will never begin to understand.

Lainey's breathing is ragged from our kiss and lust is deepening her sultry blue eyes.

She bites her lip and I groan.

She rolls her hips into me, feeling my growing erection, and she grins.

I let off an animalistic rumble and greedily ravage her mouth, forgetting whatever plan I had in mind when I tossed my keys down and came looking for her in such a hurry.

"Remington," she moans as I kiss along her jaw and lightly suck on her throbbing pulse point. "Oh, God, I miss you so much when you're gone." Her confession is like a drug. I grip her ass and haul her up, spinning around as I walk to the kitchen and place her down on the counter.

She looks like a goddamn snack, ready for me to devour, in a soft lavender sundress with cap sleeves. The cotton material under my rough fingertips feels like it's begging to be torn off of her. But I know Lainey will kill me if I do that, having just bought this dress on a shopping trip with Jess and a couple of the other fire station significant others when they had a girls' day.

Instead I slip the cap sleeves down her shoulders, the top scoop of her dress dropping slowly below her perfect round tits. I suck in a sharp breath when I see her bare chest.

"No bra?" I quirk an eyebrow at her.

"This dress doesn't need one."

"And did this dress require any panties?" My eyes trail down her body. Her chest is heaving, and it is taking everything in me not to suck her tight nipples into my mouth. But I am not ready to be done teasing her yet. I want her writhing and begging for my touch.

"Maybe you should see for yourself." Lainey drags her

own eyes over my body, lingering on the very noticeable bulge behind my navy-blue work pants.

She makes my dick throb when she takes one of her perfect, silky-smooth legs and props it up on the counter, giving me a partially obstructed view of her pussy.

I can see that it's bare.

It is also dripping, waiting to be taken care of.

I will do anything to get my hands, tongue, dick anywhere near it. *Right, and I was going to be making* her *beg?*

With a knowing smirk, like she was able to read all my dirty thoughts, she slides the dress up more, showing me the rest of the most beautiful sight.

"Did *my* pussy miss me?" I demand.

Gasping, realizing that she can tease me all she wants, but I'm the one in control, Lainey nods her head. "Yes, sir."

"That's right. Missed me so much, it's dripping all over the counter, and I haven't even touched you yet." I trail my finger from her throat, down her breast, her stomach, and over her exposed thigh with the lightest graze possible. Her whole body shudders.

"Yes."

"Beg me, Lainey. Tell me what you want. Tell me what my perfect pussy needs." I slide one finger up her calf slowly.

Moaning and trying to scoot closer to me, Lainey says, "Please, Remington, please. Your pussy needs to be touched, to be fucked," she whispers. "She needs *you*."

Her words are my undoing, and I am absolutely feral. Fisting the hair at the nape of her neck, I kiss her deeply while simultaneously sliding two fingers into her tight, soaking wet channel. The grip around my fingers is so tight, drawing me in deeper and pulsing.

Lainey's cries of pleasure fill the kitchen, and I bend to finally suck a nipple into my mouth. Her back arches, and I press the palm of my hand against her clit, working my fingers in a continuous rhythm that makes her legs shake.

"Oh . . . oh, I'm so close. I'm going to . . ." I immediately pull back, stopping all my motions. Withdrawing my fingers, a look of shock that morphs into sassy rage plays across my beautiful woman's face, and I can't help the smug grin I give her back.

"What the hell!" Lainey yelps at me, obviously frustrated.

I undo my belt and unzip my pants, shoving them and my black boxers down. Lainey's hungry, molten eyes track every single move. I step between her legs and yank her to the edge of the counter, placing my mouth right next to her ear. I rasp, "The only place I want you to come right now, baby, is on *your* cock."

Lainey sucks in a surprised gasp and says, "Holy shit, that's so hot."

"What, you think I am going to claim your pussy, call it *mine* and not expect you to be just as possessive of my dick? It's a two-way street, baby. I want to own every part of you, just like I want you to know you *already* own every fucking part of me." There is a shimmer of something deeper in her eyes as she takes in my words. Something neither of us are ready to voice yet, but I would bet my life we both feel.

I slide the head of my cock up and down her needy, wet center, making her eyes roll back in her head. "Watch," I demand. And we both do, and I slip home, fast and hard, to the hilt. I fuck her harder, deeper. My strokes feel like tides crashing over both of us, consuming pleasure rippling down my spine.

"Right there, oh, please don't stop," my woman begs.

"I'm never going to stop." I kiss her in a promise that belongs to this moment and far beyond.

"I need to come, please, please let me come, Remington."

Deep pulsing from inside of her tells me how close she is, and I am right there with her, unable to hold back.

"Yes, baby, come on *your cock*. Let me fill up *my sweet pussy*," I growl.

"Yes, yes . . ." she screams out breathlessly, and we both come together in a perfect moment.

Heat, passion, and possession.

Mine. Every fucking part of her is mine.

"Sorry we got a late start," Lainey says to me as we get close to our surprise destination.

"No you aren't," I laugh out, "and neither am I. I would take our morning a thousand times over and risk being stuck in some traffic."

She hums happily and reaches over for my hand. "Me, too."

I am taking her away for the weekend to my buddy Walker's cabin. He doesn't use it all the time, so when he's not there he rents it out for extra income. This weekend he happened to have a cancellation.

We are in the foothills of the Blue Ridge Mountains, almost four hours from home. The drive here was breathtaking, and I can't wait to be tucked away in our private cabin. Walker has done a lot of work to make this a special destination spot and has had a lot of people even book it for honeymoons. There is supposed to be an easy hiking trail that leads from the cabin to a small, but stunning, waterfall. I know that this is the perfect, romantic, special weekend Lainey and I need.

Following the GPS, I turn my truck onto the long winding

drive that leads up to a picture perfect, A-frame log cabin. It has a large front porch with four deck chairs in deep red, a mixture of colorful flowers in planters, and an abundance of windows to showcase the thick forest view all around us.

"Remington!" Lainey bounces in her seat excitedly. "Look at this place. It's like a postcard. This is the most beautiful thing I have seen."

The most beautiful thing I have seen is sitting right next to me.

"Come on, let's go check it out." I grab our bags out of the truck, and we head up the wide steps. I punch in the door code that Walker gave me, and the door unlocks and swings open. Stepping inside, my eyes are instantly drawn to the tall ceilings and the massive widows at the back of the open cabin. From the wooden exterior, you'd think the inside would be dark, but it isn't. There's a cozy airiness with mountain touches, smooth dove-grey walls, thick accent beams, and a wood ceiling.

There is a single bedroom off to the right side of the cabin which houses a massive king-sized bed, cream and olive-green bedding that blend effortlessly with the forest and give a relaxed feel to the room. The bathroom has a deep claw-foot tub that Lainey drools all over the second she sees it, which makes me laugh. The kitchen is a mix of open shelves and closed navy-colored cabinets, dark granite counters, and a small island.

The best feature, however, is the deep, dark grey sectional that faces the back windows and a wall that has a handcrafted stone fireplace. Lainey snuggles up on the couch, pulling me down next to her. I wrap my arms around her and feel all the stress melt away.

"It's so peaceful up here. Thank you for bringing us, Remington. I don't think I even realized how much I needed this until I stepped out of the truck and took in a lungful of mountain air."

"We both deserve this break, baby. The quiet, the calm. Nobody knows we are up here. We get to just enjoy each other." Kissing her temple, we sink deeper into the couch and watch the sunlight dance through the forest. "This is our first adventure like this of many," I promise her.

30

Lainey

I never want to leave this cabin. It is freaking magical. The past two days have been cozy, lazy perfection. We have spent a lot of quality time exploring each other—staying up late and sleeping in is easy to do in the comfortable king-sized bed. If there was some way to copy and paste the claw-foot tub into my real life somehow, I would do it in a heartbeat. It was big enough for both of us to soak in last night, and I'd never felt more relaxed than I did laying in that tub, Remington at my back, his strong arms cocooning me in.

Today is our last day, and Remington promised an easy hike that ends with a surprise. I don't have hiking boots, but he told me my running shoes would be fine. I paired them with black bike shorts, a pink sports bra, a loose white running tank, and pulled my hair half up in a small claw clip. When I stepped out onto the back deck where Remington was waiting for me he let out a low moan of appreciation when he took me in.

Now, we are hiking hand in hand through the quiet forest. The soft sunlight, fresh mountain air, and summer breeze are stirring up emotions in me that are hard to describe. One of the things that is so refreshing about being with Remington is that we don't have to fill time with chatter. Of course we talk to each other, and I love each conversation, but I also appreciate these moments, too. They feel so intimate and completely ours. It's as if he knows when my body just needs him, whether we are wrapped around each other in bed, him controlling every ounce of my pleasure, or if I just need his solid strong presence. Right now, it's the latter.

Rounding a bend, Remington helps me down a rocky incline, and we hear a rushing sound of water that we couldn't make out before. He grins at me and says, "Ready for the surprise?" I nod at him, and we walk a bit faster toward what I assume is our intended destination.

When we come to a bright clearing, my breath is stolen straight from my lungs. A stunning waterfall is pouring over a cliff face that must be a couple hundred feet high. The powerful water pools in a small lake of some kind where we are standing. It is not massive but is still impressive. There are wildflowers dotting the open, soft grassy area around us.

The breeze ruffles the hairs around my neck, and I shiver, not because I'm cold, but because I am trying to lock in the feeling of this moment. Looking up at Remington, I find his eyes already on me. "This is amazing," I say honestly. "It looks like a painting, but a million times better."

"I knew that this was at the end of the hike, Walker told me about it. But, yeah, it's way more than I expected." Tucking some hair behind my ear, he kisses me gently. "Come on," he says, "let's cool off our feet."

We take off our socks and shoes and I hesitantly wade into the water. "Shit, that's cold!" Remington yells. He jumps as his feet hit the water making me laugh. He looks at the glint in my eye as I bend down and says, "Lainey, don't even think—" but is cut off as a cold splash of water from my cupped hands hits him right in the chest, soaking his already sweaty shirt.

"Oh, you asked for this," he says. The look he gives me back is much more heated and determined than the playful one I delivered with my jest. I expect him to splash me back but only have a split-second to realize that's not his intention. He scoops me into his arms and we fall backward into the deeper water.

I don't have time to tell him to stop.

I don't have time to warn him.

I don't have time to try and figure out how to take a breath.

I just have time to panic.

We pop up, and I am trying to not sink back down into the lake. Coughing on what water I just sucked in, the fear is overwhelming.

I can't breathe.

I am dizzy and disoriented.

Black spots dot my misty vision.

The water is not going to drown me, but my trauma just might.

Strong arms band around me and tug me close. My body locks up in deep fear until I hear Remington's voice, terrified and gruff, right next to my ear. "I got you, baby. I got you. You're okay."

Before I can form a thought, we are on the grass next to the lake and I am coughing, crying and shaking. My heart is racing, and the fear I had in the water is still flowing through my body. I am trying to calm myself down, but I have lost all control. Remington just pulls me tight against himself and holds me through it, murmuring and reassuring me.

Eventually, my breathing evens and my shaking subsides. I have no idea how long we have been sitting here, surrounded by wildflowers, my pain, and the rushing sound of the waterfall. Birds I didn't even notice are singing, unaffected, and the sun is not in the same position in the sky as it was before.

"I'm sorry," I whisper, not even sure Remington can hear me, but when his body stiffens, I know he has.

This is when he realizes it's too much, I'm too much.

"Baby, please look at me," he pleads. "*I* am the one that is sorry. I am so fucking sorry." He grips my face, rubbing his thumb along my jaw, his eyes honey-filled pools of pain.

"I can't swim." I look away, ashamed to admit this to him.

"I had no idea, Lainey. I would have never done that, I swear. We were just messing around and then, God. Baby, I'm so sorry." Distress is all over him, and I hate that I am the reason for it.

"Remington, it isn't your fault. I never told you, how would you have known? It's embarrassing, and not something that I go around openly telling people, proudly shouting it from the rooftops. What adult doesn't know how to swim?" I look at him hesitantly.

"I'm sure a lot of people, and I shouldn't have assumed you knew how before doing that. Please forgive me." He runs his hands up and down my legs soothingly.

"I forgive you, and I also owe you an explanation."

"Lainey, you don't have to share anything you're not ready to." He strokes his warm hands up and down, still comforting me, soaking into my chilled skin.

"I want you to know all the pieces of me, even the ones that are so broken they probably won't ever totally heal. You just might not want me after you know all the damage that's been done. Like I told you before, my family is not like your family, Remington." I whisper his name painfully and look away at the waterfall in shame.

He turns my face back to look directly at him. "I have told you before, *I know you*. Who you are now, *that* is what matters to me. You're so strong and have been through so much. Everyone is a little broken, but the important thing is finding your safe place. You are mine, Lainey. And I hope I can be that for you, too." His words hold so much meaning, so much value.

My hot tears fall, and I kiss Remington. "Yes, yes, you are my safe place. I've never had that with *anyone*, and that's why you get all these pieces of me. I didn't know if you wanted them, or if I should just keep them to myself."

"Let me carry them for you, with you—whatever will make it easier for you, baby. Just let me in, please," he begs.

I nod, wiping my tears, ready to tell him what so few people know.

"I never went on any kind of family trips or vacations. I have never even been on a hike like this. My dad's job was always his priority, impressing the people around him. I was used as more of a prop and a placeholder in our family. Sit here, say this, act this way, answer this way. There were rules and expectations, and if I stepped out of line I got verbally berated, ignored, and gaslit into thinking I was the problem and a tarnish to our family name that he worked so hard to polish and perfect."

Remington's face is passive and stone-like. I can tell he's trying to control his rage and emotions for my sake, so I continue. "Everything I did was a direct reflection on my father, good or bad. And I tried *so hard* to do it all just right, to make him happy. My mom was there to poke me along and try to keep just enough peace, but it was always tense. Cal was the perfect one, and I was constantly the problem."

Pausing I take a deep breath.

"I didn't like swimming at all, but the country club they were a part of had a pool. Lots of their friends had fancy houses with pools too, including us. Swimming was a requirement, but water always made me uneasy. Instead of getting me lessons when I was really little and making me comfortable, he just threw me in the water one day."

Remington sucks in a breath. "Your dad?"

"Yeah, right into our pool. I was twelve, but he knew I never liked being in the water, could not really swim, and was afraid. He told me he was sick of me being an embarrassment, only hardly being able to doggie paddle around in the shallow end, never putting my face in, and I needed to get over it. He picked me up and tossed me right into the deep end. I thought I was going to die. Obviously, I didn't. Somehow I managed to get to the side and pull myself out, and when I did . . . he was gone. He walked away, left me in there all alone."

I can feel the anger pouring off of him now, and Remington stands up and starts to pace in front of me. "What in the actual fuck!"

"He claimed that it never even happened. I was told I made the whole thing up, because afterward he did sign me up for swimming lessons. They were at the country club, private lessons with one of his friend's older sons. He was in high school. I had to go twice a week . . . for two years." I let out a breath, not wanting to tell him more, but knowing I need to get this out. Nobody but my therapist knows this part of my life.

"I still wouldn't put my face in the water after what had happened. I was terrified. I felt like I was suffocating, and it made me panic every time I got close. The instructor told me I just needed to relax, that he would h-help me." I swing my sad eyes to Remington, and he is frozen in place.

"Lainey," he whispers, knowing nothing good comes next.

"He t-touched me." I can barely get the words past my lips. "I was s-so young, and I had no idea what was really going on. He told me that it was part of my lessons, that it was h-helping me get ready to be a good swimmer. My dad was paying for me to go to these, these private lessons, to be t-tortured and I couldn't do any-anything." A sob rips from my lungs and Remington is right there, where I need him.

"You didn't tell anyone?" he asks softly.

"I told my dad that I didn't like the lessons. That they made me uncomfortable, but he told me that he didn't have time to listen to me complain. He told me I was b-being *ungrateful.*" The shaking in my body returns as I remember that day, the hopelessness and knowing I was utterly alone.

"What happened?" Remington cautiously asks.

"He went away to college. My 'lessons' stopped, and I obviously never learned to *actually* swim." I wipe my eyes and sit back.

"Who is he? *Where* the fuck is he?" Remington's voice is deeply menacing, and his eyes are full of pain for me, a promise of destruction for the person that tortured me.

"It's okay—" I start to say but he cuts me off.

"The fuck it's not!" he roars, making me jump. "This sick bastard hurt you, Lainey, a child. And who knows if he did it to someone else—*is doing it* to someone else?"

"He's not," I whimper.

"You can't know that."

"Yes, I can," I say more sharply than I intend.

"How, how can you know that? Where is he? Has he tried to contact you?" Remington is up and pacing again, but my next words stop him in his tracks.

"He's dead."

"Dead?"

"Yes, he was involved in a drunk driving accident his junior year of college. It was his fault. I know because my dad is still friends with his dad. I was in high school, and we all went to the funeral. Maybe I am a horrible person, but all I felt when I heard the news that he was dead was relief." I look back to the waterfall where it splashes the lake and mists over the surface of the water, hoping Remington can forgive me for my evil thoughts.

"I'm glad he's dead too, but I wish I could have killed him myself." His admission makes me suck in a shocked breath.

"What?" I look at him, gaping.

"It makes me absolutely furious to know that nobody was there to protect you, baby. That you suffered in silence because there was not *one person* in your life that you felt safe with. I wish I could go back in time, but I can't." He pulls me into his arms. "All I can do is promise to keep you safe from this day forward."

"Thank you." I hold on to him and weep, letting out years of pain that had been so tightly locked away.

After some time, I look at him and say something, trying to be brave by sharing another fear. "I don't want you to treat me differently. I'm not made of glass. It took a lot of therapy for me to feel ready and capable of any kind of relationship. I just always allowed for really terrible ones up until I found you. And I also had to do a lot of work to allow myself to be, to be touched. But being with you . . . It has unlocked something totally different for me. I don't want me telling you all of this to change that or take it away."

Remington spins me so that I am straddling his lap, placing his hands firmly on my waist. "The only thing I feel after what you told me is pure fucking awe for the woman you are, gratitude that I get to be the man you allow to hold you, touch you. And I promise to worship your body every day the way it deserves, the way you deserve, Lainey."

Leaning in, we meet each other in a kiss laced with passion and healing. Healing that I never thought I would find, let alone feel worthy of. And as we lay in soft grass, surrounded by wildflowers, a soundtrack of nature, and the rush of the waterfall, Remington does exactly as he promised and worships my body.

Healing me, holding me, loving me just as I am.

And I know in this moment, that he has fully claimed me—body and soul.

31

Remington

It's late at the fire station, I should be asleep. Instead, I am up in the common area with Lainey's journals and my drawing stuff. Our trip to the cabin was perfect and painful. Perfect because we had so much quality time together and nature has a way of calming me like nothing else can. Walker's cabin was incredible. He definitely undersold his description to me when he said it was just a little place he used for a side hustle. If he put some money into a couple places like that up there, he'd have a full-blown destination spot that would be booked out months and months in advance. He told me he barely even advertises for the cabin.

The painful part of the trip was at the waterfall. I felt like my soul was being torn from my body when Lainey opened up to me and told me about her past. If that fucker wasn't already dead, I honestly would hunt him down and put him in the ground myself. I hope I never have to meet her father because I have nothing good to say to Patrick Quinn. I already had zero respect for the man, but after what I saw pour out of my beautiful woman that day—the absolute terror, the pain, the sadness, and trauma . . . I wish I could put him in the ground, too for all the sins he's committed against Lainey. He may not have ever physically hit her, but his words, emotional trauma, and neglect left deep scars that will always mark her. She deserved so much better, and I hate that I can't protect her from her past.

So lost in thought and the sunflowers that I am sketching, I don't hear Eli come up and sit down. I jolt and mess up my lines when he says, "So does Lainey know you are a little Rembrandt yet?" He casually kicks his boots up on the coffee table and puts his arms behind his head.

"Shit, you messed me up." I huff and erase my mistake, blowing off the paper and starting again. "And to answer your question. No . . . She doesn't know yet, and I'm going to keep it that way until this is done."

"What about your drawing setup in your office at home?"

"I stashed it all away in the guest closet and can pull it back out again someday. We never really go in the office anyway. Lainey took over the whole dining area for her workspace, which was fine by me." I use my pinky and blend the strokes I just made, bringing the flowers to life.

"She is going to freak out when she sees this." Eli nods to the journal.

"I hope she likes it," I admit nervously, reading the quote she wrote in the journal to accompany that day's thoughts.

"A sunflower doesn't compete with other flowers; it just blooms."

Why does everything with Cal have to be so difficult? I swear it will never get better if he refuses to realize that Dad isn't a god among men. But that's right where he's been our whole lives;

serving at Dad's altar. Cal is the golden child—the one that will take over whatever they are "building" in DC that I want nothing to do with, no matter how much they push. They hear me say no, but to Dad and Cal it just means that I am being stubborn or stupid. Having a mind of your own, according to the men of the Quinn household, is like walking around with the plague, which they are determined to rid you of one way or another. I will happily be sick the rest of my life.

I want to be my own person. Live my life away from them. That's all I have ever wanted. Is it really asking for too much?

"Are you kidding me? It is romantic as shit, Rem. I have never seen you put so much time and effort into something like this. You also took the risk of exposing your hidden talent to the whole station to be able to work on it when you're here, which I know you never planned on doing." Eli understands me better than anyone, and he also knows that my art was private. He was one of the only people on the planet that knew I could draw more than a doodle on a bar napkin, let alone that it was a serious passion of mine.

"Well, this is important. And I guess being with her makes me feel brave enough to not hide parts of myself that I should be proud of. Cora always made me feel like shit for going after the things that made me happy, the things that I was good at. Hiding the whole drawing thing, I think that was just an automatic reflex from the damage she inflicted." I stare down at the sunflowers, knowing that I don't want to hide anything anymore, including my feelings for Lainey.

"That makes a lot of sense, man. I'm happy you found Lainey. She's really good for you." Eli claps my shoulder.

"Yeah, she is," I easily agree. "Now we have to find you the right woman to settle down with."

He lets out a rough bark of laughter. "Fuuuck, no! You might be all locked down and glowing, but that is *not* my path. I am happily on the single road and never getting side-tracked."

"Sure, sure." I decide to let it go, not wanting to give him too much of a hard time this late at night.

"Haven't had any crazy Cora sightings lately?" Eli asks.

"No. We did the whole restraining order thing. Then when they went to her apartment she was actually there, which was a shock. They arrested her for the vandalism to Lainey's car. She has a court date and all that, but they don't keep you locked up in holding long for something so minor," I explain to him.

"They couldn't keep her on any drug charges?"

"She apparently didn't have any in her system at the time, and they didn't find any when they arrested her. Doesn't mean I think Rodger was mistaken. I definitely think she has a problem." I rub my neck, thinking. "Still have no idea why she is trying to make me marry her. It's creepy."

Eli shudders. "Yeah, obviously she's not in her right mind, who knows why she locked in on that. I think her dad must be right, that she's just desperate and trying to get to your money. If Cora was willing to rob her own mother? I can't imagine the lengths she would go to for more cash. She knows you were always responsible, you have the finance background. It's not like you are out blowing your money on stupid stuff. But thankfully you and Lainey got the right things in place to keep her away and documented everything."

"Right. I just hope it's enough to keep her the hell away

for good." I let out a long sigh. "Well, I think I'm gonna try and get some rest." I stand up and head toward where we rack out when we are on shift.

"Hey, Rem," Eli calls after me. "Anything you and Lainey need, you know I'm here for you, right?"

"I know, brother," I say, the term tying us together in this station and in every other aspect of life.

My sister and brother-in-law have a cute blue Cape Cod about ten minutes from my house. They live on a cul-de-sac, which is full of growing families. It's comforting that Sutton has a nice, safe area that she loves and has good neighbors looking out for her while Deck is gone, which is often. His missions and deployments are not typical since he is attached to an elite, highly classified SEAL team.

Today we are hanging out here so that Lainey can help Sutton set up her coffee bar in the kitchen for the gender reveal she wants to have ready whenever Deck comes home. She has no idea when that will be, so she wants to get all the little details "just right," as she said, so that as soon as he walks in the door she can share the happy news that they are going to have a daughter. I can't wait to spoil my little niece and was thrilled for them when Sutton shared her happy news.

The doorbell rings and Sutton's squeal of excitement can probably be heard from space. "My ears, Sut," I say, sticking a finger in one and wincing.

"Sooorrry! I am just so excited. That should be Kendra and she has my mug. It is the *most* important part of this whole setup, Rem." She rushes to the door, flinging it open to, in fact, reveal Kendra who encourages more squealing.

Lainey laughs at my pained face and says, "Let her be excited, this is a fun memory she is trying to make extra special for Deck. And Kendra has been working hard, too."

"Yeah, okay," I grumble, leaning on the counter and crossing my arms, waiting for the big mug presentation.

The girls all surround the island with the small box that Kendra has, the star item carefully wrapped in tissue paper tucked inside. Sutton is rubbing her baby bump and practically vibrating with anticipation.

Kendra gently unwraps an oversized cream-colored mug with a sturdy handle. All over it, tiny hearts painted in various shades of pink add a delicate cheerfulness. Turning the mug, the front showcases, in a bold, masculine font, the script that reads "GIRL DAD." I can't help the wide smile that spreads on my face when I see it.

Sutton sucks in a breath, and happy tears swarm her warm, brown eyes. She cradles the mug in her hands like a precious treasure and whispers, "It's perfect."

Lainey and Kendra swipe away their own tears and hold each other in a side hug as they watch Sutton examine each angle of the mug. Lainey looks up at me and I give her a wink, which makes her respond with a watery grin.

"The happiness in this moment is worth the squeals, I guess," I say, breaking the bubble the girls were floating in.

Sutton rolls her eyes at me and says, "Oh, shush! You know this mug is ev-er-y-thing!"

"Kendra's rubbing off on you," I quip.

"Damn straight." Kendra laughs.

The girls are in a fit of giggles when the doorbell rings again.

"Oh! That's probably Mom," Sutton says. "I told her all about this, and that Kendra was planning on dropping off the mug today. She can't wait to see it. She is going to *just die* over the cuteness."

She walks to the front door, mug still cradled in her grip, smiling with delight. We all watch from the open kitchen as she swings the front door wide, but it is *not* my mother that stands on her doorstep.

Two uniformed men are there.

"Good afternoon, we are here to speak to Mrs. Sutton Brooks," the first man, tall, dark, and voice like gravel, states.

"That's me," Sutton says quietly, her hand hovering over her belly. "Please come in." Both men enter, eyes surveying the room and landing back on my sister, focused and somber.

"Ma'am, on behalf of the Secretary of the Navy, I regret to inform you that your husband, Lieutenant Derek Brooks was severely injured early this morning on a mission and was reported dead at nine a.m. I am deeply sorry for your loss."

The heart-covered mug slips from Sutton's hand and shatters around her feet. Her gut-wrenching scream fills the silence that echoed through the house after the officer delivered my sister her worst nightmare. Her body falls to the floor in slow motion, and I can't reach her fast enough. The two uniformed men try and fail to keep her fragile body from landing on the broken ceramic shards. The sobs that wrack Sutton's body have nothing to do with the small cuts pooling with blood. No, she probably can't even feel those wounds as I reach her, and I wrap her in my arms, scoop her up, and bring her to the living room couch.

Her most penetrating wound is gaping open from her very soul, one that won't ever fully heal. How can it? The love of her life, her best friend and the father of her unborn child, their baby girl, is dead.

Derek Brooks, one of my best friends, and the person that always seemed superhuman, would *not* be walking in that door "any day" to the surprise we were happily creating for him moments ago. I look toward the kitchen and see Kendra and Lainey clinging to one another, crying. I want to hold Lainey too, but I can't let go of Sutton. Her cries are so painful and raw. It's a sound I didn't know a human was capable of making and one I wish I didn't know existed, especially coming from a person I love so deeply. I want to carry this pain for her, wipe away the last ten minutes and bring back the happy squeals I was teasing her about. But I don't think that happiness will run through her veins anytime soon, if ever again.

There is another knock at the door. Lainey quickly moves through the kitchen and around the broken mug to answer it. I look over, surprised to see the two men that came to notify us of Derek's death still in the room, having forgotten all about them, as they stand there holding a silent sentry over the scene. I should talk to them, but I don't even know what to say.

Tears pouring down her face, Lainey opens the door to find my mother standing there. Instantly her smile falls when she sees how upset Lainey is and she says, "Oh dear, what's wrong?" with one hand cupping my beautiful woman's cheek and wiping away some of her tears.

"Renee," Lainey whimpers. "It's Derek." She points toward the living room. My mom takes in the space. The men, the mess, her children on the couch. Her hand flies to her chest, then she rushes to us, and my arms around Sutton are replaced with hers. Sutton looks up and sees that our mother is here and starts gasping for air, like she can't get enough.

"Breathe, Sutton. Slow down, baby. Slow. Shhh." My mom calms, rocks, rubs, and soothes her daughter until she is not gulping for air. I want to throw up and run out of the room all at the same time.

Fuck, why is this happening?

I turn around and find Lainey pressed flat against the wall, arms wrapped around herself and shaking. Her eyes are wide and tears are flowing in a steady stream. The men are speaking in hushed tones to my mom as she strokes Sutton's back. I notice that Kendra has found a broom and started to sweep up the broken mug, even while her tears are just as steady as Lainey's.

But at this moment, my attention is on the one person I need in the most visceral way.

I stalk over to her, and we wrap each other in a hug. My face finds her neck, her soft hair bushing her shoulders. The sweet, honey scent of her shampoo fills my senses. She is my safe place and exactly who I need to be with, what I need in this moment of sorrow—and I fucking lose it. Sobs shake me to my core. And my woman just stands there and holds me, letting me fall apart, letting me feel every slice of pain this new reality is wielding.

32

Lainey

Never in my life have I experienced grief consume a room so quickly, so powerfully. One minute we were all laughing and talking about Deck coming home, and the next that possibility was literally shattered. The meaningful mug that was supposed to welcome him back with a special surprise smashed into a thousand jagged pieces and sliced into Sutton's skin when she fell onto it.

After I held Remington for a while, he broke away from me to call his dad. Charles raced over immediately, bursting through the door, red-rimmed eyes hunting for his little girl. She looked so small in his arms when he held her, and a fresh wave of heavy tears flowed from her body. Charles held her, looking up to the sky unable to hold back the stream of his own tears, and murmured lovingly to her.

Renee's presence in the house overwhelmed me. She snapped into a mode that I can only describe as "mother lion," taking charge. Her grief was evident, but she locked in on what needed to be done for her daughter. She asked questions of the men there, took notes, organized plans. I had no idea how she knew what she was doing in this moment when I just felt totally numb and useless. I was in complete awe of her.

The death notification officer and the chaplain he brought with him gave all the necessary information before taking their leave. I have no idea how they do that job and not fall apart themselves at the end of every day.

Kendra had found a first aid kit in the kitchen and was sitting on the floor at Sutton's feet gently cleaning her cuts. There were many, but thankfully none too deep or needing stitches.

"Kendra." Sutton's voice came out a hoarse whisper, and we all look at her, these being her first real words in a long time.

"I'm right here." Kendra grabs Sutton's hand, tears welling.

"The mug, I'm so sorry a-about the mug."

"Oh, Sutton," Kendra chokes out, pulling her into an embrace. "It's okay, the mug, it's only . . . Don't worry about it."

Sutton's whole body shakes, and Kendra looks to me and Remington, who pulls me close to his side. We feel helpless, and I know for him it's even harder to not be able to swoop into a situation where someone is hurting and save them.

Charles walked back into the room and cleared his throat. "I just got off the phone with Derek's father, Sean. He will be flying in tonight from Texas, and I offered for him to stay with us. He was Deck's only other family."

Renee nods her head and says, "That is good, he needs to be here with us. Why don't you go get the house ready for him. I am staying with Sutton. Come back and pick us up in the morning. There are a lot of things we have to do, but today she needs rest . . . for her and the baby."

Charles first kisses Renee, then leans down and whispers something in Sutton's ear. She doesn't move at all, just blinks and stares at the window like she is seeing something we can't. Charles gives Renee a concerned look, but she just shakes her head, and he nods, trusting his wife in their silent communication. He says goodbye to the rest of us and leaves to welcome another person that will need a lot of support into the fold.

The bright sun seemed like a mockery of what was happening today. Shouldn't there be thunderstorms and turmoil? It did not feel appropriate to be sitting here on such a perfect summer day. I hadn't been to many funerals in my life, and I definitely had never gone to a military funeral.

It was heartbreaking.

It was haunting.

It was powerful.

It rooted a panic inside of me that I could not shake no matter what I did.

When they played the song to honor Derek, "Taps" is what Remington told me it was called, it made a shiver crawl up my spine as tears ran down my cheeks. We sat directly behind Sutton in the family section. Deck's father sat on one side of her and Charles and Renee sat on the other. Next to us, two of the members of the SEAL team Deck was a part of sat, stoic, fierce, and sporting various injuries.

Before the funeral I told Remington that I shouldn't be in the family section, so close to the front. He growled at me and said I was going to be at his side where I belonged. I *wanted* to be at his side, I just didn't know what was appropriate and was trying to be respectful. These were uncharted waters for me, and all of my insecurities were surfacing.

Remington squeezes my hand, bringing my attention back

to the chaplain. It isn't the same man that came to the house, which I think is for the best. I'm not sure Sutton wants to see either of those men again. I don't think I would.

The American flag draping the casket stands out amongst the uniforms and sea of black that the people in attendance are wearing. Two sailors step up and methodically, respectfully, and reverently fold the flag. A hush falls over the cemetery, like even the wind and the birds know that this moment is sacred.

Leaning in front of Sutton, one of the sailors speaks to her as he passes the flag over. "On behalf of the President of the United States, the United States Navy, and a grateful nation, please accept this flag as a symbol of our appreciation for your loved one's honorable and faithful service."

Sutton takes the flag, hugging it to her chest, and she finally breaks after staying so strong during the whole service. Her cries run through the cemetery like a river, leaving no one untouched.

One of the SEALS next to us wipes a single tear sliding down his face.

Remington looks at me, and I see his handsome face, blurred through my own tears. He holds my face with his hand, rubbing his thumb along my jawline, and gently presses a kiss to my forehead. What words are appropriate to say when the world is turned upside down?

We hold on to each other, but I feel my fears pulling me apart, pulling me away from Remington, and putting me in a place that is just out of his reach.

33

Remington

It's been almost two months since the funeral. Almost two months since we stood in the cemetery and buried one of the best men I have ever known. My brother-in-law, a best friend, the man my sister was supposed to raise a daughter with. We are all worried about Sutton and the baby. She has been having extra doctor appointments, we take turns staying with her because she refuses to stay anywhere but her and Deck's house, and we just pray that our showing up will be enough to keep her going. I feel so fucking helpless, and it's killing me.

It's also been almost two months since Lainey has changed. She is still my sweet, kind, beautiful woman. But the sunshine, spark, and sass that bubbled under the surface is gone. She is keeping me at an arm's length at all times. I know that she thinks she's doing a good job masking the fact that she is pushing me away, but she isn't.

And I know why she is doing it.

She's scared.

Terrified is probably more accurate.

I like to think that I am a pretty patient man, but my

patience is running out. I have sat by and waited for Lainey to share her feelings with me, to come and tell me about her fears. That hasn't happened. After our trip to the cabin we shattered a wall that was so thick and impenetrable, one I never expected to breach. Our relationship shifted in a way that could not really be put into words. But the shocking death of Deck and everything that's been going on since shifted our focus and has Lainey building a brand-new wall, one that I fully intend on blowing up today. I refuse to allow her to sit in pain and fear alone anymore.

Lainey is curled up in her favorite spot on the couch writing in her journal when I get home. Honestly, I am just happy she is here instead of her apartment. She tried to make excuses to start staying there more often, but I know she sleeps better when she is here. I used to get an enthusiastic greeting anytime I walked in the door—a huge smile, kissing, sometimes even tearing our clothes off. Now, she looks up and gives me a tired half-hearted smile and says, "Hi" softly. I remind myself of the end goal, trying not to let my frustration bubble up before I've even started a conversation I know she is not going to want to have with me.

"Hi, beautiful," I respond with a real smile and forced enthusiasm. I stride over to where she is perched and pull out the flowers I had hidden behind my back. Her sad blue eyes widen in surprise when she sees them, a tiny glimmer flicking in their depths.

There she is.

"What are these for?" she questions.

"Do I ever need an excuse to bring you flowers, Lainey?" I remind her as she stares at them like they might bite her.

Jesus, this wall is thicker than I thought it was.

"They are unnecessary, Remington." She tries to get up, but I don't let her move away from me.

"Oh no, we are not going back to that bullshit again, baby." She sucks in a breath and really looks at me for the first time.

"I don't know what you are talking about."

She is playing a dangerous game.

"I told you a long time ago that I was going to give you any and all flowers I could as often as possible. Unfortunately, I have been slacking on my deliveries, and I'm really sorry about that. Things the past couple of months have been hard on us. I wanted to get these, remind us what our priorities are." I try to take her hand, but she pulls it back.

"Your only priority should be Sutton and the baby, Rem." Her words are like hearing another person speak.

I suck in a sharp breath.

"*Don't* fucking call me that," I say, no longer able to tamp down my anger.

"What?"

"You. Don't. Call. Me. That." I punctuate every word, trying to get my point across.

"Everyone calls you that." Lainey rolls her eyes.

Fucking finally, that sass. I want to kiss the shit out of her sexy, pouty mouth, but I hold off.

"You *never* once have called me that, Lainey. Ever. It's one of the things I love most. That you *full-fucking-name me* all the time. Hell, I realized early on in our relationship that I have a kink for it." Her shocked face is taking me in, pink cheeks heating, and a blue flame in her eyes dancing for the first time in weeks.

"Why?"

"I don't know. For as long as I can remember, everyone shortened my name and called me Rem. Then you came along and used my full name—have *always* used my full name, and you fucking know it, too. So don't you dare sit there and call me 'Rem' acting like you are just anyone else." My breathing is heavy with frustration and lust.

Tears start to swirl in her stormy eyes, and I don't want them to douse the flames that were just there, I want her to fight for us. I refuse to hold back any longer.

"Stop pushing me away, Lainey."

She stands, crossing her arms, trying to protect herself, keep the truth of my words from touching her. "I don't know what you're talking about, *Remington*." She emphasizes my name, as if proving her point.

"Ever since the cemetery." She stiffens at my words, knowing that I know, that I see her better than anyone ever has, ever will. "You think I didn't see it? That I don't see you building new walls and hiding behind your fear?"

"I'm not!" she protests, even as a tear sliding down her cheek betrays her.

I step into her space and grip her chin. "I will not let you do this to yourself, to us. I am right here, Lainey. I'm right here." At my words she falls into my arms and the tears she had been keeping at bay fall freely, soaking my shirt and baptizing me in her fresh waves of pain. "It's okay, baby," I whisper into her hair.

"It's not okay, it's not," she croaks. "It could be you."

"It could be anyone," I counter.

"No, Remington. *You* have a very dangerous job. Deck had a very dangerous job. You literally walk into fires and unpredictable situations constantly. I don't know what to do with that." The fear painted on her face and trembling under my touching is real, powerful.

"My job *is* dangerous, I won't deny that. But I can't walk into it with fear. I have to go in with confidence in my training, my brothers, and myself." I pull up my shirt and point to part of my sleeve tattoo on my inner bicep with the script under the FGFD shield that reads "If not me, then who?" Her breathing stops as she takes in the words.

"Why you?" Lainey whispers, kissing the tattoos softly.

"It's my calling, my life. It's who I am. I can't stand here and promise you that nothing will ever happen. I pray to God it doesn't. But I *refuse* to not live, to not allow myself to love you deeply and fully because of the what-ifs."

She sucks in a surprised breath. "You, you just said . . ."

"I love you, Lainey Quinn. Deeply and fully." I capture her mouth as she gasps, not giving her time to respond. I can't. I need to let the words live in the world for a moment before she has a chance to refute them or deny them. She parts her soft lips, and I deepen the kiss, giving her everything, telling her with my body what I desperately have been locking up for the past few months, trying not to scare her away.

Breathless, Lainey pulls back. She searches my face and says, "I love you, too, Remington. I don't think I even knew what love truly was until you. And I still don't feel like I am worthy to be loved by a man like you."

I cup her soft, tear-stained face in my rough hands and make sure she is looking at me when I say, "There is nobody in this universe more worthy of my love than you. You were made for me, Lainey, in every possible way. My perfect fit, my missing piece. I will spend every day, until my last breath, making sure you know that you are the treasure of my life."

There is no holding back the flood of her emotions that my words unlock within her. Lainey flings herself into my arms and I catch her, hauling her up my body and holding her tight, kissing her neck. Knowing that she has never been loved by her family is painful, but I am her family now. I am her man, her lover, her protector. I will be here and do everything I can to let our love be more powerful than the fears and anxiety that whisper to her in the darkness.

I carry Lainey to our bedroom and lay her gently on the bed. Her tears are spent, and she is looking up at me with relief. She sighs as I kiss my way across her cheeks and bridge of her nose. Contentment and comfort flow through her limbs and she melts into the mattress.

"I love you," I whisper, and she moans at my admission.

"I love you, too."

Slowly, I strip the layers she is wearing off of her perfect body. First her loose band T-shirt that was hanging off one shoulder. It reveals a black lace bra that makes my mouth go slack-jawed at the sight. I have never seen a woman as sexy as Lainey, and she doesn't even have to try. Next, I pull down her yoga pants and discover simple lace panties that match her bra. My dick throbs at the image of my woman laid out before me.

"You are stunning," I tell her as I run my hands over her body. She arches into my touch, and I know she missed our connection, our true connection, as much as I did.

"Please, Remington, I need you."

"You know I can't deny you when you beg, baby." I nip her inner thigh and then rip her panties down her legs in one swift tug.

Lainey gasps, eyes blown wide with lust and wanting. She bites her lip, a lip *I* want to be biting. I lean forward and claim her in a kiss, nipping and licking. I suck her bottom lip into my mouth and grind my erection onto her needy center.

"You are overdressed," Lainey sasses at me, giving me a small push and tugging at my shirt.

I pull it over my head in one fluid motion that makes her

groan in appreciation. I quickly shed the rest of my clothes and hover back over her. Trailing my hand to her pussy I find her already soaked and ready for me. Bringing my finger back to my mouth I suck the needy, rich taste of her arousal off as she watches my every move.

I line myself up, and Lainey grinds into me, desperate for me to fill her, but first I lock my eyes on hers and say, "No more walls, Lainey. Promise me you won't push me away again. We are in this together from now on, okay?"

Her eyes flood with emotion as her small, soft hand finds my face. "I promise," she whispers. "I love you so much, Remington. I'm yours."

"I love you," I say. "I am yours. *You are mine*," I vow as I drive home and claim her body. This feels different. No more walls, no more hiding how I feel, worried it will make her run scared.

Now, we are coming together, binding ourselves with a love that will stand against any storm. The foundation of our relationship is solid, strong, and rooted in soil that has been nourished from the very beginning, the way it was meant to be.

"I feel you everywhere," Lainey groans, pulling me closer and digging her nails into my back. I thrust deeper, hitting the spot that I know makes her see stars and feel her clench me tighter.

"That's it, baby. Don't hold back. Come on your cock." I lick up her neck and kiss the pulse point, nipping behind her ear as she explodes. I can feel her wetness soaking me, and I moan into her sweet, honeyed hair.

"More, more, please," she begs.

"Anything for you." In a swift move I flip us so she is on top, riding me and giving me the best fucking view. Her breasts are trapped in the black lace cups as they bounce up and down, begging to be freed. I reach up, unclasping her bra, and she tosses it to the floor.

Lainey's hands go into her hair, head tipped back, and mouth slightly ajar. I have never seen anything more sexy in my life. She is going to give me a heart attack. I lean up and suck one of her perfect pink nipples into my mouth, and she rolls her hips, moaning in satisfaction.

"Eyes on me, Lainey." She instantly obeys. "Good girl," I growl. "I want you to come all over your cock again, but I want you to watch me fill you while I do it. Watch as you completely unravel your man."

"God, yes." She bites down on that sexy, pouty bottom lip again, and I feel my balls tighten, knowing I am not going to last much longer.

I hold my thumb up to her mouth and she sucks on it, wetting it just like I wanted her to with a resounding pop. Smirking at her, I take my thumb and rub her swollen clit as she rides me, knowing she is seconds away from her next detonation, and I'm pressing exactly the right button.

She flutters her eyes closed. "Eyes," I bark out, unable to say anything else. We lock in on each other another, then both look down to where I am thrusting up into her tight, soaked pussy, and both let go . . . our orgasms illuminating our bodies in shuddering perfection.

Lainey collapses on top of me, her body shaking. Suddenly I realize it's not from the aftershocks of an orgasm but from tears. Worry engulfs my mind as I roll us so I can look at her face.

"Talk to me, baby," I plead, looking at her closed eyes. "Did I hurt you?"

"No, no." She lets go of a watery laugh, which is not what I expected. Looking at me finally she says, "I got a little overwhelmed that's all. It was very intense . . . and I just—"

"Just what?"

"I just love you so much," she admits, a grin lighting up her face in a way I have never seen before. "I am overwhelmed with happiness."

"Love looks really good on you," I tell her. She instantly turns pink and tries to hide her face behind her hands. "Uh-uh, no more hiding, which includes my compliments. When I give them to you, you have to believe they are true." I kiss the blush on her cheek.

"That will be hard, but I'll try." She sticks up a pinky finger and I wrap my own around it, then kiss hers.

"Good."

I pull her into my arms, and again say the words that have long been on my heart before I allowed them to fall from my lips today. "I love you, Lainey."

My eyes are drifting shut when I hear her voice. "Remington?"

"Hmmm."

"You didn't tell me about the flowers." She runs her hand up and down the tattoo inked along my side.

"What flowers?" I ask being lulled by the patterns she is tracing on my skin, knowing we need to clean up and absolutely not wanting to move.

"The ones you brought me today, sleepy."

"Oh, those." I peer at her through one eye, seeing her waiting curiosity. "I brought you a mix of David Austin garden roses. My mom has a whole collection growing in her garden."

"I thought you said roses were too easy or basic," she teases me.

"There is nothing easy or basic about *these.* They are specialty roses. My mom has been tending her rose gardens for years to make them as successful as they are. These are not grocery store roses, which *are* basic and easy to just buy. The ones I brought you today were grown with love and picked with a purpose. My dad plants her a new variety every year on their anniversary. Roses can mean a lot of things to a lot of people, but *these ones*, at least in my family, are legacy flowers."

"Wow. So, definitely *not* basic." Lainey smiles at me and kisses my cheek tenderly.

34

Lainey

A light breeze makes me cold despite the warm day, but I am not ready to go inside yet. I'm standing in the backyard of Remington's parents' house looking at all the roses. Renee's legacy flowers. The sun is setting, dipping the delicate petals in a soft orange glow making it seem like they are embers, burning in the final warmth of the day. Remington was right: These roses are not basic; they are a masterpiece. I should expect nothing less from a master gardener.

The woman herself steps up next to me, laying a soft, light throw blanket around my shoulders along with her warm arm. She places her head next to mine and we stand there in comfortable silence. Never did I think I could have this kind of relationship with someone, but Renee has made it easy to be here and open up to her.

"Saw you shivering out here in your sundress and thought this might help." Renee smiles at me.

"Thanks. I am not sure why I am cold today, but this is perfect. You have such a green thumb," I tell her. "I could spend the whole day out here just staring at all the beauty and never get tired of it. It's like a sanctuary."

"When we started our business it was so busy and all about our clients, the books, and eventually our babies. I needed something for myself, a space that could calm my mind, a space where I felt like I could take a deep breath after a long day or a hard moment in parenting." She leads me over to the cushioned swing that runs along one of the garden paths and we sit together.

"I don't have a physical place like that, but I guess it's kind of what my journals are for me. Sometimes I write my thoughts and other times I will put down things that inspire me. But this whole garden is full of inspiration I would never be able to capture." I laugh. "I guess I would just have to snap a photo and tape it to a page, but I know that still wouldn't do it justice."

"Thank you, honey." She pats my hand and takes a deep lungful of air. Her body sags with the weight of sadness from the past couple of months, blonde hair glowing warmly in the setting sunlight.

"How can I help you?" I ask her.

"Help me?"

"Yes, you, Renee. You have been going nonstop these past weeks. The strength you have for Sutton and the love you pour into your family, I—it's just hard for me to find the words to describe what that looks like from an outsider looking in," I say with a sincerity I hope she can feel.

"Loving my family is my purpose, even on the hardest days and through the darkest seasons. And, Lainey, now that includes you, too. You are *not* an outsider. I don't want you to feel that way here, and if you truly still do then I have not been doing my job very well." Her brown eyes, twins to Sutton's, look at me the way I always wished my own mother's had, with a profound love that comes from a place deep in her soul. Born of goodness, strength, and appreciation for just being here in this moment.

My emotions cannot handle it, it's too much and it feels like my damaged heart has just been split right in half with her words. But instead of being shattered and irreparable, it is like I have been gently scooped up. All the broken parts of myself have been poured into a new vessel through connecting with myself, setting boundaries, loving Remington, and allowing myself to accept his love in return.

What Renee just did was toss it into a blazing hot kiln. All those sharp, broken pieces I was so worried would cut other people if they got too close to me melt away and are shaped into something new, something that fits where and who I am now. Nobody here has once asked me to change or wanted anything performative from me. For the first time in my life they have allowed me space to just be Lainey Quinn and have loved me as I am. And in doing that, I not only feel like I fit here, but within myself as well.

Renee hugs me in her comforting embrace and hushes me. "It's okay, my sweet girl, let it go. Let it out. From the little bit you have shared and what Rem has told me there have not been very many people in your corner. That's just not how it is anymore."

Sitting back and blotting my eyes with a corner of the blanket I admit, "I told him this, but I really don't think I knew what it meant to be loved before Remington. And to have you accept me into your family, it really is overwhelming. I know that when you say it you actually mean it."

"Of course I do!"

"Well, in my family action and words never match up. I learned from a very young age that I was a problem for them, even if I did everything perfectly. Nothing was ever good enough. I thought moving to Fox Grove would make things with my mom better, easier." I look away. "I was never good enough," I whisper, not sure if Renee could hear my confession, or if the wind swept it away over the flowers.

"Lainey, you are more than enough." Renee's choked words have my attention snapping back to her. Tears are running down her face, pain from my honesty. "No parent should ever make their child feel the way that you felt, the way that you still feel."

"I'm sorry. You came out here to enjoy the nice evening, not have me ruin it with more of my tears and trauma." I wave my hand. "I am so tired of crying."

"Don't do that. Don't you brush this under the rug. You're safe here, and we are not going to judge you for having feelings or being a human. In fact we *won't* accept anything less. You asked me what I need?" Swiping her cheeks, she straightens her posture.

"Yes?"

"I need you to always fully be yourself with us, Lainey. You might not have the LeBlanc last name yet"—Renee winks at me when my jaw drops—"but you are a LeBlanc in our hearts already. The sooner you accept that the better."

She smiles at me like she just told me the sky was blue. Like it was a simple, known fact. *You might not have the LeBlanc last name yet.* The chills I have now don't have anything to do with the unseasonably cool breeze in the garden anymore.

Breaking me from the tornado of thoughts and emotions whirling around inside my body, Renee takes my hand, tugging me gently. "Come on, dinner should be ready now. You know how serious my husband is about that darn meat smoker contraption he has been fussing with all day."

We stand and walk back to the house together, and I enjoy the dreamy scene of lightning bugs glowing about the backyard. A few weeks ago Remington's parents insisted that we all start having a weekly family dinner. Sunday was the day that was picked, and even if Remington is working I still come. Renee told me that she hoped it would be a good routine to start and a way to get Sutton out of the house.

Since the funeral she has let her few employees run the store completely. Which according to Remington is very un-Sutton. She likes to have her hands in every decision regarding the store, but understandably her grief has been consuming her. We are all worried about her and the baby. She's lost weight when she is supposed to be gaining, and her doctors had been concerned about preterm labor. Her body is going through so much stress.

We have also been on rotating shifts staying with her. Between her parents, me and Remington, Kendra, and some of her friends there is always someone with her. Three days after the funeral we were there when a package was delivered. Sutton opened it at the kitchen table robotically, saying she had no idea what it could be since she didn't remember ordering anything. When she pulled out a soft, handmade green baby blanket with little white sheep all over it, Sutton looked like she saw a ghost. There was a note from the maker, a woman in England, thanking Deck for the custom order and congratulating them on the baby.

Sutton, after hugging the blanket and crying into Remington's shoulder, explained why the blanket meant so much. Apparently she saw it on an Etsy shop long before they ever got pregnant, told Deck how adorable she thought it was, and that it was her "dream" baby blanket. Sutton had no idea he'd even remembered it, let alone ordered it.

Entering the kitchen Remington immediately tracks my red, puffy eyes and comes over to me. "What's wrong?" he asks, cupping my cheek, tracing that rough, calming thumb along my jawline.

"Everything is fine, Rem." Renee pats his tense shoulders, but he still doesn't relax until I give a small bob of my own head. "We were having some overdue girl time. A little *heart to heart* in the garden, if you will." She winks at me, knowing exactly what her "heart" comment brings to mind, and I feel my cheeks heating.

"I'm good, promise." I kiss his palm. Remington pulls me into a hug, and a low rumble vibrates from his chest and rattles every one of my nerves.

Dipping to whisper to me, he says, "I love it when you blush like that. I can't wait to get you alone later and see if I can make other parts of your skin match." I can feel my blush deepen as he kisses my cheek, walks off to grab a plate for dinner, and leaves me beyond flustered.

As much as I wanted Remington to make good on his dirty promises to me, we didn't go back to his house together. He got called out to a fire on the east side of town. According to the spouse text group there was a massive warehouse fire and all the FGFD guys got called plus the crews from two neighboring towns. The girls said it isn't often for fires this big to happen or for them all to get called at once, but when they do everything is dropped and they answer the call.

Before he left, Remington quickly said goodbye to his parents and Sutton. Then he stalked across the room to me, not caring that we were not alone and kissed me deeply. "I love you, Lainey." His deep voice is as urgent as his kiss.

"I love you, too. Be careful, Remington." I lock my hands on his face, making him pause for a beat to really look at me before he rushes off.

"Always, baby." Kissing one more time, he leaves me standing with his family but takes my heart out the door with him.

I hear a sigh behind me and turn to see Charles and

Renee hugging. I know that it must be hard for them to watch their son run into danger. Sutton is sitting on the couch, staring off into space, biting her bottom lip. I go sit next to her and wonder if I can offer any comfort to her worried mind.

"She doesn't have a crib," Sutton says, her hand resting on her large belly. "He was going to build her crib when he got home. It's in her room, in the box. I can't even go in there. She is going to be here so soon. I am thirty-seven weeks. How am I going to be her mother when I can't even go in her room, Lainey?"

"Maybe we can go in together?" I offer.

Sutton nods and closes her eyes as if she is willing her grief to stay locked inside herself.

"I know it's not the same. It can't be, but we are here for you. We can make her room comfortable and special. Add some touches that will honor Deck if you want to?"

"We hadn't settled on a theme or anything like that for decorating. I wanted to wait until we knew if we were having a boy or a girl. But now . . . I think we should base it off of the blanket. What do you think?" Sutton looks at me, and the first small glimmer of something that resembles happiness or hope is lingering just beneath the surface.

Taking her hand I say, "I think that is *exactly* what her nursery should be. It's like Deck picked it himself. He knew what you loved and gave you that gift."

Renee walks over, having been listening to our conversation and bends over the back of the couch wrapping us both in a hug. "I think this baby nursery should be our special project for us to do together! A girls' project for our new little girl in the family."

"Okay," Sutton agrees. This is the most she has talked about anything regarding the baby or plans for the future. I, for one, am going to grab on with both hands and try to make this room perfect for the baby, of course, but for Sutton, too. I don't want her to walk in and feel sad. I want her to go into that room and have it feel like it's her sanctuary, like Renee's garden.

"What if we did a mural on one of the walls?" I brainstorm aloud. "We could make it look like a beautiful meadow with wildflowers, and even paint a few of the fluffy sheep to match the blanket?"

Sutton's actually getting excited at the idea, and Renee gives me a look, one that says she is proud of me for being right where I am supposed to be.

"I am not sure how we can find someone to paint a mural like that," I say, grabbing my phone so I can start a list of things to do for the room. "But maybe we can research someone local and get some pricing estimates? I can ask Kendra too, she knows lots of artists. Oh, Sutton, do you have any store connections, or an artist you know of?"

The two women share a quick look that I don't really understand—it must be some kind mother-daughter thing. Sutton says, "Actually I think I know the perfect person. Let me take care of that part, Lainey. I'll see what their availability is."

"Great!" Renee exclaims. "Charles! Bring the girls some snacks, we have planning to do for our granddaughter." Her smile is bright and contagious.

I look over at Sutton and I see that for the first time since we were all laughing in her kitchen, looking at Kendra's mug before that doorbell rang, Sutton has a real smile on her face.

35

Remington

The fire was a monster, and it took three crews and the entire night to get it under control and put out. Thank fuck there were no injuries, and the place was abandoned to begin with. That building has sat there for a long time taking up space and rotting. Nobody would buy it or fix it up. It was an obvious case of arson that started the fire. Gas cans and evident fuel trails led up to the building. The whole thing was sloppy and screamed amateur. Unfortunately, because the warehouse was not being used there were no active security cameras anywhere on the property.

Pulling into my driveway, all I could think about was another hot shower and crawling into bed with Lainey. She was probably ready to get up and start the workday, but maybe I could convince her to sleep in late. Wrapping her in my arms and smelling her honey shampoo was exactly what I needed right now.

The house was still mostly dark when I walked in, which I wasn't expecting. I figured she'd be in the kitchen making her cup of tea before needing to start getting ready for her workday. "Lainey?" I call out and then listen, thinking that maybe she's in the shower. Walking toward the bedroom I hear a weird noise, but it isn't the shower.

My poor woman is white as a sheet, sweaty hair pulled half back in one of her little claw clips, and she's on the floor, gripping the toilet like her life depends on it. Just as I fully push the door open, she pukes into the basin, her body shaking with the force of it even though not much comes out.

Realizing I am there when I smooth a hand down her damp back, Lainey startles. Looking at me with sick, glassy eyes she says, "Remington. Please . . . Go." Her voice is like sandpaper, making me wonder how long she had been at this.

"Baby, I am not leaving you like this. How long have you been sick?" I touch her forehead, and her skin feels like a scorching flame on my hand.

Sitting back against the tub she tells me, "I got back around nine last night. Your dad dropped me off since you had to take the truck. I got ready for bed but didn't feel good, so I went and laid down. Then I guess I started puking around midnight? Why, what time is it now?" She closes her eyes, utterly exhausted.

"Jesus, Lainey, it's seven. You have been in here alone, puking for seven hours?!" The frustration I feel is not for her, it's because I wasn't here, couldn't be here. *But I'm here now.*

"I wasn't puking the *whole* time." She points to a little nest of mismatched towels next to her that I hadn't noticed before. "When I wasn't expelling the devil from my stomach, I was laying down."

Filling a glass with cool water, I hand it to her so she can rinse her mouth. Then I go to my medicine cabinet and get the thermometer to take her temperature. 102.6. I hum and look at her again.

"Okay, let's take a quick shower together and then you need to rest—in bed, not your little squirrel nest you have going on in here. I am not sure you have anything left in your body to puke. We can put a pot next to the bed just in case."

"Mmmmkkay." Her head is bobbing to the side, and I know she is fading. I turn on the shower, strip out of my own clothes, and then help Lainey undress as gently as I can. The shower feels so good on my aching muscles, and I wish I could stay in here longer, but I need to get Lainey to bed. Washing her quickly and keeping her weak body upright is a challenge, but I loop her arms around my neck and we get the job done.

Wrapping her in a towel, I scoop Lainey into my arms and set her on the bed. "Thank you, it feels nice to be clean after all of that." She is watching me dry off and pull on my gym shorts. Even fevered and sick, she is still looking at me with hunger in her glassy eyes.

"None of that, Ms. Quinn. You are not in any state for me to make good on my promises from yesterday."

A wild giggle leaves Lainey's mouth that she tries to cover. "What's so funny?" I ask her as I bring out her brush and blow-dryer, knowing that she hates sleeping with wet hair.

"Oh, nothing, it's something your mom said yesterday." She sighs, smiling and looking into space like she's reliving the conversation.

"Care to share with the class?" I run my fingers through her hair, eliciting a moan from her lips that makes my cock come to life.

Not now, asshole, she's sick.

"Nope." Lainey pops the *p* sound and smiles up at me. If she wasn't so sick I'd spank her perfect ass and start something she couldn't resist. By the end of it I'm sure she'd tell me what made her giggle and give her that dreamy look.

After I finish drying her hair very carefully, having never done it before, I tuck Lainey into bed. When I bring her a large pot and put it on the nightstand she looks from it to me.

"Why a pot? Why not a bowl or trash can?" she asks out of genuine curiosity.

"It's what my mom always did when we were little. And this pot has two handles to hold on to when you're puking. Better grip than a slippery bowl. Less chance you spill on yourself."

"That's nice," Lainey says, sinking into her pillow, "and gross."

Laughing, I tell her, "Yeah, it is." I climb into bed and pull her into my arms, finally getting what I was thinking about all damn night.

"I don't want you to get sick." She's trying to pull away from me, but I won't let her.

"Doesn't matter. I need this, baby. If I get sick, I get sick." I kiss her hot temple, and she sighs. I can feel her gearing up to argue, so I say, "I hate that you were here and so miserable all alone. Please just let me take care of you now, okay?"

"Yes, sir," Lainey says, knowing exactly what that does to me.

"Sleep," I rumble, tightening my arms and letting my own exhaustion pull me under.

36

Lainey

The last thing I wanted was for Remington to see me sick like that. Thankfully by the time he had gotten home most of the puking was over. Being alone when I was sick was something that I was used to. Making my "squirrel nest," as Remington called it, was just another way that I made sure I was less of a burden when I was little, and it carried over to adulthood.

The flu or any other illness when I was a kid didn't mean Popsicles, snuggles, cartoons, and my mom staying close reading me books. I was sequestered away with my germs, checked on occasionally, and sanitized once I was better. How dare I get sick and have the audacity to bring it into the house and inconvenience everyone?

Remington's loving compassion and concern was overwhelming and unexpected. Letting someone in, letting someone take care of me, especially in moments of vulnerability, is almost impossible for me. In the past there were always strings attached that bound me tightly in guilt. This man doesn't make me feel any of that, only loved.

When I woke up I felt much better, and my fever had broken. Remington was still fast asleep, his strong, muscular body relaxed and hopefully not being rampaged by my invisible germs. Sliding out of bed as quietly as I could, I hurriedly brush my teeth, do my morning skin care, and rub the crimp in my neck from laying on the bathroom floor and all the hurling. I pull on my soft, knee-length, cotton robe covered in wildflowers—a gift from Remington. He told me it was another way he found to give me more flowers, and these ones wouldn't wilt. I love it so much.

Even though it's late in the day, I decide to make us breakfast for dinner. I know that my stomach needs something plain after the war it waged. My burning throat is a reminder of the awful night, and I slowly drink a cool glass of water, praying it won't make a reappearance. When I feel no nausea and less dizzy, relief takes over. I move about the kitchen making pancakes, scrambled eggs, and start the kettle for a cup of soothing ginger tea.

Strong arms gently wrap around my stomach and warm lips kiss the side of my neck as I flip my second batch of pancakes. "Mmmm," Remington hums into my neck. "I take this as a good sign? You feeling better, baby?"

"Much," I sigh with ease. Spinning around, I look over his handsome face with concern. "How are *you* feeling?"

"I feel great. Sleep next to you was exactly what I needed. And don't worry, so far I don't feel sick. Hopefully, I won't get it." He grips the back of my neck and pulls me into a claiming kiss, obviously not caring at all about the chance of lingering germs.

It's easy to get lost in him when his hands and mouth are on me. Hot desire pools low in my gut, and I rub my thighs together, feeling needy. Just as he is pressing his growing erection into me I smell the burning.

"Shit!" I jump away from him and quickly snatch my pancakes off of the smoking griddle. The would-be golden circles are the color of charcoal and ruined, but I can admit the kiss was worth it. Remington opens up the kitchen windows to let in fresh air and clear out the burnt pancake smell.

"Sorry." His alluring smirk tells me he's about as sorry as I am. Cleaning off the griddle, I start a new batch and sip my tea.

"I'm glad you're feeling better," Remington says. "I was so upset thinking about you here all alone and so sick. You should have called me or even my mom. Someone should've been with you."

"Remington," I sigh, knowing he won't like this. "Taking care of myself, even sick, is something I have been doing since I was a little girl. This morning was the first time, ever, someone has truly *cared* for me like that when I was ill."

The ripple of anger is unmistakable, but it is never aimed at me. It's the same one that runs through Remington's body any time I tell him something unsettling from my past. I can tell he wishes he could time travel and beat the crap out of my demons, erase the option of my pain before it was ever able to touch me. I love him even more for wanting to protect the little girl I used to be, and it's helping heal what parts of her are left in my soul.

"I'm so sorry, baby. That's unfair, and it rips my heart out knowing you didn't get the care you deserved. But that is *not* how it is going to be now. We're a team. We have each other. We also have my family. So when I'm on shift and can't be here, promise you will call them for help? My mom will be so upset knowing you were sick. Even if she didn't come over, she still should have known you weren't well to be able to check in on you with a call or text."

I plate up our breakfasts and set them on the island. Hopping up on one of the stools, I look at Remington who's still waiting, arms crossed. *Stubborn man.* "Asking for help is not easy for me, but I promise I will try and be better about it. Just be patient with me, okay? It's a big adjustment."

"Fair enough."

We eat our food in comfortable silence for a while. I take small bites making sure my stomach is able to handle the real food. When about half my plate is gone I feel worn out and ready to rest again. Even though I feel better, being so sick has drained me. Thankfully, I thought to call out of work last night when I wasn't feeling well so I could rest and recover all day today.

"Speaking of adjustments." Remington clears his throat and looks at me. My heart rate and anxiety automatically take off. He must read it on my face because he quickly reaches out, cups my face, and rubs my jaw. I melt into his touch and he kisses me softly. "This is a good adjustment, deep breath."

I do as he says, closing my eyes, and breathing in his cedar and fresh soap scent.

"Eyes, Lainey." His voice is a deep, sexy command that has me connecting my gaze to his immediately. "I want you to officially move in with me." His smile as he says those words takes my breath away.

"W-what?" I stammer, and my mind tries to catch up. "You don't think it's too soon?"

"Baby," Remington chuckles, "you basically already live here anyways. You only go back to the apartment when you need to pick something up. I think we should just call it what it is. Let's make it official. Lainey Quinn, will you please move in with me?"

I can't help the whoop of joy that fills my lungs as I throw myself into Remington's lap—good thing he's a big, strong firefighter and can catch me, keeping his balance. "Yes, yes! I will officially move in with you."

Our smiles reflect the happiness we feel, and nothing has felt more right than being with the man I love, in our home.

Maybe soon I can tell him about the other things I have always wanted but never thought were possible.

37

Lainey

Jess, Kendra, and I are dancing around my apartment as they help me pack up what belongings I still have left here. Sutton is on the couch, resting with her feet up and playing DJ. I was so happy when she said she would come hang out with us. Ever since the night we decided on a nursery theme and started putting things in motion, there have been glimmers of my friend emerging from the depths of her grief. I can't even imagine how heavy it feels to carry it around every day, but I know that she is working through a lot. She told me the other day that Deck would want her to be strong for not only their baby girl, but herself, too. Getting out of the house is hard for her, but the more she does it the lighter she seems.

"Rem's birthday is right around the corner, do you have anything fun planned?" Sutton asks me as a song fades out.

"Actually! I wanted to ask if you girls would help me plan something for him? I was thinking of having a housewarming party for us moving in together but actually making it a surprise birthday party for him. What do you think?" I fuss with the box that I am packing, wondering if I can make his party special enough without a ton of time to plan. His birthday gift I had picked out was already in the works weeks ago, but I also wanted to do this for him.

Jess claps her hands. "Yes! Oh my lord, that man *never* lets us do anything for his birthday. The most the guys have ever done is grab a beer. This is going to be so fun."

"I can't wait to see his face when we pull a fast one on him." Sutton grins, genuinely grins, at me.

"Please, please, please, plllllease let me be in charge of planning for you?" Kendra's little body is buzzing with the idea of doing her favorite hobbies of bossing and organizing.

Laughing, I give in without much of a fight. "That would actually be great, thank you. This way my anxiety over Remington finding out too easily from hearing me making calls or seeing things around the house will be reduced significantly." I mockingly wipe sweat off my brow.

Jess helpfully says, "I will take care of the fire crew and rallying all the troops. Obviously the people on shift won't be able to come, but they are all used to that kind of thing. Nobody will be upset about it. And the girls can still come even if some of the guys are working."

"He does so much for me and for everyone else. I really want to make his thirtieth birthday something he will always remember."

"Do you want me to order a cake?" Sutton asks.

"No, I think I have his dessert covered."

"Eww, Lainey! TMI!" Sutton blocks her ears with her hands dramatically while Jess and Kendra cackle.

"OhmyGOD! *Sutton!* That's NOT what I meant." I can feel my cheeks flaming. "I just meant that I was planning on *making dessert* for the party. I want to make my apple pie."

"Thank you, Jesus." Sutton is now folding her hands in prayer and looking up at the ceiling. I toss a decorative pillow at her and she giggles.

"I know that Matt will be happy about the pie. I heard all about the one you dropped off that time at the fire station, and how Remington refused to share it," Jess tells the girls, and I smile remembering that day, that pie, and that first kiss that changed my entire life.

"He tried his best not to let anyone get that pie, but Eli managed to steal a bite." I laugh.

"Ugh, *of course he did*," Kendra huffs under her breath.

Smiling at her phone, Sutton hits a new song and says, "Get ready for this one, girls!" We collectively look at her wiggling her phone toward us, then all cheer and abandon packing when Ed Sheeran starts to sing "Shivers." Kendra grabs Jess, comically trying to spin a much taller Jess in her arms, and they swerve around the boxes nearly tripping, making us laugh even harder. I never knew female friendships could be so sincere or so fun. Moments like this make me eternally grateful for these women.

A knock at my door has me dancing over more boxes and swinging it wide to find the grinning faces of three very handsome firefighters. Remington, Matt, and Eli are here to help.

Remington pulls me into his arms and kisses me as they all crowd into my apartment. It suddenly feels very small in here with these massive men, all the boxes, and my friends squeezed together. I also realize that I probably opened my apartment door for Remington for one of the last times. It's a bittersweet thought, but also one that makes me so excited for our next chapter—one that we are writing together.

"Sounds like a party in here, ladies," Eli says as he bends to kiss Sutton on the cheek.

"Hang on!" she exclaims. "I have one for you guys." Sutton is trying to hold back a slightly maniacal grin as she types. Seconds later she turns up the volume and Nelly's "Hot in Herre" is overwhelming the limited space.

"Oh, hell yeahhh, you know this is our song, Sut." Eli

enthusiastically starts dancing and gyrating his hips. Before the chorus hits, he is on my coffee table, stripping off his shirt and whips it across the room. Kendra yelps as it hits her in the face and tosses a scowl back up at Eli. The rest of us are not even dancing, we are all stuck in a trance watching our own personal Eli–Magic Mike moment and cracking up.

Remington wraps his arms around me from behind, and my whole body vibrates with his laughter watching his best friend's wild antics. The best view in the room, however, is not Eli's ripped body, as impressive as it is. Nope, it's Sutton. Head thrown back, hand on her large belly, and laughing so hard there is a happy tear trailing down her face.

This right here is the power and freedom in a family you choose for yourself. It's a place to feel safety, comfort, and allows you to ride out your highs and lows. I hug Remington's arms tighter around my middle and sigh when he softly kisses the top of my head.

I might be moving into his house today, but I know that *Remington* is truly my home.

38

Remington

I am finally so close to finishing Lainey's journal. Every shift I have at the fire station I pull it out and work on it when we have downtime. The guys have all gotten used to seeing me with my drawing stuff and are respectful about giving me space and privacy, not lingering over my shoulder. I appreciate them not razzing me about this and also not trying to peek at what I'm doing. If I was drawing for myself that would be one thing, but this is Lainey's, and it is staying just between us.

Flipping to the next page, I frown at what I see. There is a quote, which the journal has a lot of. Song lyrics are also common, and once in a while she will write a thought about her day or something random.

> *"When you realize you want to spend the rest of your life with somebody, you want the rest of your life to start as soon as possible."*
>
> *Nobody will ever love me like Harry Burns . . . I am always given empty promises and not*

worth sticking around for. No relationship I have ever been in has made me think a forever was actually possible. I can't even write down my biggest dream here, probably will jinx myself even though I don't see it coming true anyways.

Things feel off with Brett lately, so there is no way I would ever tell him what I really want. Maybe things will get better after my birthday. New year, new possibilities? Maybe?

Things *definitely* changed after her birthday, that's for sure. That idiot ruined his chance with the most perfect person on the planet, and I got to meet the woman of my dreams.

Lainey is wrong, however. *I* want a forever with her and have known it for a long time. I hope she knows that she can trust me, that I love her unconditionally, and that I am not going anywhere. Having her move in with me and officially being able to call my house *our house* is great. We're even having a housewarming party tomorrow, the day before my own birthday.

Reading over what she wrote again makes me wonder what dream she was talking about. What is she afraid to even write down in her most sacred space? I want to give her the world, including the confidence in our relationship to know that no matter what her dreams are I will love and support her through them all.

Knowing this is the last page in the journal and I will be able to give it to her soon, I can see exactly what I want the final drawing to be. Hopefully I can finish it before we get a call or I need to get some sleep.

The housewarming party is *not* in fact a housewarming party. My sneaky woman pulled off the ultimate surprise along with the help of my sister, Jess, and Kendra and threw me a birthday party. I have never been big on my birthday. Cora always made me feel like I should not be excited about my own birthday, but of course made a huge deal out of her own. It very much sucked all the fun out of my own day, so I gave up on it a long time ago. At most I would grab a beer with some of the guys, but this? It was incredible.

All of our friends—minus the guys on shift—my parents, sister, and Lainey yelled "Surprise!" to me as I walked back in the door from an urgent grocery run that Lainey sent me on for some last-minute things for the simple housewarming party she planned to have "for us" with just a few friends. I have no idea how they got everyone here and things set up so fast; I was gone less than half an hour.

Wrapping Lainey in a tight hug, I growl into her neck. "Baby, this is unreal. How the hell did you pull this off? I was just here!"

"Kendra was party planner extraordinaire. She loves to be bossy, you know." I laugh and nod my head, because yeah, I do know. "And Jess organized all the fire crew. Then we coordinated the decoy grocery run so we could get everyone here. Your mom had all the birthday decorations stashed and ready for me, so everyone helped set up super fast." Her happy smile as she finishes telling me the behind-the-scenes details makes me feel a warmth spreading in my chest.

"I love you so damn much." I kiss her, deeply and much

more thoroughly than I should in a room full of people, but it's our house and I frankly don't give a fuck.

Whoops and whistles sound out around us. Lainey pulls back from our kiss, a deep blush staining her cheeks, and she buries her face into my chest.

I cup her face and say, "Hey, Lainey?"

"Yes, Remington?"

"You know that song about it being your birthday party?"

Nodding with a frown she asks, "Do you want to cry?"

"Nope," I say with a playful smirk and tug her closer so she can feel the hardness behind my zipper. "But it *is* my party, so I'm gonna kiss you if I want to. Is that alright with you?"

I can feel her practically melt against me as she hums her consent and kisses me again, laughing behind our lips at the whoops that continue to follow.

"Are you ready for your gift?" she asks me with a shy smile.

"You are the only gift I need, baby." I plant a kiss right under her ear, making her moan.

"As sweet as that is, I think that you are really going to like what I got for you—I hope." Now she's nervous, and I don't want her second-guessing herself.

"Lainey, you know me better than anyone, so I am sure you picked me out the perfect thing." I tuck a dark lock of her hair behind her ear.

"Eli!" Lainey shouts. Our friends move out of his way as he comes down the hallway, emerging from the spare bedroom.

Holy shit. She did not.

"Happy birthday, Remington." Lainey grins as Eli takes up a place next to her and hands me the cutest puppy I have ever seen.

Black and brown fur, so soft and fluffy, fills my callused

hands. Little dark eyes, so deep brown they are almost black, look up at me and my heart soars. A pink tongue drops out of the puppy's mouth to the side making it look adorably goofy. I hug him to my chest, looking to Lainey who has watery eyes.

"He is ten weeks old. A German shepherd, black lab mix. Eli helped me find him at a special rescue place that's between Richmond and Norfolk . . ." She gives Eli a side hug in thanks as he grins down at her with brotherly affection, wrapping her tightly in his arms. Giving her more of that family connection that she so deserves.

"Lainey," my voice is rough with so many emotions, "thank you, baby. He is perfect. I love you so much. I have always wanted a dog. This is not what I was expecting at all." The puppy licks my cheek, making us and everyone around watching laugh.

"Well, I figured that this was a perfect time to make that dream come true for you with me moving in. I work from home and can take care of him when you're at the station without you needing to worry. Plus, he can keep me company when you aren't home. Be my guard dog."

I pull her into a hug, the puppy wiggling between us, making her giggle. She pets his soft head gently, kisses me, and asks, "What should we name him?"

A couple hours later I make my way outside after mingling and showing off our new puppy, Ash. I spent a lot of time eating from the spread of great food the girls had planned and enjoying having a house full of the people that I love. Locating Sutton sitting with Eli on comfortable, cushioned chairs under the shaded oak trees in the backyard, I grin and sit in the empty spot next to her.

"I really hope that one of those is for me." Sutton eyeballs the two plates of Lainey's apple pie, licking her lips. I was so shocked and elated that she made me her pie instead of cake. It is also a big deal that she made extra and is allowing other people to try it. They are unsurprisingly all drooling over how delicious it is. I decided in this moment that I want this every year—the pie, not necessarily the party.

"Yes, big sis, this is special pie for you." I hand over the plate a little reluctantly, and Sutton tugs it from my hand.

"Hey! Where's my pie?" Eli protests.

"It's my birthday, why should I be serving you? Go get some yourself. You have big boy legs."

"No fighting, ugh." Sutton grabs at her side and shifts uncomfortably. "And, Rem, need I remind you not to call your nine-month pregnant whale of a sister big?"

"You are *not* a whale, you are the prettiest pregnant lady I have ever seen." Eli stands and kisses Sutton's cheek. "Need anything else while I go get my pie?" he asks her.

"Y-yeah. UH. Sorry, my back must be bothering me from sitting in this chair for too long, and I am cramping up again. Do you guys mind if we move inside so I can sit on the couch and put my feet up? It's also getting too hot out here."

"Sure thing." Eli takes our plates and I help Sutton stand, her blue dress flowing over the swell of her very pregnant belly. Sweat beads at the brow of her blonde hair that she has in a braid, pulled away from her face. The late August sun is hot, even as it's setting.

When we start walking up to the steps of the porch, Sutton grips my hand hard and stops walking. Her eyes lock on mine. The soft brown orbs go wide with worry. "Oh, shit," Sutton whimpers.

"What's wrong?" I ask, and Eli steps toward us. Everyone else outside takes notice that something is going on, too.

"I think my water just broke," she whispers, looking up at me, her eyes now swimming with tears.

"It's okay, Sut. How long has your back really been bugging you? Have you been feeling cramps?" I ask.

She whooshes out a contemplative breath. "I don't know, all morning, all night. I am uncomfortable all over, all the freaking time. I figured it was just the next level of pregnancy torture, not the start of labor. Not like I've got anything to compare it to, Rem!" Her voice goes up, panicked with her wave of emotions.

"You got this. We're here for you," I try and reassure her. "Eli . . ."

"Yup! On it." He runs up the steps and into the house.

Seconds later my parents, Lainey, Kendra, and Jess surround us.

"I don't even have my bag here. I was supposed to have more time," Sutton says. "Ohmygod, Lainey! Her room, we didn't finish her room. Now she is going to hate me."

Lainey steps up, places her hands on Sutton's shoulders, and says, "Sutton Brooks, you listen to me. You are already the strongest mom I know. We *will* get her room ready, I promise. The only thing we have left to do is her mural wall and organizing some things. But right now, let's focus on getting you to the hospital."

Jess says, "Matt and I will go get your bags and whatever else you need, yeah?"

Sutton nods and squeezes my hand through another contraction. All our friends at the party wish us luck and congratulations as we head out. My dad stays back to lock up the house and promises to be right behind us once everyone has left. Adrian Garcia offers to puppy-sit Ash for the night. I feel bad leaving the little guy already but am thankful for our people stepping up as always to help.

I drive carefully and quickly to the hospital, Lainey in the front seat next to me and my mom in the back with Sutton. This is not how I thought my party would end, but I am excited to be an uncle and have this sweet baby bringing joy and light into Sutton's new darkened world.

39

Lainey

"Don't leave me, please!" Sutton grabs my hand with so much strength I will probably have bruising.

"I'm not going to leave the hospital, Sutton. Remington and I are going to be here the whole time in the waiting room, okay?" I rub the back of her hand hoping she will ease up a bit.

"*NO!*" She tugs on me, pulling me down closer to her seated position in the wheelchair we got her into when we made it to the county hospital. "I really want you to be in the room with me, Lainey. *Please.* I want you and Mom there. I need you with me."

"Of course I will stay with you, if you're sure that's what you want. It's kind of a big deal." My anxiety wraps around my chest in a way it hasn't in a while, that voice whispering doubts.

Why would she want me in such a sacred space with her and Renee?

"Lainey, you are my person. Practically my sister. I can't do this without you." Her eyes are mixed with so many emotions. I could never deny her request, and knowing that she sees me as an essential part of her life, her family, means everything to me.

Kissing the back of her hand, I say, "Okay, let's do this. I will be right back. I'm just going to update Remington." Bobbing her head, she finally relinquishes my hand and I shake it out as I go to the man I love. He is pacing nervously but stops when I walk up to him.

"Hi." He blows out a breath.

"Soooo . . . Sutton wants *me* in the delivery room with her," I tell him, biting my lip.

"I'm not surprised. She will have the best birth team in there with you and my mom," he says, running a strong, relaxed hand down my face and along my jawline.

"*Remington*, I don't know how to do this," I panic-whisper.

"It's not about knowing how to do it, baby. All you need to do is be the loving, amazing, supportive woman you always are. My sister loves you and she needs you because of who you are to her, not because she thinks you are going to catch the baby." Pulling me into a hug, he adds, "You are going to crush this."

I can't help but smile up at him after his confident pep talk. "Thank you. I am sorry I won't be with you, but I will update you as soon as I can." Kissing him one last time, I rush off to join Renee and Sutton as the staff get her checked in.

"It's after midnight. I'm so freaking tired. I feel like I need to push, please," Sutton begs the doctor that is checking her cervix again.

"Good news, Sutton. You are fully dilated. Let's get ready

to welcome your daughter to the world, alright?" Dr. Barrett says cheerfully behind her mask.

Renee pats Sutton's forehead with a cool cloth on one side of the bed and I stand on the other—sacrificing my hand again. I don't think it will ever be the same shape after today. Refusing any medication, Sutton has been at this for hours and is beyond exhausted. I hope for her sake it doesn't take long to push out the baby.

As the team gets into place, Sutton suddenly goes still. Renee and I look at each other. All the monitors are beeping at the same rate, but something happened.

Sutton's chin quivers, tears start to run rivers down her cheeks, and a guttural sob shakes her, choking her as she pulls in a breath. "He should be here. He-he-he was supposed to be here. We were supposed to be doing this together."

The whole room stills as her words destroy us. I look to the ceiling, trying to slow my own tears and be strong for Sutton. When I look around the room even the nurses are wiping away tears. Dr. Barrett is set up at the bottom of the bed, but time seems to have frozen.

Renee shifts, looking at her daughter. Taking her hand, she grabs on to Sutton's and she places it over Sutton's heart. "Sweetheart, he is here. *Right here*. Always. And in a few moments, when your daughter takes her first breath, when they lay her on your chest, she will hear your heartbeat. It is yours, but it also holds Derek and all the love you have for him, too. And that beautiful baby girl, she is a part of him, too, Sutton. She is part of both of you. A living, breathing representation of the profound love you have for each other. There is nothing more beautiful than that." Hugging Sutton as she sobs, Renee looks at me and sweeps away her own tears, too.

"It's time, Sutton," Dr. Barrett says gently. "You can do this."

Sutton takes a deep breath, resolve strong on her face, and she bears down. Pushing, breathing, and letting her tears of grief, sadness, and the extreme emotion of this moment flow.

Sutton is a pillar of strength.

An hour later she is *still* pushing, and we are all getting a bit anxious.

"She is right here, Sutton, right here," Renee says as cheerfully as possible.

"If she is *right here*, then why the hell isn't she coming out!" Sutton snaps.

"Sutton, focus." Dr. Barrett pulls her attention downward. "Give me one more good one, come on, girl, you got this." I can see the smile in her eyes even though she is wearing a mask.

"You can do it, Sutton. I can see her, push." I have no idea if what I am saying is helping, but Sutton squeezes the shit out of my hand and pushes. We all let out a collective cry of joy and relief as her baby girl finally slips into this side of the world, her small, piercing cry the best sound I have ever heard.

They place Sutton's daughter skin-to-skin on her chest, right over her heart. She runs her hand up and down her tiny back and whispers, "Happy birthday, Kinsley. Daddy and I love you so much."

40

Remington

Kinsley Renee Brooks. Six pounds eight ounces. Twenty-one inches long. And the sweetest, most precious birthday gift I have ever gotten in my entire life. Looking down at my perfect niece, wrapped in her special sheep blanket, I am in awe. She is so little. Her wisps of blonde hair are so soft. The pucker of her lips and the shape of her nose are identical to Deck.

Fuck, I miss him. I hold Kinsley a little tighter and wish this day was different for her and for Sutton. I can't even imagine how hard it is for my sister. She has a perfect baby girl, but the man she loves is not here. Looking down at my niece I make a vow to her and to Deck to always be here for her and protect her. I can't be her dad, but I can still be a positive male figure in her life.

After I dropped off Lainey at home so she could rest, I pick up Eli because I have a mission to accomplish quickly, and I need his help. We hit the hardware store for the supplies that I have on my list and head over to Sutton's house. We let ourselves in with my spare key, haul everything up to the nursery, and I see the room for the first time.

The white crib is pushed up against a plain white wall, waiting for me to hopefully create something special for Kinsley. The rest of the walls are a very soft, blush pink. My mom and Lainey painted them last week. They also have boxes of supplies and decorations they ordered waiting to be put up, a bookshelf, and a rocking chair that needs to be unboxed and assembled. Eli is going to tackle those things while I start on the mural.

"Does Lainey know that you are doing this?" Eli asks me as he takes in the space.

"Nope."

"Won't she ask questions after she comes over when you bring Sutton home and the room is done?" He side-eyes me, like keeping my secret will be impossible after today.

"I am just going to tell her that Sutton talked to her friend and asked me to let them in to do the work. Sutton knows that I want the journal to be a surprise and not to tell her about it. I had to explain it to Sutton about the drawings I was doing so she wouldn't let it slip. Same for my parents. They want to make sure it's special for Lainey, so they won't tell her before I do. My family, like you, knows my art is private, but I wanted to cover my bases, ya know?" I shrug.

"Yeah, well, girls talk. And *those girls* are as close as you can get, so it's not far off to think that some secrets might slip out," he says nervously. Clapping me on the shoulder he moves over to the pile of boxes, pulls out a pocketknife, slices open the package on top, and he says, "What the hell! I thought this was all decorations and shit, man." He groans as he holds up nipple cream and some kind of padding for a nursing bra.

Cracking up I say, "I don't know what's in all that. I am sure it is a minefield of baby supplies. Sutton and Lainey have been ordering things, plus friends and family that were not able to come to her baby shower have also sent her stuff. She was not really in a headspace to be able to open them all."

Eli's smile falls. "I'm so sorry. I still can't believe he's not here. It feels like it happened yesterday and years ago all at the same time."

"I know what you mean. Time feels totally off balance ever since Deck died. But it made me realize I don't want to waste it, that's for sure." I finish setting up my supplies and slide the crib away from the wall. The girls' plan is for a field of wildflowers and sheep to match the blanket that Deck sent playing out across the blank wall. Strokes and lines start dancing in my mind. My fingers are twitching and ready to get to work. I pick up my brushes.

"That's why you officially moved Lainey into your house?" Eli asks, breaking my concentration.

"It was part of it, yeah. But I want more. I want everything with her, Eli. I love her." I look at him, wishing he would allow himself the opportunity to find love and not just the chase of temporary lust.

"Dude, everyone that is around the two of you for three seconds can tell you are both over the moon for each other. You are basically a walking heart-eyed emoji following her around." He cracks himself up, opening another box; this one reveals a nursing pillow covered in little pink hearts.

"I'm going to ask her to marry me," I announce, calmly rolling paint onto the wall, never more sure of a decision in my life.

"Holy shit. Don't you wanna finish unpacking her boxes first?" He gives me a teasing grin.

"You know that's all done, dipshit. We just had the party. And it feels right. Some people might think it's fast, but I have known from the minute I met her that she was different."

"I'm really happy for you, Rem. Truly." Striding across the space, Eli clasps me in a tight hug. "Let's finish this room, yeah?"

"We don't have a lot of time, but I think we will barely make it under the wire. And then I was thinking on one of our next days off, you could come with me to look at some rings?" I can't hold back my smile when I look over at my best friend.

"Hell, yes! I have *excellent* taste . . . Um, but maybe we should consult one of the girls?" He rubs the back of his neck apprehensively.

Laughing I tell him, "Don't worry, I already asked Kendra to help me, and she said yes."

"What the fuck! You told *Kendra* before me? That's not fair, I'm your damn brother." He crosses his thick arms over his chest, ready to argue.

"Well, I wasn't going to. But she cornered me at the housewarming party demanding to know my intentions with 'her bestie,' and I just gave it to her straight. Figured that was for the best." I give him a knowing look.

"Yup, alright. You did the right thing. Kendra is tiny but can be scary as shit when she wants to be." He grimaces.

"Don't I know it."

Laughing we get back to work, making a special space for Sutton and Kinsley to come home to.

41

Lainey

Remington was scheduled to work today, but Chief let him have the day off so he could help bring Sutton and Kinsley home. The fire station is not just a job, it truly is a family, and the more time I am around them the more evident it becomes. Sutton is not even a fire spouse or significant other, but because she is important to Remington, she is important to the rest of them. Ever since Derek's death, they have all stepped up to be there for Sutton sure, but also Remington. He lost his brother-in-law and one of his best friends. Now he's doing something today that is both beautiful and difficult. We are all thinking about the man that is missing from this moment.

Earlier today Jess and Kendra came by and decorated Sutton's front yard, so when we pulled up there was an adorable wooden stork dressed in pink, a baby in a blanket hanging from its beak. Big letters spelling out "IT'S A GIRL" sprawl across the freshly cut green yard, and there are balloons tied to the mailbox by the driveway.

"Oh my gosh!" Sutton gasps when she sees the cheerful surprise.

"Welcome home," I tell her with a smile.

"This is too much, you guys didn't need to go to the trouble." She wipes a tear as Remington parks in the driveway.

Helping her out of the car carefully he says, "Sut, we are going to celebrate you and Kinsley every chance we get. Today is a special day, and we are going to commemorate it. Let's get a picture of you two by the stork!"

Bubbling laughter comes from his sister as she nods and slowly makes her way toward the lawn, Remington getting the car seat. I pull out my phone and snap the pictures of the new mom and her precious baby cradled in her arms. Remington's right. We need to keep celebrating the moments we have, even if they feel a bit hollow. Kinsley deserves the memories to be captured and the effort from all of us.

Renee opens the front door and says, "Charles, Charles! They're here, our girls are home." We help Sutton and Kinsley inside, and Remington grabs the rest of the bags and supplies. Once the door is shut, we all take a collective sigh. Kinsley is home, safe and sound. It's a new chapter for her and Sutton, one that is going to be hard to write, but we won't let her do it alone.

"Okay, Kinsley," Remington says in a sweet, low voice. "Are you ready to see your room?"

"Rem, her room is not quite done yet," I whisper to him, urgently.

"It's done." He smiles and winks at me.

"How?" I ask in disbelief.

"I spoke to the muralist," Sutton says from her place on the couch, stroking Kinsley's tiny hand. "They had time to squeeze me in when I was in the hospital. I asked Rem to come let him in so they could paint." She smiles down at her daughter, contentment and sadness washing over her features in tandem.

"That's wonderful! I can't wait to see how it turned out." I clap my hands.

"I know you are not supposed to do many stairs, but do you think you are up for the trip?" Renee asks Sutton.

"Yeah, Mom. I think I want to go up and see it. Then I can just stay upstairs, if that's okay?" She looks to Renee for permission.

"Sweetheart, you can do whatever you want. I'm here, not going anywhere. I can bring you up anything you need from down here. Let's go see the nursery, then you can set up yourself in bed and get comfortable. Rest."

Nodding, Sutton hands Kinsley off to Remington's strong arms and I swear I feel my ovaries pulse. Seeing him hold her in the hospital room for the first time nearly had drool coming out of my mouth. I don't think I will ever get used to seeing how at ease he is with babies and children. It is so sexy. He confidently walks toward the stairs, and I follow as if tugged by an invisible string tied to him.

Charles helps Sutton stand from the couch. "Easy, bug," he says gently.

"Don't you think I am too old for that nickname, Dad?" Sutton sighs, making her way gingerly up the steps.

"Never. You will always be my little bug. Doesn't matter how old you are, I am still just as old as I was when we had you and I held you for the first time. Snuggled right into me. Little snuggle bug. I don't get the snuggles so much anymore, but I'm keeping the name, bug." He smirks at her as they stop at the nursery door.

She is about to argue more, her stubborn streak mixed with the hormones rolling through her body ready for a fight, but it dies on her lips when Remington swings the door open. Sutton gasps, a hand covering her mouth, and her body does a little sway steadied by her father's strong arm around her shoulders.

Stepping into the room she whispers, "Oh my God, Rem, it's so beautiful." She looks at him, her soft brown eyes swimming in depths of emotion, tears slipping down her cheek. The mural wall is exactly what we had hoped for. A soft green meadow with gentle rolling hills is splattered with the most stunning wildflowers. The blue of the sky is dotted with soft, sweeping clouds, just being kissed with the start of a sunset. Most importantly, throughout the meadow are a few adorable, friendly looking, fluffy sheep that match the blanket that lays across the back of the cream rocking chair in the corner of the room. One of the sheep is positioned perfectly so it looks like it's peeking right over the rail of the crib that's pushed up to the wall.

Remington uncomfortably clears his throat and gives Sutton a funny look for some reason. A silent sibling conversation passing between them in a heartbeat of time, and she shakes her head.

"The guy did a nice job, I think," Remington finally says. "When he was done, Eli and I came back and finished setting the rest of the stuff up. If you want me to move or change anything around, please let me know."

"It's perfect." Sutton walks over to Remington, kisses his cheek, and takes her daughter over to the rocking chair. They settle in, and we all watch as she takes her first deep breath in her special space, her sanctuary.

42

Remington

Lainey is working at our dining table–turned office when I walked in from the grocery store. We talked about moving her into the actual home office, but she said she likes to be more out in the open, especially when I am on my days off. One of the hard things about days when I am not at the fire station and she is working is me needing to leave her alone. Watching her sit there, focused and so sexy, is too much temptation. So most of the time I try and make myself scarce, do errands, work out with Eli, go visit my parents, take Ash on walks, check in on Sutton and Kinsley. Anything to keep me from grabbing Lainey, hauling her over my shoulder and tossing her down on our bed—devouring her the way my body demands.

Ash is curled up on one of the many dog beds we now have scattered about the house, this one planted next to her feet. Having Ash here makes me feel better. He's still just a puppy, but once he is older he will serve as a good guard dog for the woman I love. Obviously he needs some major training since he stays flopped at her feet, snoozing away when I came in the door.

Thank fuck her workday is almost done, because me and my impatient dick have plans . . . big plans. I smile to myself imagining what I am going to do to Lainey until I notice her face.

"Hey, baby, what's wrong?" I quickly put down the bags on the counter and move over to her. Ash finally wakes up, wiggling over to me for attention.

Lainey looks up at me, and she is full of a despondent irritation that I haven't really seen on her face, ever. "My brother," she simply states.

"Calvin?" I rub Ash's head but keep my eyes fixed on Lainey.

"Yup. He just texted me and said he's in town and wants to see me. He said he stopped by my apartment building, but obviously I wasn't there. He's *demanding* to know where I am and why I didn't tell him I moved." Her eye roll is so hard I worry it might damage her perfect blue orbs that I love getting lost in.

"When was the last time you even spoke to him?" I ask. I have never heard her speak to her dad or brother on the phone, nor has she mentioned any plans to see them.

"I have not talked to my dad in . . ." She pauses to think, like she really can't figure it out. "Geez, I guess it's been over a year. Probably longer. I can't even tell you an exact date. I have not seen Cal, either. He will text every so often trying to make some demands on behalf of our dad. Or tell me that I am disappointing Mom in some way if he has spoken to her. Basically doing their dirty work as usual, not actually caring about me."

"Why would he show up now? It's been so long."

"He said he was here to see Mom and wants to see me, too." A frown of doubt tugs at her full lips.

"You don't believe him." I sit in the chair next to her and pull her over onto my lap.

"Everything with those people is smoke and mirrors. Double-edged swords. Dealing with them on my own is *so* exhausting. But I know if I don't see him, he will keep harping on me until he gets his way, says whatever it is he wants to say." She pinches the bridge of her nose.

Pulling her hand down, I cup her cheek and rub my thumb along her jaw. She relaxes into my palm, and I smile at her. I love that she feels so comfortable with me now, and I know how to quiet the anxiety spiraling in her system. "Beautiful, you do not have to deal with your dad, mom, or Calvin alone *ever again*. You have me, I am not going anywhere. Tell him to come over, can't wait to meet him." I wink at her.

She barks out a laugh and leans in to kiss me, emotion filling the space around us. I wrap my arms around her, holding her tightly against my body, nipping her bottom lip.

"Thank you." She pulls back, giving me her full attention and genuine gratitude.

"Always, baby. It's my pleasure to be here for you. This is our house, but you are my home. And I will always protect what's mine." I lean in and kiss her neck.

"I couldn't ask for anything more," she rasps. "I guess I should invite my brother over for dinner. In an hour?"

"Sure," I say, running my hand up her thigh, under her sundress. "Sounds good."

"You have to let me go. I need to start cooking." She giggles and shimmies in my lap, making my dick instantly hard and changing the plans.

"Fuck that. He can come over in two hours. We can order pizza. I'm having my dessert right now." I stand in a rush, flipping Lainey over my shoulder in a practiced move, making her squeal.

She spanks me playfully on the butt as I make my way down the hallway to our bedroom, Ash barking at our heels.

"Don't start something you are not ready for me to finish, Lainey." I flip up her short dress, revealing lacy pink panties. *She's going to kill me, fuck.* I crack my hand down on her ass and she moans, grinding down on my shoulder.

Laying her on the bed, I loom over her and hand over her phone I snagged from the table when I scooped her up saying, "Send that text, baby. I am going to take care of Ash, and then I'm going to make every minute we have count, do you understand?"

Batting her full lashes at me, her cheeks blooming the prettiest shade of pink, Lainey stares up at me and whispers, "Yes, sir."

As she takes the phone, licking that goddamn bottom lip of hers, I know that we are going to use those minutes multiple times over because there is no way I am going to last when she is driving me up the fucking wall—and she knows it.

I open the door a couple hours, and a few mind-blowing orgasms, later to reluctantly welcome Lainey's brother into our home. Calvin Quinn stands at least five inches shorter than me but puffs out his skinny chest as if his self-important attitude makes him tower over me. His eyes are similar to Lainey's but hold zero warmth. His thinning hair is a few shades darker, the brown a deeper dark-chocolate color. Calvin has on a pressed pair of khaki slacks, tasseled brown loafers, and a blue button-up. He looks stiff and stuffy. Not like he's coming to his sister's house for a casual dinner.

"Hey, man. Nice to meet you." I hold out my hand in greeting. Calvin, unsurprisingly, has a limp, disappointing handshake. "Come on in."

Looking me up and down, unimpressed by my damp hair, tight FGFD T-shirt, worn blue jeans. Eyes landing on my bare feet, causing him to scoff, Calvin reluctantly steps into my home.

"Um, who are you exactly? Lainey texted me this address and said this was where she was living now." He crosses his arms, as if he could intimidate me.

Nice try, dumbass. I could snap you like a fucking twig.

"I'm Lainey's boyfriend, Remington LeBlanc. We live together, this is our house." I gladly clear up his confusion, even though "boyfriend" doesn't sound significant enough in my mind for what our relationship is.

"Christ, she moves fast, doesn't she," he mumbles and rolls his eyes.

At my feet Ash growls at him. *Good boy.*

Before I can say anything or put his head through the wall, Lainey comes down the hall. She had just finished getting ready after we'd showered together. I told her to take her time while I ordered the pizza and waited to greet our *guest.*

"Hello, Cal," she says, stopping next to me, lacing our hands together. She makes no move to hug him or get close to him. "Welcome to my new house. It's nice to see you." Her smile is forced, uncomfortable, and the trembling in her fingers is the only indication that she is nervous. *I'm so proud of her.* I squeeze her hand in reassurance.

"This is quite unexpected, Lainey. Shacking up with someone already? Mom told me you were dating around again after your breakup, but this?" He scoffs at our intertwined hands.

Glaring at him, I lift her hand to my mouth and place a kiss there without any shame. "Where she lives, who she dates really has nothing to do with you, Cal. We kindly invited you to *our home* because you insisted on visiting with Lainey today.

If you want this night to continue, I suggest you leave your disrespectful attitude outside. Otherwise, get the fuck out."

"Charming," Calvin says to Lainey. "Can we talk? I have some news to share with you, and it's rather time sensitive." He looks down at Ash with clear disdain.

Who the fuck hates puppies?

Lainey stiffens next to me and motions for us all to move to the living room. She sits on the couch, and I take up the spot right next to her, my arm splayed across the back of the couch. Calvin sits in one of the reading chairs across from us.

"Can I get you something to drink?" Lainey politely offers her brother.

"No, thank you." Calvin shifts uncomfortably on our very comfortable chair.

"What can *we* do for you, Cal?" I ask, emphasizing the *we*.

Narrowing his eyes at me before shifting them over to Lainey in a way that is eerily similar to their mother, Calvin says, "Dad wants you back in DC, Lainey."

She scoffs loudly, crossing her arms and sinking deeper into my side. I dip my hand around her shoulder and rub my fingers along her bicep. *Right here, baby.*

"Well, hell will freeze over before I ever go back to DC, Cal," she says, voice unwavering.

"Lainey, this is important. You work from"—he pauses and lets his eyes roam all over our small, comfortable space, landing on the "dining office" before continuing—"home. You can work in DC, and Dad needs *both* of us, his children, at his side right now. Big things are happening."

"What's happening?" she asks apprehensively.

"He's running for office, and he needs our unwavering support, Lainey. You know how the political machine works. *Optics* are important. Family is important to the public perception, and he needs us to be on his team. It's the least you can do." His cold stare bores into my woman as a shiver runs down my own spine.

This is the kind of manipulative, twisted bullshit Lainey has had to wade through alone all her life? How the fuck did she turn out the way she has? How did she not let these wolves consume her wholly? It just makes me even more determined to protect her and give her the life she deserves. And to keep her as far from this toxicity as humanly possible.

"So let me get this straight, *Calvin*." Disgust drips off of Lainey's sweet tongue. "Dear old Dad is running for a political office." She holds up a hand as Calvin is about to cut her off. "I don't give a shit what political position it is, it doesn't matter. He should not be in charge of *anything*. He does not have my vote or my support. I will never stand beside a man that has manipulated and mentally abused me my entire life. Telling other people that he is trustworthy and good is a lie."

"You are so dramatic, as always, Lainey. Dad gave you everything and all you ever did was complain." He shoves a finger toward her, his neck pulsing in anger. "Poor little Lainey. Get your shit together for once and do something productive and helpful."

"Ab-so-*fucking*-lutely not," I growl, pushing so stand and startling Ash, who lets out a bark. My full height towers over Calvin, and he has the good sense to cower back slightly in his chair. "You shut your fucking mouth right now. We allowed you to come in here, and I warned you, didn't I? You will not speak to the woman I love like that. She is a goddamn *miracle* to grow up in your family and walk away the angel that she is."

Calvin scoffs, and I stride closer to him, wrapping my thick, callused fingers around the front collar of his shirt and twisting it, drawing out a satisfying whimper from him.

"Lainey is perfection, and you are a piece of trash. Not worthy to breathe the same air she does." I grip a bit tighter, just to make my point clear. "She is kindness, beauty, light, and goodness. *She is everything.* No doubt you and your dad want her back so you can try and pull her strings like you did when she was growing up. But guess what, asshole? She's not your fucking puppet, never has been. She freed herself from you a long time ago, and she made her choice." I shove Calvin away from me and step back.

Lainey is standing now, nervously wringing her hands, Ash, feeling her trepidation, sits at her feet. I hold my hand out to her, and she instantly steps into my arms, zero hesitation or fear. The look in her eyes when she locks in on my face is pure love and confidence in my ability to protect her, to keep my promises.

Calvin looks at us, looks at her like he has never seen her before—and it's probably because he hasn't, not this version of Lainey. This woman has changed and grown, allowed herself to let love break down the walls that she had built up solidly for her entire life, and bloomed right before my eyes. The person Cal pushed around his whole life is gone. She can't be controlled anymore and he's just now realizing it.

"Lainey is *mine.*" I look at Calvin. "And if you or your father ever come around here making any kind of demands of my woman or make her upset ever again you won't be talking to her. You will be dealing with me." Calvin gulps. His wide, pleading eyes look over to Lainey as she nods in agreement.

A ripple of anger flashes over Cal's face; blink and you might miss the glint of poison in his eyes, but I saw it. He is not a good man. He's been molded by the hands of his parents, especially the father that expects everyone around him to bend to his will. And then when he doesn't get his way, fits are thrown like a toddler not getting the prize they demanded. I imagine Cal being an even worse version of Patrick Quinn, being coddled and told how perfect and special he is in the most unhealthy ways all his life.

"Lainey, you are going to regret this. Quinns always come first. He wants you home, and you will come back when you realize that this is not the life that is expected of you. What you were raised for." Cal waves a hand around, gesturing to our life that we happen to love very much.

"Get the hell out of our house, Cal. You have worn out your welcome," Lainey says, walking to the front door.

He stands, now smartly keeping his mouth shut, and I follow him. Lainey opens the door to find the pizza delivery man, hand raised about to ring the bell.

"Oh, hello!" Lainey says, brightly. "I will take that, thank you." She takes the pizza, hands him the tip money we had laid out, and spins back to us.

"Goodbye, Cal." Lainey gives Calvin a shove out the door and slams it shut, slouching against it with exasperation.

"Un-freaking-real," she moans as I take the pizzas from her and walk to the kitchen. I set them on the counter, then I turn and wrap her in my embrace.

"I am so sorry," she mumbles into my shirt.

"What the hell do you have to be sorry for?"

"My family. He is so full of shit. So full of *himself*, always trying to get in as many digs as possible and the last word if he can." Her misty eyes look up at me with guilt that doesn't belong there.

"Well it didn't work this time. As far as I'm concerned, baby, those people gave up the title of family when it comes to you a long time ago. Blood doesn't mean family, as much as society would like to try and guilt you into believing it. You get to choose who gets your time, your energy, and most importantly your heart." I kiss her jaw, and she hums.

"That's an easy choice, Remington. You. You have my whole heart." She kisses my lips softly.

"And I promise to never take it for granted," I vow.

43

Remington

"Ohhh! I *love* this one!"

"Kendra, we are not here to find a ring for *you*. We're here to help Rem shop for Lainey, chill." Eli tries to get Kendra to focus on the task at hand—much easier said than done in a shop filled with glittering jewels.

"Maybe bringing her here was not the best idea?" Eli grumbles to me.

"I can hear you, asshole!" Kendra snaps. "And of course it was a good idea. Lainey is *my* best friend, and I know what she likes. Why are *you* here? What the heck do you know about diamonds and picking engagement rings, Mr. 'I am never gonna be locked down.'" Kendra gives Eli a smug look over one of the glass cases housing a variety of necklaces.

"I'm here because *my* best friend and brother asked me to be here. You don't have a monopoly on the future LeBlancs, Kenny." He gives her a wicked grin.

"Ugh, do *not* call me that stupid nickname." She stomps over to another section of the store.

"What the fuck, man? Why are you poking the tiny

beehive?" I glance between him and Kendra. They usually don't go at each other like this, well at least not *this* hard.

"I don't know. It's just too easy sometimes, I can't help myself." He shrugs his massive shoulders like a scorned child.

"Well, drop it and help me. Pick up your playground shit later."

"Fine," Eli relents.

I walk over to the main sales counter where Mr. Angelo is patiently waiting. He is the owner of our local jewelry store, Fox Gem and Jewel, located right on Main Street. His daughter, Michelle, graduated the same year as Sutton, and he had a son a few grades below us.

"Rem, what can I help you with today?" he asks me with a bright smile that matches the gleam of the diamond in the ring on his pinky finger.

"I would love your expertise to help me pick an engagement ring, Mr. Angelo," I tell him, a sudden wave of nerves roiling my stomach. I'm not nervous about my decision to ask Lainey to marry me, that I couldn't be more excited for. No, I just want to be sure I am picking exactly the perfect ring. She deserves it, plus it's going to live on the ring finger of her left hand for the rest of our lives. It needs to be perfect.

"Excellent! Congratulations, son. This is a big, big day. Is this the lovely lady?" He gestures to Kendra.

Eli, Kendra, and I all let out a collective laugh, and I vehemently protest. "No, no, no. This is Kendra, my girlfriend Lainey's best friend. I brought her and Eli to help me out today."

"Geez, Rem. No need to be so offended." Kendra pokes me in the ribs, smiling up at me.

"Sorry, Kenny." Eli puts an arm around Kendra's tiny shoulders, tugging her to his side as she tries to push away from him. "He is twitterpated and everyone knows it."

"Shut up, you two and focus." I turn to the huge selection of rings in the case, feeling overwhelmed again.

"Definitely not yellow gold, right?" I ask Kendra as she finally shoves Eli's big frame off of her tiny one.

"Correct, loverboy. Platinum or white gold. So this whole section is out." She waves her blue-manicured hand over the left side of the display case.

"We could always custom make something as well if you don't see the right thing here today, Rem," Mr. Angelo explains.

Nodding, I take my time to look at the other rings.

"We also have these setting options over here. And then a wide variety of stones to pick from that are not already set in place." He walks to a different display area, and we all trail him.

That's when I see the perfect setting. I point to it. "Can you please tell me more about that one?"

"Oh, yes, lovely choice." Mr. Angelo unlocks the case, pulls it out, and gently lays it on blue display velvet. "This is a band of 14-karat white gold. Obviously, no stone in the center yet, you get to pick that. But alternating on the sides here and on the band, we have pear and round-cut diamonds that will hug whichever center stone you select. It's a very romantic piece."

Kendra and Eli stand next to me, examining the ring as I pick it up. The lights in the store reflecting off of the side stones are already stunning. I can't imagine how much better it will look with a diamond in the middle.

"It kind of reminds me of a flower," Kendra states.

"Yeah, it kind of does," I breathe out, looking over to Eli who gives me a raised, knowing brow. A silent conversation between us, the meaning of her words deeper than she realizes.

"This is the one, Mr. Angelo," I tell the man, unable to contain my relieved smile.

"Excellent!" He claps. "Now, on to center diamond selection."

44

Lainey

"I always want to gobble you up," I say playfully to Kinsley as I bounce her carefully in my arms at our table in the Sugar Cube. "I can't handle all your cuteness." Her wide, brown eyes, bright and full of curiosity, blink up at me through thick lashes, reminding me of a baby deer.

"How is she two months old already?" Sutton asks me, blowing on her full mug of decaf coffee.

Kinsley wraps her small hand around my fingers and tugs, pulling on my hand and my heart all at once. "Swear she grows so much every time I see her, and I basically see her every other day," I say, laughing.

"Yes, she can't go long without seeing her Auntie Lainey." Sutton smiles at her baby girl.

"I'm not so sure you should be calling me that to her, Sutton," I admit shyly.

"Seriously? Why the he—ck not?" She catches herself before she curses, and I smirk at her.

"I am not married to your brother, so technically I'm not her aunt," I state.

Sutton rolls her eyes at me. "Lainey, please. Y'all live

together, love each other. You're end game. For the love of all things, you watched Kins be *born.* You *are* her aunt, end of story. And I guarantee a walk down the aisle is coming."

"I'm not sure I want that."

"What?!" Sutton's face pales.

"I mean the whole big wedding thing," I clarify. "Marriage, yes. All that attention, a couple hundred people in a big venue, no thank you."

"Thank God," Sutton murmurs.

"What? Why? You thought I didn't want to marry Remington?" I put Kinsley up on my shoulder when she starts to fuss and pat her on the back trying to get her to burp.

"For a second there you had me sweating, yeah. He needs to lock you down. For good. You're stuck with all of us forever."

"No place I'd rather be," I tell her with a grin.

"This is nice," Sutton says. "It feels good to get out of the house. Fresh air, other humans. I think that I am ready to start going back to the store some days. My team does a good job, but I miss being there."

"Really? I think that's great, Sutton. You love Brooks and Books, have put so much of yourself into the store. I know that you have a really excellent team in place to help you run the store, but I'm sure all the customers miss seeing you as well," I say with encouragement.

"The best part about being the owner is getting to do what I want, so I plan on setting up an area for Kinsley and bringing her with me. I just, I can't be away from her right now, but I also need to get out of the house a little bit." Her frown makes me think she is doubting her plans.

"You deserve to do the things that make you happy, Sutton. Being in the store, working to create a space that is welcoming, and showcasing the local talent that you have worked with, like Kendra, it's important." I hold my hand out to her, which she takes.

"I'm not sure I will ever truly be happy again," Sutton blurts out. "Does that make me a horrible person? An awful mother? I love Kinsley, but it is so hard without Derek, doing this alone was not the plan."

"You are the strongest person I know." I squeeze her hand when I feel her try to retreat into herself. "I am not lying to you or trying to just make you feel better. I really see it. Even before Deck was taken I thought that, and now it's been amplified. It's okay if you don't feel strong, or even happy. You are going through so much, so many changes. All you have to do, Sutton, is wake up every day, put your feet on the floor, and try your best—and every single day that is going to look differently."

"Lainey, how'd you become so wise?" Sutton chuckles as she swipes a tear away.

"An awful family and a shit ton of therapy are apparently paying off." I shrug. "It's also a lot easier for me to help other people and encourage them than it is to apply that same voice and kindness to myself."

"We can work on it together." Sutton smiles at me and then looks to Kinsley sound asleep on my chest. "You have the magic touch." She nods.

"Anytime you need help, *Aunt Lainey* is ready," I reply with a wink.

Expecting a grin or a laugh from Sutton, I am disappointed to see her look of shock. *Did she change her mind already?*

"What's wrong?" I breathe.

"Cora." Sutton's gaze is locked on the window to the right of us over my shoulder, looking out over the street.

Sure enough, Cora is right there, plastered up to the window snarling at us. Her dark hair looks messy and unwashed. She is wearing jeans and a tight, ill-fitting cream sweater that makes her skin look sallow. There is no more haughty glow of confidence around her, just a pulse of anger and disgust, and it's all aimed directly at me. According to the restraining order she can't come into the Sugar Cube right now because I am in here. She also should not even be on the other side of the glass leering at me. It's creepy and unsettling.

I hold Kinsley tighter and look at Sutton. "Call Remington, he needs to know."

Sutton quickly pulls out her phone and makes the call, filling in her brother on our unwelcome lunch guest. Cora is still rooted to the same spot, eyes boring into me as I try my best to ignore her. This interaction feels even more unsettling than any of the others, and Cora hasn't even spoken to me, stepped foot in the same space as me. But there is an inherent threat to the way she is watching me from out there while I am in here, as if I am her prey and she is biding her time, waiting to snag me in her vicious claws.

Sutton has not even hung up the phone with Remington when we see red and blue lights flashing at the curb. The noise and commotion must jolt Cora out of her trance because she looks behind her and starts to move away from the window. We see Danny and Megan get out of the police cruiser, cutting off Cora's escape. She flings her arms about wildly and yells at Danny, who just stands there like calm, cold steel. Megan glances in the window, checking on us, and gives me a little nod.

So distracted by the commotion outside, I don't notice Remington's black truck pull up to the curb. Ignoring the shouts from Cora, he blasts through the door of the Sugar Cube, the tinkling bell a contrast to the stormy rage he's pulling along with him. There is no calm to him until he sets his worried, amber eyes on me. He rushes over to our table, looking so handsome in his navy tactical pants, matching FGFD T-shirt, and black boots.

Cupping my face, he bends down, kissing me hard. "You're okay?" he growls.

"Yes," I whisper. I would say it was to keep the baby asleep, but that is a lie. The way he swept in here, protectiveness and masculinity pulsing off of him is making me dizzy and unable to say much more.

"She can't do this to you." He looks out the windows to the scene Cora is making, her hands now planted firmly on her hips. We watch as Danny steps closer to her, saying something that makes her shrink and then scurry down the sidewalk. He watches her go before shaking his head at Megan, and turning, they make their way inside.

"Hey, guys." Danny greets us stiffly.

"What the fuck was she doing, Danny?" Remington demands.

"I issued her a warning. She technically didn't break the order since she is outside on public property, didn't make direct contact, and was not inside the same place as Lainey," Danny explains.

Remington places his hand on the back of my chair, possessively. "The way she was acting, staring at the girls, at Lainey. It wasn't normal, Danny. That can't be allowed, can it? What did she say to you?"

"More crazy shit about how you are meant to be together, and that Lainey is in the way of the promises you made her. That the two of you had a plan to make her business a big success, and she needs you. I'm glad we have the RO in place, but her behavior is concerning. After this warning, if she does something like this again, I have grounds to arrest her. You guys need to be careful. And Lainey, next time *I* want to be your first call, okay? The guys at the fire station called me, but I want to hear from you immediately. You have my number, please use it."

I nod at him as he shakes hands with Remington. Megan

rubs my shoulder and gives Sutton a quick hug before they head back out the door and get in their squad car.

"I don't like this, baby." Remington sits down next to me, rubbing his hand up and down my thigh, as if he's trying to ground himself.

"Me, either. There is something very wrong with that woman. After all this time I had hope that she'd given up and forgotten about whatever weird plan she cooked up in her mind." I kiss the top of Kinsley's head.

"After what we witnessed today, I don't think she will ever let go of Rem that easily," Sutton says with a shiver.

45

Remington

Being away from Lainey ever since the day Cora was spotted outside the Sugar Cube has been torture for me. I want to kidnap her and Ash, take them up to Walker's cabin and hide out. I know that is completely insane and impractical. We also can't let the threat of one crazy semi-stalker rule over our lives.

Lainey is handling all of this way better than I am. She works at home as usual; takes care of our growing, rambunctious puppy; goes to see Kendra, Jess, and Sutton; and seems perfectly content. I insist that she take pepper spray with her everywhere, especially when she takes Ash on his daily walks around our neighborhood. When I asked her how she could be so calm about everything, she simply told me that with me she has never felt more safe, even with Cora looming over us. And fuck if that didn't make me feel like Superman. I want to be that for her always, her safe space.

I am going to take a page out of her book and try to focus on the good, what is actually in our control. Right now that is planning the perfect engagement.

"Eli!" I yell through the gym. He has a catchy pop song on repeat, trying to time his latest jump rope video.

"Rem!" he shouts back at me, a shit-eating grin on his happy face. "What's up?" He pauses the blaring music, taking a drink of water.

"I need a favor." I lean on the wall, crossing my arms.

"Sure thing. What is it? A kidney?"

"Not this time," I laugh. "But it is a very important job. Need you to hang on to Lainey's engagement ring for me. Mr. Angelo called me this morning to tell me it's ready."

"*Yes!* That's awesome, man. When are you going to pick it up? Want me to go with you?" His happiness for me and Lainey is so real. I know he is honestly excited to help me make this memorable and special for her.

"That would be awesome. I was thinking we could go on Friday. I want to try and stay out of Lainey's way while she is working. We could hit the gym, grab lunch, and then go pick up the ring?"

"Sounds like a plan." Eli clasps my hand and yanks me into a half hug.

"Get off me, you are all sweaty." I shove him.

He just laughs and tries harder to jump on top of me.

Fire alarms blare throughout the station rousing us all from sleep. I spring from my small bed, quickly marking the time on the nightstand clock—two a.m.

Fuck.

Bodies rush to the equipment lockers, and we all dress hurriedly, yet methodically. Each movement of the process is practiced, pounded into our veins and muscle memory for moments exactly like tonight. In less than five minutes we went from deep sleep to fully suited up for a fire and ready to be pulling out of the station.

I am driving our second truck, Eli riding next to me in the passenger seat. We are flipping on the sirens when we hear the callout over the radio.

Dispatch: Engine 26 and all units you are needed at residential address.

621 Meadow Lark Drive, suspected structure fire.

All the blood drains from my face. It takes every ounce of concentration to not slam on the brakes or throw up.

"Fuuuuuuuuck!" I scream, hitting the accelerator as all of our trucks race through the empty streets of our small, sleeping town.

I have never felt panic like this in my life.

This is not just any house.

This is my fucking house.

With my woman inside.

Ash.

My life.

Lainey.

I have to get to Lainey.

46

Lainey

I wake up from a deep sleep feeling dizzy and disoriented. My bed is empty, the man I love is gone, doing what he's called to do—protecting our community. The heart in my chest that beats for him pounds out an achy throb like it always does in recognition of his absence. But my need for Remington is not what pulled me from sleep tonight.

My brain finally registers the sharp alarm blaring in the house, the pungent smell, and the unwelcome thickness to the air. Smoke.

Oh my God . . . Ash.

Now fully awake, aware of the danger, I whip out of bed. I am wearing only one of Remington's old fire department T-shirts and sleep shorts. Rolling to the ground, I crawl to our closed bedroom door. Reaching up to grasp the knob, it sears my palm with its heat upon contact.

This is not good. I need to get out of here. I need to get to Ash.

I use the hem of my shirt, gripping the knob again. It barely blocks any heat, but I wrench the door open to find a wall of smoke. Gasping in a shocked breath, I drop back down to the floor as fast as I can, coughing and gagging. Heat ripples over my body from flames and fire I can't see but can certainly smell now and hear. The crackling of the burning house and the fire alarm blaring feel like spikes in my brain making it hard to concentrate. The smoke makes my eyes sting and my lungs burn.

Ash is in his crate, where he sleeps every night, in the guest bedroom down the hallway with the door shut. So close and also a million miles away. I can hear him yelping in fear, my heart ripping open at the sound of his panic.

I'm so sorry, sweet boy. I'm coming.

I can see flames now, tunneling toward me, and I scream, pulling more noxious smoke into my lungs—choking me with invisible grey fingers. A hot lick whips up my neck and jaw in a burning caress that makes me cry out.

I can't go this way. I am trapped, burning in my own home.

I scramble back to our bedroom like a crab, kicking the door shut. The room is black with thick smoke now. A glow from the flames that chased me down the hallway lights up the crack under the door like a nightlight sent from hell.

Spots blink in my vision. This dizziness is consuming, the burning in my lungs feels like being tossed in that deep water all over again. A whole different kind of drowning. Gulping for air. Praying it is all a nightmare but knowing this sharp, burning pain only comes from reality. Blackness swallows me down, and I hold on to *him* in my mind.

My safe place.

My true home.

Remington.

I love you . . .

47

Remington

Our trucks stop in front of my worst nightmare.

My house is engulfed in fire. The monster we face down every day has come knocking on my own door. Threatening the one person that matters the most to me.

My heart is trapped in that house, and I can't fucking breathe.

We spill from the trucks, and what should be natural feels like chaos in my panicked state. Eli fills my field of vision, his strong hands clamping down on my shoulders.

"Rem! *Focus*. One goal. One mission." His calm determination and leadership is exactly what I need to snap me out of my mental tornado.

All I can do is nod. I grab my gear, strap on my SCBA mask, pull up the protective hood, check my oxygen tank, put on my helmet and gloves, and ignore all the shouts and directions being given, and rush to the door—my fucking front door. I try to kick it in, but it's not as simple as it should be. That's when I notice the door has been tampered with, barricaded from the outside. *What the fuck?* Eli's right behind me with his irons, chopping through, helping me forcibly enter my own space.

The door slams open, blasting us with a wall of flame, heat, and smoke. It's the middle of the night, so Lainey would be in bed, Ash in his crate. I told the guys that on the way over. Everyone knew there was not a chance in hell that I am not going in here to try and save my woman. They all know my house, but we have no idea what we will find inside.

I quickly make my way into the house, flames consuming the spaces that I have loved. The rooms that Lainey and I made into our home, gone with each stroke of the flames up the walls and along the floors.

"I'm going to the primary bedroom to look for Lainey." I talk into the radio. "Ash should be in the spare room."

"Got it." Eli copies, and we head into the flames together. Unafraid of the fire but terrified we are too late.

I make it down the ruined hallway to our bedroom and the closed door.

Pushing it open, my heart nearly stops when I see the love of my life collapsed on our floor. She looks so tiny, so fragile, covered in soot, dark smoke blurring the room. Yanking off my mask, I place it over Lainey's face to give her breaths of the oxygen I know she desperately needs. I don't give a shit about the risk of my mask being contaminated by the fire, of what I am breathing in, or that I am breaking protocol.

I kick the bedroom door closed again and call out over the radio, choking on the thick smoke, "Ryder, back bedroom. Third window off the deck. Come bust out the window. Hallway is blocked, I can't carry Lainey out that way."

"Ten-four, we are coming, Rem." Matt's voice crackles over the line.

I take a pull of oxygen from the mask then place it back over Lainey's face. I scoop her limp body into my arms, tucking her close to my chest. The window shatters, and I see

Ryder and Jacobs on the other side. They clear the glass, and I slip Lainey out into their waiting arms. I'm next through the window, sinking down onto my knees for just a moment once I'm out before I have Lainey back in my arms, and I am running for the front of the house.

I see Eli at the end of the driveway, Ash cradled in his lap, oxygen over his little muzzle.

The ambulance is there, doors open and waiting. I place Lainey's still body gently on the gurney. Our paramedics start to work on her quickly, and I rip off my tank, helmet, gloves, and jacket. We load Lainey up, slamming the doors closed, and I am right next to her, that small hand held perfectly in mine.

I don't give a shit that we are racing away from the fire, my gear left in the middle of the street with my crew, my house burning to the ground.

None of it matters.

If I didn't get to her in time . . .

If Lainey doesn't make it, I will never have a home ever again anyway.

48

Remington

It's been well over twenty-four hours and she still hasn't woken up. The noise of the machines beeping in the ICU are not what's keeping me awake. It is the panic of closing my eyes and then waking up to a world that exists with Lainey no longer in it.

I have not left her side. My smokey hair and skin overwhelm the room with the scent of the fire that ravaged our life, but I can't leave her to truly wash it away. Even just that fifteen minutes would be too much. They brought me water wipes that did little to clean me off and a set of scrubs to change into. I stripped down to my boxers right here in the corner of the room, discarding my fire-contaminated clothes. A kind nurse wearing proper PPE bagged them up and took them away. Nobody has tried to make me leave since then. So I sit, watchful and consumed with worry.

The doctors told me that she almost didn't make it. Had we been just a few minutes longer, she would have died from the smoke inhalation. Seeing her intubated, IV line in her arm, laid out on the hospital bed makes me want to scream. I want to hold her in my arms, wrap her in a false safety that I cannot offer.

I can't heal her, take away this suffering. I can't protect her. I promised I would, and I failed her.

A white bandage on her neck and jaw makes me clench my own. Flames burned her delicate skin, touching her in the place that I have claimed as my own. The line I draw on her face to calm her, comfort her, reassure her, melt her. Now it will forever bear a scar, but I will not let it keep me from claiming her all the same.

She is still perfection, still my peace. My home.

Soft knocks at the door bring me out of my thoughts. Chief, Eli, and Danny, in uniform, walk into the room. Normally they only allow one or two people in at a time, but I guess you get special treatment when you're cops and firefighters.

"Hey, Rem," Danny says quietly. "I am so sorry, man."

I can only give him a sharp nod, looking back to Lainey, feeling tears welling in my eyes. Words are too hard right now, especially for comfort or accepting condolences.

"We have some news," Chief says, gruff and remorseful. That gets my attention, and I look over at the group of men, all their eyes already tracking me.

"What happened?" I ask.

"The fire, Rem. It was not an accident. It was arson," Eli says.

"The doors?" I wonder.

"All the outer doors of the house were blocked, tampered with, and barricaded in some way. Poorly, albeit, but still. Also, the accelerator to start the fire was gasoline. We found the gas cans," Chief explains.

"Whoever did it was not an expert in anything they were trying to do, but it was damaging none the less. And the fact that they blocked the doors? That bumps the charges from arson to premeditated attempted murder." Danny glances at Lainey. "All your security cameras were cut this time, so we didn't get anything off of them from the uploaded material."

"What the fuck," I say rubbing my hands over my exhausted face.

"I'm so sorry, Rem," Eli says.

"Well you know exactly who the hell it is," I say in a whispered shout, anger rising. "It had to have been Cora, but she got smarter with the cameras this time. Go fucking arrest her, Danny!"

He shifts on his feet. "We went to her apartment right away, Rem. Thought the same thing."

"And you arrested her, right?" I demand.

"No . . . She—Cora was dead, Rem," Danny says, quietly. The news blows me back in my chair.

"What?" I mutter in disbelief.

"Drug overdose. She'd been there at least forty-eight hours. It couldn't have been her, Rem. We also found evidence that she owed a lot of money to some bad people, like her dad told you. She had a plan taped to her fridge of ways to get money. The top one was marry you and use *your* money," Danny says.

"Then who the fuck else would do this to us then?" I lament.

"We are going to find out, I promise," Chief says, clapping his hand on my back, and I slump forward, face in my palms feeling a wave of nausea overtake my system.

"Did they check you out, too?" Eli asked, concern lacing his voice.

"They did." I nod. "I had a little smoke inhalation, but I'm fine." They all nod too, knowing that I understand the drill, what to look out for. Plus I am camped out in the goddamn hospital, if I need anything for myself, which I won't, all I need to do is sound the alarm.

"I took Ash to the vet. He said Ash needs lots of rest but will make a full recovery," Eli says. I look up at him, overwhelmed with guilt that I hadn't even thought of our dog. "It's fine." He reassures me, sensing my guilt. "You need to be here, all attention on Lainey. Matt and Jess are taking care of Ash for now. The boys are thrilled about it."

"Thanks, man," I say shaking my head, foggy with so many emotions.

"I am going to run home, then to the station and get you some things, change of clothes and all that. You need to clean up, man. Can't have Lainey wake up to you looking and smelling like that." I roll my eyes at him. "Kendra is getting a bag of stuff together for Lainey, too. She said she will bring it up later today," Eli tells me, looking over at the machines beeping next to Lainey's bed.

"We appreciate it, thanks," I say, speaking for both of us.

"Rem," Danny says, "we're gonna figure this out, and until we know who it was, I am going to place an officer outside of Lainey's room 24/7, rotating shifts, okay?"

Dread sinks deep in my gut, reminding me of just how serious this situation is. "Yeah, okay. Thank you, Danny." I stand, stiffly, and shake his hand.

Chief hugs me long and tight, making my eyes sting, followed by Eli. They file out of the room, and I am once again left alone with my worry and the woman I love.

49

Lainey

My lungs are on fire.

FIRE.

Panic races along every nerve ending in my body.

The smoke.

I am choking on the smoke.

I can't breathe.

There are lights, so bright that I can't really open my eyes. I hear shouts, feel cool hands on my skin. One voice calls out to me, calming me, pulling me from my panic.

Remington.

I cough, gag. Pain lances my throat as someone removes the tube that was helping me breathe. I gag and gasp as it clears my lips quickly. Tears sting my eyes, and I blink them away. The brightness of the hospital room lights shimmer into focus, but there is only one thing I want to see, one person. Turning my aching neck to the left I see him.

"Hi." My voice is a hollow rasp. Sandpaper and pain.

"Thank fuck," Remington cries out. His arms are around me as soon as the doctor gives him a nod, his face buried in my neck, and he weeps. His hot tears run down my neck, and we hold on to each other. My own tears burn my sore eyes, but I welcome it knowing that it means I am here, alive, whole. Complete in the arms of the man that not only loves me but saved my life—because I know without a doubt, without even knowing the story, that he was the one to pull me from the flames.

Leaning back, Remington ever so gently kisses my lips, like he's afraid of breaking me. I press my forehead to his, letting a shiver ripple down my spine, feeling calm for the first time since before this tragedy tried to take everything from us.

"You smell smokey," I whisper, my voice too tired and damaged to be any louder.

"I'm so sorry. I know I am gross, but I couldn't leave you, baby, not even for a minute." He lifts my hand, kissing the back of it.

I look at his eyes, the gorgeous honeyed-amber that I love so much is soaked in worry, red irritation, exhaustion, and pain. "How long have I been here?" I whisper.

"You are in the county ICU. You've been out for more than twenty-four hours." Remington swallows hard, lines of worry creasing his brow.

"Are you okay?"

"Baby, you don't need to worry about me. I'm fine." He leans in, kissing my temple.

"I will always worry about you, comes with the job. Signed a secret contract when I became your girlfriend." He smirks at me, happy to see that I'm still here, still me.

"Ash!" I shout in a panic and then grip my neck at the ripping pain that caused my lungs and throat.

Remington gets a cup of water with a straw from the bedside table, encouraging me to take small sips. "He's okay. Eli saved him. Took him to the vet, who said he needs rest, but he's gonna be just fine. The Ryders are looking after him for now."

I sink into my pillow, so relieved that our precious puppy was spared. "I wish I could see him. He must have been so scared," I whisper as more tears spill down my face.

"I promise we will see him soon. Jess can send us some pictures while we are here, okay? Puppies are resilient little things. He is going to get lots of love and attention. We will make sure he's fine."

Remington runs his strong fingers through my hair, but it's not the comfort I want. That's when I realize I have a bandage on my face—remember the flames licking my skin. The burning, the pain, the smell. I reach up, wincing when I feel the cloth-covered area.

"I know, beautiful, I know," Remington says, his voice full of sadness, like not touching me the way we are used to is killing him as much as it is me. "You have a second-degree burn, borderline third, there and on your neck. The doctor said there will be some scarring, but he is hopeful you won't need surgery."

I close my eyes, taking in his news. "Is it stupid to feel sad about that? I should be thankful. It could have been so much worse, *should have* been so much worse, Remington."

"Lainey, you can feel any way you need to feel about all of this. But I can tell you right now, once you are healed? A scar on your face won't stop me from touching you there . . . kissing you there. That line along your jaw? I ran my finger there for the first time, and I swear to you it was like an invisible string that connected right to my damn heart. I love every inch of you, but that is like a magnet, a comfort, a high. I refuse to let that fire take it from us, baby. Okay?"

Smiling at him, basking in his love and perfect confession, I just nod.

After that, more doctors and nurses come to check on me. I learn exactly how close I came to dying on our bedroom floor, breaking down in tears at the news that this was not an accidental fire. Sadness and shock roll over Remington and I as he tells me about what happened to Cora. As much as I hated the woman, I certainly didn't want her life to end like that. It's heartbreaking for her and her family.

A new blanket of fear settles over my shoulders when I look out my hospital door and see the uniformed officer standing guard and reality hits me.

Someone burned down our house.

Someone tried to kill me.

Kendra came to see me, crying nearly her whole visit and leaving me with a bag of her essentials from her home and clothes from Jess since she's taller and more my size. Sutton called us on FaceTime so I could see Kinsley. Jess kept sending us a stream of photos and updates about Ash. Her boys were over the moon to have a dog in the house, and Matt said they were already begging to have one of their own once they have to return Ash to us.

Remington's parents were next. Both looked haunted, worried, and relieved to see that I was finally awake. Renee wanted to stay and mother me, but Remington sent them home. I was happy to see everyone but exhausted.

Eli came earlier with much needed clothes for Remington, toiletries, all the essentials he could think of. He has been handling so many things for us, I honestly don't know what we'd do without him.

"Please go shower, I'll be right here when you get back," I beg Remington.

He looks at me suspiciously, like I might melt into the

pillow or evaporate into the air if he doesn't keep his gorgeous gaze on me at all times.

"I have a babysitter." I motion to the officer outside my door. "I really, really want you to climb up onto this bed and hold me, sleep with me. But I won't let you if you are a smokey mess." I wrinkle my nose. "Plus, you are exhausted from your heroics and bedside vigil. A long, hot shower will feel good on your body," I whisper.

"You know what else would feel good on my body," Remington says smugly, moving closer.

"Nope." I toss up my hand, halting his progress. "Shower, then you can touch me. Maybe I will convince the nurse to let you be the supervisor of my next shower when they finally let me out of this bed again? At least you aren't stuck here."

"How can I say no to that?" He smiles, kissing the top of my head, finally clean after a lovely older female nurse helped me with my own shower earlier—Remington nervously hovering barely outside the door the entire time.

"I will be so fast, don't fall asleep without me," he demands playfully.

"Okay." I hum, sinking back into the pillow, shutting my eyes, missing our bed. Missing our house. Pain gutting me to my core, knowing that place is just a pile of smoldering rubble, *a crime scene* now.

I hear the door click. My eyes blink sluggishly open, heavy from being almost asleep. When I look to the side of the bed expecting to see Remington, shock has me sitting up straight to find my brother, Calvin, at the foot of my bed.

"Cal?" I rasp out, pain shooting down my strained body. "What are you doing here?"

"Oh God! Lainey, I was so worried when I heard what happened. I came right away. Are you okay?" he asks, moving up the side of the bed, closer to me.

"I will be, yes. But I don't understand. How did you know I was here?"

"Mom, of course. She called to tell me about the fire, that the house burned down. I can't believe it. It's a *miracle* you are alive." He reaches out for my hand, but I pull back.

I glance at the door, a sick feeling twisting not only my stomach, but my very soul. The police officer that was on guard is no longer standing at my door.

Where could he have gone?

"When did you talk to Mom?" I whisper.

"Right after you were brought in, she's on your emergency contact form."

He is lying. I know he's lying because my emergency contacts, in order, are Remington, Kendra, and now Renee as of a few months ago. I changed them after the night Remington found me on the bathroom floor.

I think I am going to be sick.

"I appreciate you coming to check on me, but as you can see, Cal, I will make a full recovery." I motion to my body.

Calvin's eyes flicker with a cold malice that he's apparently masked expertly our entire lives. I knew he was never fond of me, that he was not a good person, but I didn't think he was capable of actual evil, but that is all that is reflected in his gaze now. That's the terrifying thing about masks, some people are so good at crafting them, wearing them, that when you live in such close proximity to them for so long it's only when you walk away, gain distance and perspective, you start to see them slip to reveal the real monster lurking underneath.

"What a shame that is, isn't it?" He snarls, leaning into my space.

Sweat slicks down my back. I have no place to run, nowhere to hide from the hate oozing off of him. Slowly, he walks across the room and closes all the blinds granting a view into the hallway.

"What did you do?" I plead.

"I did what any good son would do. Dad needed *me* to get you to fall in line, comply, and you *fucking wouldn't*. As usual. So I decided that if he couldn't have you by his side in the flesh, he could have you in spirit. Sympathy is just as powerful in politics. And driven by tragedy?" He chuckles darkly. "Well, that's something that could inflame his whole political platform." His grin was twisted, sick, *proud* of this awful plan.

"Killing your own sister?" I say, a stinging tear rolling free.

"You were never *really* part of our family. It was just supposed to be me. I was all they needed. All you ever were was a mistake, a disappointment. I had to tolerate you, same as Dad. Now I can be the one standing by his side, like it was always meant to be."

"I was never going to be by his side, so what does it matter!" I try to raise my voice but it just trembles.

"That's the fucking point, *Lainey*. He wanted you, too. And I only want it to be *me*."

Stepping even closer this time, he strikes out fast, like the snake he is, wrapping both of his hands around my neck. Cal is only a few inches taller than me, and by looking at him you would think he would be weak, but his rage is making him strong. I claw at his fingers, but he just grips harder. My tired, smoke-addled body can't fight back like normal.

My eyes roam to the door, praying the officer is there again, will look in here and see this fucked-up family reunion.

"Oh, he's not there," Calvin hisses. "Sent him on a nice, long coffee break. On my very generous tip, of course. How could he resist? No cop likes babysitting duty. And I assured him that you'd be safe—I am your *brother*, after all."

His disgusting grin and wild, beady eyes are the last things I see before his wrath pulls me back into darkness.

50

Remington

She was right, of course. A shower, long and hot, was really nice. It would have been nicer if she were with me, but hospital rules and all that would probably frown on that wish. I lingered under the hot spray, letting it loosen my tight, sore muscles longer than I intended to. My thoughts got lost in the steam, swirling down the drain with the soap and grime from the fire.

Exhaustion swept over my limbs as I toweled off the water droplets from my body as quickly as I could. Pulling on Eli's grey sweatpants, an FGFD T-shirt, and my gym shoes he picked up from my locker at the fire station, I felt like a new man. Clean and ready to climb into that shitty hospital bed, wrap Lainey safely in my arms, and hold her all night.

Walking back down Lainey's ICU hallway it's quiet and calm, but I feel uneasy. I can't explain it, but something in my gut is screaming at me to move faster. Looking ahead, her door is unguarded.

Unguarded. Where the hell is the cop?

Dread. Panic. Fear.

I drop my bag and sprint down the hall, catching the

attention of the nurses at their station. They call out after me, but I ignore them.

Bursting through Lainey's hospital room door, I can't believe what I am seeing. I don't even have time to process it fully before I am moving.

I lunge, tackling Calvin to the floor, and then I *unleash* myself on him. Every ounce of rage that has been pooling in my veins pours out through the bone-crushing punches I deliver.

His eyes.

His nose.

His jaw.

His cheek.

His ribs.

It doesn't matter where the punches land, as long as they inflict maximum pain and damage to this piece of shit.

He had his hands around Lainey's neck. He was choking her, killing her.

I can't stop. I don't stop until staff members yank me off of his still body. He's breathing, but completely fucked up, and I don't have a drop of sympathy.

Spinning around, I rush to Lainey's side.

God please don't take her away from me after all of this. She deserves better.

Her breathing is a thin whisper in the room. The pale, delicate skin on her neck is already darkening with bruises where that son of a bitch wrapped his hands around her neck, trying to steal the very breath that gives me life.

The commotion in the room is like the buzz in a hive to my overstimulated mind. Lainey is surrounded by doctors and nurses, her care being their main priority. A group of staff members lifts Cal onto a stretcher, assessing his many wounds. The kind nurse that helped Lainey shower guides me to a chair. Carefully, she starts to clean the wounds on my hands that I hadn't even noticed were there.

"I almost lost her again," I say softly to her.

"I know, sugar. I know." She hums. "But you got that bastard. And your Lainey is going to be more than fine, because you are her hero—so many times over."

Looking up I see the cop in the doorway, the one that was supposed to be guarding Lainey. Fury ignites all over again, and I jump up.

"Where the fuck were you!?" I scream at him. His eyes go wide, confused and afraid.

"I went to get a coffee. Her brother was here for a visit, said he would make sure nobody would come in and bother her." The young cop's face is as white as the walls surrounding us.

"He just tried to fucking strangle her to death, you useless piece of shit. Stand outside that door and don't move an inch. I am calling Danny."

"Remington?" The softest, whispered cry of my name comes from the hospital bed, and I am next to Lainey instantly, pulling her into my chest. Her sobs are nearly silent because of all the trauma to her throat over the past forty-eight hours.

"I'm here, baby. I'm not going anywhere." I gently rock her body, holding her tighter, needing to not let her slip out of my grasp.

"It was Cal," she states, shocked and broken.

"I know. I know, and I am so sorry. I don't know why he would do something like this, but I will never let him hurt you ever again." She gives me one tiny nod as I swipe away her tears.

"I know." She gingerly touches her neck and whines. "Why."

"Don't talk yet, okay? Let's wait for Danny to come so you only have to say it once?" Again she nods.

Fate. Angels. Miracles. Whatever was on our side, letting me get to Lainey not once, but twice before it was too late? I am so fucking grateful. I can't even let myself think about the "what ifs" of that timing being off. My arms firmly wrapped around her trembling body in this moment are the only things keeping me from falling apart from the magnitude of what just happened.

51

Lainey

Danny and a detective from the Fox Grove police department came to take our statements. I quietly, slowly, painfully recounted the whole story, once, like Remington wanted so my voice was strained the least amount possible. It was difficult. To speak. To tell the horrors of what happened in that room. The things that Cal admitted to. He was sick, twisted, and not the man I thought he was. Not the boy I grew up with. I knew he was an asshole, never really cared for me, and was manipulative. But never in a million years did I think he was capable of all this.

Right now he was laying in the very same hospital, guarded by cops much more capable than the one that left his position for the temptation of coffee and a break. Danny was *livid.* He felt enormous guilt for what happened to me, having picked the cops on the rotation to watch over me. I told him that he was not allowed to carry that—the weight of someone else's mistakes on his shoulders. He was too good of a man, of a cop, to let that sully his integrity.

Remington was not being charged for ripping Cal off of me and beating him nearly to death. It was being ruled as self-defense. We had a floor of witnesses ready to go to bat for him, and we are so grateful to the hospital staff for taking care of both of us.

As nice as they have been, I am ready to get out of here.

I would love to say "let's go home," but that is gone. So when they let me out of here we are moving in with Remington's parents. His mother insisted, so she is able to take care of me for now. The doctors have me on strict instructions to rest, and I am supposed to limit my speech as much as possible for the next month. My vocal cords have severe bruising and trauma—ya know, from my brother trying to burn me alive and then strangle me to death.

I'm definitely *going to need to start up my therapy sessions again. Sarcasm is not going to be enough to cope with the shit he put me through.*

"Remington," I whisper, and he's instantly at my side, his deeply bruised hand holding mine tenderly.

"Yes, baby? What do you need? More water?"

I shake my head, whispering, "These won't fit." I point to the two dozen bouquets of flowers decorating my regular hospital room. I had been downgraded from the ICU, and for the past week flowers had been showing up constantly. Some from our friends, Remington's parents and Sutton, my work, but mostly from Remington. He didn't leave me to pick them up though, he had them all made and delivered.

Staring at all these bouquets this week has given me a lot of time to ponder which flowers were my favorites. I appreciated and enjoyed them all, of course, but I think I finally decided on a favorite for myself—I just hadn't told Remington yet.

I wonder what he will think when I tell him? Will he stop bringing me all different kinds?

"Don't worry, I have backup coming to help us haul this out of here," Remington tells me as we hear raised voices in the hallway.

Kendra and Eli waltz in the door then, bickering between themselves but turning on the sunshine and smiles when they see me. "We are ready to break you out of here!" Eli grins and claps his hands.

I stand from the bed, wobbly, but much stronger than last week. Kendra hugs me, her little body squeezing me tightly. "I'm so happy we get to visit you *not* at the hospital after today," she admits.

"Me, too," I whisper.

Our favorite nurse wheels in a big cart for the flowers. We load everything up, and Kendra takes my small bag, filled with borrowed things. Eli pushes the flower cart, and Remington pushes my wheelchair, which the staff are making me ride in until we reach the hospital exit.

The sliding glass doors open wide, and the curb is filled with people—for me. I cover my face and I feel overwhelmed. Remington's parents are picking us up, which I knew about. What I wasn't expecting was nearly the entire fire station to be there, including one of the trucks. Kinsley is cradled in Sutton's arms, sleeping peacefully. Danny and Megan stand by their cruiser. Jess and her boys are holding Ash on a leash, and he's happily wagging his tail, watching all the excitement.

I stand up, and Remington wraps his arm around my waist. "I don't even know how to handle this, what to say." My voice is a soft, hoarse plea; I am sure they all can't hear.

"You don't have to say anything, sweetheart," Renee says, stepping forward. "This is what family does." She hugs me tight, and I hug her back, relishing in the feeling of being fully loved by a group of people that know the meaning of loving, cherishing, and protecting the people that mean the most to you.

Being at Charles and Renee's house, living here, and having them help care for me, it was now easier to imagine what it must have been like for Remington and Sutton growing up in this warm, loving environment. It doesn't surprise me that they turned out the way they have after experiencing being here in this way.

Renee fusses over me, feeds me, keeps me company, makes me laugh, and has become a true friend. Charles is steadfast in his protective nature, like Remington. He fills my water, makes sure I have anything I need, hugs me in a fatherly way that makes my eyes sting every single time. I feel like I belong, not just because we are staying here since our house burned down, but because these people are my true family. I fit here, and I haven't felt that anywhere but with Remington.

Knowing that makes sitting across from my mother today very uncomfortable. She came over to see me, finally fully informed of the horrors her son put me through. First she had to call me, not even knowing where to find me. Remington answered my brand-new phone that he got my old number transferred over to since my old phone was lost in the fire and talked to her since I am still supposed to be on vocal rest.

Sitting on the couch, hand laced with Remington's, my mother's eyes linger on the burns slowing healing along my jaw and neck. A permanent reminder of the first evil attempt to take my life, the faint yellow bruising ringing my throat from trying to suffocate the life out of me the second.

Renee brings me a warm cup of tea, which has been routine multiple times a day, for my throat. Gently rubbing my shoulder, she says, "You just let me know if you need me, sweetheart. Alright?" Warmth flows from her eyes, giving me the strength I need in this moment.

"Thank you," I mouth quietly, nodding as she excuses herself.

My mother clears her throat from the other couch, sitting stiffly in her discomfort. She had refused the offer of Renee's kindness when asked if she wanted tea as well or something else to drink.

"What can we do for you today, Ann?" Remington asks from his relaxed position next to me. His protective hackles are raised, on high alert, but you'd never know from his tone and body language. I know because I know *him*.

Scoffing, my mother says, "I came here because I wanted to see if Lainey was alright. I was worried!"

I roll my eyes, bristling at her sharp words. "The fire and attack were almost two weeks ago. Calvin was arrested, has been in jail for almost as long. It's hard to believe you were that concerned when you only called Lainey *yesterday*. Her father has not tried to contact her at all," Remington growls out in frustration.

"Remerton, I think Lainey can speak for herself." She looks pointedly at me, but I keep my mouth shut, happy to let the man I love speak on my behalf.

"Once again, Ann—it's Remington, to Lainey. Rem to the rest of the world. Your misuse of my name now is not a mistake, it's just you trying to be a bitch. I don't like using that term, especially under my mama's roof, but I think she'd agree with me on this one."

"Amen, dear," Renee shouts from the kitchen, and I have to hold back a snort.

"See?" Remington glares at my mother. "As far as Lainey speaking for herself. Actually, Ann, you see, she isn't supposed to talk much at all. You would know that had you been at the hospital, or around at all these past weeks. Her vocal cords sustained such damage from your son trying to *kill her* that she is on strict orders from her doctor to rest. Which means very limited talking."

"She can just whisper," my mother states. "I'm here to talk *to her*. This has nothing to do with you. You are just trying to insert yourself into a family matter."

"I *am* her family." My mother blanches. "Once again, you're making this about you. What you want, what you think is best. Your terms. That is *not* how this is going to go anymore. Lainey allowed you to come here today thinking you actually gave a shit about her, but you don't. You should be falling to your knees, begging for her forgiveness. Instead, you're here still being unkind and judgmental." Remington kisses my temple, and I lean into his warmth.

"I don't have room in my life for people that don't love me the way I deserve," I whisper, looking my mother directly in her angry eyes.

"That's unfair—" I cut her off, holding up my hand.

"What's unfair is that you went to see Cal, *in jail*, before you came here to see me. That you would even go see him at all after what he did . . ." I touch my throat, her eyes following my fingertips. Remington hands me my tea off of the coffee table, and I take a sip, trying to soothe my weak voice.

"He's alone in there. I needed to know why he did it. He is my son and, and—"

Stopping her again, I say, "And I am your daughter. But you don't deserve me."

I have no more tears left to cry for her, no more excuses to make for why she doesn't care enough, or if maybe it was her relationship with my father that made her the way she is. I won't spend any more days forming myself into a person I'm not to try and please her and gain an ounce of her unattainable affection. No, she is her own person, making her own way in the world. I am lucky enough to have found a family that knows what love really is, and they are patiently teaching me how to accept it, show it, and believe in it. I no longer have to hold on so tightly to the ropes of my own family. The ones that were silently strangling and suffocating me for years, long before my life was almost taken by someone that should have also loved me unconditionally.

Charles steps into the room, arms crossed. Stoic, intimidating, and protective. His pinched, deep golden-brown eyes and wrinkled brow hold zero warmth for my mother. He is not only here for Remington, he's here for me, too. He is claiming me as one of his own—*a LeBlanc in his heart, if not in name.* My heart pounds, trips over itself again thinking about my conversation with Renee in the garden. It feels like a lifetime ago. But after all we've been through, it also feels even more true today.

Running a strong hand over his light-brown stubbled beard, Charles says to my mother, who's still frozen by my words, "Lainey has said her piece. It's time for you to go."

She stands, grabs her designer bag from the place next to her, and doesn't look back as she marches out of the room. I don't follow, try and say goodbye, or feel any of the guilt that would usually make me chase after her. For the first time in my life I know that the guilt and burdens placed in my soul over being a constant disappointment to my parents for everything I did have evaporated . . . Because I finally understand that all along, I was never the problem.

52

Lainey
TWO MONTHS LATER

"I want to go see it," I argue, my voice feeling strong and steady.

"Are you sure?" Remington rubs the back of his neck, his handsome face filled with so much love for me I could melt into a puddle right at his feet.

"Positive. Dr. Radack says that I am ready. I have tools to help if I feel like I am going to have a panic attack. My nightmares have gotten better. And most importantly"—I step into his space, wrapping my arms around his middle—"*you* are going to be there with me, right?"

"Of course I will, beautiful." He reaches down, gently running his thumb across the rough, pebbled, pink flesh that scars my face. I swallow harshly, still getting used to it. To the new feeling, the look of it, but never wanting to let go of that special connection to Remington. I lean into his palm, placing a kiss on his wrist. My neck healed a lot better, but my jaw, my face will always bear the deeper and more obvious scars of what happened to me.

"I need to see it, please, Remington. We need to take the

next step, together." My pleading eyes do him in, and he nods in agreement.

I wasn't ready.

I don't think I could have ever been prepared properly to see the devastation left by the fire that consumed the cute little house on our peaceful street. All the other homes on the block stand untouched, happy, whole. Where our place had once stood, now there is nothing but a charred lot of land. The torched skeleton of the house had been demolished, taken away weeks ago, leaving us with this depressing view.

"I'm so sorry." I cling to Remington.

"Why are you apologizing for the sins of someone else? This is not your fault, Lainey, never was. That man will not ruin what we had here." Taking my hand he leads me to the backyard and the towering oak trees that stand sentry over the little, sad green space left on our property.

We sit on the patchy, scorched grass under the trees, and stare right out to the street. Slow minivans and sedan drivers gawk as they pass our lot. Everyone in Fox Grove knows about what happened here and at the hospital. It won't just be gossip that fizzles out after a week or so, it will be Fox Grove legend. This is not a typical, everyday, accidental fire—this was a crime scene, a near murder site. I am a walking miracle to have escaped the literal fingers of death twice. The feeling of Cal's disgusting hatred wrapped around my neck wakes me up often, leaving me gulping for air, worried that I am trapped back in that hospital room with him. Only the comfort of Remington's arms can chase the demons back to the darkness.

"There's nothing left." I breathe out. "I mean, in my mind

I knew that, you *told* me that. But being here in person, seeing it right now, *it's real*."

"Yeah, baby, it's real." Remington slings his tattooed arm around me and pulls me to his side.

"Everything we had is gone." Gasping with sudden realization I say, "All my journals!" Tears pool hot and unwelcome as I tuck my face into my knees. "I know it's stupid to be so upset, and you lost even more than me. You lost a whole house you bought and had been working on for years."

"Lainey. Look at me," Remington demands. I give him my eyes . . . my heart, my soul.

"They were just unimportant memories. I should be happy." I wipe my face, feeling embarrassed.

"What happened in that house, that fire—nothing about that was happy. I have never been more terrified. I'd gladly burn everything I own a million times over to keep you out of any more flames. But you being trapped, us losing the home and all of the things we held precious besides each other, baby? You are allowed to mourn that. I am. Nothing about the journals was unimportant to you, don't minimize them." He reaches out to gently hold my face, slowly leans in, then reverently places the most delicate kiss against my jaw.

His words tear me apart.

They also fuse me back together.

I close my eyes as a breeze ripples over the early evening air, sending a chill up my exposed arms. Suddenly a gentle weight presses down on my lap. When I open my eyes, my hands reach for my heart before they go for the gift that Remington has just given to me.

"How?" I barely let the word leave my lips.

"I didn't have it at the house. Couldn't let you see it until I was done." His smirk is so handsome and enchanting. "You might not have all of your journals, but you have this one."

This one.

It's the palest lavender, my favorite color. A creamy, soft leather cover that is embossed with one single, large flower—a peony.

"A peony." I look up to see his perfect, honey eyes anxiously watching my reaction. "How could you have known?"

"Known what?" He tilts his head in question.

"I picked a favorite, in the hospital. When I was laying there looking at the flowers, thinking about all the ones you have given me. And the one arrangement next to my bed were those pink peonies you gave me." I trace my finger over the cover, glancing up at him to find a huge, happy grin on his face.

"We found your favorite, huh?" My heart pounds in my chest, so hard and rhythmic I'm sure he can hear it.

"Yes, I guess that means you can stop giving me so many flowers now, doesn't it?" I hug the notebook to myself.

"Open it," Remington insists, raising an eyebrow.

I am excited to see my words written in his familiar handwriting, knowing that he spent his time giving me back a piece of myself.

Flipping open the journal, it nearly slips from my fingers when my eyes take in what is on the page. I gasp at the beauty. My journal entry is there, but he added to it—

"Flowers," I sob.

I keep turning pages and keep finding more. Every single one is different, stunning, thoughtful, tagged with a name and meaning at the bottom of each page. This is why it took him so long to give it back to me. He was not just simply copying what I had written, he was writing me his own love letter in return.

Iris.

Magnolia.

Dahlia.

Orchid.

Chrysanthemum.

Roses.

Plumeria.

Lotus.

"Oh my God! My perfect pie day, Remington." Apple blossoms explode across the page.

I keep flipping, each page a new discovery of his talent and his affection for me.

Poppies.

Sweet peas.

Bluebells.

Violets.

Calla lily.

Buttercup.

Sunflowers.

They just keep going. There are so many flowers, so many hours of work. It's going to take me just as long to look at each one and truly appreciate each detail.

"I can't believe you did all this, Remington. It's the most incredible thing I have ever seen. And you kept it a secret from me that you can draw? Not even doodles or stick figures, this is like *drawing drawing*." My mouth hangs open in awe with every petal he's placed on the pages.

"Baby, nobody really knew I could draw. Only Eli and my family. Well, Keller, too," he says, rubbing his strong hand up my thigh.

"Who's Keller?" I ask, unable to tear my gaze from the pages in my lap.

"My friend who does all my tattoos, lives in Norfolk."

I glance down at his sinewy arm, rippled with muscle and ink. "I have always wished I could get a tattoo," I admit to him longingly.

"Why didn't you get one?" The lazy strokes of his fingers pull a sigh from my chest, and I tip my face toward the sky.

"Judgment from my family. They were not fans of anything outside of their box. Tattoos were a huge no. I was never ever brave enough to bring it up, even as an adult." Remington's snort brings my attention back to him.

"Pretty sure I knew that from the second Ann Quinn laid eyes on me, baby. But that part of your life is over. If you want a tattoo, get a tattoo. Your wish is my command." He holds up his arm, showing off his sleeve.

"You did these?" I say, shocked.

Laughing he says, "I didn't tattoo myself, no. Keller did that. But I drew a lot of these, he tweaked them, and then did the ink for me."

A lightbulb snaps to life in my brain and I gasp. "Kinsley's room!? That was you?"

Remington nods. "Yes, sorry I didn't tell you, but I wanted you to see this first."

I can't hold back anymore, so I lean in and kiss Remington hoping he can feel every ounce of passion, awe, and love I feel for him in this moment. Time stills as he weaves his fingers through my hair, tugging just the way I like, making me melt against his body. Breathlessly, we pull apart. I want more, but we are in our burnt, open yard. Not exactly the most ideal place for him to strip me naked and make good on all the dirty promises dancing in his lust-soaked eyes right now.

"Go to the last page." Remington points to the back of the journal as I am still lost in his spell.

"Alright," I hum.

I remember the last page. It had been right before my birthday. Things were not great with Brett, and I had cried, made girl dinner, cracked open a bottle of wine, and binged classic romantic staples. I said I would never find a man like Harry from the movie *When Harry Met Sally*. I also wrote about being afraid to voice my deepest dream. I knew that nobody in my life at that point deserved to hear them, let alone hold them.

This is impossible.

There, on the last page of the journal, Remington had filled it with the most stunning *peonies* I had ever seen. Some were in full bloom, others tiny buds. And in the center of them he had written—

MY LIFE STARTED THE DAY I MET YOU.
I WANT TO MAKE YOUR EVERY
DREAM COME TRUE.
YOU CAN TRUST ME, LAINEY.
I LOVE YOU.
-R

"Lainey," he whispers, gentle hands cup my face, "let me all the way in, baby. I want to be part of making your dreams a reality."

"*You* are my greatest dream. I never voiced it because it was never possible with anyone before you. Remington, I want a happy marriage and a loving family. The opposite of the one I was raised in. I want to build a life I am proud of, a home that is happy and full of a life worth living." My voice is healed, but I feel weak finally admitting what my heart wants, terrified the world will be cruel and rip away my happiness.

"It will be my greatest honor to build that life with you. Starting right here." He gestures to the black, scraped ground. "We can start from the ground up, make our dream house. Fill it up with love, laughter, happiness, and all the babies you will let me put in you." I laugh as he tackles me back to the ground, rolling just right so I am cradled in the safety of his arms, then kisses me like he's bringing me back to life.

And I think he just might be . . . Over and over, every day when he wakes up choosing to love me, just like I always dreamed but never imagined was possible.

53

Remington

ONE MONTH LATER

I walk into our bedroom in our new apartment, in Lainey's old Fox Hollow building, and nearly trip over my own feet at the sight before me. My woman is bent over our bed in nothing but deep-purple lace panties and a matching bra.

Quietly I step up behind her, and she yelps in surprise when I band an arm around her waist, pulling her body into mine, her back flush to my chest.

"You are a little fucking tease, aren't you, beautiful?" I growl into her ear.

"I don't know what you're talking about." Her sweet voice bubbles out with a hint of laughter.

"Hmm, really? You *don't* know that we are supposed to be leaving soon to meet the contractor? You expect me to walk in here, see you looking like *this*"—I trail my fingers down her side leaving goose bumps in my wake—"and not expect me to fuck you the way you deserve?"

"I mean, if you insist." She bites that bottom lip, driving me crazy.

I pull her even tighter against me so she can feel my erection, begging to be set free. "Feel that, baby? Desperate for you, that's what you make me." I spin her around and claim her mouth.

She kisses me back passionately, just as needy for me. Her hands slide under my shirt and the contact of her fingers burn my skin with want. Gasping and peppering kisses down my neck, she says, "You are very overdressed again."

"I can fix that." I yank my T-shirt over my head as she works my belt open. Her sexy breasts shake with her movements, and I can't wait to get my hands, my mouth, on them.

I shed my jeans and boxers in record time, reclaim Lainey's mouth, and pick her up. Her curves fill my hands perfectly as I sit her back on the bed, snapping open her bra, nearly ripping it apart in my haste.

"Remmmington." She moans my name and grips my hair when I suck a pink, needy bud into my mouth, massaging her other breast with my hand.

"Perfect, baby. Every inch of you."

Her body arches off of the bed as my kisses roam over her creamy skin, stopping over her lace-covered center. Rolling my hands over her hips I look at her with a greedy smile. "Now *you* are the one that is overdressed." I rip the purple lace from her body as easily as wrapping paper covering the most precious gift.

"Remington! Those matched my bra. I *just* bought them." Lainey tries to act upset, but the lust in her stormy-blue eyes and her dripping wet pussy as I run my fingers up to her clit tell a different story.

"I'll buy you more." I settle between her open legs and kiss my way up her calf, pressing down on her hips as she wiggles on the mattress.

"Be a good girl and let me worship you," I demand, nipping at her inner thigh.

"Ohmygod." Her moans of pleasure fill our empty bedroom with the sweetest sounds while her addictive taste floods my tongue. I will never get enough of her, of giving her pleasure, and knowing that I am the man that holds all her secrets.

"More. Yes. Remington. Oh, right. Thhhere." Her body locks tight as I suck her swollen clit, rolling it over my tongue, and her orgasm crashes powerfully through her body and spills into my mouth. I lick up every delicious drop.

"I could live right here," I admit to her as she looks down at me, her chest heaving.

"But I need you up here." She pulls me to her, chest to chest. I kiss her fully, letting her taste her own release on my lips, and we both moan.

I grind my throbbing cock against her soaking wet entrance, knowing she is more than ready to take every inch. With one hard thrust I slide in deep, fully seated in my own personal paradise.

"Holy shit!" Lainey cries out. She rolls her hips, silently asking for more, and I am happy to give her anything she wants.

Our hearts pound in rhythm with our bodies, and we get lost in each other. Hands and hearts tangled in the sheets. Kisses and confessions of love falling from our lips. Heaven and home. Here and now.

"Come with me, Lainey. Let me fill you up. Feel my perfect pussy ruin me." She nods wildly, eyes pinched.

"Eyes on me, baby. Right here." As soon as her blue oceans open to me, revealing the depth of her passion, love, and our connection—we combust together, tossed over in a turbulent sea of lust. Lost to each other in the most perfect way.

Collapsing, heart racing and full, I hear Lainey start to giggle. I look over at her, brown hair a soft halo around her glowing face and shoulders. "What's so funny?"

"We are *definitely* going to be late for the contractor." She covers her face, giggles turning into full-on laughter.

Damn, it feels good to see her so happy.

We get into my truck, late, and head over to the house. Well, can't exactly call it that yet. After Lainey fully recovered, we decided to move back into her old apartment building while we rebuild our dream home. As kind as it was of my parents to let us live with them, we needed space and privacy.

Thankfully this building allows dogs, so Ash could stay with us. He's getting so big, has the sweetest personality, and made a full recovery from the fire as well. We take him to obedience classes, and he is the best one in there, not that I am biased or anything. Ash also is Lainey's constant shadow. I think they recognize the trauma that they endured, a silent bond that pulls them together. Wherever she is, Ash is steps behind. So right now he, of course, is in the back seat, head resting on the center console of the truck. His dark eyes moon up at Lainey, watchful and loving.

"Isn't it weird that he wanted to meet at dusk?" Lainey asks me as we turn into our neighborhood.

"He is really busy, just wanted to get a feel for the space he has to work with," I grumble and grip the steering wheel tighter.

"Still think it's weird." Lainey looks down at Ash, scratching behind his fuzzy ears.

She continues looking at him as we park in the driveway and doesn't notice that the contractor *isn't* here. I hop out of the truck and round her side, opening her door.

Finally looking up at our property, Lainey stumbles into

my arms in shock. "Oh my God, Remington." She looks up at me, awe and tears welling in her eyes.

I had cracked the windows before I got out; the night is cool, and I don't want Ash to run through my surprise, so we leave him in the truck for now.

Taking Lainey's hand, I walk her to where our house used to stand, where the new one will eventually be built. All over our property, every spot that was touched by the fire is now covered with arrangements of flowers—any and every variety I could get my hands on. There are also hundreds of candles, battery-operated ones thank you very much, dotted throughout the massive bouquet and lining a path to the middle where there is a large space for us to stand.

"I have never seen anything more beautiful in my entire life," Lainey says as she spins around, taking in the rainbow of colors and false flickering flames as the dusky air hums around us.

"I have," I state as she turns back to me, finding me staring at her.

"Remington," she whispers.

"Lainey, you lit up my life from the moment we met. Before you, I was existing, going through the motions of life, but I wasn't truly living. I wanted that dream you told me about too, but I was afraid to chase it, to open myself up to the possibility of getting hurt."

She wipes a tear that runs down her cheek. I cup her face, tracing my thumb along her scarred jaw. Shivers ripple through both of us.

"I had no chance resisting you, baby. This pull. This connection. You captured my heart, my very soul before you ever realized it, Lainey. I am wholly, completely yours."

Dropping to one knee, I pull out a small lavender box and pop it open to reveal the ring I have been waiting too long to give Lainey. The large radiant-cut diamond in the center sparkles in the glowing candlelight surrounding us.

"Make me the most blessed man to walk this planet, Lainey. Marry me? Be mine. Let me be the man to give you flowers and my forever."

"Yes, Remington. Oh my God, yes!" Lainey sobs as she launches herself into my arms, hugging me, anchoring herself to me.

I kiss her deeply before I pull back, and taking her left hand, I slide the engagement ring down her trembling finger.

"Remington, this is too much," Lainey tries to protest, as if it will change it.

"You deserve this, baby. I picked it just for you. Nothing is too much for you." I kiss her cheeks, blush staining them perfectly.

"Lainey LeBlanc has a nice ring to it." Her eyes shimmer with happiness.

"It sure does." I kiss the shining promise that I just slid into place on her hand.

Holding it up to the fading light, Lainey looks at the diamonds on the band meeting the center stone and grins at me. "It looks like a flower."

"I told you, beautiful. I am going to find a way to give you as many flowers as I possibly can." I kiss her soft lips.

"Forever?" Lainey asks, voice full of love and longing.

"Forever," I vow.

Epilogue

"Keller! Good to see you, man." Remington shakes his friend's hand.

He is just as tall as Remington, thicker though, like an immovable brick wall of muscle and tattoos. *So many tattoos.* You would think that would make Keller Shore scary, but looking at his face, kindness radiates out of him. He has dark hair, a crooked smile, double dimples that are sure to make women melt, and striking green eyes.

"It's been too long." Keller's rumbling voice booms through his tattoo shop.

Remington motions to me. "This is my fiancé, Lainey."

"Nice to meet you, Lainey." Keller takes my hand, shaking it in a firm but gentle grasp.

"It's really nice to meet you. I've heard so many stories from Remington." I smile at the two friends.

"Oh shit, don't believe any of them." Keller throws his head back on a laugh. "Come on over to my station, I have everything ready to go for you."

Anxiety rolls through my gut. *I'm really doing this?*

Remington, knowing me so well, runs his hands up and

down my bare shoulders, whispering, "You can do this, baby. And if you changed your mind, we can try again another day."

His unwavering love and support, always giving me the freedom to choose what I want, gives me the courage to sit down in the chair next to Keller.

Hours later, inked up my spine in shades of black and grey, resting between my shoulder blades, is a beautiful peony flower in bloom, drawn for me by Remington. Woven into the stem of the flower in cursive is the word "worthy."

Worthy.

I finally believe it.

Worthy of love.

Worthy of loving myself.

Worthy of accepting love and kindness from others.

Worthy of this life Remington and I are building together.

Bonus Epilogue

A wet dog nose pressed into my ear followed by a sloppy lick on the cheek wakes me up abruptly. Remington's deep laughter comes from somewhere nearby, and I reach over finding his side of the bed cool and empty.

"Good boy, Ash," Remington says.

I reluctantly pull myself from the last tether of sleep holding me down, open my eyes, and see the most handsome man filling our bedroom doorway. Remington's smile is as blinding as the sun that is just starting to blaze into our room through the balcony doors. In his hands is a tray filled with the most delicious smelling breakfast, coffee for him, and tea for me.

"Mmmm," I say. "This is a really nice surprise to wake up to. You and the breakfast, I mean. Ash's nose in my ear, not so much." I glance over at our very proud dog, goofy tongue floppy out the side of his mouth like usual.

"Well, to be fair, I asked him to go wake you up and he did an excellent job following directions. He *was* number one in his obedience classes for a reason." Remington freaking winks at me as he walks to our bed.

Did I mention that he's also shirtless? Blond hair perfectly mussed, muscles and every tattoo on full display . . . *I think he's trying to kill me before the day even starts.*

He sets the tray between us, picks up a freshly sliced strawberry off of the huge pile of French toast, and offers it to me. I open my mouth and gladly let him feed it to me, moaning as the tart berry runs over my taste buds. Our eyes locked on each other, licking the juice from his fingertips, Remington says, "Happy first wedding anniversary, Mrs. LeBlanc."

Grinning, I lean in and kiss him. "Happy anniversary, Mr. LeBlanc. It's been one of the best years of my entire life."

"Mine, too, baby." He cups my face, gently running his thumb across my jaw, my scar, and then down my neck.

"What is the plan for today?" I ask, sinking back into the pillows.

"Well, this." He motions to the perfect breakfast he made us. "Then I was thinking we could take a shower together. Later we are going to pick up Gino's and go to Eagle Point to watch the sunset."

"Shower together, huh?" I say with a raised eyebrow.

"Yup, all about water conservation around here." He smirks. "After we shower I have a surprise for you here though."

"Ohh! Do I get a hint?" I fold my hands hopefully.

"Absolutely not." He puts a forkful of scrambled eggs in his mouth, eyes filled with mischief.

"Well I guess we better hurry this along then," I say, taking a big bite of my own French toast, holding back a smile while Remington laughs at me.

We in fact *did not* hurry anything along—

We made slow, passionate love in bed after finishing our breakfast. It was intimate and sweet. Then we got in the shower together and Remington took me against our glass-tiled wall. It was rough, commanding, and powerful. Raw. All sides of ourselves connected, free, open, and loved to perfection within each other's embrace.

Now we are standing in our spacious living room where Remington is tying a blindfold around my eyes.

"This is fun, but I think I am a bit too sore to go another round right now, Remington," I tease him.

Rumbling into my neck, he says, "Don't tempt me, baby. You and I both know you could take it." He smacks my ass, making me yelp, then laces his fingers through my hand, leading me through our house.

Rebuilding from the ground up after the fire was a lot of work, more emotional than I think either of us expected it to be, but also really exciting. Now we are living in a house that has everything we could possibly want with plenty of room to grow our family.

"Where are we going?" I ask, feeling the fresh air hit me as we step outside.

"Patience, beautiful. Almost there. Watch your step." Remington leads me off of our deck and into the unfinished backyard.

Charles and Remington have been working on the landscaping and hardscaping to make the yard a nice place to have company and enjoy ourselves. Renee promised me she would help me with a small cut-flower garden. I do *not* have her green thumb, but I appreciate that she is teaching me and we can share in a love of flowers.

Remington twists my body into the position he wants, then wraps his strong arms around my stomach. "I love you so much, Lainey. Happy anniversary."

He pulls off my blindfold and I blink quickly, adjusting to the bright sunlight. There in front of us, in the empty dirt space that will eventually be my garden, is a singular plant—a beautiful, large peony plant, bursting with life. Deep green leaves and gorgeous pink flowers.

Spinning in his arms, I take Remington's smooth face in my hands, kiss him, and look into his glimmering, honey-colored eyes. "It's so beautiful. Thank you."

"It's our own legacy flowers, baby. Every year my dad gets Mom the new roses, right? So I thought since peonies are *your* favorite flower, we could carry on the tradition, but in our own way." He bites down on his lip and runs his hand through his sandy hair nervously.

"This is the most incredible gift you could have given me today, Remington. You never stop surprising me with how thoughtful you are." I kiss his wedding band.

"You do a good job at surprising me, too. I'm not sure a little plant can top Ash." He hugs me to his chest.

"I mean, this is our first anniversary, and it's traditionally supposed to be paper gifts. I technically made mine for you. Here." I reach into the back pocket of my jeans and give him an envelope. "It's really kind of for both of us." I smile up at him.

Carefully, Remington tears open the pale lavender envelope, slipping out the folded paper. His brow wrinkles in confusion as he takes a moment to realize what he's holding.

"Surprise," I whisper.

"We're pregnant?" Remington traces a finger lightly over the black-and-white sonogram image, showing the tiny bean shape that is our baby.

"Yes. I went for my yearly exam last week, remember? They always make you take a pregnancy test, just in case. I was not expecting it to be positive. Dr. Barrett squeezed me in for an ultrasound since I didn't know how far along I could be.

My periods have been really irregular ever since we had my IUD taken out." I fidget with my wedding band and engagement ring as I explain my appointment to my husband.

Suddenly I am swooped off of my feet and Remington's lips are on mine, drowning me in an adoring kiss. I feel swept away in emotion and happiness. His strong arms holding me and our growing baby, a place that will always be a safe haven for the both of us.

"I take it back. *This* is the best surprise of my life," Remington admits as he wipes tears from his eyes. "I'm so fucking happy, baby." Dropping to his knees, right in the dirt, he kisses my stomach. "Hello, sweet pea," he says reverently.

I run my hands through Remington's hair as he continues to kiss my stomach and talk to our baby—my heart exploding, surrounded by flowers and the precious threads of forever being grown right here from the deepest roots of love.

The End.

Afterword

Writing was a dream that I always held close to my heart. A *secret* dream that I didn't think I was allowed to chase. Reading has been a place for me to escape into. Books have been a comfort. Authors have been heroic benchmarks that I felt I could never measure up against. Long story short, I was terrified—of failure, of judgment, of critical people in my life, of not being able to write anything worthy of taking up space and people's time.

I never knew that writing could unlock not only an escape, but a beautiful space to heal as well. These characters knocked on my soul and would *not* let me run away from their stories. I decided to take a chance on myself and finally do what felt impossible—pursue that dream I had locked away for so long.

This book is truly so many pieces of me poured onto the page, but it is also uniquely the characters. They kept me up at night, popped into my head when I was driving or blow-drying my hair . . . demanding attention at the most inconvenient times. Lainey and Remington's story allowed me to be brave, believe in myself, take pride in this pursuit, and open myself up to a new world of possibilities.

I hope that if anything, when you read this book you feel a little bit braver to take a step in the direction of whatever dream *you* may be harboring in your own heart. It is scary, big, and hard to try new things—and also worth every step of the journey.

Acknowledgments

To my husband . . . None of this is possible without you. You give me the confidence to dream, to believe in myself, and to say the words "I am proud of myself" out loud and *actually* believe them. When I have an idea you make sure I hurry and write it down so I don't forget what it is. You let me write as uninterrupted as possible with three wild boys at home when ideas flow. You listen to me ramble about my fictional world even if you don't really understand what's going on. Everyone falls in love with "book boyfriends" they read about, fictional men that they wish could fulfill things that are out of reach in the real world. Those men are fun to read about, but I am so grateful to have *you* as my husband, someone all those book boyfriends should be taking notes from. Nobody could love me better than you.

To Jackie . . . Fox Grove literally would not be named *Fox* Grove if not for you. You get all my first thoughts, my wild ideas, my chapters as they pour out of me—rough, raw, unedited, and new. The way you have loved me and encouraged me to keep going, even when I felt like giving up has changed me. When I flip through these pages, stroll the fictional streets of this town, *you* are right there with me because that is what best friends do; they walk alongside you in life through the ups and downs. We get to celebrate and commiserate. We get to laugh and cry. We get to keep each other accountable and hold each other's secrets . . . and most importantly we have front row seats, cheering each other on while we chase dreams.

To Joey . . . You changed my author life with a simple question. It glued us together and now you are stuck with me. I am forever grateful for your creativity, guidance, friendship, knowledge, and support. This book baby is going out into the world bundled in the most beautiful way because of your care —of it and of me. As a first-time indie author, you took me under your wing and allowed me to have a safe space to ask all my questions, kept me from jumping out of the nest too soon, and have been a behind-the-scenes hero from day one.

To Kaitlin . . . I walked into the author world scared and unmoored. It made me so anxious to think about picking an editor, placing my book baby in the trust of someone else's care—but then I found *you.* All that worry melted away because I just knew that you were my person. The one that was meant to take my hands, my book(s), and my trust. There was no doubt that with your help I would be able to send out my work, my dream, into the world confidently. That is a gift that I don't think I can thank you adequately enough for.

To my beta readers . . . Thank you for taking the time to read my very first book, a true book baby. Your thoughtful notes, comments, encouragement, and insights have helped to make this book stronger. I am so excited about the final product of this book, which was only possible because of your kindness and care with being some of the first readers.

To my author friends . . . Thank you for welcoming me into this space and being so kind. There are so many questions, a huge learning curve, and having to take so many leaps of faith. It is so much easier to chase this dream when you have amazing friends lifting you up, cheering you on, and paving a path ahead—willing to reach back and pull you along when you are unsure where to go next. We all deserve to share our stories, and this community feels like a warm embrace when you find your people.

To the book community . . . Thank you for taking a chance on indie authors. We are little fish in a big sea of choices. When you decide to read one of our books it truly can impact our life more than you know. My goal when I wrote this book was the hope that it might become just one person's new favorite book—and that is still a goal. So readers, please feel free to DM me as you read! I would love to know that you are reading Remington and Lainey's story and to finally be able to chitchat about them with all of you!

Warmly,
Pamela

References / Attributions

"Blessed is he who expects nothing, for he shall never be disappointed."

—Alexander Pope, chapter six

"A sunflower doesn't compete with other flowers; it just blooms."

—Zen Shin, chapter thirty-one

"When you realize you want to spend the rest of your life with somebody,

you want the rest of your life to start as soon as possible."

— *When Harry Met Sally*, chapter thirty-eight

About the Author

Pamela Gauthier was born and raised in the Midwest with the love of reading from a young age. Now as a wife and a mother, she is pursuing her author dreams alongside a busy family life. She is a lover of tea, fancy chocolate, and the secret tattoo trope.

instagram.com/pamelagauthierauthor

www.ingramcontent.com/pod-product-compliance
Lightning Source LLC
Chambersburg PA
CBHW030233120726
47903CB00005B/1469

9798993267302